ARISTORN

N.A. VREUGDENHIL

Book 3
of
SHADOW GLYPH

ISBN: 1502408600
ISBN-13: 978-1502408600

For What We've Been Permitted
To Break

Books by N. A. Vreugdenhil

The Shadow Glyph Series

Shadow Glyph (2012)
Gothikar (2014)
Aristorn (2014)
Tiberon
Planned 5th Book

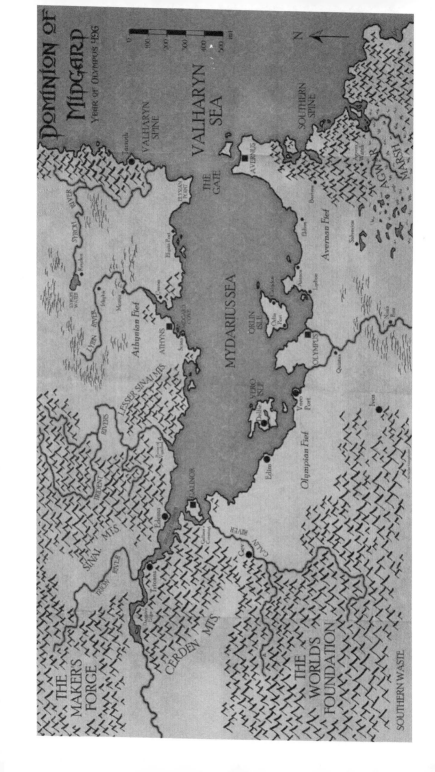

A Note on Pronunciation

y pronounced like *i* in *grin* (Dryn, Rychard, Rysarius)
Double consonants separate syllables (Ker-res or Tan-nes)
ae is pronounced as *i* in *dine* (Haekus)

A Note on Dates

Years are recorded from the founding of the Dominion's oldest city, Olympus. The Year of Olympus 0 was its establishment, which marks the end of the Age of Myths. *Shadow Glyph* was set in the Year of Olympus 588, while *Gothikar* spanned the years 539-588.

A Note on Maps

For better resolutions, please check www.ithyka.com

GOTHIKAR FAMILY TREE

*Royal Names in **bold** and dates in Years of Olympus

- ❖ Veldar ten Gothikar (m. / 404-501) married Nara ten Heth (f. / 446-493)
    - ❖ Parcep Gothikar (m. / 431-463)
    - ❖ Tamese Gothikar (f. / 478-514)
    - ❖ **Akheron** Gothikar (m. / 484-527) married Reya Edemar (f. / 497-543)
        - ❖ **Periander** Gothikar (m. / 519-) married Catlin ten Joran (f. / 520-558)
            - ❖ **Artemys** Gothikar (m. / 545-)
            - ❖ **Pyrsius** Gothikar (m. / 558-588)
                - ❖ Lanteera "Iris" Gothikar (f. / 572-)

Third, passion.

1

Akheron Gothikar breathed his last.

There were three men—two behind him, one in front, and three knives—one in his lower right side, one in his right lung and one in his heart.

The teal tunic he wore beneath the leather jerkin turned red as small frowns formed around each knife, spreading dampness down his torso. The leather jerkin was tight, but not enough to hold the blood within him. A red cape ran from his neck to the height of his knee-length riding boots. The boots themselves seemed loose. His toes had room to clench, though it was mere instinct that squeezed them. And his hands, hanging at his sides, were smooth and clean.

The men's faces were as calm as he imagined his own to be—their eyes were alert, the skin around them slack but not sagging, the stubble on their chins as smooth as the barely noticeable layer of sweat on their hooked noses. These were men who could not be remembered, with faces stolen from a crowded market or a busy harbour. They were clean, their clothes bland. The wool material matched the road beneath their feet, a dull grey. Each had a black hooded mantle and a brown leather sheath at their belt. Had they been there last week, in Salverion? Had they watched him then?

It was the year 527, and Akheron was touring the lands he had taken, the fiefdom of Avernus. He briefly thought of how frustrated his guards always were with the walks he took in solitude. A walk like this one. Even that concern drifted away.

Akheron inhaled his last breath, but it was not an angry or

rough sound. Though he tasted the blood in the back of his mouth, he stilled his hands and released the muscles of his toes. His time had come. He could see the men on either side, the one in front, the road beneath them, the oaken forest around, the Maker above. Akheron was done. Finally free. Finally going home.

He exhaled.

It had been a long journey from Agwar to Salverion that spring of the 527th year. Even then, as the caravan finally reached the farms near the lake-town, the sun was an angry red orb half sunken below the horizon. Akheron sat in the front seat of the lead wagon, his feet occasionally bumping those of the driver beside him, though both would hurriedly turn their knees aside. This man had grown up in Avernus and his name was Dourus, if Akheron's memory served him alright. Akheron had given the man little space in his mind to be remembered; though the Prince was only a man of forty-three, his mind seemed far too full of memories. He had no room for some adoring layman.

The wagon bumped again as it trundled over yet another bridge. It seemed the last hour of travel had involved more bridges than roads. The entire region around Salverion was so low and spotted with water, whether creaks, ponds, or proper lakes.

Akheron ran a hand along his collar. He was sweating in this sun. His physician had bundled him up today—Gysius had mumbled an excuse that it might help his lord's health—though Akheron doubted sweating this much could be healthy. "Where's my horse?" he mumbled.

Dourus glanced at him, a lengthy look, before answering. Finally, "You're in no shape to ride, milord."

Some of them thought it was poison, though Gysius had checked thoroughly, going so far as to change Akheron's diet. In Prince Akheron's opinion, a man could not survive on bread alone. He needed meat.

Akheron knew it was none of these things. He could not think clearly anymore, but it was not the workings of any poison. He had not eaten in a day.

He had sat upon a steed when they left Avernus last year. A tour of his province to let them all see the great Prince, their Usurper. He had known it was a celebration, a bragging and displaying of the people's idol. Akheron had been opposed to it, but his advisors had insisted—so he had set off on his own horse with a troop at his back. It had seemed he had not done so in years. Not since Reya had given birth to Periander.

The wagon bumped again, and he glared at Dourus. The man ignored his hostility. A simpleton, a strongman, a traveller.

As they reached the town gate, Akheron wondered when he had stopped riding that steed. Had he made it to Agwar last month? He doubted it. *It does not matter. I've sat on this wooden seat since the Marsh. Curse this.*

Another shudder coursed his limbs, and set off a coughing fit. They were not real coughs, he could feel it. It was a reflex of some kind. The gate guards, seemingly short men the lot of them, had to wait for his silence before intoning, "Welcome to the town of Salverion, my lord Prince Gothikar. As vassals of your realms, we look forward to your visit and hope you enjoy the feast in your honour."

"Where are our accommodations?"

The guards seemed surprised that he had spoken to them directly. One of them stepped forward, no more than a boy trembling within a cone helmet and chainmail, and bowed. "In the Lord's Hall, my lord."

"Bah!" Akheron was about to ask for something else, but coughing shook him again. He pulled his arm out from under the fleece Gysius had wrapped him within and put his coughing mouth in the elbow of the soft wool to catch the spittle.

The horse and rider that had been following behind his wagon had moved forward, and, as Akheron lifted his head from the coat of his arm, Haekus told the guards, "Your hospitality is appreciated. Please direct us to your Lord's Hall."

The guards bowed and one approached Haekus's horse to give him direction. As they pointed through the gate and spoke in hushed tones, Akheron swallowed fiercely and said, "Haekus, this is the last time you will undermine me! I'll have your hide for this! I used to live in inns! I've had enough of this—this cursed pamper—ing! I'll—"

His rant collapsed into a gag and he had to take a deep breath to calm the hot blood that had filled his face. He imagined his cheeks were flushed, taking away from the sharpness of his hooked nose. Beneath the stringy grey-tainted beard his mouth curled with a snarl. *Curse this! I'm not an old man. I used to be black-haired and as fierce as a raven.* He was only a year past forty, but his hair was dark grey and his features weathered and wrinkled.

Haekus was speaking, as he rode away—with his back to his Prince—through the gate. "...to Avernus next year. You can skin me then, if you want. I'm trying to keep you alive until then."

Akheron would remember this. Perhaps he *would* have the brooding blade-master's hide strung up. Why had he chosen the fool as his advisor? Thin red hair, curly on top, grizzly on his chin and no scars on his face—the village maidens in Salverion were already swooning. It made Akheron sick. Hadn't they learned that love was a duty? One that could only be failed?

"Perhaps the feast will improve your spirits, my lord," Dourus said.

"Hmph." Akheron beckoned for him to follow Haekus into the village. "My spirits aren't the problem."

"Aren't they?" Haekus called back.

"By the Maker and his Great Glyph, I'll have your tongue too!"

That quieted him. Akheron Gothikar *never* spoke that curse. Never spoke that name. He had killed men for less.

The streets of Salverion were barely wide enough for the wagons to turn. His caravan had five, two for supplies, the rest for persons. As they made their way through the muddy ruts that served as roadways, Akheron looked at the sky. It was the dry season. In the northlands, there were cold and warm seasons. This far south, it was only dry or wet. The wet season was a sopping, soaking, raining curse. The dry season left your mouth parched, the sky grey, the sun angry. Even now, as the sun dipped its last rays below the flat horizon, the sky was a pale shade, similar to ash, or Akheron's hair. Any further in that direction and you'd be in the Olympian fief, where Odyn's men might as soon feed you as they would string you up. They were a suspicious, superstitious lot. Burning the Kinship Steads had been risky there.

Finally, they reached the Lord's Hall. It should not have taken so long in a village this small. It was larger than their northland counterparts, the walls higher, the populace more abundant, but it was nothing compared to Eldius or Avernus.

Akheron's neck itched and he raised his right hand to scratch beneath the hemmed collar of the tunic he wore. His weathered skin had become so irritated. He wiped his hands on his knees.

They left the wagons in the yard surrounding the Hall. It was a single-storey building, but with a very high roof, almost like a second layer. It was almost entirely dark oak wood, but had grey stone brickwork in the corner. Lord Rodis's banner hung on either side of the double wooden doors; it was a dark blue with two black birds, crows perhaps, above a white sun. A column of smoke rose above the structure and the air smelled of fresh meat and bread.

Some of their entourage were dismissed into the town to find inns and food on their own. Akheron's inner circle proceeded inside where they were greeted by warm applause and cheers for the Prince. Akheron waved his hand until they stopped. The room was large enough for a hundred party-goers. There was a table occupying most of the floor space. Around the exterior of the room were various doors or divisions. Some areas were simply cordoned off by a curtain. Akheron eyed them suspiciously.

At the head of the huge wooden table, Lord Rodis stood to his feet. He was an old man, old enough to be Akheron's father. He had a receding hair-line of snow-white hair and eyes set so far back into his head, beneath bushy silver eyebrows, they were barely visible. "Welcome my Prince!" he called over the din and the noise gradually quieted. "I trust your journey went well?"

"It could have been smoother," he replied. "My physician tells me I am in poor health and my guard tells me I am in poor spirits."

Rodis bowed his head and raised his cup. "Perhaps our feast will help with the latter. And even the former... a toast to our Prince's health!" he cried and the room uproariously agreed.

Drinks were drunk. Akheron and his men were seated.

The feast carried on as the last one had. Akheron was fed more than anyone else, but he ate the least. He spoke the least, and jested the least. But everyone seemed delighted by him.

He knew it was their fear. It disgusted him and, strangely, made him miss Reya a little. She no longer feared him. She had told him what he was. He missed her.

As servants took away the first course of the meal, a man stepped out of one of the curtained corners of the room, a cubby near the door.

Akheron stood up, fast enough to send his chair screeching back. Silence fell as all eyes followed his gaze. The man held a book under one arm and a heavy amulet dangling from his neck. He was bald, but seemed about Akheron's age. His eyes had huge rings around them from reading by candlelight. "What's your name?" Akheron asked.

The man had no trouble hearing him and stammered, "Thoral, my lord." Those dark-rimmed eyes broke their lock on Akheron's and glanced at Lord Rodis.

"And what book is that?"

Thoral blinked back at Akheron. "'Tis nothing my lord. A history of no significance."

Akheron ran his tongue along his gums, then sucked in a deep breath. "Haekus!" The man was standing near the door, amidst a circle of guardsmen. "Read me the title of that book!"

Haekus stepped toward Thoral—his presence was like a giant seizing a child—and roughly grabbed the book from the man's arms. A sigh escaped Lord Rodis; Akheron glanced at the slight tremble in the man's lower lip and the flush creeping up the man's neck.

Akheron's blade-master examined the book silently, oddly quiet. "Well, what is it?"

Haekus glanced up at him. "The title is *Reasons for the Kinship*, my lord. Should I take this man to be flogged?"

Akheron closed his eyes. He could hear Rodis stuttering; he could imagine the man's bumbling excuses before any words broke the silence. He had seen behind that curtain when Thoral had stepped into the central Hall.

"My gravest apologies," Rodis said, rising to his feet. "I have allowed select members of my council to continue their religious beliefs... I did not see the harm in it. Thoral will be reprimanded, I assure you. I, myself, do not practice such beliefs, in accordance with your laws, my lord. I truly do apologize..." He went on like this for some time, until eventually rejoining the silence.

Akheron finally opened his eyes, but looked at no one. He slid his fingers behind his collar and pulled at the material uncomfortably. Now he stared towards that curtained chamber. The silence became so loud that the crowd shifted in discomfort, until at last:

"Get out! All of you, out!" Akheron's voice was a roar like a bear or a wild cat. Like the tide, the tables of the Hall emptied until Akheron and Thoral were the only two remaining, the latter trembling in fear and the former in ferocity. Akheron's voice dropped to a guttural rasp. "You too."

"My lord?" Thoral questioned, surprised. Even as the words left his mouth, he was already moving at a brisk walk towards the door.

"Out!"

Thoral ran, and Akheron waited until the oaken doors thudded shut before moving. With more weariness than he had shown even on the wagon-ride, he lifted himself up and out of his chair. This had been long coming. Far too long.

He moved with a limp, teetering towards the veiled chamber. When he reached it, he took a deep breath before pulling the curtain aside. He remained frozen at the opening, his mind as still as his body.

The shrine was small, likely out of fear. Akheron had made worship a dangerous offence. The traditional glass circle was set on a shelf against the log wall of the Hall—he had not seen one of them in years—and on either side of it were the normal totems. On the left was a glowing candle and a cupful of water. On the other side was a slab of rock and an identical chalice— this one full of only air. Below this altar was a table. There were books there of which Akheron had tried to burn every last copy. Some even looked singed, such as the copy of the *Book of the Glyphs* that was set out front.

His hands burned here. He wiped his palms.

There were other artefacts and treasures within the shrine— drawings, one of a woman he did not recognize, most of them more significant Kinship figures; food such as the loaf of bread on shelf nearby; a cushion for knees in prayer.

Akheron finally took a breath, releasing the red flush from his face as he sucked in the air he had just refused for many moments. His mouth remained open, tasting the tears that had appeared from nowhere. He fell to his knees, the curtain catching on his feet as a frame-shaking sob escaped him. He reached his hands to his collar once more and tore the wool from neckline to his waist before falling onto his elbows.

"Maker," he gasped, unable to hold any breath. "Maker. Forg—" The word caught in his throat. "For... Curse this voice!" This was a short shout, like one word, then his words returned to a rasp as he struggled for air. "Forgive me."

Finally saying it sent him into the throes of passion. His frame switched between sobs and silent trembling. "Forgive me, forgive me, forgive me please."

He had been telling himself lies, trying to forget the truth that the Maker *could* forgive him. Saying these words—words he had thought would destroy him; he *knew* now that he should have said them a long, long time ago. He looked back up at the artwork, the sketch of the woman and then back down at his folded hands.

He took a deep breath and a shriek came out of nowhere, without his permission. "Forgive me!"

And the Maker *did*. It was as clear as a voice. And the relief in its wake as clear as glass or the water from a fresh spring. Washing him clean.

He was himself again.

3

Agwar Marsh was a long cry from the comforts of Avernus. A thick mist rose into the air for as far as Akheron could see south. It was considered one of the Dominion's natural wonders. Scholars had long come to study it. It covered at least three hundred square miles, more than any other swamp in the land. The lowlands here were soaked by two rivers that sought the Valharyn.

Though it was considered one of the significant holdings in Akheron's Princedom, the town of Agwar Watch was not like any respectable city anywhere else. The streets were little more than piles of dirt high enough to stay above water, the wealthy houses sat on stilts, the rest sat in mud. It appeared ahead, crooked roofs rising out of the mist

"Do you miss your son?" Haekus asked, from his saddle.

Akheron scowled. He was tired of Haekus's questions. Yesterday, Akheron had almost fallen from his saddle. Gysius had insisted he spend the rest of the journey on one of the wagons unless he regained his strength. "Not my son," he said. "Reya's."

"And yours," Haekus said. The bruises from their fight weeks earlier had finally faded.

They kept going in silence. Akheron missed Reya's warmth. He supposed he did miss his son a bit, little Peri.

The sun was directly overhead, and Akheron started to sweat. When had he let them pick at him, tell him what to wear, tell him how to behave? That was the real reason he had teetered in his saddle. Their pampering was making him weak. It had made him weak.

He trembled. "Haekus," he said. "Go ride in front."

Haekus stiffened at Akheron's voice. "Very well."

"Very well, sir!" Akheron barked as his guard rode ahead. Haekus glanced back and, with a glare, repeated the Prince's words. The man driving the wagon, who sat brutishly beside Akheron, glanced at him nervously and then back at the road. Akheron had not bothered learning his name yet.

They reached the ring of shoddily-angled palisades on the edge of the town. There were two posts on either side of the road, rising twenty feet into the air. Near their tops were two crackling braziers that guided lots of travellers out of the marshes. Akheron wondered how they kept them alight. *Probably magic...*

Haekus spoke to the guards a moment later and their caravan was welcomed to the town of Agwar. *Some welcome*, Akheron scoffed to himself.

As they rolled past, Akheron glanced back, around the corner of the wagon's cover. Sure enough, there was a set of glyphs carved into the base of each post. Akheron cursed magic under his breath. They loved to meddle in what was natural. The Maker should never have given them glyphs.

The people in the streets cheered when they saw him. Some called compliments, praise. Some just stared. As they neared the Lord's Manor, a two storey wooden building raised two feet from the mud beneath it, their din grew to a new crescendo.

"Enough!" Akheron shouted at them. "Get back to work. There is nothing here to see. I'm just a greedy man like you lot."

This only made their adoration increase. They saw him as *theirs.* He was one of them, a grumbling but aspiring commoner who had taken one of the most powerful seats in the entire Dominion of Midgard. His words also drew an uneasy glance from Haekus, whose hand wandered toward its sword.

"Tell us how you did it!" someone cried.

"Haekus," Akheron barked, standing up from the worn wagon bench. "Grab him."

Haekus slid from his saddle in a fluid movement and strode into the crowd. Alarmed, their din quieted and they made way for the blade-master. Haekus loomed over them; he was taller than most of the crowd by a head and shoulders. He was not a thick man, like the cowering wagon driver, trying to avoid the gaze of the townsfolk around them. Haekus was gaunt, almost lanky, but this made him no less fearsome.

The man who had called to Akheron was dragged forward. He was thin and trembling, with brown chops on either side of his mouth and a thick brow. "Sorry, milord, apologies please."

Akheron dropped from the wagon onto the soft grass. The soil was moist enough that he felt his sandals sink a bit with each step. He only moved one or two paces from the wagon. He had the strength he needed now, none of this saddle-sickness or pampered sweat. He had his *ferocity* again. "You want to know how I did what?" Akheron asked, with as much gentleness as he could muster.

"Became Prince, milord," the man quivered. "Defeated the Maker..."

Akheron kept walking forward until the man said his second phrase. He froze. The crowd went silent. The man had said the Maker's name in front of the closest thing to a devil any of them had known. They loved their devil. Akheron abhorred him.

"How could I defeat him?" Akheron asked the man. It was one of his many phrases. He could not speak the truth that was in his head for none of them could receive it. But he could speak his mind in a way they could misinterpret.

The man stammered a reply that Akheron expected, "Of course, milord, if something's not real, it can't be destroyed."

Everyone breathed a sigh of relief. Except Haekus. He kept staring at Akheron, trying to understand him. Akheron shook his head and turned his back on Haekus. "You're all fools, the lot of you!" he shouted. His voice echoed off the wagon covers of his caravan and then off the buildings that surrounded them.

From the direction of the Lord's Manor, another voice called, "Apologies, my Prince. My subjects should not ambush you so."

"Glyphs," Akheron said, quietly.

"Welcome to Agwar Watch, Prince Gothikar," Lord Ahryn said. He was one of the Three Nobles of Avernus, and the lord of Agwar. From here, Akheron could only see his braided brown hair and burgundy cloak. "May I receive you in my Hall?"

"You may not," Akheron said. "Not yet. I need some time

to clear my head. I'm going for a walk, and I forbid any of you to follow me." He ignored the eyes of his men, the crowd, and the lord, and walked towards the edge of town. He could see it clearly from the road where they had halted, straight ahead, a gurgling steaming swamp.

"Sir," Haekus said. His eyes looked so haunted. When had Haekus become haunted?

Akheron strode past. "Don't," he snapped, now several paces through the crowd.

"Stop," Haekus said, still trailing him.

Akheron spun on him. He raised his hand, for Haekus was taller than him, and struck his guard with the back of it. The force of the blow knocked Haekus to his knees. The blade-master had not time to blink. Akheron could remember the first time he had moved that fast and Haekus had called it faster than lightning. That was back in the days when they fought side by side. Haekus spat blood into the mud and glared up at Akheron, his Prince.

"Stay down," Akheron said. "Dog."

Haekus shifted his weight from his outstretched and muddied hands to his legs, but paused. His eyes met Akheron's with a baleful fury and then with fear. This was not a drunken, self-destructive Prince, not now. This was the fiery Gothikar. Haekus stayed down.

Akheron turned his back on the blade-master and strode down the road. None of the crowd dared to follow him.

The marsh made walking difficult. Akheron sometimes stepped from rock to rock to cross a watery gap. He could only see a short ways ahead or behind him. There were hounds howling in the distance and, occasionally, birds singing. Life kept going, despite the darkness that surrounded him.

"Glyphs," he said aloud. "What am I still doing here?"

Was he going to rot away, into a wiry, wrinkled fruit? Like shrivelled old Leto, the Crown Magician, now stinking in her grave? Would he watch Weveld grow old? He reached up to feel the wrinkles on his face. "Will I watch my son become me? Or can my son bury me? Please, let him bury me." It was the closest he had come to a prayer since he had watched the last Kinship burning—eight years ago.

It felt like a long time. He ducked and shouldered his way

through the scratching branches of a small sickly tree. He couldn't tell if it was the husk of a dead tree or the sleeping spirit of an ailing one. Eight years. He himself had sunken so far during that time. If he had 'killed the Maker'... he had killed himself in doing so.

He saw a little earth-spawn scamper away through the fog. He had not seen one of them in ten years. He remembered, as a young boy, the infestations of them in the city alleys and the tribal settlements they made in the hills. He had, honestly, come to believe they were all dead. Soon its figure faded into the swamp and Akheron was alone again.

But only for a minute. Another shadow cast itself on the mists and a man approached Akheron from the south. "Who goes there?" Akheron asked, gripping the hilt at his side. It wanted to be drawn. His knuckles turned white.

"No need to be afraid," the voice called. "You may call me Terrus."

The man, once Akheron could see him clearly enough, was wearing off-black pants and an elaborate orange tunic, full of criss-crossing folds of cloth and blue-embroidered patterns. He was not armed. He had short brown hair and a thin band of scruff across his chin, save a line on his cheek where no whiskers grew.

"Your name's not Terrus," Akheron said. This brought him back almost twenty years, right to the beginning of everything. Most of those memories were buried in his mind, walled off so they could not harm him; so they could not break him. *Glyphs, they almost did.* This man however—the recollection of him came quickly. "It's Arad."

"Arad?" the man asked, confused. He did not remember Akheron. He scratched his chin.

"Yes..." Akheron said. "We have met before. Fifteen years ago, at least. You have not aged at all!"

"You have?" Arad asked, his voice stretched thin. He glanced into the fog, but Akheron saw nothing there. "Arad was a friend's name. He seems so far from now."

The words were a jumble that made little sense to Akheron. "I'll warn you," he told Arad, "I'm a much darker man now than when we first spoke. Do not expect warmth or insight from me this time."

Arad raised a hand. "I must think about this for a moment. If you've seen me before, I must visit you again later. No, earlier. I'll recognize you that time, but you will not recognize me."

"Glyphs—what?" Akheron asked. He sounded more muddled and confused than Leto had, at the end.

"Forget it," Arad said, lowering his hand. "May I walk with you?"

Akheron shrugged. "Why?"

Arad started walking, so Akheron matched his pace. "I've studied you. Not from books or rumours, but... your actions."

"Great Glyph, why?"

"I wanted to understand you. During my travels," Arad said, "I've become very good at reading people. But I can't read you."

Instead of asking if that's why Arad was here again, out of time, talking to him, Akheron asked a question far closer to his mental barricades. Close enough that he could feel the tremors. "Why would you want to know anything about me? So you can *be* like me, like that crowd back there wants?"

Arad glanced at him. In an instant, the scattered Leto was gone and an incredibly empathetic intellectual was there instead. "No, so I don't become like you."

Akheron stopped walking, his heart pounding and his eyes threatening tears from nowhere. Weveld had made him feel the same way, but more aggressively, not fully understanding Akheron. Even Arad was not fully grasping what hid behind those walls. Would he someday? Akheron remembered Arad's confusing words earlier... perhaps Arad had fully understood Akheron the first time they spoke. "Thank you," he found himself saying.

Arad kept walking, so Akheron had to stride to keep up. "I saw you sing hymns," Arad said, "as a young man. You were simpler then, weren't you? I could read you then. You believed those words you sung, didn't you?"

Akheron didn't reply. He didn't want to remember that version of himself. Thinking of that young man gave him hope and he didn't want any of it.

"You used to believe in so much—the grace, will, truth of the Maker. Now you don't believe in anything. The only truth you believe in now is that you cannot be saved," Arad said. This time he stopped walking, for he knew Akheron needed it.

"I can't be," Akheron said, when he was able. He was holding his sides and he felt sick. "I can't be."

"What if you can?"

Akheron spat to the side. "Don't," he said. He opened his left hand and stared at his palm. So much blood. "I swear to all the glyphs that I will kill you if you speak of redemption to me. My damnation is all that I have left."

Arad sucked in his breath sharply, and started walking again. Akheron pressed his fingers to his eyes and then wiped them dry on his brown cloak. He wasn't weeping, he *wasn't*. He followed the mysterious man again. They passed a fallen tree and walked across a pond on it. The bark was cracking away, revealing what was inside its dead shell. As they dropped off of the log and onto the soft soil on the other side, he asked Arad, "Are you a believer?"

It was a complicated question. Akheron's revolution had put to death so many people who had answered 'yes' to that question. Akheron himself had killed because of it.

"I did not realize until recently that I *was* raised to be a godly man," Arad said. "But I am not a religious man."

Akheron smirked. "Most don't realize the difference. There's also a distinction between religious men and believers."

Instead of replying, Arad asked, "Are you a believer?"

Akheron did not stop walking this time. Though no one had asked him this before, he replied without hesitation. *"With all my soul,"* he said.

They kept walking in silence for a while. They must've been close to an hour's hike from the town now. Haekus and the others would be worried. Though Akheron did not feel at peace, he felt alive again. The logical next question for Arad would be to ask Akheron why he acted the way he did, if he truly believed.

Instead, Arad said, "A... wise man once told me, 'you have to choose to be a god or a devil. You can decide not to choose, but then it will be decided for you.' I think you could learn a lot from him."

Akheron paused again, staring at his free hand. He had chosen already. He had chosen to be a devil. And then he had forgotten that there was a choice.

"It's not that simple—" Arad was gone. Akheron was alone in the marsh. There was another crooked tree nearby and a rock next to it, covered in pale green moss. In the distance, another hound started barking as it caught the scent of its prey.

"This changes nothing," he said, to the same person he had addressed before the appearance of Arad. The man seemed as ethereal as the fog now, but when he had talked to Akheron, he had been as real as the sword hilt still gripped in the Prince's white-knuckled grip.

He turned, and set off toward the town again. What a madman he must be.

"What does this one say, Father?"

"It says how Tiberon Odyn won the Battle on the Lyrin. King Nerik and King Gothikar were allied against him, holding the mouth of the river from the southerner's fleet. They had only twenty ships, and the King's Alliance had thousands of men," Akheron said.

"King Gothikar?" Peri asked. He was seated on his father's knee like he owned it. This was his throne until he fell asleep.

"Your great-great-great...-great-grandfather," Akheron said, counting on his fingers. He pointed to the dark armoured man in the background of the book's illustration and made his voice gruff. "Ursun Gothikar."

"Was he a good King?" His son glanced to the right, halfway between his father and the book, at his bed chamber.

Reya had told Akheron they were raising a good, democratic son—the Triumvirate's son—so he told Peri, "No, Ursun Gothikar was an evil tyrant. He made his citizens unhappy. And he very much wanted to stop Tiberon Odyn from setting up the Triumvirate."

Peri nodded solemnly. "But Tiberon won, right?"

"He certainly did," Akheron said. "He defeated both of the bad kings."

It was not a story often told, as though, somehow, remembering they had once been monarchs would fuel even more Gothikar ambition. The whole world was waiting to see what Akheron Gothikar would do next. It would take them far longer than necessary to realize that he was burnt out, soured, and spoiled.

"Good," Peri said, turning the page in the book that Akheron held. The next was an illustration of the first Crown Magician, Anaia Desser, clasping hands with her successor. "And this one?" Peri asked.

Akheron closed the book. "No more, Peri," he said.

"Fine," the boy said sternly, though he leaned back against Akheron's chest gently. His head fit snugly between his arm and torso.

Akheron closed his eyes. *What am I supposed to feel now?* he wondered. *Joy? Completion?* He felt nothing. No one had told him that once depression and anger and action had all taken their toll, there would be nothing left. *Is this what King Gothikar felt when Tiberon Odyn came for his head?*

It was a large stretch of time between them, three hundred years give or take a few. One Gothikar had lost everything. And Akheron had reclaimed it. Because he wanted to?

No. All I wanted was an end to it. An end to what I felt.

"And I got it..." he whispered.

"What?" Peri asked.

"Periander..." Akheron breathed. "Set your mind to something and you can achieve it. Choose how you want the world to be, and make it that way. They'll say I'm ambitious. They'll say I'm great. By all the glyphs, they might even say I'm a sinner."

"Father?" Peri asked, sitting up and twisting to see him.

"Just remember this," Akheron said. "You can be *whatever* you want. You just need to try."

"Thanks..." Peri said, leaning back into his breast.

Within ten minutes, his son dozed off and Akheron carried him to his bed. It was still early in the evening so, once he was satisfied that his son was soundly asleep, he strode past the chamber's guards and toward the royal tavern. He could see their latest stable hand in front of the nearby building, watching him. The boy's name was Dobler. He was a natural with horses, despite being younger than ten. Dobler watched Akheron with wide eyes.

The Royal Tavern was not a large building. Its size, however, received no complaints from the noble patrons it served. They all appreciated a certain measure of discretion.

Akheron paused before the door and looked back at his Keep. He tugged his gold and green cloak tighter around himself; the temperature was falling as the Valharyn's winter arrived. There were guards patrolling high above, pricks of orange torchlight meandering left and right along the ramparts of the four-storey Keep. It had been only two storeys when the Aristorns ruled here. He shivered when that name entered his thoughts.

I hope someone destroys it, someday, he thought. On second thought, he reconsidered. He had added the top two storeys, and those were what he wanted destroyed. *My achievements. My mockery.* He had intentionally instructed the masons to build it in mimicry of the preceding floors. *Someone burn it down.*

Dobler was still watching him, but Akheron returned his eyes to the tavern. It would shake him from this cursed reverie. And it did. He got the whole bar to himself; everyone else left it within the first half hour. He was already three mugs of ale in, by then. He used to hate the stuff. Anything alcoholic had turned his gut. It had never had anything to do with the taste though. He drank another.

At one point, he found a tiny barmaid on his knee. His hands explored her, exploited her. She seemed happy with it, and everyone else did too.

Of course they did. He was their glorious and valiant hero. He was their Prince and he could turn them into skeletons with a word or lords with another. He felt sick. He picked the girl up with both hands on her shoulders and set her aside. He did not shove her. He did not harm her. He drank more ale.

He swallowed an entire keg of it as the night went on.

Haekus finally left his peripheral vision and stepped into focus. He had been there, in the edge, since Akheron had left the Keep. Now, he took Akheron in an embrace and, supporting his weight, led the way to the Prince's chambers. "Why do you do it?" he said, at some point. Akheron had no idea where they were. There were stone walls around him, his Keep, but he didn't know which hallway.

"I made a promise," he said, voice slurring. *Should I be hearing my own voice slur?* a lucid thought asked, but drifted away like a snowflake on the breeze. "A promise to myself."

"Here you are," Haekus said. He said it immediately after Akheron's words, but they were at the Prince's quarters now. This was his door.

"Thank you, ol' friend," Akheron opened the door and lost balance, then righted himself by leaning on the doorframe. He turned his head over his shoulder and snapped, "Now go throw yourself off the Keep, you fool."

Haekus shook his head and walked away.

Reya was awake, which surprised him. She looked at him with pity. He scoffed and sat down on their bed. He waited for her to speak. She was just a dark shadow on the other side of the bed, looking at him with pale white eyes. He couldn't see pity. *What am I thinking about?* he wondered. He yanked off his boots and tossed them at the wall.

"How many this time?" she asked.

"What?" he replied. Glyphs, he was tired. And drunk. "Drinks?"

"Whores."

"Glyphs!" He stared at her in the dark. Was she crying?

"You go from reading to our son, to passing out?" she asked.

"What do you want from me?"

She snorted and threw up her hands. "I'm going to sleep in the other room," she said.

"No!" he shouted. "What, by the Great Glyph, do you *want from me?*"

The door creaked as a concerned guard stuck his head in. The Lord and Lady Gothikar never argued. Akheron released a knife from his sleeve with a blur of his hand and it struck the wall somewhere. He had been aiming for the guard, and the door slammed shut without a word being spoken.

The *Lady Gothikar* flinched at the noise.

Akheron stood up, beside the bed. "I told you what I was before you got into this! I told you I would hurt you and fail you. You didn't have an issue with my drinking back then! Nor with my whores!"

"You're a real earth-spawn," she cursed. "You're worse."

He grabbed her face, roughly, in his hand, her chin gripped between his thumb and his fingers. He leaned in close enough for her distraught expression to twist from his stench.

"You're damned right I am," he growled.

Again, he was careful not to shove her away from him. He released her and turned his back on her. "We've both known that since the beginning," he said. "Don't pretend this is a surprise. I told you what to expect and you said you loved me anyway. I told you that you were a fool, Reya. And you married me anyway! Did you think that fixing me was part of it?"

She was trembling. He wondered how many people could hear his shouting. He yanked his knife out of the wall and looked at the blade. He could never harm her. It was his own heart he contemplating freeing.

"I thought it was your fight with House Aristorn, and your issues with the Kinship! You told me you would always believe in the Maker." Reya had to gasp for air. "I thought it would pass in time. Your bitterness, your... violence. What happened to you, to make you this way?"

He glared at her. "I told you to never ask me that. I told you... a hundred times, I told you."

"No one is this... tortured! What did you bury within you?"

Akheron trembled, but kept his baleful eyes upon her. He had killed the last person that had asked him twice. He had bashed that man's skull against an altar until the whole world turned red and forgot the Maker. He finally glanced down at his hands, sliding the knife back up his sleeve, and then wrung his fingers together until they felt clean again. *What did I do? What tortures me?* he asked himself. *I* mustn't *remember.*

He turned his back on his wife and opened the door into the Keep's corridor. Haekus entered the room as he left, to check he had not harmed her. They should all know better. Akheron never harmed women. But Haekus had to check, so the Prince cursed him as they brushed past one another.

Akheron awoke in the Barracks that morning, halfway through the day. There were guards sleeping nearby, but they had given him a private area of two or three beds. He sat up, and fought his way out of the blankets. The night was a blur to his pounding head, but he remembered what he said and what he did.

He smiled, though he wanted to weep. Reya's hatred was what he deserved, wasn't it? For all the pain he'd caused. For all the pain he'd continue to cause.

Haekus was standing outside the barracks, with his back to it. When Akheron walked past, he fell into his usual spot a few steps behind. He was Akheron's personal guard, no matter what. Akheron chuckled as he walked. "Anything to say?" he asked, before they reached the Keep.

"No," Haekus said, in stride alongside him, "sir."

"Would you like to tour our lands? The Nobles have been bothering me since I got back from Delfie. They want me to ride around like some pompous fool so that all my idolizers can weep and cheer all over me. I think it's a cartful of manure, but it might be nice to visit the different areas again."

"I'd like that," Haekus said. "To get out of Avernus again, for a while."

"Are you going to put a knife in my back?"

Haekus staggered. "What! Of course not, you pompous fool."

Akheron laughed enough to wind himself. He sucked in his breath. He felt weak, like he had been for the past few years. He had bouts of strength, like last night, but he spent his days wasting away. He shook his head. "I was really hoping you'd be the one, Haekus, to put an end to me."

"You were?"

"I don't want to live as old as my father did. I've kept you around and made your life misery so that you might be the one," he said. It felt very odd to be saying these thoughts aloud. Even before he voiced them, he had not given them a place to live in his head. It was best if things did not live in his head; he spent a lot of his energy avoiding thoughts and memories he feared.

Haekus just shook his head. Akheron didn't meet his man's eyes, though the blade-master was staring at him. There was a moment of silence. "I don't think I will be."

"I'm sorry to hear that," Akheron said, glancing at his friend briefly. He scratched his chin through the scruff on it and looked back at the Keep. He'd have to tell his wife they were leaving. He shivered. Haekus was still waiting for his words. "Now, go saddle your horse," he said.

5

He had not believed Leto, when she said she was going to step down. He had thought she was playing a scheme. All magicians had schemes. They were smarter than everyone else— Akheron was certain of it—so they made schemes no one else could follow. Bluffs, plays, pawns. That had never been Akheron's way. It was too weak for him. He had always enjoyed looking his foe in the eyes before they danced to death.

So now he was surprised. Leto had impressed him with her frankness.

The rooftops of Delfie were dark in the rain. In Avernus or Eldius, roofs shone in the rain for they were often shingled and caught the setting sun or the torchlight from the streets. Delfie's houses were thatched and turned a dull brown as the summer storm soaked them. A spell, compliments of the Avernan Guildmaster, kept Akheron's party dry. As they walked, Akheron analyzed the town with skepticism. Delfie was a tiny town. Just a port, really. There had not even been a Stead here, during the burning of the Kinship.

Akheron glanced into the sea, briefly. Across that water, on the mainland, was Edim. He had heard that the city there had become so deserted since the Great Stead fell, that now only two villages remained: Greater Edim and Lesser Edim. The rest was empty ruins.

The other day he had heard someone call it the Revolution. The People's Revolution. What an awfully poetic way of recounting the story. It made Akheron queasy. *It wasn't a Revolution, it was a massacre.*

Up the hill, Akheron could see the School. They would be there soon. They were expected and they were late. There was a good fifty feet of forested ridge between the School grounds and the town. Vero Isle was a rough rise of land. There was a lake somewhere much farther uphill, and a river that ran through waterfalls to the beach. The arm of land that extended to Akheron's left, on the horizon, was a single rocky mountain pointing toward Galinor. That was how he always remembered it, from the maps.

The forest here was not unlike the forests of the Avernan inland. The coast itself was full of rolling elevations and scattered copses of wood. But the lands between Salverion and Eldius, between Bertren and the Olympian rivers, were full of warm deciduous: oaks and sycamore. The Olympian peninsula was tropical—another secret of the Magician's Order, no doubt.

But the forest that Akheron, Haekus, his guards, the leader of the Avernan Guild and all his ilk walked through was alive with the monsoon's water. There were tulips and foxglove dotting the green foliage, drinking deeply.

It looked so refreshing, which just made Akheron feel more dry.

They walked in silence, mostly. Haekus spoke occasionally with one of his soldier friends, a man named Ennys.

A metal fence and gate emerged from the forest ahead of them. The narrow cobbled path ran right to the gate, which was a good arm's length taller than Akheron. An orange robed monk opened it for the party as they arrived. "Welcome to the School of Delfie, my lords and my Prince."

"Thank you, Sentinel," Haekus said, though Akheron walked past without so much of a glance in reply.

The new Crown Magician met with them in the Order's Council Chamber on the third floor of the Hall of the School. It was not a tremendously old building. If Akheron were to guess, most of the campus had been renovated or added to during his own lifetime, excluding the Tower, whose ancient quarters had always been home to the Crown Magician.

Haekus opened the door to the Council Chamber for Akheron, but did not enter. The room had been rearranged for their meeting—the new Crown Mage was meeting with all Three Princes as they became available—with a narrow table in the middle of the room and the chairs rearranged for their group. The table, a fresh wooden construction, was populated by a variety of pitchers and mugs, a map, a collection of books and the smooth hands of the wizard who awaited them.

"Akheron Gothikar, I presume," the man said, with a clear voice. He had a long face with deep set eyes and thick brown hair. He reminded Akheron of Ivos, one of the lords of his own court. "Allow me to introduce myself. I am Weveld of Quintus, now the seventh Crown Magician." He extended a hand for Akheron to clasp, and then invited them all to be seated.

They sat for a moment in silence. This Weveld eyed Akheron over at length, while Akheron gave him only one look and then moved on to more interesting matters, like the rain dripping from the eaves outside the room's only window. He didn't need to examine the Crown Magician. Weveld was a boy with the stern jaw of an ambitious man and the deep set eyes of an aged scholar. Maybe in twenty years he might have the right to analyze Akheron like an open tome in a library, but he certainly did not now.

"I'll not discuss the weather with you, mage," Akheron said, with a sneer.

"Good," Weveld replied. "Allow me, then, to be absolutely transparent with you."

Akheron looked at the guild-master that had accompanied him from Avernus, shifting uncomfortably in his seat. "This should be intriguing," Akheron jeered, and glanced back at Weveld.

"The past twenty years of this Dominion have been chaotic and, frankly, unacceptable."

"I'll be sure to pass your message along to the commoners."

"Don't play revolutionary with me," Weveld said, sternly.

Akheron shifted in his chair and rose from his lounging posture to meet Weveld's unwavering glare. "Go on."

"You are the cause of this chaos. You're a plague, Prince Gothikar."

Glyphs, yes.... His knee shook.

"As Crown Magician," Weveld said, "it is my task to make decisions for the benefit of the *Triumvirate*, not the sadistic rule of the mob."

Akheron leaned forward. *Yes...*

"You have been idle for more than five years now, Prince Gothikar. I would encourage you to remain so. If you disturb the peace again, I will force the hand of the Triumvirate and we will deem you a traitor of the Dominion."

The blonde-haired guild-master coughed. His apprentice and he tried to avoid looking at either of their superiors. There was a war being fought in this room, and they had not been prepared for it.

Though Weveld's unveiled threats were exactly what Akheron wanted, exactly what he deserved, he decided, *why stop at threats?* He glanced back at his opponent. "You think that the other Princes would dare raise a hand against me?"

"I will raise a hand against you."

Akheron smiled, though he tried to cover it.

"Is this a joke to you? A game of some sort?"

"Others have threatened me," Akheron said. "The fanatics, the 'sadistic mob' as you call them, put those people to death. Do you really think you could get close to me?"

"I am right now."

Akheron laughed. "You have nerve, I'll give you that."

"And the brawn to back it, let me assure you."

Akheron raised a hand. "I am not doubting you, mage, but appreciating you. There are not many that speak back to me anymore. Take this babbling fool, for example. You."

The guild-master spattered, "Me?" as all eyes in the room turned on him. In a last ditch effort, he tugged the hem of his tunic and thrust his shoulders out. "I-I am—"

Akheron grabbed the master's apprentice. "Kill this man, now."

"What?" everyone asked in unison.

"That will not be necessary," Weveld retorted.

The guild-master's eyes were locked on Akheron's though. Had he seen the Kinships burning? Had he wept on the Grey Night, like all the rest of them? "Your Prince, the Fury of Avernus, as I have been called, is ordering you."

The man pulled a knife from his belt. The apprentice squirmed in Akheron's hand.

Sickened by them, Akheron released the apprentice, who knocked back his chair in his frantic dash for the door. "See?"

Akheron asked. "It's pitiful. Put down your knife, you useless lout."

Again, the guild-master did as ordered. "You're dismissed," Weveld said. The man disappeared, and the Crown Mage said, "I was wrong about the mob. It was your madness not theirs, at fault."

"You've only words? After that show?"

Weveld shrugged. "It was only a show, Prince Gothikar. I am not one of the fools you surround yourself with."

Akheron poured himself a drink from one of the pitchers nearby. "Would you like one?" he asked.

"No."

"It's only a light ale."

"I'm not thirsty."

"Do you not partake?"

Weveld raised an eyebrow. "Not in the company of Princes."

"I could order that, too."

"Do you have a death-wish, Prince Gothikar?" Weveld seemed to be asking a genuine question.

"If I wanted to die, I would not have picked my cursed war with a church," Akheron said, as he took a drink. He could taste the hops in it. Most of the alcohol on the island would have preservatives. Akheron doubted there were vineyards here for the academics.

"No. But with an Imperial House or the Buccaneer's Navy instead?"

Akheron lowered his cup toward the table, but it hovered above it. "Do you have a death-wish, mage?"

Weveld finally gave a slight smirk. It seemed he appreciated cleverness. "Not I, sir. I simply wanted to be blunt with you today. If you start valuing the Triumvirate above your own desires we will get along comfortably. If you cross the Triumvirate, you cross me. And I will not be a pawn in your games and revolutions."

Akheron pursed his lips and nodded slowly. There was a long moment of silence, so he had another drink. When he finished it, he stood up to leave. He felt oddly proud of Weveld. A man with good values in his heart. There were not many of them.

"Do you value the people that little?" he heard himself ask. He was already halfway to the door, but turned back to the new Crown Magician.

"Pardon me?"

"The Triumvirate *is not* the people it governs. It seems for you, the former takes priority. I learned very early that the Triumvirate has no power, and the people have it all."

"Only if we acknowledge they do," Weveld said.

Akheron frowned. "Madness."

Weveld laughed this time. "You sit down here, argue with me, threaten murder and ruin the relationship of two others, then laugh, and you're calling *me* mad?"

"What happens on the day that the people govern the Triumvirate? When all the money, influence, and peace lies in their hands and their expansion?" Akheron's war on the Kinship had been a revolution of sorts, but not a true, political revolution.

"I pray such a day does not come," Weveld said.

"Think on this," Akheron said, ignoring the prayer. "On the day we must choose between citizen and state, we *must* fight for our people. Even if it means fighting the Triumvirate itself. Anything else would be madness."

Weveld blinked as he devoured Akheron's words. But then his ambition returned. "This is philosophy. I do not deal in the hypothetical, but in the tangible and pragmatic. Live in peace now, Prince Gothikar, or we will ensure that you do."

Akheron shook his head and opened the door with a light push. The damned doors opened with magic here. It made his skin crawl. The hallway felt cold after the argument. There was no sign of the guild-master or his apprentice in the ornate wooden corridor, but Haekus fell into stride behind Akheron.

"Are we returning to Avernus now, sir?" the lanky guard asked. The tapestries that adorned the walls seemed so out of place after Weveld's discourse; here was a hero fighting on top of a hill, and here was a man on a sailboat, crossing the Mydarius for the first time.

"Not yet," Akheron said. "I would like to pay a visit to Leto first. I will miss that woman."

Haekus hummed instead of laughing. "Haven't heard you say anything like that in twenty years."

"Don't get used to it. Weveld put me in a good mood."

Akheron led the way down the staircase to the Common Hall on the first level of the building. Here, students sat at tables and ate, studied or talked.

Leto had apparently not yet accepted her retirement. She would most certainly seek out a coast-side estate somewhere off the island, but for now inhabited a tiny cabin on the School's side of the village. He would have considered it a shack, but the thick posts on either side of the deck gave it a very sturdy appearance. Haekus knocked for him, while Akheron stood on the steps to catch his breath.

A middle-aged woman opened the door. "Visitors?" she asked.

"Prince Akheron, to see her," Haekus said.

"Who are you?" Akheron demanded. "Leto, you're not even opening your door anymore?"

Her aide threw up her hands when Akheron took the door from her. He found the old magician in the main room, lying lengthwise on a cushioned bench. A bed to die upon.

Glyphs, she's ancient! Leto wore a beige gown, but was wrapped in a blanket. Her skin, on her face and the hands that clutched the blanket, was bumpier than the crusted wax of a candle left burning far too long at the head of a shrine to the Maker. Like that first shrine, if Akheron's memory served him. Everything served him.

Leto certainly had. Until she was a feeble old hag.

"What?" she asked. Her voice still held the quiver he had noticed the last time she joined them for the Imperial Council. "Don't look so surprised, Akheron."

He was speechless. He glanced back over his shoulder. Her aide accepted Leto's nod and stepped outside where Haekus was already slouching against the wooden beams. Akheron looked back at the rag of a woman on the couch.

"I held my position at court for as long as I could, but my service to the Triumvirate is done," she said. "I warned you it soon would be!"

"I didn't believe you, old friend." Akheron said.

"Old friend?"

"May I seat myself?" he asked, grabbing a chair from near the wall. *How delightfully polite of myself!*

"I certainly hope so. Since when have you asked

permission for anything?" Leto asked. "For that matter, since when have *we* been friends?"

"Always!" he exclaimed, sinking down at her bedside. The chair he had chosen was made of solid oak and had the angles to break his back if he sat too long. He resolved to keep it brief.

"Not three years ago, you were cursing my futility in front of two other Princes," Leto noted.

"Not three years ago, you were sitting with the Three Princes!"

Leto shook her head. There was a wide window beside her. It was as long as the bed she lounged in, and Akheron was certain she could see the ocean from it. She gazed out for a few moments, then turned back to him.

"What do you want, Akheron?" she asked. "To say farewell, or congratulate me on my career?"

"No, it's your replacement," he lied.

"Weveld?" she said. "He's a tough dog. He'll bite back if you nip at his heels. I'm sorry to leave you with someone like him..."

"No, no. I like him."

Leto raised an eyebrow and took a moment to judge if he was serious. He didn't know why she needed to; when did Akheron deal in sarcasm? When she realized he was stoic, she laughed. *Why?* His sarcasm would undoubtedly have been received with less mirth.

"He might actually stand up to me, you worthless wimp," Akheron said.

"Ho, now," she smirked. She held up a finger to reprimand him. "Please, on my deathbed, enough of our games and banter."

That sobered him. "Your deathbed? Are you ill?"

"No," she said. She looked back out the window. "Just tired. So weak, and tired."

"Glyphs," he said, rolling his eyes. He stood up restlessly. "You think I'm not tired?"

"You're young yet," she said.

"I thought you were better than this," he said, brandishing his own finger upon her. "I thought you were clever, old woman. You don't know what exhaustion is. You've seen a fraction of the darkness of this world and it has weakened you this much? To lie in a bed beside the ocean and call it your deathbed?"

She stared at him.

"You're a damned fool, Leto. You've seen the Prince, you've seen the revolutionary, you've seen all the facades to me, but you haven't seen *me.*" She couldn't meet his eyes anymore. She looked through her window more. Akheron collected himself once more. He sank back into the cursedly uncomfortable chair and, with a sigh, said, "That's true darkness. That's true... *exhaustion.*"

Leto shook her head. "You're right, of course," she said. Her gaze didn't leave her window. What was out there? Did she see something in the street, the sea, the horizon?

For a long moment they sat there, both in great discomfort. *Is there companionship here?* he wondered. *We share something, but is it only this uneasiness?* He wished dreadfully that they shared a real companionship and not just awkward silence.

"What do you want, Akheron?" she asked with a tremble, and looked back at him. He had never noticed how blue her eyes were. It must have been the angle of the sun.

"To lie here and die with you," he said.

She gave a dry chuckle in reply.

"You're right, we've always been tense debaters at Council and shared opposite points of view, it's just—"

"And why is it that you want to die, so badly?" she asked him. "I've seen all that you've seen and more. I'm twice your age."

"You haven't," he assured her. He squeezed his eyes closed. He could still feel the plaster of that statuette, and the pulse. Glyphs, the pulse. He banished the memory from his mind. He had to.

"Man up," she said.

"What?"

Leto shook her head. "Something in this world showed you what it's made of, the darkness and evil that's in it. So what? Look around you, at this world of men who get over it."

"Cowards, who would not face it," he said.

"Heroes, who keep the peace."

"Fools. There is no peace."

Leto shook her head. "You're one angry child," she said.

"No," he retorted. " Children become angry because the

world isn't the way they expected it, isn't as good as they wanted it to be. It is not this immaturity that plagues me. It's the truth that comes with age, instead, that tortures me. That there is *no* world. There are only men. I don't mean men by our sex. I mean, there are only humans. There is *no* darkness in the world, there is only the darkness in men."

She mulled over his words for a few minutes longer. "Have you tried to be good?" she asked.

"I—" What could he say? How did one answer this question? "Maybe," he began. He paused again. "Maybe, men don't get to be good."

"What, by some cosmic design?"

"By some cosmic joke."

"One that makes you want to kill yourself?" she asked.

"Yes," he nodded. He shivered, then added, "though I've never thought of it so blatantly. This is the most unfortunate conversation I've ever had."

"What are you waiting for?" she asked, leaning toward him. Her jowls shook. "You're wearing a sword. Too many social implications?"

He shook his head. "You know I've never cared for 'social implications'."

She smirked. "Then you need poetic justice? Hang yourself. Or... poison? That's got a great ring to it."

"Glyphs. No. I don't want to kill myself," he decided.

She chuckled again. "Now what, Gothikar gone coward?"

"Ha, no," he laughed. "If I wanted to kill myself, it would mean that the world had won."

"But you said there was no world."

"Then it would mean *I* had won," he rephrased, impatiently. *It would mean the darkness had won. I will* never *secede.* There was the anger again, the volcano he had imagined in his youth. It was fading to bitterness in recent years, but once the very thought of the darkness in this world and within himself demanded the fury to annihilate it all.

"You're one twisted man," she said. "This conversation has been intriguing, depressing, *long*, and, once again, exhausting."

Akheron nodded, and stood. "Very well. I should return to my own ocean window."

"I'll leave it with this," she cackled, with her old woman

voice. "Rest in peace, my old friend."

He glanced over his shoulder at her as he left. *Glyphs, that feels right.* "You as well," he said. Outside, Haekus was smiling and jesting with Leto's servant. So lively. Akheron closed his eyes and sighed.

6

At the annual meeting of the Triumvirate Council in the 520th year, Akheron Gothikar was the last to arrive and the first to leave. It was not that he had little interest in his responsibilities of state, but rather because his fellow Princes's antics wore away at his patience. From their Council Chamber in the Tower of the Throne, Akheron could have looked into the Mydarius Sea and watched the gulls spiral, the ships sail, and the girls swim. It was the summer and the capital smouldered like the embers of the Grand Stead. Those who lived here loved it; men and women alike stripped down to swim in the salty coastal water or one of the dozen pools that dotted the city and nearly everyone in the city spent their time outside. Once, priests would have criticized them for it, but their liberties were unhindered now. Akheron imagined Olympus had been such a paradise, though its age had started to rot its innards. He imagined it could get a lot worse, but if he had to bear the heat, he would bear it here in Galinor.

Instead of gazing out at the beauty, he was watching the sweat bead on Prince Verin Theseus's forehead. Odyn, the burly boar of a man, did not sweat at all. *Odd... I wonder why.*

"...thought that hiring corsairs to kill corsairs had it wrong," Theseus was saying. He was an old man now and his voice had become nasally. Leto, who sat against the far wall, was just as wrinkled as he. *They would make a good match,* Akheron decided, *if Verin were not already married to one of his wrinkly bark-skinned northerners.*

"So the rumours are true?" Odyn asked.

Theseus nodded. "We paid the Wave Riders, but now they have stolen our gold and joined the enemy."

Akheron was so dreadfully bored that he continued thinking about sweat. *Odyn the Tenth is from a city that sweats, so maybe he's already sweat all he can.* "Damn Buccaneers," the boar said, as if on cue.

Akheron had seen the Olympian Court a few times over the years. The Prince of Tiberon's dynasty spent his sessions of audience lounging on an ornate throne. It was carved from some sort of wood—many scholars claimed it had to be everwood, because of that throne's miraculous age—but was so thoroughly covered with golden plates and designs that it looked like a golden throne. There were two cushions, though they rested upon the chair, rather than being upholstered to it. They rested on the throne, like the near-monarch who rested while his court sweat.

Akheron moved his watching eyes to Theseus. In the North, heat like this never forced the inhabitants of the region to shed those gaudy furs they loved to decorate themselves with. Though the Mydarius Coast was fair year round—Athyns with it—Theseus would be finding the Galinor summer as uncomfortable as Akheron found it.

"What now? The Navy must be stopped." Leto said. She was always the one to speak such nonsense. *She insists on her own world.* Akheron loved her for it; she would not settle to live in the world they lived in. *She's like Reya: decidedly deluded.*

Thoughts of his home life briefly distracted him. His son had turned one just before he made the journey here. He had a son. The thought still twisted his stomach. He was drawn back to the council meeting by the silence of his colleagues.

"Stop trying," Akheron said. They glanced at him. He was not particularly talkative at these meets. "Corsairs will be corsairs, bandits will be bandits. Organized or not, there *will* be crime."

"And attitude like that is what permitted the Grey Night. I thought *you*, of all people, would understand that," Leto retorted. "We must not allow the Navy to continue defying us."

"Must you always be so damned futile?" Akheron demanded, glaring at her. "Stop wasting the Triumvirate on vain things like crime and revolution. They will run their course."

"Says the revolutionary," Odyn sneered.

"Bah!"

Theseus and Odyn shared a glance. The former leaned toward Akheron and said, "We may have tolerated your attitude during the revolt, when millions supported you. Now   "

Akheron stood up and planted his hands palm down on the clear everwood table. He glanced at the Throne, then back at his opponents. Would they have this bout again? "I could kill...." He chose his words carefully when Leto took to her feet. If he had tried to attack them, she would have been the biggest threat. The Crown Magician was no priest, but a warrior. "You think the mob doesn't support me still? If I stood above the City Gate and bellowed down at the people to seize you two and hang you... do you think you would survive? Your guards would certainly protect you from the rabble, and the magicians would grant you the air-crushed or fire-scorched flesh of *hundreds*. But how many would die before you surrendered? Do not forget who *I* am. I am the usurper of Avernus, the Maker's Bane, and the champion of Midgard, and you and all your lackeys would tremble if I raised my fist." He slammed the table once and then turned away to the window. Verin jumped in his shoes.

"Those are treasonous words you speak," Leto said, after a moment.

Akheron hadn't even looked out the window; he spun on her. "So go ahead and stop me. Cast some spell. Bind me up in the air. Or you, Odyn, livid red in the face, strike me down with all your brawn." He waited a moment. "What's that? Not a word? The Triumvirate is a system of governance by the people, no matter what you say. It is rule by wealth: not our wealth, but the people's. You three must hate me, but you cannot reprimand me."

He turned back to the window. Would they attack him? Would Leto follow him once they left this 'sacred' chamber and demand his arrest?

Outside, he could see tan bodies lounging on some of the rooftops. The Tower of the Throne was several storeys tall, but this chamber was not in its highest layer. He watched the waves of heat rising above the buildings, snaking tails into the sky. A wall stood between him and the shore. He could see the ocean, but not the beach. *Glyphs, now I'm sweating.* He ran a hand over his forehead and it came away dripping. He remembered licking sweat this thick from a woman's back. Not his wife's, he suspected, though the memory was too murky. He felt slightly aroused and very sick.

The meeting recovered from his outburst. "Akheron's... 'contribution' aside, we cannot sit idly by. Let's commission some of the Royal Fleet to patrol high risk areas. If we cannot hunt the Buccaneers without our guides turning cloak," Theseus said, "we can, at least, protect our merchants and travellers."

Good luck with that, Akheron wished them. He watched a bird sail toward the port. There were many ships anchored in the Galinor harbour. One of them was his, the *Sky Hound.* Theseus and Odyn each had Crown Magicians because neither of them had studied magic. Akheron had no magic nor a Crown Magician. Glyphs were for him to curse by, not live by.

It was a long journey, one that he often wasted with short outbursts in Council and noisy stays in an ale or a pleasure house. Whether at sea, at court, or at home, he was a lonely man. *I've always been,* he thought. He looked at his hands, still sticky with sweat and wrung them in the corner of his tunic to clean them.

"Are there other matters to discuss?" Odyn asked.

After the meeting, as Akheron made his way toward his inn, Leto fell into stride behind him. She walked with a grace he envied, smooth, no matter how the road turned or bumped. She was silent until he spoke.

"Come to arrest me for my treason?"

"No," she replied. "You're right. You own the Triumvirate these days, for you own the people. I pray that you die soon, though none of us will have anything to do with it. Glyphs, the people may blame us anyway."

"You pray?" Akheron asked. His voice was low now, a hoarse wind whistling from his depths. "Pray to whom?"

There were two guards with him. Akheron had given his usual bodyguard the day off to enjoy the sights of Galinor. It was the sort of thing that Haekus enjoyed even more than his Prince. The guards with Akheron tensed at the tone in his voice.

Leto stopped walking. "The Maker," she said, calmly.

Akheron shook his head. "You dare speak that name to me? Guards."

They drew their weapons, but waited for instruction. Leto stared at him with something between shock and resignation. She trembled.

"Arrest her," he said, ignoring her unvoiced plea. The guards seized her arms; she did not resist. "If you were a commoner, I would kill you, Leto. If you were a lord, I might call upon the mob to do it for me."

"You would be breaking the law," Leto told him.

"Since when has that stayed these hands?" he held them up for her. Could she see what hid in the cracks? "If I told this guard to cut off a finger from one of yours, he would."

They had drawn a crowd now, a mix of soldiers from the courtyard and citizens watching from the guarded gate. Unless he summoned them, they were not allowed to enter the Palace's grounds.

"I'm getting too old to play these games with you, Akheron," she said, growing irritated. She did not struggle against the guards. "Soon, I will retire."

"That would be true treason, wouldn't it? To retire without permission, from a position of state?"

Leto smirked. "You're getting good at this," she said. She shrugged her arms against her captors. "What's your decision, Prince? Will you truly depose a loyal Crown Magician?"

Akheron stared at her. He glanced at the growing crowd. There were children there, all of them half-naked. They reminded him of little Peri, a helpless worm with a plump belly. They were watching a man of legends, the Usurper, and waiting to see what would happen. He glanced back at Leto. "You will spend a fortnight in a cell for insulting me—your Prince," he said.

"I will step down from my position of Crown," she said, without blinking.

He laughed as he walked away. With a mild scuffle, the guards dragged her across the courtyard. "Two fortnights then, the second for lying to your superior!" he called back.

When had Akheron become so cursedly sad? Once he had been angry, once terrified, once idealistic—foolish. *Glyphs,* he thought, *I was a fool. I thought I knew love. I thought I knew courage. I thought I knew fury. I thought I knew what it was to be alone. I thought I knew my god.... And here I go again. Sad.* He wished silently to become bitter. If he was a thorn, at least he might do something. At least he might be able to sleep.

He lay beside his wife in the middle of the night. Her stomach was the moon. Before the moon waned, he would be a father. *I thought I knew love.* Reya was not the first. Not even the second. He had loved Illa. He had loved Mavas. He had loved Tam. But once he had loved... *her.* He dared not think her name. He rolled away from Reya and thought of *her* again. Tears wetted his pillow, and he forced himself to close his eyes.

Did my father weep? Did Aristorn? he wondered. A horrific thought occurred to him, one that might seem insignificant to him tomorrow, or to any other man. *Will my son weep?* He wished it would be a daughter. Since Reya had told him she was with child... he had whispered his wish to all the night-shadowed walls in his palace. *Then my child need not feel ashamed to weep,* he told himself, as he bit his tongue and dried his eyes. *And a daughter would not have to carry on this damned name.*

Reya stirred in her sleep. She had started having trouble sleeping because of her growth. Akheron watched her for a moment. She could, at least, keep her eyes closed. He could not.

She was a strong woman. So much stronger than he. He

could tell her anything and she could bear it like the child he had given her. With grim determination, if the matter was hard, but with capability nonetheless. He admired her. But he felt terribly alone at the same time. She was too strong for him. His mind could not imagine someone with her... greatness. It denied everything that he thought he knew of this world and, for that, he had married her. Like everything he had touched, he knew it would end poorly.

The next morning, he watched her awake. He watched her walk across the room, her belly swaying like a sail. *I thought I knew courage.* A servant helped her dress, while Akheron still lay there. *Enough of this,* he decided. *It's time to stop this moping.*

"I'm going down to the port today," he told her. She raised an eyebrow. "Don't try to stop me."

"Have some food first, at least?"

"No." He put on his own breeches and jerkin. The servants had learned the hard way to not come near Akheron Gothikar in the morning.

"You can't live on air," Reya said.

"I'm not the one with another person to feed," he said, though their treasury was abundant. "I can get by on air, just fine."

"Did you even sleep last night?"

"Enough," he said.

"You'd think I would be the moody one," Reya said to the servant, a prim little woman with greying hair who favoured Lady Gothikar with a curt smile in reply. Akheron shoved his feet into a pair of boots while the servants tightened the ties of Reya's under-dress where it was right to do so. Fashion was much different for pregnant women, but Akheron had never made it a point of attention for himself. As he watched his wife don a blue and white gown, he thought, *Maybe I should have.* Reya glanced at him and smiled. "Instead, I'm the reasonable and practical one in this marriage."

"Ha." He stopped himself from saying, *Because marrying someone like me was such a pragmatic decision!* He made for the door, despite Reya's disappointment. They did not spend much time together, for a married couple.

"Have a smooth day," she called after him.

He did not reply. The hallway outside of his room always felt cold on the skin of his balding forehead and the tips of his fingers. He brushed them against the smooth material of his jacket. He paused to look at the painting of his father that he had recently had hung outside his door. Veldar ten Gothikar had been an insignificant man and had died when Akheron was young. The painting showed him in front of a shop with a dirty apron on. Akheron only gave the piece one quick inspection and was then on his way again, striding toward the staircase and down into the Hall.

A tanner by trade, Veldar had never come close to royalty himself. Even his eldest son was long gone, drowned when ferrying his father's goods westward along the Mydarius coast. The only time that Veldar had ever spoken of Parcep to his younger brother Akheron, he had said, "And we lost a damn large shipment of leather too. Almost put me on the streets, that boy's stupidity." Akheron and his sister had been born years later, when their mother had decided to cling to her youth, despite Veldar's irritated final years.

His father was nothing like old man Aristorn.

Somewhere between the Keep and the Palace Gate into the rest of the city, Haekus fell into pace in his usual spot behind Akheron. Irked, Akheron held out a pouch to him and said, "Go find a dice table or a harlot's bed on my coin. You won't be needed today."

Haekus stifled a chuckle and folded his arms behind his back. The sword at his thigh clinked as he increased his speed to walk beside the Prince. They left the Palace guardhouse and entered the streets. "Why is that?"

"Why is that, sir."

"Why is that, my royal Prince?"

"Glyphs." Akheron shook his head, but did not pocket his coin yet. He gave it a shake to make it heard.

"I've no interest in either of those activities, sir."

"I thought you gambled," Akheron said.

"I used to," Haekus said. He was sporting a short goatee these days, like a little envelope for his mouth. It looked ridiculous, though Akheron's layer of untidy scruff likely looked worse. "But you won't be rid of me today, sir."

"I could order you." Akheron led the way around a

merchant's wagon. It was a noisy house on wooden wheels; the windows had been turned into counters for business and a host of trinkets and foods were offered. A massive man that weighed the equivalent of three of Akheron was shouting about pearls from Tarroth. The city assaulted all of Akheron's senses.

"You could order me," Haekus said. "Where in this fine city are we bound today, sir?"

"The port."

"Are you looking for a fight?" Haekus asked.

Akheron slowed down and looked at his guardsman. "Not this time. Are you offering?"

Haekus smirked. "Course not, sir."

Akheron shook his head again. *I thought I knew fury.*

They passed a bakery that warmed the entire street with freshness. His stomach growled. He wondered absently how long he could go without eating. It felt like he had been awake for more than an entire cycle of the moon now, and hadn't eaten for days.

The port of Avernus was down a long flight of stairs built into the Avernan cape. The cliffs were alive with gulls, rodents and children; the lord and his guard got quite the collection of eyes as they descended. It was the fall, and the port was brimming with the year's traffic. As an Imperial City, Avernus was a major centre for trade simply because of its populace and political popularity. Within the fortnight, the harbour would empty completely; many captains would head west to Olympus or Galinor. Some would set course for Athyns. A few would press north through the Gate for Tarroth, the infamous free city.

Akheron remembered that city clearly. It was like one massive rock that put this stone-hewn stairway to shame. How a place as heavy as that mountainous settlement could claim to be 'free', he would never know.

His empty stomach gnawed at him. *When* was *the last time I ate?* he wondered.

They reached the port, a collection of wooden buildings with a few stone structures appearing as the place grew. There was a large courtyard in front of the docks, with enough space for returning crews to rendezvous with loved ones or for merchants to unpack their cargo ships. The looks that Akheron and Haekus received now were unlike those of the climbing children they had encountered earlier. Everyone here was armed, and more than a few eyed Akheron's jerkin jealously. Those who recognized him were much more adoring. Why did he attract so many worshippers? *I thought I freed them of worship...* He had never considered that such a task might be impossible. It was those that did not know which lord walked into the yard that noted his coin purse or his jeweled sword scabbard.

"Perhaps I was wrong," he told Haekus under his breath. "Perhaps I am looking for a fight."

Haekus didn't even tense. His hand remained on its hilt, where it often did and his face did not express anything more than his patience. "Whatever milord fancies," he joked. Akheron's stomach was a fiery pit now, turning his insides to ash.

The tavern that Akheron chose was called the Gatehouse. It was one of his favourites. Avernus spoke of this establishment in the common rooms on any street. It was one of the places that spread its name beyond the walls of this city alone. The Gatehouse was a two storey tavern—it had no rooms to sleep in, only bars and tables to carouse at. By the owner's motto, 'If you want to sleep, find an inn. If you want to share a drink with men from every port on either sea, find the Gatehouse.' The storeys were built from rough stone, designed intentionally to look like a primitive dwelling. Someone had once told Akheron that the only people who find it comfortable are those that have just arrived across The Gate.

As they crossed the marble slab that served as threshold, Akheron saw Haekus shake his head. This was no place for a Prince to go. Especially in the morning.

Within, Akheron defeated two burly doormen with a dry smile. The owner of the institution made an elaborate bow and attempted to speak polished words to the Usurper. Akheron gave him no more than a glance and started his rounds of the place. He was looking for someone. *Well, anyone would do,* he decided.

The first floor was a single massive room, large enough to seat a hundred men. A fog of smoke hung from ceiling to Akheron's belt; he could smell tobacco from the Edimi flatlands, fierce weeds from Elysia and the soft, telltale whisper of an Agwarian pipe. Those, though Akheron had not experienced it firsthand, were said to give a man a dream of himself dreaming. The smell of alcohol dominated all of these, and the din of harbour-shouting and metal-hammering were drowned out in the deafening hubbub of drunkards and whores.

Akheron Gothikar drank it in.

A servant girl asked him if he wanted a spot at the bar or a table, and if she could get him a drink. He said, "Fly away little one," and she did.

Haekus stayed close. Akheron was an acquired distaste: almost everyone seemed to love him, but those who did not... did not. Among his enemies, Akheron imagined none would hesitate to kill him, even in this public place. A little knife in the ribcage, a drop of something in his drink, or maybe a cord around his neck.

A man in one corner gestured his chair excitedly, and Akheron rolled his eyes. He kept walking, up the staircase to the tavern's second floor. There was another bar here, full of noisy men and clouds of tobacco. It was all Akheron could do not to cough. This building disgusted him. Here men were their true selves. They were rotten, half-lucid vermin. Grovelling for their next fix, alcoholics and cutthroats dined in their paradise and Akheron was right there with them. This reminded him what he was.

Once, he thought. *Once I was above this all. I thought I was. I prayed I w...* he cut the thought off.

Haekus was there, quietly, at Akheron's elbow. Waiting. He coughed quietly.

Once, Haekus would have asked me why we were here. Why I was looking for things in the bottom end of the world. He knows me better now. "Haekus," he said, "when did you get to know me so well?"

Haekus scoffed. "When did you let your guard down?"

"What's that?" he asked. Someone was waving from the bar, but he was asking what Haekus meant.

"I haven't learned how to interpret you any better," his friend said. "You've gotten careless at pretending to be something you're not."

Akheron smiled. "Careful. That almost sounded like a compliment."

Haekus laughed. "And what would be wrong with that?"

The waving from the bar became furious. It was a man tanned from hours in the sun, with curling squid's arms tattooed across his bald head. "What would be wrong with that, *sir*," Akheron reprimanded, giving Haekus a firm glance before striding toward the bar.

"Akheron Gothikar!" the man exclaimed, once they were close enough to be heard.

"Sathius Miroso!" Akheron returned. Most of the nobility from Tarroth assumed the usual title *'of Tarroth'* for none of them had royal names and none were widely known. Sathius was neither a commoner nor a noble. Once, he had—fiercely—told Akheron to call him by his last name, not his place of birth.

"Am I allowed to call you Akheron?" Sathius asked. He offered his hand as Akheron seated himself next to his old comrade, in seats that had been vacated by the Prince's dark glare. "You're not here to arrest me, are you?"

The barkeeper gave them a glance.

Akheron clasped the hand and patted the shoulder. "You can call me whatever you desire, my old friend!"

"Haekus," Sathius said.

"Miroso," Haekus replied, "haven't seen you in some time."

"All we need now is Edemar, and this would be a proper reunion," Sathius said, and took a pull of the tobacco pipe he held. "I heard he's your treasurer now, and that you married his daughter!"

"That I did," Akheron said.

"I'll be—"

"And this would not be a proper reunion without Demetas, may he rest in peace," Akheron said. *I thought I knew what it was to be alone.*

"Demetas? Peace?" Haekus asked. "That's unlikely."

"And you, certified blade-master, are a pacifist?" Sathius retorted. He ran a finger along a scar on his arm. Looked like a new one. "Akheron, dispose of your stiff shadow. I'd prefer to catch up with my *friend.*"

Haekus chuckled and sat down at the bar. "Mead," he called. The barkeep rolled his eyes and filled a mug. It was reasonable to drink mead in the morning, but not profitable.

"I'll have a straight Orlin brandy," Akheron said, which got him a small smile. He had once seen a man blow a cloud of fire from his mouth after lighting a match to his cup of brandy. Had it been a dare?

Haekus shook his head. "Don't you think it's early, sir?"

"Don't you think I told you not to come, sir?" Akheron mocked.

Haekus took a drink of his mead.

"I thought to myself," Sathius said, "wouldn't it be ironic if I came here to Avernus and ran into Akheron! And here you are. Bloody Gate, what are the chances?"

Bloody Gate, Akheron thought. *There's one I haven't heard in a while.*

"I said to myself," Sathius lowered his voice, "remember that time we did that job and made Akheron a Prince of an Imperial City?" He laughed, and took a drink of his own. The barkeeper finally procured Akheron's.

Akheron examined the small quarter-filled glass. Not many men got actual glass. "I remember it well."

Haekus laughed. "'Course *you* would." He put out his hand for Akheron's drink.

"You should have said to yourself," Akheron said, "Remember that time we found the Buccaneers?"

Haekus's hand was still hovering and Akheron's mood was sinking. "What?" he asked his body-guard.

"You know."

Akheron set the drink down on the wooden bar top. He must have set it down hard, for he got a few glances from around the room. There was a group of young sailors nearby who had recognized Akheron when he first arrived. "I ordered you not to come. Then I ordered you to leave. You honestly think someone will poison me? A knife works just as well and is a whole lot less dramatic."

"Maybe it's your dramatic enemies I'm concerned about," Haekus said. He took a drink and winced. "That's strong."

"But not deadly, I trust?" Akheron asked. He looked at his glass as Haekus handed it back, and the fingerprints that now decorated it. "Now I have to drink from the same glass. That's the real poison," he scoffed.

Haekus stretched his lips and went back to his mead. "I'm certain you'll survive."

"You two haven't changed a bit," Sathius said.

Akheron drank his whole brandy in one mouthful. It was smoky and sharp on his tongue, a mix of fire and vapour. Sharper in his empty stomach.

"Don't talk about the Buccaneers no more," Sathius said. "I'm done with them."

"Really?" Haekus asked. His next words were hushed: "But you're still a corsair."

"What else would Sath' Miroso be?" Sathius asked. "After Demetas, things were different. I tried to keep a hold on the whole Navy, but I've never been a lord in any sense of the word. You need a proper commander for a fleet like this."

Akheron nodded weakly. He put the glass down carefully. His throat was burning while his stomach felt worse.

"So who's in charge of the thing now?" Sathius asked, rhetorically. "Glyphs, if I know."

Haekus shook his head. "We've lost control of it. The whole forsaken thing."

Akheron lurched to his feet. He was going to be sick, but he couldn't; his stomach was still empty, more or less. His comrades stood just as quickly.

"Akheron?" Haekus asked.

"I'm fine," he gasped. "Air." He made for the stairwell. The room felt off. It was slanted. No, it was skewed. The smoke in the air was so strong, filling his lungs. It was the smoke of the Great Stead, or the smoke of the Grey Night. And the alcohol in his veins was the tears of children running in the streets and in the canyons of Akheron's fingerprints. Why could he feel the sweat in his fingerprints? He tried to wipe his hands on his jerkin, but it didn't work this time.

The first floor was noisier now. Somehow. Its noise pounded on Akheron's temples. Haekus had his arm and was trying to take him to the bar for water or bread to absorb whatever he had consumed, but Akheron was walking for the door and Sathius was opening it for him.

He slipped on the two-tier steps in front of the tavern; he slipped or he lost his strength altogether. He didn't hit the ground, for his friends held him. But somehow, the sky was so far away. The ground was so close. Haekus had drank from the same glass, but his support was strong—he had not been poisoned...

Akheron closed his eyes.

When he opened them, he was lying in a feather-down bed. His bed. There were low voices nearby. Men talking. Everyone always said that women liked to chat, but it seemed to him that men's chattering was worse.

"What happened?" he asked, as he opened his eyes. Haekus and Gysius stood over him. The latter's grey moustache was particularly bushy from this angle. His mouth was bone dry and he took a drink of the water canteen he was presented with. It tasted pure and stayed in his stomach comfortably. He pressed his hand to stomach. Beneath the blanket, his cotton shift and his muscled abdomen, he could feel a full stomach. "Did I eat?"

"We had a magician give you food," Gysius said, "for we could not wake you."

Haekus said nothing. He looked grim.

"Glyphs! Someone used magic on me?" Akheron asked, starting to rise. He felt fine. Better than fine. He felt alive.

"I understand you don't like it," Gysius said. "But you consumed strong alcohol on a starving stomach. You poisoned yourself, in short."

Akheron shook his head. "Say that again, and we'll poison you next. No one hears about this."

"I'm afraid several have already," Haekus said. "Though I will quell any further—"

"What do you mean, several have?"

Haekus shook his head. "My apologies sir. It was necessary to tell your wife."

Reya? "Haekus, if I did not find your mere existence to be humorous and entertaining, I would have you thrown from my Keep!" he shouted. "Why, by the Glyphs, was it necessary to tell my wife?"

"She can answer that better than I, sir."

Akheron trembled. "Out. Both of you!" His pride stung. But he had never cared much about it.

They moved briskly to the door.

"Wait," he said, with a forced calm. "Where is my Lady wife?"

"A servant waiting in the corridor will take you to her,

milord," Gysius said. He patted his robe. "What a day!" he let out under his breath as the door closed behind him.

Akheron clambered out of bed. He was still clothed, which was a pleasant surprise. He looked about his room. Through the window, he could see the sun was now past midday; the Keep's shadow was cast across the Palace walls. His boots were sitting neatly at the end of his bed. As he forced his feet into them, he wondered about Sathius. *Likely, he dared not accompany my unconscious body around the town,* he decided dryly. *Unless Haekus threw him in jail once we got here!*

"Take me to my wife," he told the servant who waited outside. It was that frail gray-haired woman again. He almost said what he thought of her out loud, that she was a twig to be broken. He had seen it too many times when they brought down the Maker's Kinship. She should be at home under lock and key, not trying to guide corrupt lords around.

She led the way down the hall to a room guarded by two men that Akheron recognized as true veterans; they were men that had served Lord Edemar and Lord Edemar's father. They had seen their share of conflict, between the rebellion against the Kinship and the raids before that. But why would two elites be guarding his wife?

"Did something hap—" Then it hit him like a clap of thunder. "The child came."

He had stopped walking, and the elderly servant waited for him without a word. He looked down at his feet. He forced one step forward, into the doorframe. *I thought I knew courage.*

Reya waited there, with their son. She smiled when she saw him. *Can there be hope? Can this be a good thing, to have brought another into this world? Will I be a good father?* He had so many questions. He had never imagined himself a father. *Will he bury me?*

Will I tell him about the day of his birth? What I did, this day? He looked down and straitened the hem of his pants with his palms. He looked at his hands. *I thought I knew fury.*

He stepped forward again. "You deserve better," he said. "I'm a drunk fool."

"It doesn't matter now," Reya said. She had always been far too forgiving. "We have a son. Come and see him. *You* have a son."

He stepped forward again. Who was this little person? A pink babe, eyes squeezed shut against the light of the world. *Dare I?* he wondered. He reached out to take the child, but could not touch it. Instead, he knelt beside the bed and took hold of his wife's hand. He had spent so long trying not to feel that now he didn't know how to. He didn't know *what* to think.

"I love you," he told Reya, or the child, or neither of them. Perhaps it was a memory, he told "I love you."

"And I you," she replied, and gave him a kiss.

I thought I knew what it was to be alone, Akheron thought. *Glyphs, I am such a fool.*

8

"I'm just so tired," Akheron explained. He was lying on his stomach. The bed was somewhat firm, it was not his and he guessed it was likely full of cheap feathers instead of down.

"Of course," Illa said, as she pressed and folded the skin of his shoulders. He could feel her warmth in the lower curve of his back, where she sat with a leg on either side of him. Her grip was firm, working the stiffness from his shoulders.

"How's your brother?" he asked. Her brother was a guardsman in his hire; some lords might have blackmailed the woman to sleep with them, but Akheron did not mind paying.

"He's well," she said. "I've never asked you if you have any siblings."

"I had a brother that drowned long before I was born, and a sister that died a few years ago," he said. "Now it's just me."

"And your wife," Illa said, tapping her hands gently against the back of his neck.

"Yes, I suppose," he said. "And my wife. Reya."

"What's she like?" Illa asked. Her hands paused. "Is it alright, my asking? I know some men are sickened by discussing their wife in the presence of their..."

"No, that's fine," Akheron said, opening his eyes. There was a nightstand beside her bed and an intricately carved wardrobe against the wall. "I don't care. She knows I come here."

"She does?" Illa exclaimed, leaning down on him. He could feel her whole torso pressed against the skin of his back. His muscles tensed again, undoing her attempted massage, but it

felt good. "You told her you spend time in a brothel?"

Akheron smirked. He had been resting his chin on his hands, but he stretched his arms out like a bird. "She's known that about me since we met. I was leaving one when I first met her. From there, I went to the courtyard up the street and gave a speech inciting revolution." It was a paraphrase.

Illa laughed. Her voice was higher and softer than Reya's. Sometimes it felt fake, but most of what she said seemed genuine.

"She knows I could've married one of you, or some other girl," he said, "but I married her. I chose her."

"But if you aren't exclusive to her, what kind of choice is that?" Illa asked. "I mean, the only difference is that she'll bear your children..."

Glyphs, children? Akheron wondered. He had never thought of that. There was no risk of children with strumpets, for glyphs warded the rooms of brothels from conception. "Are you really debating the integrity of men? Here? With your legs wrapped around me?"

She laughed and sat up again. She started tracing the muscled lines of his back. "No, I'm just curious. Like what would life be like, from your perspective? What is your wife's like?"

"You shouldn't ask these questions," Akheron said. "You wouldn't like my life. Even I don't."

Her finger paused again, right between his shoulder bones. She shifted across the bed, untangling herself from him. "Then why don't you change?"

Akheron glanced at her, a tiny naked thing on top of the blankets. She had bright brown hair, almost blonde, and sharp brown-green eyes. She was more expensive than a drink, but accomplished the same thing for him. It both helped him forget his failures and embrace the comfort in being a failure. "Because I don't want to," he said. "Because nothing is worth it, and even if it was, the amount of strength required to change is an insult to my morality."

"So you call yourself a bad man—"

"I am a bad man. I've burned men and women alive and murdered even more with my bare hands."

"So you're a bad man," she said, un-phased. She knew who

he was. "Because you're rebelling against all the bad men in the world?"

Akheron chuckled. He rolled over, closer to her, onto his back. "Something like that. The world wanted to corrupt me, so they could defeat good. They did. They won. That can't be undone. No matter what I become, or how much I change... I already failed and the war is already lost."

"That's depressing," she said.

"Terribly so." Akheron put a hand on her hip and drummed his fingers against her buttock. "Which is why I spend time in brothels and taverns and my wife doesn't care."

"But still," she said, "why marry her?"

"A debt," he admitted at last. "She loved me, probably still does, and I owed her father a Prince's favor."

She laughed and pulled her hair back behind her shoulders, inching closer to him. "A Prince's favor," she said. "Could I earn that by fetching another one of the girls to join us?"

He stared at her. "Glyphs, no," he said. "I'm not interested in anything like that. I didn't even know that was accepted enough to ask..."

"It is now," she said. "Now that the Kinship is no more."

"I'm more of a Kinship sort of man, I suppose," he said. He found such deviance to be tasteless and unappealing. He considered himself a man of tradition.

Illa laughed. "Oh, clearly. Your friend Haekus is interested in... 'things like that'," she said.

Haekus always accompanied him on his outings; more often than not he waited outside of the brothels, but occasionally—like today—sought out his own companionship. What a terribly lonely life it must be, serving as Akheron's shadow. He hadn't thought about it much. He blinked though, trying not to picture what Illa was telling him.

She pushed him into the bed and put a foot on the floor as they shifted their weight.

After the soft thump of her foot on the carpet, there was a thump of the door. Wood splintered. Hinges creaked inward. A man stepped in, garbed in grey. He held a wicked dagger with a curvy blade, the sort that could saw through fingers stretched out to keep death away.

Everything slowed down. Akheron had to decide how to

act. There were two ways this could transpire, two ways that he saw.

The assassin took a step forward.

In the first scenario, Akheron would let himself die. He had waited so long for this assassin. The knife would cut him quickly. The stranger would drive it into his heart, perhaps, and the bed would fill with blood. Finally, Haekus did not stand between him and the final peace he was waiting for.

Death came a step closer.

Illa was between him and the assassin. She would die. There was no way around it. The knife would arc into her neck, beneath her chin as she turned to confront the assassin. Blood would splash down her neck as her knees hit the rug.

Another step. Illa turned toward her killer.

Akheron could not save her. And that meant he could not let himself die either. He had no qualms about the killer getting free after murdering the Prince, but he would not let Illa's murderer live. He could not.

The man shoved his knife upward, into Illa's head. Akheron shoved the whore, hard, to the left—away from the assassin. The knife went with her, smashing against the wall with a sickening thud.

Akheron punched the man in the throat and followed his opponent through the stumbled back step. The assassin took a swing at the Prince with his empty fist. Akheron went under, and swiftly slammed his shoulder into the assassin's torso. The man grunted. As expected, he brought his elbows thundering down at Akheron's exposed back. Akheron dropped nimbly to his belly; he wasn't wearing a thread and moved with the dexterity of a serpent.

The man's missed elbow-swing pulled him off balance. Akheron reached up from the ground and grabbed the man's belt, throwing him into the room. The motion forced the man further off his heels. He tripped across Akheron's side and tumbled into the bed.

Akheron stood up and reclaimed his composure as much as he could. He stepped forward. The assassin was leaping back to his feet, at a speed that would astound most men. For Akheron, in this moment, the man was moving like an elder. Like a priest. Slow. Methodical. Predictable.

Akheron grabbed the man's throat and pressed it back into the feather mattress. He ignored the flailing arms. All men were the same when they died. They could thrash left and right and slam punches into Akheron's gut. But they could not escape this grip. It was the grip of time on the world, pulling everyone to their graves. Everyone but Akheron.

"You damned monster," he said to the desperately struggling man. "You couldn't do this right. You couldn't find me alone. You won't die in peace."

The man's eyes were starting to lull, though he still struggled. He clawed at Akheron's face, drawing blood from the Prince's nose or from the furrows he dug into gaunt cheeks. Akheron did not flinch. He took a deep breath and said, "What do you think lies beyond the veil?" he asked. "On the other side. Not where the good men go, but where the bad men go..."

His nails dugs holes of their own in the neck of the monster until there was no more breath in him. Then, Akheron sat down on the harlot's bed beside the murderer's still corpse. The moments shuffled their feet across the bloodied carpet. A voice—his voice—choked out, "I'll be there, waiting to torment you."

He eventually inhaled, though he did not feel like he had been holding his breath. His face had not turned red, only grey.

Illa was watching him. She was just a body now, not a soul. Would she find a seat in heaven? He doubted it. She had died a sinner, and, like Akheron, was bound for a darker destination. But none of that was what he looked at now. He looked at an empty husk of flesh. There was blood covering her nakedness. The knife was just a black spike under her mouth. An hour ago, that mouth had been kissing him. Now it was just a bloody frown.

The room gradually crowded, though Akheron remained seated on the bed. He draped a bed linen across his waist. Haekus was there, his shirtless body a sharp collection of angled muscles and sweaty surfaces. He was holding a sword, having run to his liege at the first noise. "Are you harmed?" he was asking.

Nothing had changed for Akheron. This was exactly the world he had explained to Illa. His head was full of dead men and dead women and he was living—or something that looked an awful lot like living—surrounded by empty spaces.

A healer fixed the lines that had been carved into his cheeks. Reya gave him a long kiss when he got home. They ate a quiet dinner together and she offered him companionship after. He told her he only wanted silence and spent the night in the chair of his study.

When he finally climbed into bed, she said, "I wish I had known her."

"Why?" His voice was hoarse.

"Because you loved her," she said. There was a distant bitterness to her voice, but a controlled calm as well. "And you fought to avenge her."

"I would fight harder for you," he said. "That's the truth."

Beneath the blankets, her hand found his. "Why won't you ever confide in me?"

"I don't know," he lied. In his head hid the dead, and all around were empty spaces.

9

The world had not been the same since Akheron had defeated the Maker. It was still in shock, though Akheron himself was never shocked anymore. Parties filled the nights— lavish, sinful parties to distract the citizens of the Dominion from the absence of their religion. They called it freedom. They had always called it freedom.

What would they do with the two extra afternoons? There was no need for the Eve of Reflection and the Eve of Preparation for there were no Kinship services left, and no one was really certain what they should be doing with the latter half of those days. Some tradesmen had already started working full days instead of the Eve of Reflection. Of course, the day of rest that preceded the Eve of Preparation was still necessary. People could not be expected to work all seven days of the week!

This was one such issue brought to the audience of the Prince this day. It was the middle of the summer and Akheron sat uncomfortably on the stone throne of his Great Hall. He ran two fingers behind his collar. They came away sticky, no matter how he wiped them on the linen sleeveless tunic he wore.

"Master Tierres has demanded my brother and I keep mining," a short excuse for a man said. He was covered head-to-toe in soot and dirt, and barely resembled a human at all.

He reminded Akheron of an earth-spawn, almost. *All miners must be earth-spawn*, he thought. *All lumberjacks are giants, of course.*

"Even on the day of rest!" the man said.

"Milord Prince," the employer said, a good two arms-lengths from his worker. "I see no reason to cease work. There is no Kinship to attend. Your highness's mines can produce an extra seventh of their output if you permit this."

Akheron rubbed his temples. *Who cares?* he wanted to demand of them both. *What would be fair?*

The court certainly sided with the poor worker. There were over a hundred in attendance. Most were middle-nobility from Avernus, employers and merchants of reputed families. The wealthiest were always in attendance for matters discussed here were often of significance for them. There were colorful visitors from Olympus—their bright red, violet, and teal dresses blinding Akheron. The men of Olympus wore stiff dark coats, bound at the waist with vibrant sashes that matched the decor of their wives or mistresses. A few guests were from Athyns, where leathers and hides were far more commonplace. The only Noble in attendance was Edemar, Akheron's father-in-law, who sat to his right without a sound. Edemar had become a quiet and brooding man over the years. His short brown hair had all but left him now, and his face was hewn with wrinkles and whiskers. He watched the court with thinly-veiled disgust.

"My lord?" the miner asked. "Please, my brother has fallen ill and we need a day of rest."

Akheron turned back to the issue at hand. He slouched back in his chair and said, "Master... whatever by the Great Glyph your name is. If you want to put your miners to work on the day of rest, you must work harder than them all on that day. Doing *their* work, not yours."

"What!" The taskmaster was appalled.

"This will be a law for all my lands. Business can be conducted on the day of rest, only if it is conducted by all men. Equally," Akheron said. *They like equality,* he told himself. *It's part of the freedom they won with the blood of holy men.*

Lord Ivos stepped forward. He was still a young man, but a very involved one. He was friends with Edemar, and the other two Imperial Nobles. He would be Akheron's replacement, which served Akheron just fine. "My Prince, what will keep the Masters from just entering their workplace and doing no work?" he asked.

"My Prince," one of the wealthier lords said and stepped into the open audience floor beside Ivos. "Perhaps we should give the right for commoners to bring plights of this nature before their lords."

Another lord stepped forward, but Akheron stopped him with a hand and a glare. "Very well," he said. He had learned how to speak at court long ago, so his voice echoed around the Hall for all to hear. "Workers may report their Masters in groups of three. Masters are not allowed to reprimand workers for this. Master... miner, here, perhaps you would like a day of rest."

The Master was flushed red with anger, but the court adored Akheron still. The commoners considered him their hero, as always. "I will take my leave, milord Prince," the man said, and backed out of the audience clearing.

The commoners on the opposite side of the room shuffled and made way for the next issue. Many of the lords were sitting. The Great Hall doubled as a feast-hall and a public audience hall, with a raised dais and head table for Akheron and the upper nobility, a few side-tables for other lords, and a cleared area for the crowd that filled the chamber for audience.

The next man had a stocky build. He was well-fed, but had a sickly yellow complexion. He was wearing an off-angled hat and a short cape. He looked like a problem on legs. "My lord," he said, loudly. "My neighbor worships the Maker still."

The Hall fell silent. No one spoke that name in the Prince's presence. No one. A few of the commoners booed. Akheron sank deeper into his chair, his arms still gripping the intricately carved armrests. There were phrases in the old tongue written there. Akheron had made certain that the only Ancestral tongue left in the Triumvirate were the mottos of the Houses. It was one more curse against that which the old language had originally served, for now it only served the fame of men. Etched into the arms of Akheron's chair was the phrase *"Decadus abrikorbios"*, "Conquest stands alone."

"His name is Bernyn," the bold man said, unhindered by the court's reaction.

"Is this Bernyn here today?" Ivos asked. He seemed like a good, ambitious man; Akheron did not mind the thought of Ivos reigning as Prince after the unfortunate, but brief, interruption of the Gothikar Princehood. Ivos' sister had married an Olympian lord who had named a city after her, and now their House's tenants were scattered between Avernus and Olympus. Once they had been Princes in the fief of Athyns, but the man in Akheron's court was the closest they had come to reclaiming their glory.

"I am here, my lords," came a wavering voice. Bernyn came forward, slowly. He was an elderly man, with a crook in his back. He came to the first man's side and resolutely took his stand there.

"And how do you reply to your accuser's claims?" Ivos questioned.

"I don't believe them to be accusations," Bernyn replied. "A man must believe what he must. I have not harmed my neighbor."

"You have judged me," the first man said.

The crowd's noise was growing, but the argument could still be heard.

"I have," Bernyn said. "Are you such a weak man, that you cannot believe something and hold that belief despite the judgement of others?"

Akheron closed his eyes. Here was a good man. *And, by his own definition, strong. By my definition also.*

Ivos spoke up again. "You have broken the law," he said. "How do you reply to that?" The crowd shouted at the man, questions similar to Ivos's. This was the mob. Akheron thought he had finished with mobs, when he had shown the rioters outside of the Great Stead his handiwork.

"I refuse to," Bernyn said. "Tell me where to live, that I may believe what I will."

Someone shouted, "Akheron Gothikar said, 'any man who believes he is better than all the rest is a liar!' You're a cursed liar!" And the crowd took up the chant, just like in the old days.

The first man shouted at Bernyn. "Take your Maker with you when you swim into the sea—that's where you can live, old man!"

Akheron stood up, and the hall silenced. Someone coughed, and it echoed off the pillars and walls of the Hall. Then there was quiet until Akheron spoke.

"Hang 'em both," he said, and sat down again. He ignored the dismay of his wife, who sat on his left. Edemar only sat at his right-hand because this was a court of state not an event of family.

For some inexplicable reason, the crowd cheered. The guards dragged the two out; the first man went shouting and screaming. Bernyn went without protest. As the two left, the chanting continued until Edemar raised his hand. Everyone quieted and the next plight for the Prince approached.

Akheron, meanwhile, looked at Edemar. They had once been close friends, plotting against the Aristorns together. Edemar had always been a Noble, but he had not always been a satisfied one. Then, they had become acquaintances. Akheron had married Reya, and uncomfortably accepted Edemar's role as a father. But by the time the Great Stead burned, they were no more than politicians.

Edemar met his gaze as he lowered his arm. He did not approve of the Prince he had made. He ran his fingers over his round scalp and then looked away from the Prince.

Akheron didn't care. He looked back at the court's floor. A woman wearing an elaborate orange and turquoise gown took the floor. She had long black hair bound behind her head with two angled pins and a smooth face. Because of the dress she wore, Akheron could not tell her height. He could, however, see her proportions and he liked them.

"My Prince," she said, in a loud clear voice. "I am Lady Lyris Karcamus. I hope my repute has preceded me to your fine city; I am a popular painter from Olympus. My family has been painting the Odyn family line since the days of Tiberon."

He was still examining her physique. He had an interest in her, but not in her trade. "Welcome to my court, Lady Karcamus."

"I myself have proven my skill with the brush and canvas with many noble paintings of his lordship, Odyn the Tenth." She knew she had his eye, so she paced forward more. "But these are the days of change, and you have conquered tradition. It is time for the Karcamus family to move on. You are the new Tiberon, the first of a new dynasty."

Akheron shook his head. She was wrong, the poor, cute idolater.

"I would like to paint a new masterpiece," she said. "I would name a nominal fee, and begin offering my artistic services in this city, the new heart of the Dominion."

Akheron leaned forward. "While I certainly welcome you

to Avernus, my court, and even my table...." Edemar shifted uncomfortably while Reya did not. Akheron had to mask a smirk at those two. "I have no interest in my portrait lining the halls of *any* keep."

"Such work would sell for a fortune, I assure you," Lady Karcamus said.

"I'm certain it would," Akheron said. "But I have no interest in it."

"My lord," she insisted.

"I do not want this face to be remembered," he said, sharply. A few murmurs began, but he quieted them with a loud declaration. "That is all I will say on the matter. Please enjoy your stay, in my Palace or wherever you desire. I am certain you can make a good fortune off the other lords and Nobles of my lands."

She bowed, without arguing more, and backed out of his presence.

10

The horizon had disappeared behind a veil of smoke. Before Akheron had entered the massive temple—now burning and collapsing—he had seen a beautiful panorama. The magnificent city of Edim sat on the soft south-western coast of the Mydarius Sea. Inland stretched the Olympian heartlands, flatlands that were dotted with farms and unplowed green stretches. The trade port in Edim was a major exporter of food, though Gev, further inland, bought a lot of it. Those fields had looked so pristine and idyllic; in a rocky place like Avernus, such a vision only existed as an artwork.

Seaward had been an equally majestic vision, an open view of the ocean: bright blue waves that only greyed near the horizon where Delfie lay. When they had arrived in Edim, the waterways were heavily travelled; the ship's captains knew what had been coming. Everyone had known what was coming. Despite the reasons that fleeing white sails had dotted the horizon, it had only added to the beauty. Perhaps that was why the Great Stead had been built in Edim, hundreds of years ago.

Akheron had brought that whole history down as ashes. He forced his fists to uncurl. The cool winter air felt cool on his sticky palms, even though it was warmed by fires.

The courtyard in front of the burning Stead was full of dead bodies. There were fewer Defenders scattered in the dirt than Akheron's mob, but there had been fewer Defenders to begin with. Around each armoured corpse was a halo of commoner's corpses. How could their armour still shine, after killing the rebels and bathing in their blood?

The ringing in his ears began to decline and he could hear the sounds of fighting somewhere. The crowd that had cheered when he carried the body out and dropped it on the steps of the Stead had already dissipated, running past Akheron with shovels, clubs, and makeshift blades lifted.

The panorama was lost in the smoke and so was Akheron Gothikar.

"We won," Haekus said. He was standing beside Akheron, though his arrival had gone unnoticed.

"We did," Akheron said.

"Are we done now?" his friend asked.

Akheron looked at him, and then back at the bleak cityscape. Beyond the walls of the courtyard, he could see empty streets and rocky buildings of Edim, draped in a soft ashen snow. He started walking, though he did not know what his destination was.

"We defeated the Aristorns." Haekus was matching Akheron's pace. "And now we defeated the Kinship. Do you have to kill anyone else?"

Akheron stopped. They had reached the broken wooden gate that the mob had rammed down with a wooden pole, their makeshift ram. He still didn't know where they had found the thing, but it had certainly been effective. He glared at Haekus; the blade-master knew that this was not some glorious quest to free the people of the Triumvirate. He knew this was just about killing people. "I did not want to kill those that taught of the Maker, I only wanted to kill him."

Haekus nodded. "I know."

"And now that he's gone," Akheron said, "No one knows what I did. I think I *am* done. Glyphs. Can I have peace, at last?" It was such a relief to think this, like the weight of the whole Great Stead had been lifted from his shoulders in one glorious moment and he could soar above the bright blue sea. But it could not be so simple, for the Mydarius was shrouded by the smoke of holy wood and holy men.

"I know." Haekus's voice was quiet.

"What?"

"It's not that complicated. I've been at your side for twenty years now."

Akheron stared at him and, in shame, looked away. *Haekus*

knows? He reached for his sword and Haekus tensed. He shouldn't have been so surprised. This man had spent every waking moment watching Akheron. He just wished that Haekus could've been more blind.

"Wait," Haekus said. "I know you can kill me. I may be better trained with the sword than you, but I know that nothing can stand in your way. I have seen you defeat men ten times your skill. Let us not fight."

"Perhaps I will let you win," Akheron said, drawing his sword.

"Please," Haekus said. "I will not strike you down. Do not fight me. Our friendship must mean something."

"It means nothing," Akheron said. "Am I your Prince?"

"Yes."

"Swear to me that I am your duty and your life," Akheron said.

"I swear it."

Next he was going to order Haekus never to speak of this, but that was an order that Haekus already lived by. He did not speak of what he knew any more than he spoke of Akheron's goal of killing the Maker to the freedom-fighters that served them.

"I will not argue with you," Haekus said. "I will not tell you how you could improve your life or how you have lost your beliefs because of your actions. I will not tell you the truth, because you will not accept it."

"Doesn't stop you from bringing it up now." Akheron sheathed his sword. He could kill Haekus. If his friend ever stood in Akheron's way, he *would* fall to the Maker's Bane. "You will never speak of this day to me," Akheron said. "And I *may* permit you to live. Guard me until the day you must kill me."

"Glyphs," Haekus said. "That day will never come."

"It will," Akheron said.

"I pray it never will. Even now, I am too loyal."

"Why?"

"Your dedication drives you to greater skill than even I possess. I *must* respect that," Haekus told him.

They fell silent, listening to the screams of the mob.

"Do not pray again," Akheron said a moment later, as he

walked through the gate and into the now sinful city of Edim. "Our days of prayer are done. We will burn in the Maker's wrath, Haekus. We will *burn* for what we've done. Then, at last, will all things be made right."

Haekus said nothing. Akheron did not know what Haekus thought of these actions, of their lives. He may have respected Akheron for becoming Prince, but not this. Akheron did not want to know what thoughts Haekus had to live with now.

When the smoke settled on Edim, Akheron and his entourage lay quietly within the inns there. Akheron spent that night alone, for once, though he was truly looking forward to the return home the next day, and Reya's warmth. He did not know, or care, how Haekus spent the night. As he watched the fire in his inn-room burn low, Akheron quietly pondered that his friend now bore his secrets too. *I will make him hate me,* he decided. *I will make him kill me, or, in the very least, let me die.*

He closed his eyes and pretended the Maker was not still alive.

11

Above the masts of the *Sky Hound*, seagulls circled and shouted down at the shivering crew. It was the winter of the year 518. Though the coast of the Mydarius was mild, the open sea breathed a sharp breeze upon Akheron's face. It felt like a mask now, frozen upon him. How long had it been since the lookout shouted, "I see it! Land ahead!" and the troop in Akheron's service had scared the gulls away with their cheers?

They passed another trade cog, buoying its way along the coast. "Do you think they know?" Akheron asked. His mask creased as he spoke. The cold skin of his cheeks was stiffer than his legs and his back. It would all be loosened up soon, though.

Haekus glanced at him. The lanky warrior bristled like a deadly insect: he had a sword on one side of his waist and knives on the other, like pincers. Another blade hung around his shoulders. "They know."

Ahead, the sprawling city of Edim offered its port as a feast for the gulls. And the vultures. On Akheron's right and left, there were banks of rock, glyph-cast into the sea, and walls built on top of them. Within were more ships, some already rowing towards the Sea Gate, where the *Hound* had invaded.

Akheron risked a glance at the cityscape. The Great Stead stole his vision; it rose above the other rooftops with a massive tower of dark stone bricks. A ring of white bricks, perhaps quartz, was built into the tower's face, visible even from here. It looked like a makeshift Circle, the symbol of the Maker.

"Sir, look at—" Yory, the *Hound's* captain said. She was a plump corsair woman, with an axe at her belt and a thick fur cloak. She extended a short finger toward the docks.

There were crowds on the wharfs. Some lifted bloody weapons—had there already been fighting? As Akheron came within fifty feet of the dock, he saw men and women part ways for an armoured man. They drifted closer. *That's not an armoured man,* Akheron realized. He shivered. *It's a corpse!*

It was the corpse of a Defender, his dark grey armour trimmed with thick gold and white paint. They brought him to the very end of the pier and then dropped him into the water, with a shout. "Maker's Bane! Down with the Kin!"

A hundred voices took up the chant. Akheron glanced at Haekus again. *Today, the Kinship ends.* He doubted if even he could stop the mob now.

Haekus did not nod or console him at all. He met Akheron's eyes briefly, and then strode toward the bow.

"Ropes!" Yory shouted. The crowd's cheering made it hard for the crew to hear, but they complied. Ropes sailed through the air, to be grabbed by the flailing arms of Edim's citizens. The ship began to move sideways until it bumped the dock.

"Gothikar!" someone bellowed and Akheron raised his fist in reply. This brought on a huge applause. He remembered Mavas's question. *"Why do they want to kill the Kin so much? Why do they hate the Maker?"* It had been an odd question, coming from one of her profession. Certainly, she would understand. Akheron had replied as best he could: *"Because we're all alone and the Maker made us that way."*

He heaved himself onto the handrail, standing at waist level of the *Hound's* crew, and balancing with one hand on the rope rigging. "How many guards hold the Great Stead?"

"A hundred!" someone shouted back. A few voices seconded it. The rest remained silent, as though surprised that the Usurper of Avernus had no words of inspiration or welcome.

Akheron nodded. "We'll break them!" he hollered. He gave them a moment of cheering before raising a hand. Silence began to creep amidst their murmurs, and then something cold and hard hit Akheron's face under his left eye. He raised a hand to wipe away mud or dung; he didn't care which. Someone shouted some curse upon the heretics.

The hundreds crowding the docks surged inward and tore the attacker limb from limb. More bodies fell into the water.

Some of them swam and climbed back up, having fallen in by
accident.

Akheron laughed, to ease the crowd's discomfort. He
blinked his left eye and lifted his hand to quiet the harbour again.
"Trust me," he jested, "I'll be muddier than this by the day's
end." The mood lightened briefly.

"We'll do the fighting for you!" someone shouted.

"I hope not all of it," Akheron said. "Now, where does the
city guard stand?"

"Nowhere!"

"The cowards have locked their doors!"

"Should we kill them too?"

"No, no," Akheron assured them. "No one needs die unless
they protect the Maker from me. Let your comrades-at-arms stay
behind their locked doors!"

A few supporters clapped.

"We'll need arms for anyone without," he declared. "And
we'll need a ram!"

"Ursyn found a building with columns that might work!"

"Go bring them, then! We'll attack the Stead in an hour!"
He dropped back to the *Hound's* deck with a wooden thud and
nodded to Haekus. "Clear the way."

"Sir," Haekus said. Was he nervous? Was he disapproving
or just nervous?

I won't die today, he wanted to tell his guard, but didn't.
He didn't know for certain. "Glyphs." He clenched his fists. His
voice quivered with anticipation and his muscles ached to be
used.

Ten Avernan soldiers marched around Akheron and
Haekus. Also within their circle was the magician Nyrus Daren.
Akheron hated magicians, but to strike the greatest stronghold of
the Kinship required precision and the element of surprise. Their
entourage had teleported from Avernus to Delfie, the closest
Known Location to Edim. Once, it was said, men could teleport
directly to Edim. But the spell had long since been lost.

As Haekus led the march through the mob, hands reached
for Akheron, dragging across his cloak, his shoulders, his hair.
What they found desirable about him, only the Maker knew. *And
you won't know it much longer,* Akheron said to himself. *When
not a single Stead stands, you'll be dead. What is a god without*

a worshipper? What is magic, without glyphs? What is love, without sex? What is the world, without mankind?

He wanted to curse at them to stop touching him, but he let them. Today, one last day, he would give to them of himself.

"Sir," Haekus said. "The *Hound.*"

Akheron glanced over his shoulder but didn't stop moving. They were in the streets of Edim now, marching between storefronts and double-storey residences. The *Sky Hound* had cast its moorings and was drifting into the harbour again.

"I told Yory to," Akheron said.

Haekus raised an eyebrow and then bobbed his head inquisitively at Daren.

Akheron nodded.

They reached a small square and were confronted by a small gang of Kinship supporters. They brandished mallets and knives mostly. The first man to charge at them fell to Haekus's fist, flattened to the ground with at least a broken bone or two. The rest soon followed and Akheron did not even draw his weapons.

Above the rooftops, Akheron could see the spire of the Great Stead. They were more than halfway there. The mob pressed ahead. They were joined from an alleyway by another group of men, those who had gone to find a ram. They bore three long wooden poles. By Akheron's standards, those were not columns.

"It'll have to make due," Haekus said. "There's no stopping this crowd now."

Akheron shrugged and, in anticipation, drew his sword. A ram was the difference of a hundred lives, at most. It would not stay the Kinship's demise.

Ahead loomed the gates of the Great Stead. There was a fair sized ground around the temple proper, protected by a twenty-foot stone wall. Two dozen Defenders stood in shining gold-trimmed armour on the battlements, readying those arrow-throwing contraptions.

Crossbows. Akheron could clearly remember the first day he had seen one. *Five years ago.* His subordinates brought many treasures of interest to the Prince. One of them a new technology invented in one of the Academies of Gev. He had been appalled by the strength of the weapon. The bolts could punch through a shield if released within range.

The crowd halted under the walls, readying their ram. More weapons were being passed out, as Akheron had instructed.

"Citizens of Edim," a voice echoed. It was loud enough that it must have been enhanced with glyphs. The speaker was nowhere in sight; he must have been hiding within. "Lay down your arms and return to your homes. Your sins may be forgiven if you yield this foolish task now."

"Down with the Stead!" the crowd chanted in reply. "Down with the Stead!"

"Then die and be damned!" the voice boomed. The Defenders raised their crossbows and death rained upon the mob. Akheron saw a man go down with a bolt in his head and a woman clawed her way to the ground after him, trying to cradle his scattering life. Half a dozen fell.

The ram surged forward toward the gate and another volley picked off every man who was touching the wooden pole. Those who stepped in to fill the gap left by fallen companions were pierced full of arrows too.

The crowd only grew more angry. Stones and knives clattered off the armour of the guards. Not even one fell. The shouting escalated, but the guards retaliated by picking off those who were loudest, while keeping the wooden ram haloed by bloody corpses.

"Come down and fight us like men!" a young woman screamed. The guard stationed directly over the gate lifted his crossbow and took aim. The bolt struck the girl in the neck. She clutched the shaft, and fell slowly below the shoulders of the men between her and Akheron.

"Glyphs." Akheron unsheathed his sword. He told Haekus to follow him with a glare, and marched to the nearest building, a residence with a locked door. The rebels made way for the Prince. He planted the point of his sword above the latch and, in a fluid yank, splintered the wood and pulled the latch off. His boot drove the door inward.

He grabbed the first piece of furniture he saw, a wooden table and shoved it into the street. Haekus took it without question and passed it ahead into the crowd. Akheron grabbed a wardrobe, kicked off the doors, and dragged it outside too.

"Take this one, for cover," he told some of the peasants.

He preferred the table for its manoeuvrability. He scooped up the front of it, and Haekus took the rear, and tilted it up.

"Grab the ram again!" he bellowed, running forward. Haekus and he took the right side of the ram. The men with the wardrobe struggled to keep up and the first flurry of crossbow bolts almost had a free sight of Akheron's vulnerable side. As it was, two struck the underside of the table near his hands and the rest of the volley was absorbed on the tabletop itself. The makeshift shield quivered. "Glyphs! Someone get the ram!"

The crowd surged against the table in an attempt to pick up the wooden column. Akheron was practically standing on top of it. He was abruptly shoulder to shoulder with people he didn't know, men and women of many ages. They scooped up the pole from the ground, peeling it from the hands of the corpses beneath Akheron's feet. He tried not to look down.

He took a step forward, and was jostled by the next release of the crossbowmen. "Curse you cowards!" he shouted. This was a slaughter.

The ram-crew stumbled to keep up on the uneven ground. Akheron felt a man's buttocks against his, through the leather coat he wore. A moment later, the man was dead from the crossbowman that could see between the two wooden shields.

Even if he craned his neck, Akheron could barely see the wardrobe carriers. If they fell, so would he.

Another round of bolts snapped into the wood. They were less than ten paces from the gate now. Soon the ram would be slamming the gate. The mob filled in the positions of those who fell. Now a woman was pressing against Akheron's shoulders. Haekus cursed, and Akheron glanced his way. There was a hole in his padded jerkin, though no bolt; he had been holding the table too close and the crown of a crossbow round had pierced through. They were puncturing the wood deeper, as the ram reached the gate.

"Rocks!" someone above ordered. The wooden pole slammed against the gate with a lousy crack.

"Tilt your cover more!" Akheron shouted to the other team. Even as he spoke, a heavy weight slammed against the table top. Akheron fell to one knee, then shoved upward to his feet again. In that lull alone, one of their rammers sprawled to the ground.

"What about Daren?" Haekus asked.

"I'm not risking him!" Akheron shouted back. "Ram!"

The ram slammed the wooden gates again. How thick was the beam on the other side? How many guards waited there? Another volley of bolts fell, and a sharp pain appeared in Akheron's right arm. He ground his teeth and did not let his grip on the table shake. Again they slammed the gate. This time, they were rewarded with a loud boom. A man at the front of the ram let go of the pole and shoved himself into the opening that appeared in the gate. He became a porcupine of spears.

"Ram again!" Akheron shouted. More rocks fell, but as soon as they faltered, he released the table. He had to pull his arm free of the bolt that had pierced the wood. Warm blood soaked into his leather sleeve. He was sweating, and the salt stung his wound.

He drew his sword, and Haekus followed suit. The crowd behind them had allowed a small gap as they feared the attacks of the Defenders; they closed it quickly as they saw the gates caving.

The ram crew burst into the yard and were cut down in seconds. Akheron was next through the gate, with Haekus and a hundred bloodthirsty rioters on his heels. The yard within was full of soldiers. This was the Great Stead, and it was protected more than any other religious site in the Dominion.

With an incoherent shout, Akheron cut down the first Defender to charge at him. The man swung a bastard sword at him, and though he raised his shield, Akheron's parry took off his sword arm. The rest held their ground as the crowd charged them. Many fell in the first wave, simply running into their spears and swords.

As a line of corpses formed, arcing into the courtyard from the broken wooden gates, Akheron and Haekus stormed the wall. There was a stone stairwell on this side of the wall. It led up to the ramparts, where crossbowmen continued firing down upon the mob. Half of the Avernan guards that had disembarked the *Sky Hound* with Akheron had already fallen.

As Haekus and Akheron charged upward, two steps at a time, the Defenders came down to meet them. A heavily armoured guard parried through the first flurry of Akheron's attacks; two swings glanced right off plates of his heavy iron breastplate. Impatiently, Akheron put his weight behind his sword and knocked the man from the staircase. The body landed on a commoner, likely breaking limbs as the two collapsed.

Haekus grabbed Akheron's shoulders to stop him from falling too. He would have.

He watched his guard swiftly thrust his blade through the next Defender that charged them. Haekus had the finesse to find holes in any set of armour. He had a keen eye.

Together, they cleared the battlements. There were a few dozen guards up there. Many fell to their deaths, but a few bled out against the wall. It was hard fighting because Akheron's arm continued to bleed. He wondered if anything major had been cut.

By the time they stumbled down the stairs to the courtyard again, the battle was over.

"We won!" he hollered and the crowd joined in his cheer.

"There's more of them garrisoned inside!" someone replied.

Akheron held his hand, and walked through the crowd. There were dying men in the courtyard. The crowd was dragging them aside, looting them for coin, armour and weapons. Now there were swords mixed through the group. They quieted, as he climbed the steps in front of the small tower. The doors were closed, and locked. They were small doors though, and were not barred. "They are cowering within, and they know now that they cannot defeat us!" he shouted. Haekus wearily climbed the steps beside him. "How many Kin reside here?" he asked.

"Four!" someone returned, as Akheron's guard began wrapping his arm with a clean rag.

"One for each element!" another cried.

"How many have we killed already?"

"Got one here!" the crowd said. "Another over here."

"And here's the third's head!" shouted a young woman, lifting a bloody head from the base of the stone stairs right in front of Akheron.

Akheron waited a minute, until people started saying "three" to themselves and then declared, "Then one priest still lives. I will kill him myself to end this *war* of ours!"

Their excitement deafened him. Weapons were lifted high and hands lifted in praise. "Akheron!" They shouted. "Maker's Bane! Down with the Kin!"

Have they no creativity? They have been chanting the same

thing for years! Akheron thought. He glanced up and met Haekus's eyes. "I'll go in alone," he said.

"No, sir," Haekus said. "I will—"

"Haekus," Akheron said quietly. "You are torn between your loyalty to the Maker and to me."

"I am loyal to you, sir."

"And that bond will win, in the end, unless you were a 'man of faith'." Akheron said. "But you're a man of the sword. When I step within this temple, I will be a demon. A demon for swords to kill, not serve. I will not have you spill holy blood for me."

"There will be more Defenders—" Haekus looked back at the crowd. He very rarely showed this sort of distress. It made Akheron feel... dangerous.

"If I die," Akheron said, "I will die. If the Maker decides to kill me, no blade-master can or should stand in his way. Let me go, my friend."

Haekus blinked. "I will have failed my oath," he said. "But if you order me to stay, I will."

"Stay, then," Akheron said. "And do not let any come after me."

He stepped past Haekus, toward the two locked doors. The left door fell to his kick. He could feel the nerves in his leg dancing up into his spine.

Within the antechamber, three Defenders in full plate armour stood guard. One thrust at Akheron with a spear, which he hacked downward at with his sword. The metal on shaft of the spear snapped, breaking both weapons. Only a foot-long spire of broken steel remained of Akheron's sword. He grabbed the broken spear's length and pulled. The Defender at the other end stumbled forward. Akheron drove the broken blade of his weapon into the face-slit of the man's helmet. A scream tore the air and the body began convulsing. Arms jerked upward, releasing the wooden shaft in Akheron's hands.

He stepped back as the other two Defenders advanced. *I liked that sword,* he thought. He had wielded it throughout this entire rebellion. Now it was a broken shard of iron in the face of a faithful man.

"The Maker will protect us," one of them said, coming at Akheron with a sword. Akheron raised the length of his makeshift staff and, swinging it like a sword, knocked aside the man's swing. He let go of the spear's length and stepped closer to the Defender. The knife at Akheron's belt moved into his hands, and then into the Defender's neck, sliding horizontally and spilling blood all over the golden armour.

"Then the Maker will burn you," the third said. He swiped forward with a one-handed battle-axe. Akheron ducked. The axe embedded in the side of the soldier who's throat was slit. Akheron kicked the Defender backward. As the warrior released his axe and stumbled against the wall, the dying body finally teetered to the ground. It took the axe with it.

Akheron stepped forward as the Defender swung a hand at Akheron. Akheron caught the fist in his palm, twisted it, then slammed his opposite arm upward. His first swing broke the man's arm, but bloodied his fist on the iron vambrace the man wore.

This Defender was remarkably tough. As Akheron released the Defender's broken arm, his foot knocked the Prince backward. His sword-arm hung limply at his side, but his off-hand was folded at the elbow and ready to defend him.

Akheron, bent at the waist from the man's kick, charged forward and planted his shoulder into the man's abdomen, knocking him back against the wall. The plaster broke, spilling dust into Akheron's mouth. Then, the Defender brought his armoured left elbow down into the back of Akheron's ribcage.

Blinding pain lanced through him and he found himself clawing in the blood of the men he had slain. A kick. He knew it was coming, so he prepared his hands and braced himself. A moment later, he gripped an armoured boot and a broken rib from the kick. But he had the foot. He lifted himself upward, throwing the Defender off balance. The man teetered, inevitably losing his footing and plummeting onto the body in the middle of the room.

The Defender landed on the sword hilt, pushing the broken blade deeper into the corpse's head. The pommel dug into the split between the fallen Defender's breastplate and back-plate. Akheron could hear the gasp.

Akheron yanked the axe out of the other dead soldier. *Glyphs,* he breathed, as the Defender reclaimed his feet, unarmed and dazed. *Where did my dagger go?* He had lost it in the scuffle. But the battle-axe would suffice.

He nearly took the Defender's head off with it.

After catching his breath, he stepped into the Stead. It was a circular auditorium, as was customary; pews in ranks filled each section of seating around the room's circumference. The main aisle ran from the front anteroom, now bloodied, to the altar and dais in the middle. Akheron slowly made his way toward it. He was a sight unseen here, the killer in the temple. Blood dripped where he walked, from the spittle he sent to the floor to the film of red-stained hair on the end of his axe. He was breathing heavily. He paused halfway to the Circle in the middle of the Stead to run a few fingers under his shirt and feel the bumpy bruise where his rib had broken. Then he stumbled further ahead.

There was a priest here, as the mob had suggested. He was kneeling calmly in front of the altar where the Four Elements sat. Praying. *Does he think the Maker will save him?* Akheron wondered. The man had to know that Akheron approached him.

"Here we stand," Akheron said, before the Circle of the Great Stead. The Kinsman did not flinch or look up. "At the end of the world."

"Here I kneel," the man said, nodding gently. Was he the head of the Kinship? Or just some priest who was in the wrong spot at the wrong time?

"I don't," Akheron said. He smashed the tainted axe into a nearby pew and pulled off his gloves, dropping them to the ground.

"You should. His words created magic, created the world, and created all of us." The words were ripe with passion and strength.

Akheron looked down at the man. He was not as old as expected, probably only ten years older than the Prince of Avernus. "His words made the world, but they cannot make me kneel again."

"What did he do to you?" the man asked, rising to his feet without quaking.

"Nothing," Akheron said. "It's what he let me do. I cannot kneel to a being so... calloused."

"You would rather he had... what?"

"He should have stopped me. He should have struck me

ARISTORN

down!" Akheron said. He started walking toward the Circle and the Four Elements. The Kinsman stepped in his way and tried to stop him. "He should have burned me to ash and thrown me into the wind! I'll break everything he's ever loved for what he has made me!"

"Freewill is a gift."

"Freewill is a damned curse," Akheron snarled and shoved the priest aside. "And I'll make him believe it before I'm done with this world!"

He reached for the Circle. The large wooden ring sat on a stand beyond the altar.

"What did you do, then, to hate him for your own deeds?"

Akheron froze. He turned around. The Kinsman stood not two paces from him, a look of genuine concern on his face. Not concern for his own life, but concern for the world. "Do not ask me that again," Akheron growled. *"Do not ask me that again!"* He had the priest's throat in one hand, forcing him down. He dragged the Kinsman to the altar of the Great Stead, where the Four Elements sat on narrow tray. Fire: a brazier flickering away; water, a steep bowlful; air, a bowlful of it too; and a smooth cube of rock, fashioned from some sorcery. Akheron smashed the board off the altar with his free hand. Glass shattered on the ground and the embers of the brazier lit the dry carpet instantly. *Do not ask me, I will not remember!*

"What did you do?" the Maker asked him again with a quivering priest's voice.

Akheron screamed incoherently and slammed the man down onto the altar. The stone was bloody when he lifted the Kinsman back toward his feet again, and then back down. There was a sick crack this time. "Why?" he shrieked. *"Why* are you?"

The corpse hit the altar again, the head only held together by the hood it was caught in. There was blood all over the podium, and fire was licking Akheron's feet. He threw the Kinsman aside as he reclaimed his axe from the pew a few feet away.

"What kind of... *sick* abyss have you made?" Akheron cried. He split the wooden Circle in two and a loud snap echoed throughout the entire Stead, louder than the fire or the priest's head. The narrow wooden halves tumbled into the flames.

Akheron planted his bloody palms on the red altar and

91

roared, "What kind of sick abyss have *we* made?" He then threw the altar remnants into the flames.

He stood in the burning Stead until he could not feel his pulse anymore. His hands were clenched into fists still, and he felt truly alone now. He had won, and that made him feel sick. It could have been the smoke he was breathing, the broken rib, or the cut in his arm; he teetered on his feet. He had won. He had killed the Maker. He shrieked until his voice broke. It was a haunting sound, echoing throughout the remnants of the Stead.

Embers of burning temple began to fall around Akheron. Would he burn with the Maker? He imagined the auditorium as a tomb. *It would have a certain measure of completion, wouldn't it?*

But what of my world? Did I not do all this so that I can live in peace? He had been fighting so long he had forgotten. *Now no one knows, no one but me. Now, at last, peace...*

He looked at the bloody body. Did he still believe in peace? He had fought the Maker to free himself. The mob had only been a means to that end. A live ember landed on his shoulder and he knocked it off with a sticky hand. He started wiping his hands on his tunic, and they began to cleanse.

Akheron had fought the Maker because the Maker had seen what he had done. Now it was finished.

"Maker," he prayed. "I do not know if you can hear me still. Honestly, I do not know what I would prefer. Your world has chosen, and it has not chosen you. Goodbye, my Kin." He paused. "Please, *destroy* me for this."

He started to walk toward the broken doors, but paused. *The mob wants a body, though.*

He picked up the poor priest. One hand supported the man's back, while the other fit in behind the knees. Akheron carried the Kinsman like a child out of the burning Stead. *Glyphs, it is hot,* he realized as sensation began to breathe through the adrenaline.

Haekus was the first to see him, as he walked out of the antechamber. His friend only stared, and eventually looked away from the bloody sight. He knew this was a dark day.

The mob cheered. There were two hundred men and women in the courtyard, all raising their hands into the air. Some were injured, but they rejoiced too. Akheron spotted a handful of turncoat Defenders in the fray, praising him like the citizens were.

The rioters felt more than Akheron's inner peace—the calm after the storm. They felt the ecstasy of victory and the urge of celebration. For this, they would party in the blood of holy men. There were still Defenders fighting somewhere, and more believers than not lived in this city. Edim would bleed into its streets and sewers. Akheron dropped the Kinsman's body onto the steps with a thud and raised his arms to give the mob the vindication they wanted. He thrust his fist into the air and hollered in unison with them.

12

"I swear, Akheron," Verin Theseus said, "You have gone too far."

They were standing on a balcony of the Avernan Palace, looking out at the hanged man. It was a gruesome sight, for other criminals hung above the arch of the Palace gate as well. A rope ran between the two guard towers on either side of the gate, and from it hung the criminals and the man who had said, "the Maker." Even looking at the raven-pecked body made Akheron think of it.

"Have I? Should I not be feared, if I am a killer?" Akheron asked. His voice was calm.

"He committed no crime!" Verin Theseus retorted. He drank more from the canteen he carried. It was alcohol of some kind, Akheron was certain.

"I have never pretended to be just," Akheron said. "But I have also not harmed the society I swore to protect. In fact, my citizens cheered when we knocked the man's support out, and he hung."

"The mob is not society," Verin argued. The Prince had arrived late the day before, through a teleport from Athyns.

"And I am not a Prince," Akheron said.

Verin glanced away from the Palace wall at him. The northerner had pale skin and a dark grey beard. It was not thick, like some Athynians preferred, and gave the Prince a very distinguished look. He raised a thick eyebrow at Akheron's words.

"Nothing is what it should be," Akheron elaborated. "But

we must live here nonetheless." He shifted his grip on the wooden railing back and forth, feeling the grain of the world. He broke his gaze from Verin's and stared at the hanged man again.

The other Prince put his forearms on the rail and looked down into the yard past his folded hands. "Reports trickle in, from across the north, of men and women butchered. The Steads burn. One by one, they are *all* going. Leto thought we could stop it from spreading into my lands, but we couldn't."

There were some soldiers sparring in the cobblestone yard for a crowd of onlookers. A groundskeeper picked fruit from a few apple trees that grew near the wall. He stood on a rickety ladder, with big wicker baskets tied to his hips.

Akheron turned around and stepped inside the guest quarters. He didn't have any particular destination in mind; he simply wanted to get out of the outdoors. There were chairs he could sit in, and a table he could sit at. Tapestries adorned the wall, though a dust-framed hole remained where one of them had been taken down. When Akheron had become Prince, he had burned anything of the Maker's here. "Theseus, are you here to voice your desire for retribution? To claim it? Or are you complaining like Odyn did?"

The echo of Verin's reply followed him. "Nothing like that. Just getting it off my conscience. These deaths are not on me. They're on you. That's what I came here to say."

Akheron smiled. He sank into a cushioned chair and met Verin's glare. Verin was no saint, but he was one of the better rulers in their present day. He stood in the door to the balcony with one elbow leaning on one side of the frame and his opposite palm gripping the other side. Akheron said, "They are. Sleep easy, Theseus. Your wife need not blame you for it. You can both blame me."

In thoughtful silence, Verin seated himself in an adjacent armchair. These were the royal guest quarters on the second floor of the Palace. As part of the old Keep, not Akheron's new storeys, this room dated to antiquity. Its wealth reflected its age, in the gold gilt that swirled in the etched lines of the wooden arms that supported him. Too much detail was ill-fortune, so the room sported simple engravings.

At last, Verin spoke. "Does your wife?...Blame you?"

Akheron frowned. He pulled at his collar. He always felt

stifled indoors, but felt vulnerable out. *Since when I have cared about feeling... stifled?* He shook his head. "Reya," he said, "thinks I am an angry old man. She is an... innocent, I think, and I tolerate it."

"You tolerate your wife's offences but not your subjects'?" Verin asked.

"Is that not always the case, at court?" Akheron said, though that made him more uncomfortable than anything. "She tolerates me, which is something the Kinship never did."

"Do you mean politically?"

"No, personally. They called me a sinner, which I am. But Reya never has." Akheron smiled. "I don't think she has a bone in her body that cares what sin is or is not."

"You seem to appreciate honesty. You are a very blunt man," Verin said, moving toward his point. "Why do you reward her blindness, and criticize it in others?"

Akheron laughed. "Because I am a hypocrite. Do I approve of Reya's liberalness, her nonchalant lack of moral cynicism? Not in the least. But she tolerates my flaws, and I owe her a likewise tolerance." He clapped his hands for a servant.

A young woman came in, a beautiful little creature. Akheron did not hide his interest in her and stared at her blushing. He did not care if Verin saw his blatant lack of honour. That was the context of their conversation. "We'll have some wine," he said. "Fit for Princes."

She bowed and withdrew. She kept her mask of calm, despite his eyes and intimidation. He could only fathom the stories the commoners told about him. He was a god to them, with all of the love and fear that combined for such a deity. Did she feel exhilarated, or offended? Did she feel lucky, or just plain terrified? Did she feel the least bit aroused?

"Well," Theseus said, drawing him back to their conversation. "I do not share Reya's ignorance. I know good, and I know evil. I will not voice my beliefs, lest you hang *me*, but I know the lines. I will teach my son what I know, and I will teach him to live by the lines better than I have."

"And he will die alone, in a world that has lost its soul," Akheron said, quietly. Sadly.

"Glyphs," Verin cursed. "That's not a friendly thing to say, about another's child."

"Wait." Akheron sat up straight. "You have a son?" he asked.

"Three years old now. Erykus, named after one of my uncles," Verin said.

"'Glyphs' is right. I apologize. I'm some bitter whelp next to you, and I have no right to make such offence," Akheron said.

"That sounds awfully close to respect," Verin smirked.

"Your wine?" Haekus asked, stepping into the room from Keep's corridor. The door creaked, ever so quietly.

"What, where is the serving woman?"

"She asked me, very politely and full of 'milord's', to bring this in." Haekus set a tray onto the short round table between Verin and Akheron. There was a narrow necked bottle between two minimally engraved tin chalices. Elaborate designs were ill fortune for the upper class. A single phrase of glyphs amidst an ornate artwork were enough to kill.

"She was that scared of me?" Akheron asked.

"She didn't tell me."

"Hang her!" he ordered. Theseus stood up and Haekus tensed.

"Do no such thing," Verin said.

"Now you have two Princes giving you contrary orders," Akheron said. He shrugged. "Hang her, or don't. She's no longer welcome in this Palace, and I'll not have her attending in my court."

Haekus bowed stiffly and walked away. The door thudded closed. Akheron did not care what his friend chose to do. Haekus did not approve of his Prince's habit of extreme punishment, and had an excuse, with Theseus' words, not to carry out the order.

"Glyphs," Verin said, sinking back into his chair.

"Wine?" Akheron asked, pouring for them both.

"Please." Where had the other Prince's small silver canteen gone?

Akheron handed the dignitary his cup. They drank in silence for a while.

"I have offended," Akheron said, at last. Verin set his cup down. "I will take my leave now. I trust I have been a sufficient scapegoat for your guilt? Do not worry, the Kinship will be gone within the year. I have already begun making plans for the Great Stead."

Verin opened his mouth, but Akheron did not let him speak.

"Do not ask about it. It would only weigh on your conscience," he said. He finished his wine in a gulp.

"Akheron."

"Will you at least join my wife and I this evening, for supper?"

Verin frowned. "Do you love her? Reya, that is. I no longer love my wife," he said.

"Glyphs, no," Akheron said. *I still miss Mavas too much.* That was a fresh pain. He missed Tam too, but Tam was different. Reya was special to him, an innocent ideal that threatened to give him mild happiness. But she was too deluded, too foolish. "Someday I might. If she ever stands up to me."

Verin laughed, but it was the laugh of a man who pities another for his backward ways. He took another drink of his wine. Akheron had left him the whole flagon and Verin Theseus, reputedly, would enjoy finishing it himself.

"I have matters," Akheron said, raising his hand dismissively.

The hallway was deserted. Presumably, Haekus was with that serving girl. He was either carrying out her execution or escorting her from the palace grounds. Did she have a lover, to drag down with her when she sunk from this rot-filled height of the world? "Glyphs," Akheron said, to the empty hallway. "I'm becoming bitter..."

"Milord," a girl's voice said, from behind him. It was another young woman, taller than the other and more ample, but of an age with the first servant. She wore a thin wooden frame around her neck, open in the front—the sigil of a servant. It was neither uncomfortable nor humiliating, in fact the opposite. It prevented any sort of awkward misunderstandings with the palace folk. The girl bowed to Akheron and said, "I am Thera, milord. I will be your new waiting servant in Banna's absence."

Akheron stifled a laugh and continued down the corridor. "Of course you are!" he exclaimed. He humorously asked, "Will you flinch at my favour and hide when I look where it is impolite?"

"No, milord," she said, confidently. He didn't need to look at her to trust her lack of modesty.

"Good," he said, quieter, more sadly. He wiped his hands on the tunic he wore, against the weave. "Go, attend Prince Theseus."

"Milord," she bowed.

He continued down the hallway alone. He went down the stairs, through the doors, past the sparring men and under the hanged. His city was alive. He liked to think that people went about their lives easier thanks to him. Or at least, enjoyed their nights easier. One of his advisors at court thought that the full impacts of the decline of the Kinship would not be fully realized for years to come.

Despite this, wherever Akheron looked, he saw happiness. He saw children playing a game of handball, running through the streets and splashing in the puddles. Merchants' calls and hammer-falls filled the air with an amiable din, and the smell of fresh food drew Akheron further into the town.

He sought out the Bard of the Valharyn. A significant meeting place for business doings, drinks and beds, the Bard sat on the border of the Residential and the Merchant Quarter. He passed a mother and daughter that were coming out of the inn on the wide entry steps.

The large common room was not abundantly full, but there were a few rings of dice-players and the bar was crowded enough. All the regulars, likely. A stiff waiter asked if Akheron wanted anything before he could even reach the nearby window seat he aimed for. The man had a moustache and a small copper pin in his earlobe. Akheron waved him away and approached the bulky short-haired woman that sat by the window.

"Yory," he said.

The corsair looked up and smiled. Yory had a double chin and a bit of stubble above her lip, but her eyes were as sharp as Haekus's. She looked at him with a keenness and a strength that was ready for whatever he threw at her. "I got your letter. Please sit, my Prince."

He shook his head at her mockery. He sank into a chair. "Perhaps I should have ordered a drink after all."

She raised her own cup. "How is your dear wife?"

He rolled his eyes. "How is your late husband?" he retorted. That silenced her leering. She took another drink from her cup and shook her head. She had married one of Demetas's inner circle, though the man's name escaped Akheron.

"I hear they've renamed Trionus's Upper City the 'Mountain's Grief,'" she said. "After the mob burned the Stead there. We all know who lit the torch."

Akheron shrugged and folded his arms.

"Why am I here, Akheron?" she asked. "You need me to sail you somewhere again? How much longer am I going to be ferrying you around?"

He smirked. "The only corsair who serves the Triumvirate."

"No," she said, setting her cup down firmly. "I serve you, not your government. Your gold is good and we have history, but I tire of being your 'court' captain."

Akheron frowned. "Only once more then," he said. He sat with his back straight and his hands folded in his lap, under the table.

Yory blinked in surprise. "Where?"

"The Great Stead."

Her jaw dropped and her chins bounced. She glanced around the common room. Akheron glanced behind him, at the bar. Her two men shifted uneasily; they were too far to hear but close enough to react if they were needed. He nodded to them and then turned back to Yory.

"You've a keen eye, as always," Yory said. "By the M... glyphs, you're really going to do this, aren't you?"

"If you won't or can't land us in Edim's port, I will find someone who can," Akheron said. He glanced out into the street. Haekus would be looking for him now. Though his guard knew of the plan, haggling with Yory was simpler without Haekus's brazen wit.

The corsair raised a meaty finger. "It is not a matter of can't. Nor a matter of won't. How much?"

"Twice what I paid last time."

"So, a hundred Imperials? Half before, half after?"

Akheron nodded.

"Done." Yory slammed her elbow onto the table top and offered Akheron her hand. He clasped it. She pulled his hand to one side and glared at him over it. "But this is the last time, Akheron."

"Very well," he said. "But I keep the *Sky Hound.*"

If he won and he burned Edim down, he would have no reason to navigate the Mydarius again, save to reach Galinor for council meetings. Any captain would be sufficient for such a task. Yory could do as she pleased if the Great Stead burned. Only his... less than legal missions required a corsair.

And if I do not win, if the Great Stead stands... Well, Akheron would be dead and the world might get on alright. And Yory could do as she pleased with the *Hound*.

"Very well," she said. "I'll have enough for a better boat thanks to your coin." She raised her cup to her lips again.

"I think I *will* order a drink after all," he said. He stood up.

Haekus appeared through the front door, barely containing his frustration. "Akheron. Yory," he said as he approached.

"And now I will have to share my drink," Akheron said. He sat back down.

13

The Defender came at Akheron with a fury, smashing at him with his shield. Akheron stepped back and to the left, rolling on the balls of his feet as Haekus had taught him. He twisted at the hips and slashed outward with his sword. The Defender parried the strike and his blade clanged off of Akheron's small buckler next.

Someone was chanting nearby, a rhythmic reciting of the glyphs written on a scroll. *Curse your glyphs, priest!* If Akheron did not put a sword in the mage, the Kin would finish his spell and bring some divine magic to drive Akheron from the Stead. The Defender would not let him past. As hard as Akheron hacked forward, the armoured knight defended his ground.

Nearby, Haekus grappled with another. He had managed to lose his sword in his conflict and was brawling with the man.

The Defender thrust at Akheron with a short sword. The Prince riposted after he blocked it. His opponent's shield was too large. All of his attacks were knocked high or low by the metal edge.

"Azor-arnar!" the Kin shouted. As if on cue, the Defender fell to his knees, like he was praying. Perhaps he was.

A blinding radiance was released from the Kin's raised palms. It was as bright as the dazzle of the sun, but hotter. Akheron raised his shield and squeezed his eyes shut. The spell was burning him. Scalding pain gripped his arm. He ground his teeth and tried to keep his arm raised still, but it was like holding one's hand in an oven. He hollered and flailed his arm up and down, opening his eyes enough to squint at it. He stared at what he saw. Between the blinding rays of light above and below his arm, the metal shield was beginning to warp. The metal was seeping against his shirt, burning through it against his skin. "Glyphs!" he cried. His hand was half covered in malleable, faintly glowing iron.

Then the light went out.

He dropped his sword without looking at it and, with that hand, yanked at the cords on the underside of his burning forearm. The distorted buckler shield fell to the ground; hot metal thumped against the wooden floorboards instead of clanging.

Haekus stepped up behind the kneeling Defender and twisted his helmet to one side until a resounding crack could be heard. He released the dead man. "I'm growing too weary for this," Haekus said, dryly.

"What?" Akheron gasped, looking around Haekus. The glyph-user was lying on the floor boards as well, completely still.

"Are you hurt?" Haekus asked, bending and putting a hand on his Prince's shoulder.

"Glyphs," Akheron said again. He picked up his sword again and sheathed it. It was still warm, but unscathed from the heat, thankfully. It had been a gift from someone at court—as he recalled it—from before the riots had begun. It was lightly etched upon, but heavily jeweled with small rubies and topaz. Some of the gems were missing after its heavy use.

He glanced around. There was a broken wooden shelf crashed over the body of the Defender that Haekus had been fighting. They were in an arched entryway to the Stead's sanctuary, between cold stone walls and a wooden roof. Haekus stepped forward into the aisles of the Stead, where the chamber opened up into a tower. Akheron looked down once more; his shield was just a peculiar lump of metal, with only a vague outline of its original shape. Bits of leather strap stuck out here and there.

Akheron shook his head and followed Haekus. He stepped over the body of the priest. The middle-aged man was drooling blood; Haekus must have broken something in his throat. "Sometimes they break," he said.

"What breaks?" Haekus asked. He glanced up into the lofty

rafters. There was a stairwell that ran around the interior of the circular tower to the roof, accessible by a ladder nearby. Ahead, in the centre of the Stead, sat the shrine to the Maker. It waited for them quietly, unlike the fresh decoration of the entryway.

"The Kin," Akheron replied. "They profess patience and faith. Most of them believe that the Maker will strike me down for my crimes, and will not raise a hand against me to give the M— their god his due wrath. But sometimes..."

Haekus glanced back at the priest that had attacked him. "Sometimes, they break."

Akheron nodded and met Haekus's eyes as he passed. He let the way to the altar. Haekus followed, but not as far. "Do you think he will stop me?" Akheron asked.

"You know I am not a man of faith."

Akheron grabbed an unlit torch from nearby. The Steads were often too large to be lit by windows. He held it over the shrine, over the candle. The torch's fuel whispered to life. "Will he stop this from burning?" He set the torch on one of the wooden pews, on its side. Immediately, the wood started blackening. In a few minutes it would catch fire too.

"This place will collapse," Haekus said. He was looking around at the wooden columns that helped to support the tower.

"I'm counting on it," Akheron said. But he was looking at his target. *Will you stop me?* He stepped toward the shrine again and threw the altar, with its elemental symbols onto its side. It knocked down the Circle with it. The wooden ring rolled away from the toppled shrine. It spiralled in a wide oval before it clattered to the floorboards.

Disappointed, Akheron turned back to Haekus. "That's done," he said. He brushed past Haekus and passed the bodies of the fallen on his way. The doors of the Stead and the barricade behind them were broken open—one of them was missing a hinge and tilted inward. It occurred to Akheron that the mob was oddly silent as he clambered out of the Stead.

He understood why once he was clear. A young man stood in front of the mob, with his arms crossed and his legs firmly planted apart. He distilled the very epitome of force. His long black hair was bound behind his head with a golden clasp and the sword at his waist was a smith's masterwork that matched the yellow and black coat he wore. Unlike the other lords of towns that Akheron had incited to riot, Trion did not bend to the whim of his people—instead, he set their whims.

"Ernes Trion," Akheron greeted as he wiped his hands clean. He extended one arm for his fellow lord to take.

Trion begrudgingly accepted his gesture. "Gothikar," he said. They separated, and Trion raised his hand to pat the stubble on his cheeks. "You've set fire to one of my buildings."

Akheron turned around to look at the column of dark smoke already rising from the Stead [The Stead has no windows—see previous page]. A few birds frantically evacuated a hole in the brickwork at the top of the Tower. He turned back to Trion. Most of the time, the politics of these scenarios transpired a little differently. The regional lord would usually ignore Akheron's actions so as to not cause an international issue. They did this, usually, by keeping a distance from the riots and attributing the destructions of lands and the murders of the clergy to the mob itself.

Trion was not looking the other way. He crossed his arms again and looked right at Akheron. "It was an ugly one," he said.

Akheron sighed again, just as he had when the shrine of the Maker had toppled without ramifications. The crowd gasped a breath of relief. Someone said, "Couldn't choose between the two, if I had to!" and his comrades laughed. Trion was the frontier conqueror, but Akheron freed their hearts and minds.

"You should have warned me you were in town though," Trion said. "I would have given you a place to sleep and some soldiers to deal with those troublesome Defenders."

"No, you wouldn't have," Akheron said. "You can say that after the fact, but you wouldn't have before."

Trion blinked. "I had heard you were direct, my Prince." His voice was more articulate than Akheron's; he emphasized each syllable like it was its own word. Haekus must have reacted sarcastically to Trion's words, for the ambitious lord said, "And I had heard you were clever."

The blade-master smirked and glanced reservedly at Akheron before saying, "I prefer witty."

"Hah!" Trion turned and lifted his hand toward the enormous fortress up the hill. "Allow me to give you a roof and I will throw a feast in your honour!"

"I have no honour, sir," Akheron said. The crowd stirred.

Everyone always reacted to Akheron's darker side differently. Some laughed, some sighed—most remained silent.

"But we would be *honoured* to accept your courteous offer," Haekus said.

Akheron glanced at his guard sharply. He did not like it when Haekus spoke for him, but he held his tongue. The sun was almost touching the mountains behind them, casting shadows onto the slope of Trionus city. Below them, the town looked eerily quiet, as though twilight had already sent the inhabitants indoors. Trionus was not a large place, but it had not been there ten years earlier, which said something about the intellect that Trion had to back his ambition. Akheron kept his eyes on the lord and said, "Of course. Lead the way."

"This way then, highness."

"Believe what you will now," Akheron called to the crowd. "You will hear no more of the Kinship, nor its god."

They cheered for him, and then he followed Trion. There were stone steps, each of them an enormous block, that led from the upper city to the castle. He imagined men hauling them up here like the slaves of antiquity. Before the days of the Triumvirate, or even the Kingdoms that predated it, slaves had been owned by the wealthy and forced to work by Skin Casters—men and women who had tattooed glyphs upon their bodies to cast magic without writing spells down. "Were these steps made by magic?"

Trion turned and smiled. "They were. Your friend Leto, in fact."

"No friend of mine," Akheron said. *Damned magic.* He had few reasons to truly dislike it. Instead, glyphs were a minor irritation to him, a reminder of the Maker's pervasion into everything. He could see the Maker's hand in everything, and now he was starting to see his own hand in everything. *I've been around too long,* he decided. He was having a bad day, for some reason. For starters, his forearm still itched from its burn.

"Welcome to the Strait's Sentinel," Trion said.

The enormous stairwell reached a short wall, patrolled by guards, where the slope flattened into a wide courtyard. Akheron saw a stable, a sizeable storehouse and a bustling tavern in front of the Keep, while Trion's castle itself rose up at least three storeys and dwarfed all three of the former.

"That's certainly a dramatic title," Haekus said.

"I have an appreciation for such things," Trion said. "Two things will leave one's mark on the world: action and reaction. Achievements and reputations. Drama will help the latter."

Akheron smirked. "No wonder you shed no tears for the fire I set earlier."

They were halfway to the Keep by now, but Trion paused and decisively raised a hand in front of himself as he turned toward the Prince. "What do you mean by that?"

"In your world, there is no room for faith. No value. Only acts."

"From your tone, my Prince, you criticize this. But allow me to point out your own life," Trion said. "I take an inspiration from you. I borrow your ambition."

"Bah," Akheron said.

"You have changed the world with your actions and everyone knows your reputation," Trion insisted.

"And no one cares for my faith."

Trion gaped. Likely, he thought Akheron spoke like a madman. Akheron was changing the world, indeed. It would forget the importance of faith. It would forget the importance of inner passion. It would forget that things known only by the Maker himself *mattered*. Only achievements shown to society would be considered acts at all.

And now, this man, this shallow creature of sin and betrayal... he spoke of faith? Trion shook his head and kept walking. He had no words to reply. He preferred the reputation of Akheron to the fiercely incomprehensible man that he had invited to share his roof and his food.

"Thank you, Lord Trion, for the quarters to sleep in. I will speak to your chamberlain when I require them. For now, I would like to take a walk." Akheron glanced at Haekus. "By myself."

Haekus blinked and analyzed Akheron's look briefly. "One of *those,*" he said, and turned back to their host.

As Akheron turned away, he heard Trion ask, "Does he do this often?"

He did not wait to hear their reply, but turned around and walked past the guard-patrolled wall again. He heard the massive doors of the Keep creak open and bang closed as they entered. This place was even more outrageous than the extra storeys that Akheron had added to his own palace.

He wasn't sure where he planned to walk; he never was, on these escapes. He was restless and frustrated. Haekus had once told him that these walks would get him killed one day. Sometimes, his guard tried to object. Haekus was far too loyal, as Akheron saw it. Perhaps, one day, Akheron's enemies would kill him. He hoped it was not before he had done the things he wanted to—the things he had decided he *had* to.

He did not walk to find his death. He walked to find his life.

There was a square in the middle of the upper city, where two main roads intersected. He wandered around the square for a while, looking at the stalls of any merchants that were still open. Many of the men and women recognized him. A young boy came to thank him, though the child could scarcely understand why he was giving thanks. Akheron liked that; he did not understand why either. This was part of the reason why Akheron was so beloved by the commoners: he walked and talked among them, instead of above them.

He glanced toward the remains of the Stead when a loud boom echoed off Mount Trion's face. It was starting to collapse. The roof of the entryway was falling inward and the tower starting to lean. Live fires could be seen, reaching skyward. The Stead was hard to see from the square, as the sun was setting in that direction. He meandered toward it.

He was not certain how long he sat beside the wreckage. He planted himself on a fence nearby and watched until it was dark and there were only smouldering ruins. He felt sad and happy at the same time. Two parts of himself were at war with one another. *It is amazing,* he said to himself. *That I can still care, after all of this.* He lifted his hands and studied them. *There should only be one part to myself.*

He stood up and started to wander again. He decided to go down further, into the Lower Wall. Trionus City had enormous defences, to keep out any rabble and mountain tribesmen that might bother the area, and an entire half of the city was built into it or in the narrow band of lowland that hid behind it. Only the wealthy could afford life in the Upper City, where they could see over the wall. As Akheron meandered his way down Leto's spell-cast stairs, the mountains vanished behind the wall and the smell of the town enveloped him.

"Want some keynen?" a hooded man asked Akheron as he walked by a single-storey wooden lean-to.

"Keynen?"

The man held up a little bundle of smooth, narrow wooden sticks. They were out of the way of the torchlight and Akheron could not see anything more than the man's dim eyes and his 'keynen'. "Just break the stick and inhale the contents," the man said. "And you'll forget all your troubles."

"Even the Maker cannot do that," Akheron said. "Now scurry away, before I step on you."

The vermin said no more, and vanished into his hovel.

Akheron carried on down the main street as the moon peeked above the Lower Wall. He saw only a handful of guards. They all carried torches. The nightlife hid from the light whenever they passed, so Akheron did the same. He drew to the side of the road, and loitered with the beggars and drunks.

He came upon a two-storey building, neither large nor small by Trionus' standards, lit by the warm glow of colourful lanterns. The sign that hung outside read, "The Magenta House".

You're married now, he told himself. He stopped walking toward the place. *Reya Edemar is waiting for you in Avernus. Reya Gothikar.* He leaned against a lantern-post and his palms itched. He tried to imagine Reya to convince himself not to sin, but imagining her with her legs open to him made him equally uncomfortable—not because he did not desire her, but *because* he did. He had said the Maker's name earlier, to that scoundrel. He had not spoken it in so long. He was lonely and broken. "Maker, I'm lonely," he whispered. He entered the Magenta House.

14

"You're leaving, aren't you?" Reya asked. She set down her fork and regarded Akheron with her wide dark eyes. She was a sharp woman, with sharp eyes, sharp bones and a cleverness that could cut. "Every time we get close, you find some reason to leave."

Akheron pursed his lips. The taste of spiced beef and gravy still danced in his mouth. He put down his own cutlery and picked up his warm mead.

"Is it the rebellion? Or you just want to get away? Can the mob not murder old Kin without you?" she asked. Her cheeks were beginning to flush, and her hand, still on the table, trembled. The clinking of utensils echoed in the quiet dining hall. They had been married for less than half of a year, and she was not yet confident to stand up to him.

Akheron took a quick drink of his mead, but savoured it in his mouth before swallowing. A grated fire warmed the whole room from the nearby wall.

"I'm sorry," Reya said. What kind of man was Akheron? She had treasured her wedding to a Prince. She had dreamed of Akheron like every young woman had in the past five years. But what kind of man was he? Did he beat his wife, like many did? Did he always ignore her? Would he want children? How many?

Akheron had been living with her for the equivalent of a month during their marriage, and had left on three separate outings. Whenever he spent time with her, he could see the questions streaming through her head.

He put down his mug. "Reya," he said.

She quieted her fretting and dropped her hands to her lap.

"A home life does not interest me," he said. He leaned forward. "I may, in time, come to love you, once I know you. But I may never, truly, live with you. Haekus knows I can't stay still. He has to follow me on my walks, whenever the whim arises."

"I-I do not need your love," she said, "but I do like your company. If we have children—I know you don't want any—they need a father."

"I am not comfortable with your company," he said. She protested, but he raised a hand. "I am not comfortable with anyone's, because I am not comfortable with my own."

"Why not?" she asked.

"Reya..."

"I know, I know. Never ask you that."

"Never ask me," he repeated. "Look at what I have done, what I am doing! This is the man you made your oaths to—a killer, a cheater. I will sleep with anyone that will let me! I will kill anyone, if I... must, whether they are man, child, or—woman."

She barely batted an eye at most of it. "Would you kill me?" she questioned, with both hands parting her dark hair out of her face.

"Glyphs!" he cursed. "No. Never."

"Why not? You do not love me, and you will not give me a child, and I only complain about your travels..."

"You're my wife!" Akheron snapped.

"Which means nothing," she said, not with anger or frustration. Almost indifference. The nearby fireplace crackled loudly.

Glyphs. Care, Reya. Care! He took another quick swig of his mead again. "We made an oath, by the Maker and his glyphs!"

"And a few words before the Maker mean something to you?" she asked. "Since when!"

"Since always," he said, standing up. His chair skidded back from the table with a loud grind. "Enough of—"

Reya stood too, keeping him at eye level. "Do you believe in the Maker?"

"Always!" He planted his fists on the table. "I will always

believe."

Reya's mouth dropped.

"I may not like him, I may not," he paused, "follow him. I will *hurt* him and I will *end* him. But I will always believe in his existence and his power."

She nodded, and, for a silent breath, they only gazed at each other. "Now I understand," she said.

"You do?"

She looked down at their table. "Well, I didn't know I had married a believer. You know I am not. And I don't understand why you want the things you want. But you're more real to me now."

Akheron sat down again. "Glyphs," he said. "I wish I wasn't this way. I wish..."

For a long time, they were quiet. Reya took a delicate sip from her drink. She was still standing nearby, but they both looked into the nearby fire.

"I have nothing else to say," she said, and turned toward the door.

"Reya." He leaned forward, his eyes on her.

She glanced back at him. "Yes?"

"You said—you said that you do not need my love. You certainly do not need my power or wealth; your father provides both of those," he rambled. "Why marry me? Why did you want to, before?"

She stared at him.

Akheron frowned. "I'm sorry, I just—"

"It's fine," she said. "I may not love the 'personal', real man, but I love the public one. I love the man who went from a tradesman's son to become a Prince, because he wanted to."

"I never wanted to," he said.

"I love the man who saw in our people what they wanted— freedom from the Kinship's clutches—and showed them how to get it."

"I'm not doing that either."

"I know. You're not the man I love."

"Huh," Akheron said. He leaned back in his chair again, fingering the handle of his cup.

The corners of Reya's lips folded up in a small smile, almost a sad one. She opened the door into the Palace corridor and disappeared. Akheron sat at his dinner table and closed his eyes.

The fire crackled quietly and, somewhere in the Palace, a dog was barking.

"Have a good evening, milady," a smooth voice said, muffled by the aged door.

"You too, Haekus."

Akheron opened his eyes and finished his cup, without rising from his slouch. He felt like curling himself deep into the seat of the chair until he was no more than a cushion upon it.

"Haekus," Reya's voice said.

"Yes, milady?"

"How do you react to him, when he's in his moods?"

There was a pause, then Haekus said, "There's a balance to him, somewhere between what he does, who he is, and what the world sees of him. Usually, I just ask myself where his balance is, and protect him from all the rest."

"Does he talk to you, then? Does he tell you of those different parts?"

"Milady?"

"Does he lower his armour for you? I am always trying to chip through it."

There was another pause, with a distinct chuckle in the middle of it. "No, Lady Gothikar. I am only his guard. He confides more in you than in anyone I know of."

Akheron sat up slowly, peering around the empty room. Did they know he could hear them? Haekus must. He must've heard the entire conversation between Reya and her husband. If Akheron could hear the corridor, the corridor could hear within.

The outsiders were quiet for a few breaths more, then Haekus said, "Rest well, milady."

"Thank you," Reya replied, and there were no more words spoken beyond the door.

15

The Steads were falling. One by one. The Kinship was breaking. Akheron's grip on the world was turning it red. *Let go.*

He walked with his head down and his shoulders turned in. His arms dangled by his sides. Beside him, snaked a tail of blood. It was a serpent, slithering its way between clumps of ash and soot. Akheron matched its ponderous pace. He watched the tail turn right and left, around a splintered block of wood. It knew where it was headed. Downhill. Everything in this world seemed to know to where it was moving, but Akheron spent his energy trying to believe he was standing still.

Behind him walked Haekus, bloody sword drawn. Behind the guard was the din of fighting. A man was screaming as an axe buried itself in his shoulder. Another was shouting curses as he slammed an armoured corpse against a fiery wall repeatedly. This side of Quintus was on fire. Many Olympians had picked up arms to burn their Stead down. Many more had fought to stop them. The commander of the city watch had ordered his guards to contain the carnage. Two hundred trained soldiers had flooded the streets and set up a five-block radius around the Stead of Quintus.

"Where are we going?" Akheron asked the blood serpent. It was all he focused on. It kept winding its way down the slope. *Down,* the blood told him. Akheron kept his head down. He kept his spirits down. It found a pond of blood, mingling into the sickly swamp around a slain Defender. The Olympian arrows bristling from the warrior's torso told Akheron that the damned quarantine had killed this man.

If I keep walking, will they dare raise their bows? He turned right. He did not advance toward the Quintus guard. He did not follow the blood *down.*

"You're him," someone said. A middle-aged man stood in the way. He wore a small silver Circle on a necklace.

Akheron met the loyal man's eyes, and put all he had into that gaze. He showed the believer everything. He showed the man everything that the Maker had taken. He showed him everything that had broken—everything that Akheron had broken. Akheron showed the faithful man his own faith, his own prayers, his own darkness.

"Is *nothing* sacred to you?" the man asked. "Is nothing holy?"

"My love was sacred. My love was holy. My guilt is—" his voice broke and he looked down. He held his hands up to inspect them, but he did not see them. He only saw *down.*

The man charged at him, brandishing a broken wooden pole.

Haekus just watched. He did not raise his sword. He did not try to protect his Prince and friend. He just watched.

Akheron killed the faithful man.

16

The everwoods caught the sunlight and cast upon the wedding a golden aura. The leaves were in full bloom, a bright orange gleam that blinded the eyes of any who looked up from their theatre at the enormous trees. With a raised dais in the middle of an elaborately tiled floor, the Royal Castle of Performance was the perfect venue for the joining of royalty. Of course, it was only because the Kinship of the Maker would not provide a sanctuary of their own.

Akheron looked up through the glass ceiling at the trees of Galinor until his eyes watered. He looked down from those heights to his wedding and saw spots, blocking everything out.

As they withdrew, his wife came into view. She wore the traditional Gothikar colours: green and black over a white blouse of some sort. The rich pine green robe, with dark frills along the hems and shiny black gemstones at the neck and adorning the cuffs, wrapped around her body like the frock of some religious garb. Her hair was pinned behind her head with black painted pins; on top of each sat a small stone of malachite. Around her neck and above the collar of the green robe, was a white-gold clasp that matched her white shirt.

"... and the groom," Odyn said, "Akheron Gothikar."

Akheron stepped forward as he was cued. His wife and he stood on the stage, surrounded by the royalty of Galinor. Marriage was traditionally under the governance of religion, but it was administered by the state and all the Princes held the authority to conduct it. Akheron could conduct his own wedding, which was his original intent—the trip to Galinor presented an opportunity to more than satisfy his debt to his wife's father. The Princes had summoned Akheron for a meeting of the Council, and House Gothikar had extended an invitation to the Edemar family to have a wedding made of dreams.

Haekus, standing next to Lord Edemar and his other daughter, nodded to Akheron. He was wearing the same stiff black tabard that hung from Akheron's shoulders. He had a green sash, and a dark red cape. Akheron had insisted only on black, but had allowed them to wrap a forest green silk around his neck.

"Do you have any words for your betrothed?" Odyn asked.

Akheron closed his eyes. *It was supposed to be Mavas!* he wanted to say. Mavas had dark hair too. But even when Mavas had held him, marriage had not been the plan. He corrected himself, for the one it really *was* supposed to be. *It was supposed to be* her. He remembered her soft red hair and her smell.

But he didn't say either of these things. He just wiped his hands on the black he wore and looked Odyn in the eye. "I do not," he said.

There was a quiet murmur from the audience, but many were not surprised. Anyone who knew anything was aware that this was a token wedding, a political tribute.

"And Reya Edemar, have you any words for your husband-to-be?"

Reya caught his eye, and held it. She was brimming with joy, her cheeks flushed and her eyes wide. "We all know what this union is," she said, with her head held high. "But no one knows what this is to *me*. This is not fame or fortune I have won. This is not a large mansion, promised to me by oaths taken before my lord Princes. This is not a safe life for my children nor a wealthy necklace against my skin. This is the *dream* of our age: change, desire not denied, passion unhidden and unhindered. You are the noble commoner, and I will cherish you."

Akheron's face burned. He opened his mouth and breathed, "There's nothing noble about me."

Only Reya and Odyn could hear him. The other Prince raised an eyebrow. Reya only held her smile. *Glyphs,* he thought, *she's a strong one. Almost as strong as...* He wiped his hands on his tabard, further wrinkling it with his fidgeting.

"And now for the Joining," Odyn intoned. These were ceremonial words. Everyone in the room shifted uncomfortably, knowing what was to come. *"Ta shen tu Thoanus anos."*

Akheron and Reya lifted their hands and folded them over their own hearts. Akheron tried to ignore the tension in the room. The ceremony was conducted in both Common and the Ancestral Tongues, just as the Kinship conducted their preaching. The marriage would also include oaths to the Maker—Akheron hoped that the audience would survive their fear of such words, the fear he had instilled in them.

Odyn was an enormous man, practically a giant, and to hear him speak Ancestral was entertaining to Akheron. "Before the Maker, swear to always protect and to care for your betrothed. Swear to the Maker to be faithful to your betrothed." Again, he recited the old tongue. *"Seros tu Deyvas, o hesh vanon tao gendro anos qisti vinday orgos. O tu Deyvas o nowus septay o kos orgos."*

Akheron took a deep breath. "I swear it by the Maker. *Osa ert tu Deyvas orgos."* He watched Reya, with her hands above her left breast, ready herself for the vow. *The Maker did not keep his promises to me... I need not weight my oaths to him with any truth.*

"I swear it by the Maker," Reya said, and repeated the Ancestral oath.

The Kinship does love its languages, he thought, as she spoke. *The language of Glyphs, Ancestral, Common... if I had not broken their following, they would have continued adding to it!*

"Now take the hand of your wife and take the hand of your husband. Kiss, and be joined in matrimony," Odyn said.

Akheron lowered his hands toward her. He felt dizzy. He opened his palms and let Reya take them. Did she feel the sweat? Her hands were warm too. She leaned close to him, and he closed his eyes. He wasn't certain who it was that he imagined kissing him, but it was not her. When he opened his eyes and she pulled away, he knew that it was her—Reya Gothikar—and he found himself anticipating her once again. Ever since they had met, Akheron had desired her. She was pure, in his eyes. She was something denied to him until this day.

"Wine!" Odyn called. "For Lord and Lady Gothikar!"

The room cheered, a din of noise that reverberated off the glass ceiling. Odyn shook their hands, boomed praise and went to celebrate. Akheron broke from Reya's gaze and looked up into the golden leaves above them. How unrealistic. How cruel.

"We should speak with our guests, my husband," Reya said, taking Akheron's arm. Holding his arm out awkwardly, he looked down at her hands. She leaned closer to him, pressed herself against his upper arm, and whispered in his ear. "Don't be so uncomfortable with this. I'll be touching a lot more of you tonight."

Akheron raised an eyebrow, and did as he was told. He relaxed his arm, and put his other hand on hers. Together, they drifted down from the dais and into the mill of royalty. Many of the nobles of Galinor were unknown to Akheron; he had enough trouble keeping the upper class of Avernus straight. He was a commoner by birth and had not been raised amongst them.

Reya had been raised at court, and she would provide an invaluable service to Akheron's reign as Prince. As Edemar had told him, "There are countless reasons for this favour." As they were congratulated by the lords and ladies of Galinor, Reya recognized some of them. She would give them kind words and ask about their son, their aunt, or their business.

"I am so bad at this," Akheron told her under his breath.

"That's no issue," Reya said. "I can deal with the noble persons. I will leave the destruction of civil institutions to you."

Akheron laughed. Whispering back and forth gave him a slight lift to his stomach. It made him feel that this *was* his wedding day. He almost felt a slight joy, somewhere in the background.

"Akheron," Verin Theseus said. "Congratulations. And to you Reya."

Leto was in tail with him, and Akheron suspected they had other motives than kind words by the narrow line Leto's mouth was drawn into. "Reya," Akheron said. "Perhaps your father would like to embrace you."

She smiled. "I'll leave you to your politics," she said. She gave Theseus a glare and said, "Do not keep my husband too long."

Theseus shrugged, as she went her way.

"What do you two want now?" Akheron asked.

Leto's hair was thoroughly grey now. She was starting to show the signs of her age, but looked as serene as ever in the red garb of the Crown Mage. With a fierce inhale, she told him, "The Stead of Athyns is closing its doors now. There's civil unrest on the Eve of Reflection and feasting on the Eve of Preparation."

"I have not been to Athyns since I was first elected Prince!" Akheron retorted. "You would blame me—"

"Do not play meek with me," Theseus said. "And do not let your bloody rebellion mar my doorstep!"

"You denied me landing," Akheron said. "I sailed for your city, and found the harbour under the lock-and-key of your guard. So I turned my ship around—"

"Your corsair ship," Theseus said. His words were slurred a bit. He had been drinking throughout their entire Council this morning. He held a cup again already.

"I beg your pardon?" Akheron snapped. "You have no grounds for such an accusation and you know it. If any have reason *not* to work with corsairs, it would be me. Were you there, on the Grey Night? Did you see the blood in the Palace?"

Verin cursed beneath his breath.

Leto raised her hand toward the latter. "Don't—"

Theseus leaned closer to Akheron. "Interesting how the Grey Night ended and you were Prince."

Akheron's fist sent the other Prince reeling backward, clutching his nose. "They burned my home!" he shouted. His estate had not burned until the first riots, but Avernus was his home.

Theseus, stumbling against a small wine-table, rose to Akheron's strike and reached for his sword. Haekus appeared out of the crowd. His own blade was already drawn.

"Enough!" Leto screeched, stepping between the two sword-bearers with her arms raised.

Verin Theseus wiped blood away from his nostrils. His stubble was stained, making it look dark orange.

"I am... astounded by you two!" Leto's voice did not waver. In the crowd, her apprentice turned away. He was a distinguishable man, with dark hair. The two seemed akin in their wit and *disappointment*. "To exchange insults and blows on a man's wedding day, let alone in the city of our forefathers! I am not the mother of the Triumvirate. I will not treat you two like children. I will only say: enough!"

Theseus sneered and stumbled away, lurching drunkenly. Haekus sheathed his blade.

"I-I demand an apology!" Akheron stepped fiercely after Theseus; he ignored the appalled faces of his wedding guests. "I am a Prince of the Triumvirate! I will—"

"Give it a rest, Akheron," Leto said, lowering her arms. Her eyes pleaded him.

Akheron looked around for support. Odyn had followed Theseus out of the auditorium and Haekus's face was serene and unhelpful. He turned away from Leto, and found Reya right behind him. His movement took him too close, and bumped her arm. She nearly spilled her glass of wine, but his heart was pumping adrenaline and he caught it without losing a drop. It could have spilled all over her white blouse.

"I apologize, my wife," he said. "This wedding was almost red."

She was unaffected—a shrug, a narrow smile, a confident hand on his arm. "Let's go away," she said. "You need not face these people if you do not want to."

"But this is your day," he said.

"Don't be so old-fashioned. It doesn't suit the Maker's nemesis," she teased.

His mood was improved, by only a few words. "Where should we go?"

"Home?" she asked.

He stared into her wide, waiting eyes. His home was hers now. She had nowhere else to go than where he took her. She was his, and he was hers. "You are my wife," he marvelled. It was as horrific to him as it was pleasing.

"I am," she said.

"Leto!" Akheron called. She was now talking to one of the dignitaries in attendance. "Teleport us to Avernus, please."

The Crown Magician eyed him for a moment. "Already?" she asked.

"I only do as my wife tells me," he said.

"I did not tell you to strike your fellow Prince," Reya said, earning some chuckles from those close enough to hear.

"Congratulations on the marriage," someone nearby called,

and it was echoed by many. Akheron thought he saw Lord Trion to be the first to raise the toast. One of the most famous men in Galinor.

"As feisty a marriage as it is," Akheron said, in retort to his wife's taunt. She only smiled back at him.

"Does anyone else want to travel to Avernus?" Leto asked. It was a custom of courtesy that dated back to antiquity. There was no point in travelling from one end of the Dominion to the other if a magician could connect the two places directly.

Lord Edemar stepped forward, his emerald-cornered robe flowing after him. Reya's sister followed, as elegantly adorned as the bride. For Edemar, this was a great opportunity to advertise her to possible suitors. "We would, of course," the Noble said. He gave Akheron a snide frown. "I intended this celebration to last longer, my Prince."

"You do not control me, old friend," Akheron whispered to Edemar, as Leto wrote her spell. It was the way of the world for the Nobles to control the Princes as much as they could. When Edemar had decided to back Akheron, their relationship had changed. Akheron had become Edemar's man, though he would have none of it. "Do not forget it."

"I wouldn't *dare*," Edemar said. His face did not smirk, though he meant it in humour. He had become such a dryly sarcastic man in his old age. *Haekus, Edemar, Yory... they're all becoming such bristly people,* Akheron thought. *What made them this way?* That only made him recall their heated words, a few months ago.

"Farewell for now, Prince Gothikar," Leto said. She breathed a string of ancient words beneath her breath and the air around them seemed to shift.

It took only a second, and, like the movement of a cracking joint, the panorama of Avernus replaced the everwood auditorium. Akheron closed his eyes. It made him ill, almost. He shook his head and looked at Reya who still held his hand.

Then he looked up. The Known Location, where teleports arrived, was atop an old building and Akheron could see almost an entire full circle around the city, interrupted only by the Three Towers of Avernus, his Palace. The Keep, the Barracks and the Library. None were exactly towers, but they were built upon the highest hill of the city.

It was like a dream that he desperately wanted to wake up from, but couldn't. Around them was *his* horizon. From the north blew a cold wind. The ocean stretched away, grey and impenetrable. The horizon of the Gate was only blocked by the Valara Isles. The two enormous rocks rose out of the water to the north-east of Avernus, one wide and one narrow.

Reya squeezed his hand. She was warm, despite the chilling breeze. Her skin pulled him back towards his immediate reality. As he turned toward the stairwell from the building's roof, he looked east across the Avernan Chase and south at the Southern Spine mountains, curved rocky peaks that were always trying to claw a sky they could not reach.

"Come away from here," Reya said. Edemar and his other daughter were already descending the rooftop. A moment of wind flapping their cloaks passed. "Are you crying?"

He closed his eyes again.

"Glyphs," she said. "On your wedding day?"

"It's not you," he said.

"I know it's not," she said. "I'm a beautiful and willing young girl and we've only just been married."

He forced a smile.

"What is it then? Am I allowed to ask that? Is it Tam again?"

Akheron turned to her, taking her hand with both of his. "No. It's... my lover. She left me."

Reya blinked. She turned to look eastward with him. For a while they just listened to the wind howling over the rooftops of the city. Haekus waited by the stairs, leaning against the old stone railing.

"I told her, what you told me," Akheron said, though now he *was* talking about Mavas. Tam, recently slain. Mavas, who left him. And...*her,* long before both. His breath caught, and he forced him to think about the conversation with Mavas. "That it was no issue to keep our own... relationship, when I married."

Reya nodded. He could not tell what she was thinking. At least she was interesting to him. He would have been bored to marry someone predictable.

"But she was not comfortable with it," he said. "She left me." Then, quieter, he repeated it. "And *she* left me." Not Tam, not Mavas.

"What was her name?" Reya asked.

Did he dare speak it? His pain was filling him again, like it did on the days he killed things or on the days he was alone. Would he be lonely, with Reya at his side? If today provided any foreshadowing, he would be terribly lonely. He wanted to kill something, already. He had been trying not to think about it all day. But now he wanted to feel real warmth on his hands—not Reya's softness. *Glyphs*, he thought. *Strike me down.*

She started, "It's not an iss—"

"Her name was Mavas," he lied, jumping back to memories he could still comprehend. Memories that stung like death, but did not make him desire it.

"Mavas," Reya said. "What was she like?"

"Why do you want to know?"

"Because she was important to you."

"Glyphs, I have no honour, no integrity, and you still *care?*"

Reya looked away from the horizon at him. "Look around, Akheron. Your life is full of people who care. Did Mavas care?"

"No," Akheron said. "Not in the end. She left me, remember?"

"I know, I meant..."

Akheron shook his head and turned toward Haekus. "Let's go," he told his wife. "We have celebrations ahead of us."

Haekus led the way down the stairs without a word. Reya followed him, while Akheron delayed a moment on the haunting rooftop. It used to make him feel comfortable. This used to be *his* horizon, *his* city. He had given it to someone else now, no matter what anyone said. He felt the urge for one of his walks, but subdued it.

He started down the stairwell and muttered under his breath, "Mavas stopped caring. That's why I loved her."

17

Akheron had been a Prince for five years now for it was the Year of Olympus 516. Two years of bloody riots against the Maker—*Glyphs, has it been so long?*—and three years of trying to get used to a throne. *Tam,* he thought, *why did you think this would be a good idea? I can't even leave my house without reasons now!* The guards wanted to know where he was going, when and why. Haekus was smart enough to not ask questions. He knew Akheron's urge to get out of the Palace. He probably felt it too. He followed Akheron from a distance as the Prince walked innocuously down a crowded Avernan street.

But Tam was gone now and he could not blame another soul in the world for a thing, save himself. *Why won't you stop me?* he prayed for the hundredth time. *You should have stopped me sooner.*

Tam was gone, and soon Mavas would be as well. One by one, his friends were slipping away—or dying off. *Only myself at fault,* he repeated in his head. "Only myself."

A passerby gave him a concerned eye, then widened his eyes with recognition. The man, with sandy hair and slumped shoulders, straitened his back and nodded to Akheron. Thankfully, no more attention was drawn to the Prince than that.

"What are you doing?" Haekus asked. "This isn't one of your normal walks."

"No, it's not." Akheron stopped to look through a jeweler's stall he had spotted. The private guards that stood there stiffened. They did not trust Akheron. They also did not know him—this must be a travelling merchant. She was an old woman, with two big circular earrings made of copper. They almost resembled Circles like the Kinship's. She must have thought the same thing, for she removed them before coming to speak to her customer. Clearly, she had more of an idea who he might be.

"Good afternoon, milord."

"Season's greetings," he said. It was almost Autumn.

"Are you looking for anything particular?" She noticed Haekus, but didn't say anything about either of them. Akheron suspected she recognized him as the Prince, but she did her best to treat him as he clearly intended to be received.

"A ring," he said. "Something that shows love."

"Romantic love? Or political love?"

"Dedicated love," Akheron replied. "Price is not an issue. But I want to send a message that nothing could change. Nothing could touch or hurt this love."

He was acting on a whim. All day, he'd been acting on a whim. Since he had told Edemar he intended to marry his daughter, as their pact had determined, he had spent all his effort staying away from Mavas. He had left on Yory's ship and raided the northern coast of the Mydarius, not in the way they used to raid. They had burned Steads all along the way, delivering speeches where necessary. Inciting the tension, feeding the flames. Since returning from the voyage, Akheron had spent his days avoiding any meaningful exchanges with Mavas. Obviously, they still slept together regularly, but he could not bear to have a down-to-earth conversation yet. Reya would be his wife, and he needed to find a way to tell Mavas.

"I can't lose her," he said out loud.

"Ah." The woman nodded as though she heard these things each day. She began looking through her glass cases. She must have been a successful jeweler—glass prices weren't what they used to be, but they were still high.

Mavas could always find him at the Palace. His guards let her through any door, at his own standing orders. He could not revoke them without her knowing something serious was afoot. *I don't want to revoke them,* Akheron thought. *I want Mavas with me all the time.* This was no mere infatuation, Mavas had been his for six years now. Since before the Grey Night. He shuddered to remember it.

"Perhaps this," the jeweler said, with her silver tongue. She set into his hand a small silver ring, with three tiny rubies on a triangular face. Gazing into those gems, Akheron thought about Mavas's words after the first riot. They had not been the same since then. She did not approve of his new war. But in these stones, Akheron remembered her words. *"How red will your hands be, before you are done? I thought you had to remove House Aristorn. I thought we did that out of ambition and necessity. But you're just a simple killer."* His reply had been a retaliation, but he trusted Mavas enough to consider telling her the whole truth now. The whole story. The first loss, not Tam, though Mavas understood that loss in a way very few did. *Glyphs, I lose everyone I love. Can I keep Mavas?*

Their relationship began as sex. Sex between two killers. When had it become something that could be damaged by more sin? But he knew it was.

"Well?" the jeweler asked, gruffly. "If you look at them any longer, I will write you a receipt for a viewing."

"Akheron!"

Mavas came striding down the street. She had the spring in her step that had first caught Akheron's eye. Just a little bounce that he was not used to in a girl. Especially one that wore such a sleek sword on her belt, or had her soft black hair cut short enough to wear beneath a helmet. She was biting her bottom lip. "What are you doing here?" she asked.

"I could ask you the same thing," he said.

"You could." She peeked around him and winked at the jeweler.

"I got you this," Akheron said hurriedly, taking Mavas's hand and sliding the ring on. He shot Haekus a glance and tilted his head back at the jeweler.

Mavas lifted her hand to her face. "You know I'm not one for trinkets," she said after a minute, "but this is adorable."

Haekus gave the merchant a handful of coins, and they made their way down the street.

"The guards at the Palace said you two left not too long ago. I came from the Gatehouse, so I knew you had not walked that way," Mavas said.

"Were you following me?" he jested.

She gave him a look of mock guilt. "I confess, I am always

prowling after my Prince."

"I wouldn't have it any other way," Akheron said. Haekus resumed his distance. "Now you've got your ring. Where would you like to go now?"

"I don't know," Mavas said. She kissed the hand he had wrapped around her shoulders. "Depends what you would like to do." She looked him in the eye, without blushing.

Akheron swallowed. He was nervous. When was the last time he had been nervous? When she had been his first time? "I think we should talk."

"Oh." After a moment, she added, "I think that's for the best."

"Where would you like to go?" he asked.

"Let's go up the Tower," she said.

It took them most of the hour to walk across the city. The walls on the south-west side were the tallest, where a single guard tower rose higher than the whole city, except the Palace of Avernus, now that Akheron had added storeys to it.

There were usually two guards stationed here. Today there were three. They had become accustomed to Akheron's unplanned visits, so there was no scramble to look orderly when he arrived with Mavas on one arm. He got a salute, a 'How-do-you-do?', and was let up the stairs without question or concern. The guards greeted Haekus with a clasp and a pat on the back. He sat down at their table as Mavas led Akheron up the stairs.

"Perhaps you could tempt me to do more than talk," he said, and pinched her backside through her flowing green skirt.

She turned around in mid step, though Akheron couldn't stop in time. He found himself closer to her than he anticipated, their legs touching. "We've done more than talk here," she said. "Beneath the stars."

He kissed her and held her. As they separated, he bit her lip. The taste of Mavas stirred him up inside. *I don't want to lose you,* he thought. "We might again," he said, but left the phrase hanging.

"But first we talk," she finished. She took his hand and led him past the look-out room and onto the balcony roof of their Tower. Someone had dragged a cot up here! Did the guards think it was part of their responsibilities to make this a comfortable place for him to bring his women?

Mavas laughed. "We could definitely do more up here," she said, sitting down on it.

Akheron took a deep breath. "Not yet."

"What?" she asked. "I'm not a fool. I know you've been avoiding me. Now you don't even want me?"

"Glyphs," he said. "Did you not feel my kiss? I want you more than anything."

She pulled off his ring. "And this? Is this supposed to apologize for the last few weeks? Months?"

"No, just for this." He palmed his forehead.

"For what?"

He took a deep breath. He forced himself to see clearly. He forced himself to see her clearly. He looked past her, and into his city. *Glyphs, do I love it more than her?* Not even close. He had once said goodbye to his city, without any intent to return to it. He could never do that with her, could he?

"What?"

He looked back at her, and took another breath.

She confronted him, "Why are you so scared? You've never been—"

"I am going to marry Reya."

There was a beat of quiet. Her eyes narrowed slightly, barely perceivable. "Who, in the Great Glyph, is Reya?"

"Edemar's daughter."

"Damn it, *Mar's* daughter?"

Akheron nodded. "I told him that if he supported us then, I'd support him now. I told him he could ask any favour of the Prince, and it would be his."

"I remember," Mavas said. "Because I was with you *then.* Even then. What's changed, Akheron?"

"Nothing."

"So you always planned on marrying her?"

"I never planned. I made an oath. You remember, you were there."

Mavas shook her head. "So you're telling me you're going to go through with it? You're going to marry this girl?"

"I must."

"Do you *want* to?" she asked, pulling at her short dark hair. She was heaving for breath. Akheron's had become shallow, too.

"No! I want you. I have for six years and five cycles.

Nothing has changed."

"You want me."

"Of course." He stepped toward her, but she stepped back.

"Since when have you done anything else than you wanted? That sounds like something has changed," she said.

"I *have* to be more than what I want," he said. "Surely, you understand that. You once called me nothing but a simple killer. I am more."

"Do you remember how you replied to that accusation? You told me you were exactly nothing but a killer." She was shaking her head. "Do you want me, or do you just want yourself?"

"What!"

"Everything you do, you do carelessly. Because you're so... forsakenly strong, or something." Her chin trembled. Her eyes were fiery.

"I do *nothing* without caring." These words were rough. Fierce. "Nothing."

"What about your war against the Maker?" she asked. "You told me you were a believer. You told me you had always been, and always would be."

"I believe that the Maker made all of this. This whole shadow-pit of a world. He made all of us, and let us be—what we are." Akheron's head sat back into his neck. He felt ill.

"But you fight the Maker for *you*. You alone. I asked you to stop. I pleaded with you. I said, 'sins are sins, but this is something else.' I asked you to be at peace, for me."

"And I told you, there will never be peace for me. No matter how bad I want that, I cannot have it. I will not."

"Why?" she asked.

"Don't ask me why."

"Glyphs. Here we go again."

"Yeah, there we go again," Akheron said. "I thought you loved me."

She slapped him. Slaps were not Mavas's way. "I do, you heartless spawn."

"I love you," he said. "Reya will be less than an acquaintance to me. She will be an oath, she will be a burden, she will be my wife. But you will be my love. I never have to swear to love her."

She shook her head. "Then why can't you be at peace?" She over-enunciated each word.

"Because of the first woman I loved. And because of Tam. Because of the Maker. Because everything I love is taken away from me." Akheron said. He had never been so vulnerable. He hid it behind his anger. "Because I hate this world and everything I am. All of it a failure to what I *could* have been."

"What do you want from me, Akheron?" she asked. She held up his ring. "Was this supposed to be payment, for services rendered? Or just an attempt to keep something that makes *you* forget how miserable you are?" She flicked the rubies over the balcony.

"I want someone, anyone, to hate the monster inside of me as much as I do. I am selfish, like you say. I am uncontrollable. I am sinful."

"Enough of the *I's*!" She struck him again, this time with a fist. He fell down on one knee, his hand holding him up on an angle. "Enough of your cursed whining! Enough hurting me." She struck him again and again.

He lay on the wooden beams of their Tower's roof, coughing and spitting blood. His nose was bleeding.

"I hate you at last," she said. "Is that what you want? Do you want me to kill you while I'm at it?" She struck him again. He thought his nose was broken. She had once told him that if he crossed her, she would kill him. "I love you enough," she said, "that I'll do whatever you want. You want me to hate you? It's easy enough."

Akheron let the tears come at last. Maybe this was it. He loved her more the more she spoke. "Yes," he sobbed.

"You want me to kill you?" she asked. She pulled a knife from her belt and held it above him.

"Please," he whispered, but the word was lost in bloody gurgles. To be hated for what he was. To be removed, left in a pool of blood, like the stain he was on this world. A stain amongst stains.

She looked over him, at the ramparts of the tower. "If I do, I'll jump," she said. "You're what I want, but you want me to not want you."

"I'm sorry," he said. "Curse the Maker, curse him, I'm sorry."

She slammed her unarmed fist against his chest. Her knife—still held high—trembled. "Damn it, I hate you."

Akheron closed his eyes.

With a shriek, she brought the knife down, but it pounded against the wood beside him. Then her weight was gone, her warmth, all of her.

Haekus hauled Mavas off of his Prince, and threw her down nearby. She collided with the stone battlement. Akheron's breath caught. Haekus was at Akheron's side, on his knees. The knife vanished over the rampart. The guardsman lifted Akheron's battered head, one hand on each side. "What happened, Akheron? Glyphs, what did you do? Are you cut? Are you hurt?"

Mavas reclaimed her feet, holding her shoulder. "Why do you defend him, you fool? He told me to. All of this. Just another one of Akheron's fateful plans. You're the dumbest blade-master I know. Must've taken one too many blows to the head when you were being trained."

"I have to be more than what I want," Akheron sputtered. "I'm tired of just being my hate."

"You'll never die with Haekus behind you, Akheron. But, by the Maker, I hope you do. Because you will never be more than this." Mavas spat on him and then she was gone.

18

He hadn't saddled a horse in eight years—until now. There were always stable-boys or servants or Haekus to bend their backs instead. Akheron crept out of the inn before light; after the sun rose, his men and he would ride into Edessa. His scouts had returned the night before. They had arranged for him to deliver a speech outside of the Arena. His speeches were becoming less and less necessary, and his adventures becoming more and more exhaustive. His wayward urge pulled him up early in the morning—today it manifested itself as a ride, not a walk.

They had been sailing across the North Coast on Yory's *Sky Hound*, looking for Stead's to burn, though the wildfire was spreading faster than the wind bore them.

When Akheron sauntered out of the stable door with a horse in tow, the lantern he had lit was sputtering out. There was a band of dark burgundy on the horizon, dividing the sea from the sky; the sun had not shown itself yet. It was a quiet trot to the edge of the fishing village. The tiny harbour was busier than the main street of the town, where boatmen were preparing their rigging and folding their nets. As Akheron led the steed onto a dirt mountain trail, he watched a man down the green slope pulling a line of traps out of the shallows. In the poor light, the Prince could not make out any crustaceans within.

Saddling the horse had put him in good mood. He clucked his tongue behind his teeth as he swung one leg up, over the smooth rump of the animal. For the first few minutes, they galloped. They drank deeply of the cool morning.

He remembered a day, long ago, when his sister had shown

him how to saddle.

She was eighteen and Akheron was twelve during the year 496—it was only five years before their father had died. The old man was stuffing himself with food, like he always did, while Akheron played a game of sticks with his friends. They tossed a handful of twigs on the ground, and had to pick them up before the ball they threw landed.

"Child mine," Akheron's father sneered. "Bring this letter to Avary."

"Avary lives in the Residential District," Akheron complained. He stumbled away from his friends. "I won't be home until dark!"

"You lout," his father said. "When have you ever done anything worth the time and pain it took to bring you into this world?"

Akheron took the letter from his father's hands.

"Your mother's been dead three years," Veldar ten Gothikar said. "And you still shirk her responsibilities. Your responsibilities. Great Glyph! If you're so lazy, take Bannie."

"Will you saddle her?"

The old man sputtered on his stew. "Get going you earth-spawn!" he spat after he had swallowed his mouthful.

Akheron and his friends ran outside. They stood around in front of the door, talking quietly so Master ten Gothikar would not hear them. The "estate" was a large house, but not a mansion like those in the Residential District. It had two bedrooms, a kitchen and dining hall, a storage closet, and, outside, a livestock stall.

Akheron was trying to persuade his friends to come with him on the adventure across town when his sister came home. She had spent the night out, apparently, with her betrothed, an annoying carpenter named Barun. Their father would reprimand her for her ungodly behavior, but to the group of young boys she was a goddess, a graceful and attractive creature who denied their pubescent understanding; she had the curve of a woman to her, dark hair and elegant hips. Akheron tried not to let the stares of his friends bother him, but, even at a young age he felt protective of his older sister.

In short order, she learned from them that Akheron had

been sent out to deliver the letter, and that he was delaying the journey. "Carry on home," she ordered his friends. "I'll teach the merchant's son to saddle."

She led him into the stall, where their horse was tied. Bannie loved Akheron's sister—the mare's ears picked up whenever the girl approached. After a quick look around the horse, checking its hooves, his sister grabbed the old leather saddle off the stall's wall. She gave Akheron a dry look. "Ak, you're going to have to try harder with Father. He's an old man and he's lost a lot. We both need to try to help him out now."

"But you're never home anymore."

"Look, you got to start on the left side," his sister said, leading him to the proper side of the mare. "If you had a sword, it would get in the way on the right side."

He reluctantly took the saddle from her. It was heavy, but he could handle it. He heaved it up onto Bannie's back after his sister put a saddle pad beneath.

"Do up the girth cinch, under here," she said. "Father asked me to marry a ten Gandyr. Most parents don't request this of their daughters; they just send them away."

"Do you love him?"

"I'm starting to, Ak. Someday, you'll understand." She grabbed the bridle from a hook on the wall and handed it to him. "Just give Bannie the bit. We're commoners, but we are well-to-do, you see. Hey, gently, gently. Bannie will take it." She took a breath. "We need to be thankful for what we have, instead of fighting it or craving more."

Bannie's breath was warm. Akheron lifted the rest of the bridle, and gave his sister an inquisitive look. "Here?" She nodded, and he fit the straps around the horse's ears. "Does the Maker really command us to be satisfied?"

His sister sighed. "I believe so, and you know father certainly does."

"But he never *acts* satisfied."

"He lost our mother a few years ago, and he lost your brother before he even married her. He probably doesn't have lots to be satisfied for."

Akheron sighed. "I wish the Maker would just tell us how life should be. It would make things simpler. I never understand the Kin, even when they speak the Common language."

"Wait until you get older," she said.

Akheron climbed into the saddle. His sister grabbed the bottom of his foot to lift him, and he steadied himself by clutching her shoulder.

Akheron and his steed were trotting beside a brook now, a little stream that ran down the slope to the fishing village and out into the Mydarius Sea He glanced back over his shoulder; already he could see more fishers and tradesmen moving about the small northern settlement.

He had missed his sister ever since that horrible evening that had taken her. The Maker had seen fit to rob that of her, as penance for Akheron's sins. He and the Maker were locked in a battle. "So be it," he said aloud, as the horse he had saddled sauntered uphill. Akheron found the movement soothing. "You wanted a war, and I gave it to you."

Talking to the Maker made him uncomfortable. He had not wanted the blood of the holy on his hands. He had only wanted to close the eyes that had been open on the day that taught Akheron what he was, but when their gaze had been shut, his sister laid dead.

"But the Maker's eyes were open that first day," he reminded himself. "I must close his eyes too."

The first of the mountains, the shoulders of which held their camp, was more dirt than rock. The peak was like that of a hill, round and smooth. There were very few trees, just scraggly coils of trunk that sported clumps of leaves and did not even reach as high as Akheron's saddled arse. There were taller more jagged mountains somewhere north, but Akheron wanted to get a good view, so he kept riding upward. Whenever the going became too steep, he began zigzagging. He took it slowly. He did not want to work the horse too hard. A morning ride should be relaxing, he believed.

He pulled on the reins and look back over his shoulder. The sun was starting to rise, and the sash of burgundy on the horizon had been lost in white, radiant clouds. It was beautiful. It brought back memories of the sea, another flashback.

It was three months after Akheron left Avernus, three months after that dark day of epiphany when he had lost his true love. Akheron thought about all of his loss as he stood at the edge of a stone Point of Tarroth. There were thirteen such overlooks in Tarroth, three against the waterfront, where Akheron stood, four looming three storeys above him with enormous walls at his back, and four more above that. Then, at the top of the enormous rock city, stood the other two, pointing from a ninety-degree angle out into the Valharyn.

Standing here, at the base of the enormous machine-like city, Akheron felt so incredibly lost. Out there, he knew, as he stared into the ocean, was his home. South. His family and friends, his aunt Iarn, an old woman, and Tam, whom he so terribly missed. Tam had friends, and a lover, and a life now.

Akheron had thrown everything away.

His stomach hurt, but part of it was hunger. He had only the clothes on his back and five gold coins, tucked inside his left boot. The sovereigns would last him a long time, but he had just arrived in Tarroth. He had spent a long time marvelling at the city, walking the streets—tunnels through rock more often than not. The city was shaped like an "L". At the intersection of the enormous rock Points was the Crown of Tarroth. It was a city that claimed no debts to the Triumvirate; the corsair colony scraped by on crime, exports from its rich marble, salt, and silver mines, the fishing industry in its port, or on the steep taxes imposed by the ruling class, a group of Families that held the cold city in their rock-hard grip. He could make his coins last, but his stomach would not stop hurting anytime soon.

Bad fish, sea illness, and guilt—these gnawed him from the inside, but nostalgia was in his head, and it hurt the worst. Neither the rocky claws of the Valharyn Spine rending the blue skies, nor the smoking trail above Mount Aesiar, nor the stone ground under his feet and above his head were familiar to him. This was not his home. This was not even a place he liked.

"It's a place I deserve," he whispered. Then he shook his head. "No," he said. "It's not enough."

"What's not enough?"

"Sorry," Akheron said, as he turned, not caring who was stumbling by and what they thought of him.

The man who had spoken stood behind him with a sarcastic smirk on his face and a leggy, scantily clad woman under his arm. She was clearly not the reputable type, and, judging by the man's black headdress and silver tooth, neither was he. The woman smiled at Akheron—he was a young man with fierce dark hair, clear eyes and an unmarked face.

Her smile made his stomach clench even tighter. It was enticing, but sickening to him.

"Sathius Miroso," the man introduced himself, extending a jewelled hand to Akheron. The young man must've been years younger than Akheron, barely a man, though he had the mannerisms of one.

"Akheron ten Gothikar," Akheron replied, "milord."

"Oh please, I'm no lord," Miroso said. "He thinks I'm a lord!" The prostitute giggled. Miroso demanded, "Tell me what I am!"

"A corsair," she laughed.

"You see? So, if having not enough is your problem, just say the word and Sath Miroso is your man. I am always looking for able bodied men on my lady, *Salty Shadow.*"

"Salty shadow?" Akheron asked.

Miroso released his woman and glided toward the rampart that Akheron had been standing at. His hand on Akheron's shoulder, he directed the lost man's eyes to a two-mast galley in the harbour. It openly flew its black flag. "There, my boy. The real beauty."

"She's a fine ship, sir," Akheron said.

"I'll knock your teeth out if you call me sir or milord one more time. Call me Sath," the corsair told him, with a suddenly dangerous drawl. He reclaimed his arm-candy, swooped her about himself with a flourish and said, "Come along to the Royal Rogue with us, Master Gothikar!"

Master Gothikar, Akheron thought. It had an anxious ring to it, something that stirred Akheron's innards. He chose his words carefully. "Thank you for your kindness, Sathius, but I am no corsair... I am an honorable merchant's son. Or I was. I've got none of that left save the calluses."

"A merchant's son," Sath said to his girl. "And a hard-worker, nonetheless. Very well, no piracy for you. But at least come down and see the corsair's life. Ursha?"

The girl laughed, and swung from the corsair's caped shoulder and onto Akheron's. She was all skin, tempting him. *I am a godly man,* he reminded himself. But he knew why he had fled Avernus, and it was not his belief in the Maker that had banished him. *My first bedding will not be with a prostitute,* he decided, but let his arm sneak around her hip nonetheless. *Maker, that feels good.*

"Here," Sath said, and flicked Akheron an iron coin. He had never seen one, but heard talk of the corsair's coin. He glanced at it quickly, but then tried to return it. "No, you keep that for a drink. If only to buy Ursha a drink, should you be too *honourable* for alcohol."

"Too inexperienced, in truth."

"I am rich with experience, with women, with coin, with life!" Sath declared, drawing looks from the passersby. "Just a sip is all you will need."

Akheron bit his tongue, fearing the promise to be too true. *I know what I am—an animal, a monster, a man. Perhaps that means I'm already a corsair.* He glanced back into the water one last time, and realized that the best cure for his nostalgia and his guilt was action. He turned back to Sath and smiled.

The further away from memories of that ocean sky that Akheron got, the more he was drawn back into the real world, to his ride up the mountain. He was almost at the top. He couldn't make out any of the fishing town anymore. There were some mountain goats up here, and he passed an animal hole, perhaps a gopher's or a groundhog's. Yory and the crew might wake up soon, and they would come looking for him as dawn arrived.

From the top of the enormous hill, he could see the larger mountains north of him, the Mountains of Sinai. They held his view for a long time. There were many with just rock, rising into points that jutted into the sky. Some sported snow and one or two glaciers.

"I don't think Haekus would let me go on a walk that long," he chuckled to himself. His horse was panting a bit, so he dismounted and stood there for a bit.

Gradually, his gaze fell down the mountainsides. He could see half a dozen valleys from here, branching away from a lowland and lake directly down the hill from him. *In the rainy season, that must flood,* he thought. *And run into the sea.*

There was a settlement down there, to his surprise. He couldn't make out any details, but there were a few thin tendrils of smoke, and a cluttered arrangement of what must be shelters. Perplexed, he tried to remember if his scouts had mentioned it, but the place looked tiny. Not even a village.

"That's our next destination," he said, patting his steed's sides.

The horse *hmphed* on cue, saying it did not want to go down there.

"Well, then, do you know your way back home?" Akheron asked.

The animal's ears perked up, and it looked at him with enormous brown eyes. "Careful on the slope," he said. And released its reigns, giving it a gentle slap on the flank. The horse trotted off with a wagging tail. It stopped a few dozen paces later, and looked back at him. "Get going," he called, waving his hand about like an imbecile. The steed neighed and then walked away.

Akheron wandered down the hill at his own leisure. The settlement he had seen was on his side of the lake, tucked against a cliff. He didn't imagine it would be too difficult to reach. Sometimes he had to kneel and drop off a boulder or slide through some dirt. The hill wasn't too steep but there were treacherous sands in some areas.

When he eventually reached the bottom of the slope, he was probably a whole mile off track, so he had to set off to the left. There was a woodland here, but it was dry and sparse. The Sinai mountains were hotter than most of the northlands—hence the famous vineyards they sported along the Trident Rivers.

After a few minutes walking, the place he had spotted came into view. When he realized what it was, he almost laughed.

There was an earth-spawn colony in this valley. They lived in the cliff's caves and the ragtag shelters he had spotted from above, with spruce branches arching together, tied with sinew and covered with animal hide. As he approached, he began to draw some attention. The earth-spawn here were paler than the ones around Avernus where he had grown up. He had thought the spawn were all gone, years ago. These ones matched the sandy dirt of these lands, which made sense to Akheron. He had once seen an earth-spawn eating; the little creatures feasted upon a variety of mosses and roots, even eating mud if they had to. Too much moisture could kill them, but they needed some to survive.

Akheron couldn't believe his find. "Good-day," he called.

Some of them cowered at his exclamation, some tried to reply with guttural croaks, others just stared at him blankly. As far as Akheron knew, the earth-spawn were no more capable of communication than dogs. They could exist in a group together, but they could hardly sport civilization let alone engage in a conversation.

"How long have you been living here?" he asked. *In this world of impermanence, these runts of life managed to find their place!*

Two of the braver spawn approached him, rasping away in their voiceless language. One had a lump of rock above and beside his chin, distorting what would have been a human's chinbone. The other was a darker shade, there were strands of grass sticking out of the corners of his mouth.

"Do you have names?" Akheron had always wanted to know if earth-spawn had names.

They were standing right next to him now, looking up at him with black beady eyes, as small as his smallest fingernail. Could they even comprehend him?

He pointed at them and then made an open-handed shrugging motion.

The first one's eyes widened, the sandy skin morphing upward above his brows. The eyes themselves remained the same, like little beetles in their sockets. He pointed at his friend, and voiced a nasal word, "Bansh."

"Kurn," said the other, pointing at his friend.

Their concept of names seemed entirely tied to a reference of the other. Perhaps they did not understand names as a part of identity, but only a call word.

Bansh, with the grassy mouth, pointed at the Prince and said, "Min-go."

Akheron smiled. Somehow, their uncomprehending attempt at communication, their innocent wide-eyed trust—*in this forsaken world*—brought a tear to his eye. Did they know whom they were speaking to? Even if he told them what he had done, were they capable of understanding the bodies he left in his wake? The red footprints he tracked into their vale? *Do they know that I have brought the wrathful eye of the Maker to them?*

The other earth-spawn in the settlement seemed bored by the newcomer, and returned to their caves. One of them started throwing rocks, just an occasional snap of stone on stone, though he often threw into the underbrush.

"No," he said, shaking his head. "Torment," he said, pointing to himself.

"Tomen," said Kurn.

"Misery."

"Mizee," the earth-spawn said.

Akheron could tell them anything he had ever wanted to give voice to. He smirked. "Sometimes, I wish I had never met Mavas," he said.

They said nothing, simply watched him. Bansh mimicked his mouth movements, without sound. Akheron led them to a rocky boulder three times his size and sat down on it. They just stared at him. Did they think he had something for them?

"She is everything that the animal inside me wants." Many considered the earth-spawn animals, living based on only instinct. But these two, dawdling like children, were far too innocent for a comparison to Akheron.

"Perhaps, if I had never met her, things would've been...." he trailed off.

"Bin!" cried Bansh. He frantically looked into the settlement, and repeated his exclamation. Eventually, one of the other earth-spawns, a larger one, stopped repairing his animal-hide tent and looked their way. Bansh clapped his hands, and Bin replied in kind.

"No," Akheron decided. "Things would've been exactly the same."

Kurn started picking bugs off the rock and squishing them in his hands. It took Akheron a minute to realize the significance of this. He was not eating them. He was just killing them.

Akheron laughed. "Sometimes, I regret what I am doing to the Maker's world. But right now, I do not."

"Mika?" Bansh said. Akheron thought he might be talking to another spawn again. But he wasn't. He was still watching Akheron's mouth move. Was he getting something out of this?

"Yes, the Maker," Akheron told the creature.

"Mika." Bansh nodded. His bottom lip jutted over his top one, like an expression of solemn agreement.

ARISTORN

Akheron shrugged. *Whatever that exchange meant... it escapes me.*

Bansh copied his shrug. Kurn sat down beside the rock, looking bored. He had tired of killing bugs.

Akhcron was sitting in the Stead, with his hands folded in his lap. He had not been back in Avernus long, but this felt right. He was comfortable here. He had sailed the seas, raided with the corsairs, killed men, and lost his virginity to a woman who could probably kill him with a knife in a sword-fight. All of this hung, like a storm cloud in the distance, in the back of his mind. It tugged him away from his calm. But here and now, he had come home to the Maker.

The Kin finished their sermon with a loud chorus of syllables that Akheron could not understand, though he was sitting close enough. The sermons were preached in the Ancestral tongue. Akheron knew some of it, but he was not fluent. Every family had honorary words, and the Gothikars' were, *"Tu grunay nassi tu grunay ayen welkos,"* or, "The greatest passion wakes the greatest pain." It was a curse after they had lost their first motto, and their monarchy, to the Triumvirate, hundreds of years ago. Once, their words had been about conquest. Or so Father's old book explained.

"And now," cried Lork, an aged Kin, returning to the stage as the other Kin took their seats, "we will reflect upon the wisdom granted us by our Kin and the hallowed Maker, in the words of the common man. As our Kin recounted, the Maker has promised to all of us that he will never give us more than we can endure. As his servant, Tahelion, spoke to the Gathering on the Forgotten Plains, 'The Maker has written out the annals of this age and the age to come. He has given to us each a Struggle for us to overcome, but has also given us the tools to overcome it.' Tahelion's words may mean the *thoughts* to outsmart our challenges. Or the *friends* to see us through."

Lork was a fool. Did Tahelion's Teachings truly promise such a thing? It was a passage popularly cited, but rarely addressed so directly within the walls of a Stead. Akheron grabbed the Book of the Glyphs from the nearby shelf and opened it. There were three chapters in the sacred text, and any child could explain their differences: The Creation, which spoke of the origins of the world; Tahelion's Teachings, which outlined the fundamental tenants of the religion; and Malya's Directives, an ancient sermon that explained how to use the gift of the glyphs, as well as how to live holy lives. Akheron flipped to the middle chapter, with a familiar ease he had not drawn upon in years.

Lork, meanwhile, continued with his point. "We have all lost loved ones," he said. "The Grey Night took so many of them from us. Our fathers, our sons, our husbands, our wives, our mothers, our daughters, our brothers and sisters. And our beloved Prince Aristorn, murdered by the ungodly invaders. Instead of our Prince, we had Nobleman Ahryn conduct today's Sanctification. In our Prince's absence, a hole has appeared in Avernus, one that represents the losses of all our loved ones. And we desperately need the Maker to give us a leader to fill that hole."

Akheron found the passage. On the right hand of the page was the Ancestral tongue, on the left, the Common. Lork's words seemed to become distant as Akheron read the script:

> *The Maker has written out the annals of this age and the age to come. He has given to us each a Struggle for us to overcome, but has also given us the tools to overcome it. He will give no man more than what that man needs to make him a good man, a man of the Maker. Our Struggles, respectively, will make us who we were meant to be. The Maker will always give us a way, if we ask him for it, for in the tomes of time he wrote, the way was already there.*

Akheron stood up. He received a few odd glances. As he shuffled to the end of the bench and into the aisle, he was greeted with sighs and an "excuse you," from an elderly woman.

He reached the aisle, and looked back at the podium. Lork gave him a quick glance, but paid him no mind and continued talking about the losses of the city. There were the five symbols of the Maker: the four elements, and the Circle. *I have asked you, so many times. I have begged you. Teach me how to be more than this. Teach me how to be a godly man.* The very phrase made his stomach twist.

He wanted to say something. To raise his voice. *Where is my way?* he would demand of the vacant onlookers. *Where is my rope or hand to pull me from this pit to the Maker's side?* But he didn't say a word. *When do I become 'who I was meant to be'?*

He wandered out of the Stead and into the streets of his city. They were streets he had bloodied, and he felt welcome in them.

Akheron forced the cold memory from his mind and glanced back at Bansh. The earth-spawn was still watching him, though Akheron had said nothing. He was just staring emptily at the ground, his mind hounded by memories he feared. He forced a smile. "Where's Kurn?"

"Kurn!" Bansh said, and ran toward the settlement.

Akheron let him go. The earth-spawn had caught a few rabbits, it looked like, with their thrown stones. They didn't eat them, but used their skin and sinew. He wondered what they did with the meat. He saw one of them carrying a few red little bodies out of the settlement. Maybe they used them to lure away potential predators. Or maybe they just wasted them.

He started wondering how long it had been since leaving the village. As if on cue, he saw a man clambering down the hillside toward him. Dawn had awoken the crew of the *Sky Hound* and they awaited their Prince.

"I was worried about you," Haekus said, emerging from the woodland a few minutes later. He had a trickle of sweat on his forehead. Had he run the whole way, or just ridden hard? Why did Haekus care so? Akheron remembered the look on his face, shortly after they had met. A look of disbelief, respect, and jealousy. No one saw Akheron's great passion, because none of them spoke his language. Haekus had seen that passion when Akheron had first bested him in a fight, for it was a language they both spoke.

When Akheron had become Prince, he had changed his family's words to the phrase the Gothikars had once held: *Conquest stands alone.* But right now, he remembered his old words. *The greatest passion wakes the greatest pain.*

He stood up from the boulder, squishing an ant between his fingers. He looked at Haekus with a grim face and remarked, "I was worried about you, *sir.*"

19

"By Olympus," the porter said, "who hails at this hour?"

Akheron smiled. "Your Prince," he said. He got a stern look from Haekus, but shrugged amicably.

The doorman stumbled out of the door, still trying to shut the sliding peephole. "A-a-apologies, milord Prince, sir," the poor servant stuttered. He bowed sloppily, while inviting them into the courtyard he guarded. The man had black hair with a few silvery flecks in it and a wrinkled forehead. It was at least an hour after civilized folk had locked their doors for the night, and the porter had likely thought it was a beggar at the estate's door.

"Has your Lord already turned in?" Akheron asked.

The servant shrugged. "I doubt it. Lord Edemar finished dinner earlier, and half of the House is already asleep, but his lordship is likely in his study still." He latched the door behind Haekus and the Prince, and, bowing again, said, "I will show you the way, milord."

"Excellent," Akheron said. He glanced at the door as they walked away. Lord Edemar's estate was barred by a heavy oaken plank—none could be blamed, in Avernus, for excessive security. It was ironic to see in Edemar's House, however.

"At least Edemar's nightlife is not as prolific as your own," Haekus said. It was almost the year 515 and they had already burned a few Steads, but Akheron was still the champion Prince of Avernus and was welcome at the estates of its Nobles. He spent most of his nights in dens that no lord would seek out.

"...as your own, *sir*," Akheron said, glaring at his guard.

"As your own, sir," Haekus drawled.

"Careful, dog," the Prince snapped.

The porter, who was already leading them to a side-door of the estate's main building and regarded them with a wide eyebrow. "I know nothing about any of that, sirs, but I can tell you about our history here."

Akheron shrugged. "By all means." This servant was rather peculiar.

"Lord Ahryn used to own this property, you see," the doorman told them. He calmly drew a ring of keys from his belt, and began flipping through them, one at a time. "Before the Grey Night that is. He spent his summers here, when the great swamp becomes unbearable and Avernus becomes a paradise. Such is the way of young men, I suppose. Though, he's getting older now..."

"How did Edemar come to live here?" Haekus asked. He folded his arms.

"Well," the servant began, but he paused as he found the right key. He unlocked the door and led them inside. Edemar's hold was warm and lavish. The floor was composed of vibrant marble tiles—likely imported from the mines on the Elysian Point, and the walls were adorned with golden tapestries. The air was scented lightly with lavender, for it was the hour of sleepiness. In truth, it was the hour of forgiveness, according to the Eve of Reflections and the traditions of the Kinship—for those who observed such rituals.

They turned left immediately, instead of progressing down the hallway, and their guide led them up to the second floor. "The place was robbed on the Grey Night. Completely sacked. It's a wonder the brigands didn't make off with the flooring itself!" They ascended a spiral staircase. The moon was shining in from a painted window, casting eerie shades of crimson and starlight across the sooty waistcoat worn by the porter.

Akheron glanced back at Haekus. His guard was shaking his head about the story being told. *He shouldn't concern himself with things like this. There was nothing he could do.*

"Lord Edemar," the servant said, waving his hands, "bought all of this for a single gold coin, or so they say. Lord Ahryn had given it to some of his common folk, but they could not afford the taxes, let alone the repairs. *My* lord fixed it right up, and moved in from his north-side manor. He still owns that property too. So many...." The man hesitated, and, seeming embarrassed, corrected himself: "I'm certain your highness owns many lands as well."

"I do," Akheron said. "But once, I could barely afford the taxes for my own home."

The man turned to Akhcion and gave him a smile, as though they shared a secret. He searched for words of praise or respect, but Akheron spared him the trouble. "Is this your lordship's study, here?"

"Er-yes," the porter nodded. He tapped on the double door, peeked through the left side, and asked, "Might I show Prince Akheron in, milord?"

"Akheron?" came a muffled reply. "Glyphs, of course!"

Akheron did not wait for the doorman to 'show him in' and pushed through the opposing door. He was presented with a cluttered room. There were three desks, one in the middle and one on either side. Waist-height bookshelves ran between, and tall, leaning shelves covered the far wall completely. Edemar sat in the midst of it all; he rose to his feet at the Prince's arrival and extended a hand to clasp his old friend.

"Akheron!"

"Edemar," Akheron returned.

The Noble had short brown hair, trimmed tight against his head like a military man; his hairline had drawn back another inch since Akheron had seen him last, and there were wrinkles appearing in the corners of his eyes. "It has been far too long since you visited," Edemar said. "As a Noble of Avernus, I was worried we might need a new Prince!"

"Oh, most humorous." Akheron's voice was dryer than he intended, so he clapped his peer on the shoulder and said, "Keep up that thinking and I might plot to have a new Noble."

Edemar chuckled. "What brings you to my estate, at last?"

Haekus cleared his throat.

"I swear—" Akheron began, assuming that it was his guard's usual antics, but stopped. The doorman was still standing in the corridor. Haekus smoothly closed the double doors, leaving Edemar and Akheron alone in the study. "Quite the fellow," Akheron said.

"I owed his father."

Akheron suppressed a chuckle. "Debts," he said, looking

down at the books and scrolls on the table.

"Indeed." Edemar turned back to his desk, and grabbed his chair. He set it down closer to one of the other tables and invited Akheron to sit with him. "Look at this," he said, bringing a book from where he had sat.

"The Journeys of Oban Hokar," Akheron read, crossing his legs in the provided chair. "It's a popular story; what of it?"

"I bought it for twenty coins. Twenty *silver* coins."

"What?" Akheron opened the book. The pages seemed a little thicker than the parchment he was used to, but aside from that he found nothing amiss with it. "Where?"

"Delfie," Edemar said, grinning. "The mages came up with a way to make it with magic. They produce the parchment, the binding, the ink! They can create dozens of books a day!"

Disappointed, Akheron put the book down. He had been hoping for some sort of underground book market. He didn't read much, but he liked to know of the Triumvirate's crimes. He shrugged. "Does this mean the price of knowledge went down?"

"I don't know. It will be a long time before scholars figure out what this *really* means for us."

Akheron smirked.

"Enough of this fascination," Edemar said, tossing the book recklessly to the other desk. "It's only twenty silver," the action seemed to say. "What brings you calling, after all these years? And at such an hour?"

"I will marry your daughter."

Edemar's eyes widened. He leaned back in his chair, then spontaneously stood up. In the corner of the room, he opened a drawer and poured himself a stronger drink. He poured one for Akheron, though no words were spoken. Akheron savoured it; his nerves began to quiet almost immediately. "By the Great Glyph, Akheron," Edemar said. "You haven't contacted me personally in five years! I had only your oath, and my sway as a Noble."

"You're the one who took this whole royalty thing so seriously! I had beer with Yory the other day! And Mavas still carouses the town with me."

"*Mavas?*" Edemar exclaimed, sinking into his chair again. "Glyphs, man."

"I will be completely honest with... your daughter,"

Akheron said.

"Her name is *Reya!*"

"Reya." Akheron had heard her name before, but he rolled it around in his mouth for the first time. *The name of my wife...*

Edemar shook his head and took another drink. "You'll be honest with her about what?"

Akheron closed his eyes. *Not that. Everything but that.* "I will tell her that I love Mavas, not her. I will tell her that I will give her whatever life she desires, if I can. Any wealth or fame or influence—it can be hers. I will tell her that I am a monster, who burns priests in the night. I will tell her what I am."

Edemar drank more, and poured more. "Why?"

"Because I believe in clarity and hon..."

"No, no," Edemar said. "Why do you want to marry her?"

Akheron stood up, his chair nearly toppling behind him. "I *swore* to you that I would."

"And what does a promise mean," Edemar asked, "to the Fury of Avernus?"

"Is that all I am to you?" Akheron questioned. "We were brothers, Mar! And you asked me to marry your daughter, to *pay* for being brothers. Is it any wonder it took me five years to come to terms with my *vow?* Is it any wonder I did not visit you?"

Edemar just kept shaking his head and drinking.

"Glyphs, I am—"

"Somehow, I'm the villain in this, aren't I?" Edemar said. "Despite everything you did, I'm the one who ruined our brotherhood."

Akheron winced.

"I went back to being a civilized human being again," Edemar said. "And you blamed me that I was no longer part of your wolf pack." He raised the flask, offering Akheron more alcohol for his cup, but Akheron would have none of it.

"Wolves shouldn't get to be men again," he told Edemar, his voice dripping with fire, his fists clenched and his fangs barred. "We *don't.*"

Edemar stared at him.

"If you don't want your daughter to marry the Prince, I'll marry Mavas. Just say what you want, and I'll be gone, 'Lord Edemar'," Akheron said. "I will leave you, and your estate with its gold and incense and fool doorman and... your damned

Reya."

Edemar threw his fist up. Akheron saw it coming, but didn't stop it. He stumbled back a step and tripped across his chair, hitting the desk behind him with his tailbone. Dazed, he clutch his left jaw. His neck hurt too. *That was a good blow.*

"You will not speak of her that way, if you are to marry her. You will not speak *to* her that way, either." Edemar seemed remarkably sober now, and Akheron felt ashamedly drunk. His face smarted. "You will marry her, and then you will be *my* Prince. My wolf."

Akheron shook his head. He picked up the chair he had knocked and set it on all-fours again. "I am a mad wolf," he said, leaning toward Edemar. "I have rabies, and I've infected the whole pack now. No one controls me. But, for Reya, I must and will be a pretty puppy she can pet. Not for you, not for her, but for my oath and for my long lost brother."

Edemar's grim look broke; he looked ready to weep. "May he rest in peace." He raised his drink.

"Fool," Akheron said, and turned his back on the Noble and went out.

In the hallway, Haekus was listening to another of the porter's stories. "Let's go," Akheron told his guard. With long strides, they left the corridor and the servant behind. On the stairwell, the painted window had become dim. The moon was behind a cloud now.

"Thank you," Haekus said, "For rescuing me from that... lunatic."

Akheron scoffed. They left the main building and entered the courtyard. A few beams of light broke through the clouds here and there, but it was a dark and windy night. As they let themselves out of the gate, Akheron looked back at Edemar's estate.

A girl was watching him from a window, illuminated by what must have been the only shaft of moonlight against her white nightgown. Her hair was as dark as the night and her expression too distant to read, but Akheron saw two things: her strength and her beauty. He froze.

"Is that her?" Haekus asked. His question went unanswered.

It was not love that stalled Akheron's pace, nor the lust that coursed through him in the same instant. It was a purer joy than he had ever felt before, even with the first one. *Glyphs, not even with her...* How could something so tranquil and hopeful have been born of this nest of snakes, wolves, and worse?

Akheron did not pray often, anymore, but he prayed now, quietly so Haekus would not hear. "Let her be heavenly in her thoughts, let her curse me and forsake me when I am of the earth and let her be with me when I am of you, and only then. Maker, please. Do not let her be one of *us.*"

20

It was a long night and a longer day that followed. Akheron had grown weary of everything—especially sleep. In his dreams, she found him. Her, and Aristorn, and the Maker himself. Sometimes Tam was there, and he awoke with that most recent pain. Sometimes Mavas was; in those dreams they were together, their mouths, their loves, their lives, their souls. Those ones were the worst, because of the sickness that Akheron awoke with. How could something so right be so wrong? He was weary of this confusion. He was done trying to make sense of this world and his life. Some nights, he just wanted to light a fire.

He sat on a wooden wagon seat that should have been uncomfortable, if things like comfort registered in Akheron's head when he was in moods like this. He was stronger than the wood. He was sharper than its splinters and rougher than its grain. So much rougher. The wagon was passing through the city gates, like the maw of some animal. This was Eldius, a quickly growing highway town, and the new defences had risen out of the night with a chilling gleam. There were no rain stains in the stone yet, and no wood chipped away from the oaken gates. The guards there did not stop them, they saw only their friend the farmer, and a dirt-stained man sitting beside him. In the darkness, they did not see the sweat on the farmer's brow or the men hiding beneath his sacks of grain.

Yseth was not sweating for fear of Akheron. He was fearful of the guards. He was willingly smuggling the Prince and his men into the town, men who would raise more questions than answers.

"Late day?" one of the guards called.

"I'm exhausted. The dogs had me up before the sun!" They were almost through the gate.

"By the Maker!" the guard replied. The farmer cringed. "Get some rest!"

"Of course. You too! Though, er, not on duty," Yseth replied.

The guard chuckled, but his laughter was lost to the wheels of the wagon, groaning along the cobblestones.

They crossed town quickly, as quickly as they could without raising suspicions from the sleeping town houses they passed. The Highway ran through the centre of town, right past the door of the Inn. It was joined there by another road—at the end of that street was the Stead. Akheron's stomach quivered with anticipation. Bertren had been easy enough, but this was a larger town, bustling at its newly-crafted masonry seams.

There was no moon tonight, for low clouds hung over the rooftops. The furnaces and fireplaces of Eldius contributed their smoke to the haze—the air was heavy with humidity but cool dew formed on Akheron's brow. He spat into his hands, and scrubbed them clean. Then, he cleaned his face. He needed to be the Prince again, not one of Yseth's hired hands. Once he cleaned the dirt from his cheeks, he cleaned his hands again, furiously wiping them on the lower back of his tunic. His hands never cleaned quite to satisfaction.

"Almost there, sir," Yseth said. "I will be in the crowd on the morrow." The hard-working farmer had a northerner's accent.

"Be safe," Akheron told him. "You have a wife and daughter."

"A man needs to make some statement, especially for his family, and yours is the only statement I will proclaim anymore."

Akheron shook his head. *What a waste.* "Do you think he's still awake?" he asked, decidedly not voicing his thoughts. The Great Gambit came into view, a few blocks ahead. There were some carts and stalls here, covered with bed-sheets or hides to protect them from the elements.

"He'll awake for patrons and newcomers. He's a true man,

close to the earth and those who walk it," Yseth said. "Which is why I know he'll hear you out."

"If he doesn't, we'll be forced to—"

"I'd rather not know. Whoa, whoa." The farmer pulled at the reins.

"Very well." Akheron bit his tongue, and smoothly dismounted the wagon as they rolled alongside the old walls of the Great Gambit. He jogged a few steps alongside the wagon as its workhorse huffed to a stop. "Up you come, my girl," he said.

He wasn't speaking to the horse, but to the back of the wagon. Mavas heaved out of the heavy sacks, sitting up at the waist and smiling sarcastically to Akheron. "I think your guard tried fondling me," she said, gesturing rudely between her hips.

"I did no such thing," Haekus retorted, coming out of the grain.

Akheron shook his head; he couldn't help but chuckle. He grabbed Mavas where she had pointed and above her elbow, and pulled her off the flat wagon's bed. She dropped gracefully to her feet.

"Ooh!" she whispered, pressing her lips to his. "So that's what we'll be doing if we get an inn room."

Haekus grumbled, and slid off the wagon's bed, along with Norind, another of their trusted guardsmen. "Glyphs, I hope it comes to a fight instead," Haekus murmured, pulling his sword out of the bed of grain. "So I won't have to listen to you two."

"I hope it does too," Mavas said, arming herself. She gave Akheron a smirk and then feigned innocence at Haekus. "Then you can listen to both."

The guards followed her up the steps of the Great Gambit reluctantly, while Akheron tossed a small sack of coin at Yseth. "For your family."

"This is too much! You're a cause I believe in," the farmer responded, raising his hand to throw it back.

Akheron turned his shoulder, so as not to catch it. "I am not a cause," he said. "I'm just a man." He followed his friends up the steps without waiting for his admirer's reply.

The entry to the Gambit was unlocked, and Akheron led the way inside. The massive common room was completely deserted, as expected and planned. A cloud of smoke hung against the ceiling. The metal braziers that hung there shone through it all faithfully, illuminating the cleanly polished tables.

Akheron forced himself to relax.

"Welcome," someone called from the other end of the bar. The illustrious counter stretched away from the doorway, down the wall to a corner room, and then out along the opposite wall. There were three doors across the empty room from it, leading to the inn's rooms. The bar tender was too far away to make out, leaning on his counter and speaking to the room's only patron. He called to Akheron again, "Take a seat, and I'll send one of the girls out."

They did not take a seat, but walked down the length of the bar toward the two. Akheron glanced at Mavas and smiled. She was a little grimy from her wagon ride—there was dirt on one of her cheeks and her hands, though they rested comfortably on her sword. Could anything be more attractive than a woman at ease with the steel at her belt? She winked back at him.

He wrung his palms in his tunic, though they were not dirty like hers.

"Can I pour you something?" the innkeeper said, once they got closer. Akheron recognized the man as Nallar ten Eldian, the Great Gambit's proprietor. He was also the town's mayor and founder.

"I'm not thirsty," Akheron replied.

Nallar and he had met before, and, between Akheron's slow approach and his voice, recognition dawned on the charismatic man. The man, face turning pale, turned hurriedly to his patron and said something that Akheron couldn't make out. Akheron reached for his sword.

The patron didn't like what Nallar had said. He shook his head and asked, "Why?" Akheron was close enough to make him out now. He had a long face, with a scar on his cheek and messy brown hair. The man seemed familiar—Akheron could nearly swear he had seen the young man before.

Nallar slammed his hands onto the table. "Why! Because I told you to. Great Glyph, get out of my damn inn!"

That got the man moving. Without a word, he rose from the bar and drifted past Akheron quietly, giving him a short nod.

"Do I...?" Akheron began, but the man didn't wait, and slid through the door into the night. A name was on the tip of his tongue, but he had nothing to say. He was still turned looking at the door when Nallar spoke up again.

"You've got a lot of nerve," Nallar said, "showing up like this, in the middle of the night. Showing up at all."

Akheron sat down on a stool in front of the sturdy man. Nallar had a well-groomed beard, thick eyebrows and the calloused hands of a tradesman. "You've got a lot of nerve talking to your Prince like that."

"Well, perhaps I'd give you the respect of that position if you came to me in that position. Not like a group of thieves in the night," Nallar said. He got out a single glass and poured himself a drink. "Have you heard what I did with the last brigands to come in here? Thought to themselves that here was an unlocked inn, with an innkeeper to be robbed, and him, the master of the whole town. Sure is alluring, isn't it?" He smiled at Mavas.

"You buried them behind your inn the next morning. Never been robbed since. Or so the story goes."

Nallar put away the bottle of alcohol he'd been pouring. "I can show you where, if you like, though there's no stones to mark it."

Akheron grabbed the cup before Nallar could. He took a long drink of it before giving the surprised innkeeper a smile. "I don't bury the men I kill."

"Is that a threat? Are you here to trade threats with me? You and your... lackeys?"

"No, we're here to burn your Stead," Akheron said, sliding the remnants of the drink back to its owner.

"Oh." Nallar pulled up a stool on his side of the bar. He sat down, looking rather contemplative, and waited.

"I want to know whom you'll be standing next to. You don't strike me as the type who will sit indoors while the riots are out."

"Perhaps I don't want riots," Nallar said.

"Your citizens do. A good leader puts aside his own desires for theirs. What will it be?"

"You'll make me a lord," Nallar said. "I'll be Nallar Eldian."

Akheron snorted.

"You're a dark man, Akheron," Nallar said. "Some call you a curse, some call you a devil. I've half a mind to throw you out of my inn."

"You know we wouldn't hesitate to stay," Akheron said.

"Not exactly the 'honor of a Prince', and all that. The Code of the Triumvirate, it was once called," Nallar said. "Almost forgotten now."

"I have no honour and no man could understand my code," Akheron said. "No code of Tiberon Odyn could touch the world I live in."

"It was not his code," Nallar said. "It was written by another man, a man with a heart as black as yours, until he met Tiberon."

"Haekus, are you my Tiberon? Will your continued efforts to protect me eventually make me a better man?"

"Likely not," Haekus said. Norind the guard smirked nervously. He was uncomfortable with skulking around at night.

Akheron turned to Mavas. "And you?"

She laughed. "I'm his code... and you wouldn't like me."

"You're not my code," Akheron said, insulted. His tone must've reached her, for she raised an eyebrow and backed off.

"Enough," Nallar said. "Tomorrow, one of my town's buildings will burn. I will not have you burn the rest. As a hostage I will stand beside you tomorrow. My citizens will see and hear a comrade, not a prisoner. And the Maker will forgive me these sins, for the good I have done in this world. Eldius will always be a good town."

"Wait until you see the devils you rule," Akheron said. "Then you can worry for your salvation."

Nallar shook his head and walked away. "Room keys are behind the bar."

Haekus said, "Norind," then set off across the common room to one of the corridors. After he had checked the coast was clear, he waved them over.

"You have a code?" Mavas asked as they left the common room.

"A code of who I should be," he said. He corrected himself, "Who I should've been. It defines me, by reminding me I am not him."

"And why aren't you him?"

He pinched her. "You'll find out, I'm certain." Haekus must've had a long night, too, to turn in so quickly.

Restlessly, Akheron spent the night with her. They did not sleep much, but when she eventually gave in to rest, he lay there plagued by his memories. His hands stuck with sweat, his breath stuck with her smell, his heart stuck with his rot. *Tomorrow,* he thought, *I teach the choirs of the damned. I teach them who they are. I teach them the code.*

Nights that wasted by like this terrified him. How could he finish this rebellion? They had burned a few Steads. There was discontent seeping through the Dominion. But he was wearied by it.

Days like the one that followed this particular night filled him with such fire that he could fight the Maker himself.

Akheron awoke at sunrise, and dressed again, in silence. Before going for the door, he sat down on the bed. Mavas hugged the blanket around herself. The inn room was a little chilled in the morning. "What?" she asked.

"Why don't you come?" Akheron asked. "You're eager for combat, even against an innkeeper. You're... amazing at night. You're ruthless, no matter what you do, and I love you for it. So why do you have such an issue with stopping some self-righteous men to stop judging us?"

"That's not what this is about," Mavas said. "You aren't destroying the Kinship because of the men who lead it. Knowing you, that attitude would lead you to become their leader, not their murderer. I know what it's really about. I heard the first speech."

"What about the first speech?"

"You showed us all the deepest part of yourself, and the deepest part of ourselves, and not a man or woman liked what they saw. Then you told us to embrace it."

Akheron sighed. "And everyone did."

"Not you. I live with you. I see who you are. I know you. You've never embraced being some sinner."

"I am a sinner," he said.

"Yes, but that is not something that makes you happy."

"And it shouldn't. But the Maker failed our world, Mavas. He failed us the moment he let us be sinners." Akheron had to stand up.

"You speak like this world is done. That the Maker is not continuing to forgive the sins of men."

"What I showed people at the Avernan Stead was that not one of us has been forgiven," Akheron said. "And that is the part that no man or woman liked. Look at this world! Who cares about 'liking' something? Enough of happiness! I'm damn tired of it being our goal. Perhaps a measure of satisfaction would make the world a better place."

"Satisfaction? What do you know of satisfaction?"

"Those who lose it, know it the best," he said. "Listen, I share an intimacy, a personality, a depth to the crowds out there. I thought the woman who shares my bed and my lust might like to share in that, too."

"I may not be a holy woman; I'm certainly not much of a believer. I've got my fair share of failings," Mavas said. "But sins are sins, and this is something else entirely."

Akheron felt satisfied, but he dared not say so. Though she did not hate the core of him, the part that wanted the world to burn for taking everything from him and for letting him become one of *them*, she did hate the part of him that would rid the world of the Maker. He turned toward the door. "Alright, then it *is* for the best that you do not come along on my rebellion."

"As I've said," Mavas said "but I will still be here when you return."

Akheron did not respond, but merely stepped into the corridor. Haekus and Norind were waiting out here already. Akheron knew Mavas would still love him when he returned, but a big part of himself prayed that each of these riots would be the last. *Stop me, please, Maker, stop me.*

In the common room, Nallar leaned against his bar. He wore chainmail and tanned hides—a sword hung at his belt. None of his equipment was fancy, though he could certainly afford more elaborate accessories. He made use of simple and accessible things. Without a word, he led the way.

It was a long walk to the Stead. As they went, the street became more crowded. Men and women were out already, despite the early hour. Some were tradesmen, with white or brown aprons, and leather gloves or tools slung over a shoulder. A few were merchants, softly dressed and softly mouthed. Many were revolutionaries, watching their champion approach. He got smiles, raised fists, even a few cheers. How did the town know already? Had they spent each day awaiting his arrival?

In front of the Stead, two Kin and a dozen guards waited. They stood on the steps while the body of citizens in front of the building murmured. The Stead of Eldius was wood and thatch, a freshly built building like many in Nallar's town. A pity it would not serve its years of intended use.

"All are welcome," the taller of the two Kin was saying. Nallar seemed to falter as they reached the steps. His eyes seemed doubtful; he had not expected his people to make such a turnout, already.

Akheron led the way past him and up the steps of the Stead.

"Greetings, Prince Akheron," the taller Kin announced. The sun was shining brightly, so he raised a hand to shield his eyes. "We were just telling our people that all men are welcome before the Maker and the Maker's forgiveness. You may enter our Stead, if you wish it, though these good men and women did not think we would permit it."

"*Your* people?" Akheron said. He glanced at the crowd— some were smiling, some watching quietly, yet to be swayed. The courtyard was quiet, even the holy men hung on Akheron's words. "Are you the Maker's people?"

The crowd stared at him. None wanted to answer that question.

"Are you this priest's people?"

"No," someone said.

"Not his," said another.

"Are you not *your own* people?" Akheron asked. He shrugged his hands away from his sides inquisitively.

A few cheers echoed the plaza. They were not swayed yet, but they were lured. Curious. The hook was planted, as a fisherman might say. Akheron had known fishermen growing up. He had known merchants and woodsmen and farmers. He had known *these* people, and the Maker did not *own* them.

"The Maker has claimed them," one of the Kin said.

The crowd did not respond to the claim.

"How were these priests telling you of your possession?" Akheron asked. "In our language, or in the language of old men and celibates?"

"The Ancestral Tongue is holy," the Kin responded. His square comrade was shifting uncomfortably. He would surrender first.

"How many men here speak Ancestral?" Akheron asked. "Three? Myself and these two. Anyone else?"

"Four!" A balding man at the back of the crowd joined his count.

"Five," said Nallar.

Akheron raised an eyebrow. "And how many of you speak the common tongue?"

That got a louder response.

"This is a childish argument," the Kin responded. "Everyone knows the Ancestral Tongue is hallowed for the Maker's praise." The crowd muttered.

"It is a code to hide truths," Akheron said. Men and women added a chorus of approval to his words.

"It is a song to sweeten the ears of our god," retorted the holy man.

Tradesmen were shaking their heads. Women were shouting. Akheron raised a hand. "It will be a language for the praise of men," he declared. "When the Kinship is no more, and the Steads are all ash, the Ancestral Tongue will forget the Maker. It will only adorn the walls of palaces and proclaim the glory of mortals—my glory. *Our* glory!"

Applause.

The Kin stuttered. Appalled. His shorter companion was trembling, and at last spoke up. "The Maker will strike you down for such blasphemy."

Would that he would. But the Maker did not end Akheron this day, nor for many days to come. "Listen to me, blasphemous and unworthy," Akheron said, calling to the crowd. "Perhaps the Maker forgives our sins, as the Kin would have us say. Perhaps, every day of our lives is a tear on the Maker's cheek, as Malya's Directives teach us, tears that he wipes away when he welcomes us to our divine resting halls."

He glanced at Haekus. *I have given the Maker so many tears,* he thought. *Red tears upon my hands.* Haekus nodded, understanding the fires that Akheron felt. He had seen those fires, once.

Akheron looked down upon the people. The broken, horrible people of the world that looked up to him with hopeful, thirsty faces. *How dare the Maker hold his tongue? Feed us!*

Feed these husks until they bear colour and music once more.
How dare you do anything else?

"I am no holy man. Nor will I ever be," Akheron confessed. He lifted his hands above his head. "These hands are red with the blood of holy men. This mind is filled the ravings of a lunatic. This heart," he split open his tunic, tearing the garment to the waist, "is the black and broken heart of a *sinner,* and the Maker has not repaired it. Perhaps he gives me some heavenly splendor when I confess these things to the Kin. Perhaps, in some cosmic realm, my soul is washed clean."

The crowd was growing with his words. Oddly, the Kin themselves were silent. "But I will not take a promise in another language from a man who cowers before the doubts of sinner, to convince me that I am not a *man.* And I will not follow a religion that lies to me."

"Here, here!" someone shouted.

"I won't bow to a liar!"

"Down with the Stead!"

Akheron held up his hand. "You are all sinners," he told them. The best arguments hinged on truth. They were all evil, and he was the worst of them. "You are all bad men and women. *We* are all the earth spawn of the world, and until the Maker walks among us once more, *we will not be clean."*

"You are all clean," boomed the bold Kin.

An apple rolled across the steps in front of him, smearing the marble with spittle. "Liar!" someone shouted.

"Do not lament," Akheron told them. "Do not be ashamed. Do not let these liars tell you to change your ways; do not let them convince you to surrender to your flaws. Your flaws define you. Without our flaws, we would all have the depths of these men." He gestured to the Kin. *We would be good men. We would have the Maker's depths. Without our flaws... we would be the sun itself, not... this.*

"I will not follow a religion that lies to me," Akheron repeated. "And I will not worship a Maker that leaves me dirty, broken and sinful. I demand a Maker that tells me himself that I am forgiven."

"Tells us in common!" shouted another man.

"Tells us with his own lips, not an old man's!" hollered a middle aged woman.

"The Maker does not intervene," the Kin declared. His cowardly friend had backed up behind the line of Defenders, who clinked in their armour as the army of commoners cheered and shouted. "If he made us good, we would be all the same. We would all be drones, mindless. It is our minds which bring him the greatest praise."

"Which is it?" Akheron asked. He had very gradually taken the middle of the steps, while the priest had moved off-centre. "What brings the Maker the most praise? Our unique minds, or our lack of sins? Our dedication or our words? Our lies or your lies?"

"Answer us!" shouted another commoner.

"Get down from there, you fool!" bellowed another, and a brick struck the breastplate of the Defender nearest the priest. "Let Akheron teach us!"

The Defenders lowered their spears on an order barked by the one struck. They were on guard now, ready for the riot.

"I have nothing to teach!" Akheron cried out. He spread his arms wide, his torn shirt hanging open. "I offer all that I am, for you people. Look at me, the worst of men, and know that I demand more than this Maker has offered! Look in me, and see yourself. Then you know that we will all burn for our sins if we let these old priests lie to us a day longer. They tell us we are forgiven, and without blinking, we sin again. The world is getting no better under their leadership. Only by living with your sins can you learn not to sin."

"You will be consumed by your sins!" shouted the Kin.

"I have nothing to teach," Akheron repeated. "For you have all the answers already. You have all the keys to being the holy men of our age, for you are the greatest men and women to walk our world. You have a choice: strike me down for my crimes or strike down the Kin for theirs! You are the judge—not some cosmic being that has never taken your hand or defended your home."

Seeing an opening, the Kin shouted, "Yes, strike him down! He will lead you away from the Maker and any hope of salvation. Strike down the sinner!"

With a roar, a volley of fruits and sticks and rocks rose from the crowd, pelting the Kin and his Defenders. Men and women charged up the steps, knocking aside the spears of the

Defenders where they could, or charging into them in a frenzy. Two men died in their own blood before the crowd had so crammed upon the steps that use of a spear was useless.

The bold Kin died first, broken by the baker's board and bloodied by the farmer's pitchfork. His cowardly friend screamed and fled into the Stead, while the guards found their armour torn from their limbs.

Nallar was pale and sweating. His hand clung to the hilt of his sheathed sword lest he need defend himself.

The crowd poured into the Stead like an ocean wave. In their wake was no tidal driftwood or smoothed stones, but footprints bloodied by the lives of holy men.

Akheron sat down on the steps. He was exhausted. He got pats on his shoulders as men stormed inside and out. Someone with a torch ran past, mumbling and laughing like a giddy child. The people had judged wrong. They would search the town for any men still faithful once they were done here.

The priest was still alive, somehow. He lay there, with a pitchfork in his torso and whimpered. After a moment, he sucked in a fierce breath, and, with a face turning red, said, "You led them astray. How will they find salvation now? How...? You led them all astray... You led..." At last his voice quieted.

"Glyphs," Nallar said. He stumbled down the steps, looking back at the Stead which had started to smoke by now. He reached the courtyard and stood at eye level with Akheron, but his gaze was angled above at the building. The Prince sat with his back bent and his hands dangling over his knees. "Glyphs," the mayor mumbled again.

"See?" Akheron said. Nallar had not believed it would actually happen.

"I have not created *anything* good. I have just brought together enough evil to feed upon itself," Nallar said. He sounded like the priests who caved to Akheron's arguments. Unlike the two he had defeated today. The ones who decided their lives had been dedicated to folly—the worst of believers.

"You can be a lord," Akheron said.

"What?"

"You're Nallar Eldian now," Akheron said. "We'll need the Nobles to officialise it, of course. But you asked to be a lord, and now you are. Lord of Eldius."

"Eldius is a den for wolves," Nallar said. Bloodied men dashed by them in a craze. The din of shouting, screaming and dying almost drowned out his words. "Wolves, spawn, and devils."

"Then you may be the king of devils, if you like," Akheron said. He touched his heart with a dirty hand, feeling it pounding through his chest. "Once the old king is dead."

"Long live the king," Nallar prayed.

21

"Are you in here?"

The voice was soft and scared. Should anyone interrupt the darkness and silence within this room? Even the Maker dared not visit within. He had broken what lay here, and was content to leave the shattered remnants to rest in the shadows.

"Akheron?"

Akheron opened his eyes. Like a puddle of writer's ink, the darkness that covered him refused the light that streamed past the speaker from the open castle corridor. Only the ripples of him caught a gleam from the torches outside: his dishevelled hair, the whites of his eyes—now squinted, his fists clenching the armchair.

Mavas stepped inside; she looked in his direction but didn't make eye contact. Perhaps she couldn't see him. Perhaps she didn't want to.

She closed the door.

"Haekus still out there?" His voice surprised him; it was little more than a hiss. There was no strength to it. "I need a drink." He lurched to his feet. There was water in a pitcher nearby. He poured himself a mug on trembling legs, his free hand not holding the cup he poured into, but clenching the edge of the table.

"He is. He's worried about you."

Akheron took a drink of his water and said nothing. Then he spat the mouthful out onto the floor, spraying water everywhere. "Move," he said, throwing open the door. He could barely see—a torch blinded him from both sides of his door. He squinted at Haekus and said, "Bring me ale or beer or something."

Haekus didn't look well either. His skin was pale and his hair a mess. He had whiskers on his chin and stared at Akheron with surprise. "You hate alcohol."

"Get out of my castle if you're not going to obey, dog. Bring me a damn drink or get out!" Akheron shouted, then slammed the door closed.

Mavas stared at him with wide eyes. They were now standing close, and her eyes were becoming accustomed to the darkness. "Akheron..."

"Shh."

Haekus's boots scuffed past the door as Akheron's friend went to find a drink for the mourning Prince. Once he was gone, Akheron finally met Mavas's eyes. Her dark hair was bound behind her head with a small bone clasp and her eyes were rimmed from tears. "Why are you here? Here to tempt me once more? Or just to make me weep? We're alone now. Completely. So let's hear it!"

"She's been dead for weeks," Mavas said, stepping back from him.

He struck her with the back of his hand. She stumbled against the table in the middle of the room, twisted at the waist from his strength. She had not seen the blow coming. His speed was unparalleled when he had nothing to hinder him—even Haekus could not understand Akheron's abilities. He was not governed by the laws of normal men, but by the laws of some evil.

She recovered quickly, rubbing her cheek. Her face looked so surprised. The only women that Akheron had ever harmed himself were those Defenders who had fought in the riot. That horrible, horrible riot. He had never harmed Mavas, and she stared at him with the tears of betrayal in her eyes.

He broke the painful silence. "Don't you dare to speak of Tam."

"You need to wake up," she said. "You have to find something to fight for. Fight for me, fight for Haekus. Fight for Tam."

"Damn you," he shouted, and grabbed her by the throat. They crossed the room in a blizzard of broken dishes, spilt water and toppled furniture. Somehow, through his rage, he realized what he was doing and stopped before they struck the wall. He did not release her throat, but clenched her face close to his. "You are nothing," he whispered. Their eyes were locked. "I would work for you, I would love you, I would kill for you. But compared to her, you are a common *whore!*" His fingers dug into her neck, like the armchair he had dominated earlier. "I would *kill* you in an instant if it would save Tam."

Something struck him in the stomach and his hands slipped from her throat. Another blow struck him; Mavas's fist slammed his teeth together and sent him reeling. Off-balance, he fell. He landed on his hip, and his shoulder slammed against the granite floor tiles.

"Akheron," she said. There was a trickle of blood from her nose. Her blood on his hands.

He rose from the floor with a limp and an incoherent shout. His fist was raised, but Mavas's arms looped around it as she stepped past his charge. She braced it back until the bones screamed, and hurled him to the side. He slammed into his armchair and the wall. Wooden slats shoved into his flesh. His anger was wavering. His sadness was rising. With one last ounce of fury, he reclaimed his feet and advanced on her.

Mavas ducked under his swung hand and swiped his legs out from under him. Once again, he crashed to the floor.

This time, he had no motivation to rise. He lay there. His unfed muscles screamed at him. He could feel bands of bruises coiling up on his shoulder and his hip. He closed his eyes until Mavas spoke, then looked up at her.

"Tam *has* been saved. She remained a good woman, a true and holy one, to the very end. She is with the Maker now, far from your reaches and the reaches of the men you inspire. *She* is saved. You," Mavas said, "are the one who needs saving."

Akheron chuckled. It hurt, but not enough to propel the tears that now rose to his eyes.

"If you let this crush you," Mavas said, "You will be damned, and you will ruin the very last memory of Tam. Glyphs, Akheron. I have been here for you the whole time, and I know that whatever we have is about sex and crime and not much more, but I am not going anywhere. When you are ready to leave this dark room, I will be at the door waiting for you. But I cannot enter this pit of yours. You are not hiding in here because of what Tam experienced. You are in here for you. And only you."

She started to leave. "Mavas," he said. She stopped. Akheron took a deep breath, staring at the back of his eyelids. "When did you become so wise?" he asked, releasing a drawn out sigh. He climbed to his feet slowly, tremblingly.

She was halfway to the door. She turned back to him. The dark room seemed empty, besides them. The table had been toppled and the other chairs broken.

Akheron shook his head. "Mavas," he said. "I lost her. And, for the second time in my life, *I* am to blame. Glyphs..."

Her arms snuck around his torso. So gentle in comparison. It was this that had first attracted him to her—how could someone as deadly as himself be able to care as genuinely as she did? "Akheron," she soothed.

He embraced her and held her against him. He could feel the firm muscles in her back and shoulders, and her chest pressed against his ribs. "The Maker did this," Akheron said. "He took her from me in retaliation."

"Must every event in your life have cosmic significance? I hope I still speak wisdom, but.. can't Tam's death be a horrible, unfortunate loss that happened without sense or reason?" Mavas asked.

"Nothing happens without sense or reason. That is the core of my beliefs," Akheron said. He remembered that realization: *This is the pain of belief.* "Would that I could change my beliefs. Then nothing in the world could touch me."

She tried to pull away, but he kept holding her. After a moment, she hugged back again. For a while, he simply cried into her dark hair, like a snivelling child. "I'm sorry," he whispered.

"You don't have to be," she said. "It's just hair."

"No, I'm sorry for hurting you. I'm sorry for hiding here for so long and keeping you away," Akheron said. "Tam is in such a better place, and I was blind to it. You held the key to my sight, and, in the darkness, I would not let you near."

She pulled back from him, and he let her. "No matter what it is, you have to find something to fight for."

"I have a good idea for what I will fight," Akheron said. Memories of the mob terrified him, but he embraced them. The

Maker had taken everything from him now, everything except Mavas. *I will take from you,* he decided. *I will take from you until you take the very last of me, my life. Let me burn you, my God,* he prayed.

Mavas could see the returned passion in his eyes, even in the dark. "There's the fires I fell in love with," she said. "Fight, Akheron. It will keep you alive, and the memory of Tam. And all the rest you must keep alive. Fight!"

"I will," said the Maker's Bane. "I swear it."

22

Akheron did not consider anything to be unusual that day, though the words he spoke today would shake the foundations of the Triumvirate near breaking. He awoke as he had for the hundred days prior: in the shadows of his Palace, waiting for the Maker to take his hand or strike him down. He opened his eyes in that tomb and whispered the prayer he whispered every morning. Before his shuttered window, he took to his knees and said, "Maker, teach me. Speak to me. I'm here listening. I'm here waiting. What more can I give? How else can I learn? Please, tell me how to change! Please. Please..." From the slants of sunlight came no answer. From the cold stone flooring came no lessons. From the musty castle air came no words. From the sunrise came no aid. Nor from the sunset.

It was the Eve of Preparation, the same as every other. It was during the Year of Olympus 514, and Prince Gothikar had attended many such ceremonies. He dressed himself in dark clothes—black trousers and a grey tunic. He shrugged into a dark mantle with a forest green cape, and then sat uncomfortably on the edge of his bed. How many days had he continued this ritual? His servants had stopped bringing him breakfast. He never ate it. He buckled short ankle boots to his feet and then stood for a moment longer in the chilled room.

Soon, he sat before the shrine in the Stead of the Maker.

"So we call Akheron Gothikar our Prince, leader, and brother, to *lead* us in this ceremony," intoned the old Kin. The Stead of Avernus was a silent building usually, but today it was busy. Any day that the commoners knew Akheron would make a

N A V R E U G D E N H I L

public appearance was a busy day. He was their champion. As he stood at the invocation of his name, he drew in the wide-eyed faces around him, as though he could take some energy or inspiration from their adoration.

"Akheron Gothikar answers your call," he returned. He was familiar with the rite. He would set up the shrine of the Elements, and invite the Maker to glorify their week. Next week, on the Eve of Reflection, the candle would be extinguished, the water spread for all to drink, the air released, and the rock returned to the world beyond the sanctum of this Stead.

Akheron made his way to the aisle. The men and women he had to cross in front of moved their legs out of the way without complaint. They were careful not to get in his way. He was their hero, and they would only dare touch him if he bade them.

"We meet here today not to honour our days past, but to prepare for the days ahead. Tahelion taught us that it is our acts that bring glory to the Maker. He told the Court of the Age that true praise was attained by a resistance to this world and a striving for greater achievement through hard work. Hard work carefully prepared for," the Kin said. His beard was short save a soft white tendril descending from each cheek. He wore a ceremonial cap on his head, the imperial white and gold cloth that folded down over each ear. "Tu Deyvas o'nolson deyn nen qisti jannas, nasathi ta kyrin benus qi," he intoned, in the Ancestral language.

The Maker knows. The half-remembered thought troubled him.

Akheron waited in the aisle of the Stead. The Avernan building was just outside of his Palace, with its own small town to attend it. It had stood here for centuries, ready for the attendance of its Princes. For most of those years, an Aristorn had waited within this aisle. The mosaic ceiling was two storeys above—it depicted a divine victory between the Maker and the darkness of his absence.

Sometimes the attention bothered him. He was just a man who did not want to hide anymore. He had not planned to become a Prince. He had not planned any of this.

A young man brought him a bowl of water. Akheron quickly dabbled his hands in it and wiped them on the towel over the man's shoulder. *This is supposed to clean them of the crimes of the mundane world. Clean them enough to act on behalf of our God.*

"Prince Gothikar now receives the first of the Maker's creation. The formless air within which our *Deyvas* placed us. My Prince, please bring us the air to remind us that our Maker surrounds us all the time." The Kin in the centre of the circular Stead bowed his head.

Another Kin made his way to Akheron and handed him an empty sphere of glass. The top was open, but there was only air within. Akheron bore it in both of his hands. Quietly, he made his way down the aisle of the Stead until he reached its middle. There was already an elaborate board of wood there to receive the elements. Glyphs were carved across it, and the elaborately curving letters of the Ancestral Tongue, a hundred prayers to sanctify it from the sins of Midgard.

When Akheron reached the shrine, he lifted the sphere of air above his head. He looked up past it, at the small hole of sunlight that streamed in from the roof. "Bless us, holy Maker," Akheron intoned. Then he set the glass gently upon the wood, in a short metal stand for it. There was another stand on the other end of the board for the final element. The Eve of Preparation was all about blessings. Hopes and delusions that the week would be better. Akheron knew what his week would hold: days of unanswered prayer upon the cold floor of his castle quarters, Mavas's warm flesh to receive his most base desires, delicately served meat to fill his sated body, gold and silk to soften his mind, and silence to remind him.

The Kin raised his head for the next phrase, but Akheron turned back down the aisle before he risked meeting the priest's eyes. Kin Geanar had been in charge of this Stead for decades; he had little respect for Akheron's fresh reign, nor the rarity of the Prince's confessions. Akheron walked back down the aisle with the Kin's words on his heels. "Next, the Maker gives us the world. Rock, stone and grass, this place that supports us and upholds us. Without the frame *Deyvas* made, we would only be able to drift within the world. My Prince, please gift us the ground to keep us here."

Into his hands was placed a flat rock. Moss grew on one corner of the stone, and it was cold to the touch. Would this piece of earth give them strength this week? Or was the dirt simply a reminder that they were all stuck here?

He journeyed back to the centre of the Stead with this second passenger. He held the rock in front of him, and walked with the slow pace of ceremony. Eventually, he reached the front of the Stead and placed the second element beside the first, after lifting it above his head and praying the words.

"Third, the Maker made fire to warm us and give us inspiration. Fire made us alive, fire made us hungry, fire made us fight for his favour!" The priest's voice did not quiver, but rung against the high roof of the building with the ferocity of a larger flame than Akheron was presented with. "My Prince, bring us a reminder of the Maker's fires. Remember, this week, that it was the first spark that taught us how to burn with life and passion."

It was simply a small candle. The white wax sat within a small gold cup on a little plate, and a small point of light flickered on its wick. Akheron held it in his hands and felt a little silly. Such a small sign of fire. But the candle was made from sanctified wax and the tongue of flame lit by holy hands.

He bore it to the shrine for them as well. It was expected. He was tired of being expected. He had once been unexpected: that day he stepped inside Aristorn's manse. Now he was just the Prince of the people, the one they had made. Maybe this was Akheron's little candle, all that was left of the flame.

"Bless us, Maker," Akheron said, staring upward. The Maker was portrayed as a man made of light on the ceiling. His head was the opening, where the sun shone in and his hands were full of fire. Akheron had missed a word. "*Holy* Maker."

The Maker knows.

Quietly, he set the candle onto the slab of wood. The Maker was not here. These were just some little pieces of the world. And the Maker was not the world. He was so much more—he had to be.

"But the fires burned us and left us craving, dry and thirsty in this world." Geanar's words echoed against the mosaic above them.

Akheron's back stiffened as he walked to those words.

"So the Maker created water to sooth us. Water to quench our mouths and heal our burns. He softened the earth with water and distanced the fires with water. He saved us with water."

Akheron stopped walking. He hadn't quite reached the end of the aisle where the last element was waiting. Regardless, the assisting priest took three steps down the aisle to hand him, with a shake of the hands and nod of the head, a sphere of water. The top was open and the water within awake with ripples.

Akheron stood there for a moment staring down at the water in his hands. *This is the Maker's healing?* It felt a little cold, and smelled faintly like incense. *How dare I take this?* Akheron had never healed a thing. Not in years, at least. He trembled as he turned around. This was wrong. No holy water could cleanse his hands. None, unless the Maker's own hand had blessed it.

"My Prince," said Geanar. "Please bring us the waters of our *Deyvas* to ease our thirst this week and sooth our burns."

One step. He closed his eyes and swallowed.

Another step. Then another. Very slowly, Akheron made his way into the centre of the Stead. With each lurching movement, the divine water sloshed against the sides of the glass sphere.

He reached the centre of the Maker's Stead and looked up. Daylight poured upon him and his glass of water. He closed his eyes. Then forced them open again. He lifted the water up for its blessing. *I am no holy man. I am no healer. I am no child of the Maker. Because the Maker can never love the heart of me, and this divine water cannot heal me.*

"Maker..." he said, mistaking his words. "Bless us—"

Geanar glanced up at him when he stuttered the second time. This was the most sacred ritual of the Kinship. No man was closer to the Maker than the man who blessed his shrine.

Akheron's hands could barely hold the slippery sphere above any longer. He began again. "Ble—"

He let go of the holy water.

The sphere did not slip. Akheron did not falter it. He simply let go of it. Down plummeted the Maker's healing. Down fell the completion of the shrine. Down went creation. With a piercing bang, the glass shattered. Water and shards of relic splashed against Akheron's buckled ankle boots. Drops of the ceremony splattered against Akheron's green cape and black trousers.

The silence after the shatter was almost as bad as the fall

itself. No one in the Stead made a noise. Akheron slowly looked down from the skylight; Geanar was staring at the broken glass. A stain of water was seeping into the carpet in front of the shrine.

"I—" Akheron said. His stomach was rending itself to pieces. *What is there to say?*

"The glass..." Geanar said.

The crowd started murmuring to itself. "Did you see?" someone asked. "He dropped it."

"No," someone said, "he threw it down."

"You broke the glass," Geanar said. His face was red. "You spilled the water."

"No vase of water is sufficient for me or my kind," Akheron said. He wasn't sure why he did. He wasn't sure when he had come up with such a concept either.

The priest's jaw dropped. "What! The Maker's water quenches all thirsts."

I must own this, Akheron thought. *Then they will all know me in truth. Enough of playing Prince. I need to be* me *again.* He stepped back one step, and his foot crunched more glass. "The Maker has never forgiven me," he said. He held out his hands, as if the Kin could see upon them what Akheron had done. "The Maker has never given me water that will heal these burns."

The crowd's mumbling instantly shifted from curious words of wonderment to controversial surprise. "Not here," someone said. "They won't let him say that here."

"I—what—My Prince... this is no place for a theological discussion, nor a confession. This is the Ceremony of Preparation. You have ruined the ritual, and ruined the week. You have disgraced yourself. You should ask your people for forgiveness to reclaim your honour." Geanar spoke quietly, as though he was conversing only with Akheron.

Akheron took another step back. This was all wrong. *The Maker knows.* He thought he was going to pass out. He glanced back down the aisle. All the faces were staring at him. They weren't admiring him. They were waiting to understand him. Haekus had made it to the aisle and was advancing toward Akheron. To protect him, if need be. Akheron held out his hand toward his guard and his friend stopped in his tracks. *If they want to kill me for what I say, let them,* he inwardly begged his friend. Haekus would stand by him to the end, he knew, even when it was foolishness and failure. *But I must say it...*

"This *is* the place for a theological discussion. This is the place for questions, doubts, and answers. Does the Maker have any for me? He must answer me here. Now. *He must!*" Akheron declared. He believed it. Across the whole world, this morning, holy men prepared the week's blessings. Akheron had stopped one ceremony, and stood before the Maker's eyes and the eyes of many of his followers. "Answer me, *Deyvas!*"

"My Prince, I must insist... you cannot disrupt this service! I will call the guards."

"Why won't you answer his questions?" a lone voice shouted. It was Haekus's. The crowd turned their eyes upon him, briefly, and then back to Akheron, who stood trembling before them. "You represent the Maker, why won't you answer?"

Geanar's words tripped over his tongue. But Geanar and the Stead were distant to Akheron now. His god was so much closer and real.

Akheron stared upward and asked, "Why won't you answer? I can't keep guessing how to live. None of the words written in your books, and none of the words spoken by your Kin have helped. Why do you let me continue this... this lie?"

"Guards!" Geanar called. The Defenders appeared in the aisles, marching toward the centre of the Stead. "This is the sanctuary of the Maker, not a courtroom where you may do as you please..."

Why? Damn it, I need you to answer! "Please! I need you."

The sky only gave him silence. Silence and light that hurt his eyes. He could barely see through the shimmering on his eyes.

Silence.

Geanar stepped forward and grabbed him by the arm. "Enough!" the Kin ordered, his face furious.

Akheron turned to shake his arm free, but Geanar, stumbling to avoid stepping on the glass, ended up tripping away from the shrine. Into the arms of the crowd.

First, a man caught him and helped him reclaim his balance.

A woman shouted, "Defend Akheron! Protect our Prince."

A shorter man grabbed Geanar a bit more roughly, and held

him away from Akheron. The aisles filled with citizens, obstructing the advance of the guards.

"Does he speak to you?" Akheron demanded, looking away from the mosaic ceiling. He advanced on the Kin.

"What?"

"Does the Maker speak to you? Do you hear him? Has he ever once quenched your thirst or answered your prayers?"

"Of course he answers prayers—"

"Does he speak to you?" a fierce old man asked, stepping toward Geanar. "Simple question..."

"Release me!"

"Why won't he talk to us?" Akheron asked. "I want to know. The real reason." *Because we don't deserve him to...*

"Because if he talked to us, none of us would find him. We would all fight his voice. Look around," Geanar said. "We are children! If he told us exactly how to live, we would *never* do as he said. He gives us teachings, but he can't *make* us better. *We have to do that.*"

Akheron shook his head. "I don't know how."

"Answer him! Answer him!" some of the crowd started chanting. The Defenders were trying to fight their way through—no weapons had been drawn—but the crowd held them back.

Geanar found himself pulled by three men, one of whom came face to face with him.

"Leave him be," Akheron said.

"Where is this Maker?" said Geanar's confronter. "Why doesn't he come teach us himself?"

Akheron looked around. The broken glass. The lost water. The Maker was around them like the air and beneath them like the stone. But he had given Akheron no warmth in a long time. And he had certainly never given Akheron healing waters.

"The Maker is here, in this room," Geanar said. "He can hear you, but he will not answer you unless you are holy enough... none of us are."

"Akheron is," said one of the men. "He's the most honest and humble man among us, and he's the Prince!"

"No," Akheron said. "I'm not honest."

"Get the Maker to talk," said one of the burlier men. "Or he's as much of a fraud as you." A woman was trying to pull the man off the priest, perhaps the man's wife. "Off me, woman," the man said. The woman went reeling away from his hand.

"No!" Akheron said. He tried walking ahead. "Geanar, I'm sorry. Maker, I'm sorry! Maker!"

"I want to hear him too!" shouted a boy in the aisle. A guard shoved through the clutter of crowd between the aisle and Akheron, knocking the child off his feet. A common man with the *Book of the Maker* in his hands smashed the guard down to the floor.

Akheron heard a sword drawn.

"Let me go!" shrieked Geanar. He was yanked into the crowd, and that was the last Akheron saw of the Kin he had always known.

"What is wrong with you?" Akheron demanded of the crowd. He tried forcing his way forward, but could not. "He was innocent! He was a priest!"

"He was a liar and a sinner too!"

"Look at his work!" a woman lifted the dazed and bleeding boy that had been shoved aside seconds ago.

"I am worse!" Akheron shouted. "I should pay!"

"That's the sort of man we can forgive, though!" returned the thick man that had shoved away his wife. "Everyone, enough of this place! Enough of this Maker!"

"Glyphs, glyphs, glyphs," Akheron whispered. His mind was racing. He put his hands on his head and tried to calm himself.

"Down with the Stead!"

"Down with the shrine!"

"I just wanted you to hear me," Akheron whispered. "I wanted you to see me..."

"Down with the Stead, down with the shrine!" repeated the mob.

"Akheron, Akheron!" someone cheered. Somewhere was the sound of fighting. Swords clashed. Someone screamed.

"Why won't you stop this? Why won't you stop us?" he asked the Maker. "Do you truly not care?"

"Down with the Stead, down with the shrine, down with the Stead, down with the..." on and on it went.

"I can't *try* anymore," Akheron said. "I need you to stop me, if I do something wrong." He stepped toward the shrine, to the rising chants of his people. His lost and sinful people. "Stop me, please."

He put his hands on the wooden board. *Stop me, please.*

"Down with the Stead, down with the shrine!"

"Speak to me," Akheron prayed, one last time.

There was only the anger of the crowd. And his own anger, waiting there. Unanswered and ready. So ready.

"Down with the shrine!"

He threw the wooden board and the elements into the air. The glass of air shattered, releasing its holy contents. The rock rolled and the candle sputtered out, against the floor.

"Down with the stead!"

Akheron threw over the table with a roar. "Answer us!" he shouted.

"Answer us!" replied the crowd. The guards were slain. The mob was toppling their chairs and shattering the windows. Any artwork on the walls was torn down. Someone was brandishing a torch in the doorway, running in to set things afire with the passion of man.

Akheron stood in the midst of it with his head reeling in a daze and his shoulders turned down. "I'm sorry," he whispered.

"Answer us! Answer us! Answer us!"

Out into the city echoed the cheers of freed people. The chorus of the holy men ascended—screams of pain as the riot gripped Avernus in its fiery palms. The crowd led Akheron out into the smouldering city. They pushed him in front of them, making him their champion once again. He did his best to step over the bodies as they led him into a new world.

The street was nearly abandoned now. There was a curtain of smoke across it, draping softly against the edges of silent buildings. Akheron had never seen Avernus so haunted. He walked past a gutted body. A dead merchant, it looked like. He must have pledged his faith to the wrong side. His blood was mingled with water and spit in the cracked cobblestones of the street.

"Leave us be," Haekus growled.

Akheron glanced over his shoulder. His guard had levelled his sword at the group of men and women nearby. They backed off as ordered. Unlike many they had encountered recently, these men were careful enough not to challenge a tear-stained blade-master.

Mavas walked beside him; she had said nothing to Akheron since yesterday. But she had raised her blade properly the last time they had been attacked. She was with him still, though he knew not why.

Akheron closed his eyes. "Haekus. What have I done?"

"You were honest with your people," Haekus said, approaching. Akheron heard his boots dragging; the Prince was too busy staring at the wide, glazed eyes of the slain merchant. "And then they were honest. None of it was good, but all of it was true."

"Why wouldn't the Maker stop us?"

"They say freewill is important."

"They are wrong," Akheron said. "Let's go."

They carried on. Evening was beginning to bury Avernus's sins in the darkness. No one knew what the dawn would bring, but, from the sounds of bloodshed that echoed through the city even now, none of the Maker's devout would see it.

As they advanced down the street, a group of children ran by. They gave Akheron and his friends a wide berth, picking their way past the hungry maws of alleyways and the doors of abandoned houses. Akheron was tired of seeing his home like this. Twice in the past five years Akheron had seen smoke in his streets and dead men lying there. The Grey Night was all too familiar to him.

Haekus and Mavas had passed him and were now waiting for him to catch up.

"Akheron," Haekus said. His voice sounded distant.

"What?" Akheron asked. Then he saw the door of his family's estate, lying in the street. He shoved Haekus aside. "No!"

There was smoke rising above the house. He could see firelight against the open entry corridor. Inside, he found the fire, crackling in his family's kitchen. His brother-in-law was sitting against the opposite wall, his eyes closed.

"Barun!" he gasped and dropped down beside the man. There was blood dripping from his nose and from a small wound in his side. He did not look that wounded, but when Akheron touched him the man fell over. As he toppled to the floorboards, his back left a red streak across the pale blue wallpaper.

"Glyphs..."

"Akheron, you should go outside," Mavas said. "I think there're people upstairs."

"Glyphs."

"Don't go," Mavas said.

Akheron stood up and looked at Mavas. Her face, smudged with dirt, pleaded with him. 'Don't,' she mouthed. Akheron looked away from her. "Tam?" he shouted. He ran through the rest of the dining room, ignoring the licking flames.

"No," Mavas said. "Haekus!"

There was a staircase past the dining table where once he had resisted his father's orders. He could remember that day, when his sister had taught him to ride. Up the stairs he went and caught the first of his rioters coming down. The man's throat twisted sideways, and his bones broke as he fell downward. Akheron noticed Haekus following him. To protect him. These spineless men needed protection *from* him.

The second of Akheron's godless men came at him with a steak knife. Akheron felt it clip his shoulder as he put his foot behind the man's heels. Then he slammed the man into the floorboards hard enough to break them. He knelt down, broke the man's arm, and drove his own knife into his chest.

Two more men were in the upstairs hallway, staring at him in shock. Akheron rose from his brutal kill, with barely a tremble.

"You must be a man of the Maker," said one. "That's why we killed these people. We'll kill you too."

"Don't you know who that is?" said the other in terror. "That's the Prince!"

Akheron strode forward, through the blood of their comrade. He heard Haekus ascend the stairs behind him, and the men he advanced toward turned to flee. There was nowhere to flee, just the two bedrooms up here, and the closet.

The first man, who had spoken of the Maker, died against the wall, his head slammed there a dozen times until Akheron's hands slipped off.

The second man tried escaping through the window. Instead he fell to the street below, spilling his brains across the cobblestones. Akheron took a deep breath of smoky night air from the window and turned back inside.

"Stay there, Akhe—" Haekus said. Akheron strode through the second room. It was the old bedroom, where once Akheron's father and mother had slept; even Akheron had occupied this room since then. The other room was his sister's. Haekus stood in the doorway to the hall.

He pushed Haekus aside.

Tam was on the floor of her room. Her dark hair was sticky when he knelt and cradled her. He hated bloody hair. He bent his head down until his forehead touched hers, looking into her vacant, still eyes. He brushed them closed, nearly sobbing at the feel of lashes. Tamese Gothikar was dead.

"Akheron..." Haekus said.

"He did this," Akheron growled. His sister lay dead within his arms. Her clothes had been roughed, though he was relieved she had not been raped. He lifted her as far as he could, pressing her stiff body against his chest. His hands were wrapped around her head. He could see one of her eyelashes on his red-stained finger. He heaved as the tears came. "He did this. I took something from him—his city or his daughters or his servant, Aristorn, or something. I burned the Stead and he burned my family. Tam..." he cried. *Where now?* he wondered. "Is this supposed to teach me?"

Haekus said nothing. Akheron wasn't even sure if he was there, in Tam's bedroom. Maybe he had backed away in sorrow.

"Are you trying to make me a better person?" Akheron asked. "Because you're just breaking the pieces. Pretty soon, I'll have nothing left. Pretty soon, there'll be nothing left of me to fix. You did this, *Deyvas*. You took Tam from me. First my love. Now Tam. Glyphs."

23

Akheron spent the afternoon in the council room. Odyn insisted on an offensive against the Buccaneer Navy; for once, Theseus concurred. This war at sea had lasted four years already; it was the Year of Olympus 514. The corsairs had laid siege to his harbour last month. Their daring had not returned to the heights that burned Avernus a few years earlier, but even boarding every ship to leave Athyns was unheard of for mere bandits.

Leto kept trying to bring Akheron in on the conversation. She paced beside the everwood table, ignoring her chair. Since the start, the Crown Magician had adored the commoner Prince. By her position, she was to remain neutral. "Does Avernus have troops or ships to commit to a direct offensive?"

"A direct offensive?" Akheron asked, leaning forward. He shivered in his cloak. Even the Council Chamber of Midgard was cold at the outbreak of winter. A few braziers had been set up, but it was a drafty room in the sky. "Have we discovered some stronghold to attack?"

Prince Verin Theseus rolled his eyes. "We do not appreciate your sarcasm, Akheron." He sat to Akheron's left. Between them sat the Throne of Midgard, a plain wooden chair on a dais near the Council table. Across the table from them, and the Throne, sat Odyn's monstrous frame.

"Leto does. Or she wouldn't ask," Akheron retorted. They glared at him. He was just an upstart to them. A controversial upstart that they would cut loose if he overstepped himself. "The Navy avoids us when they should and attacks us when they should. They are smart, and we are not. No 'direct offensive' is going to accomplish anything. We need to send scouts out across the two seas, a hundred of them. If fifty galleys return, we'll find the Navy. Even if only twenty last the voyage, we'll have a place to send our scouts."

"We cannot spare a hundred ships, especially with survival odds projected so low," Theseus said. He took a drink of the water in his cup. A pitcher of water and its three mugs were the only objects on the Council table.

"I want to fight, not explore," Odyn said. The enormous man shivered under an ample bear-pelt—his home was the warmest of the Dominion, no matter the time of year. Galinor, the capital, was not. "War, not games."

"The Navy is out there," Akheron said. He stood up. Behind Odyn was the room's best view. "Look."

The small window across the table from the Throne of Midgard looked eastward, across the grey Mydarius Sea. Odyn turned in his chair to look out, while Theseus stood with a grumble. The city was wrapped in frost and not a soul moved through the streets, as far as Akheron could see from here. Beyond the city walls was a stretch of land covered with evergreens and a rolling hill. Against the green swath lapped the icy waves of the ocean.

And halfway to the horizon drifted a ship. It was too far to make out as any more than a black-sailed boat, but a scope on the city walls had confirmed that it was an unmarked corsair vessel.

"They are out there, and they know precisely where we are. They even know who we are," Akheron said. "Do we know the same? You say we cannot afford to lose a hundred ships, but we are doing that anyway! Every month they board and burn a dozen merchant and passenger ships. Our citizens are demanding our money to pay for the expenses of longer land travel, because they are *scared* to sail! We need scouts, spies, magicians, secrets, not raids."

"If Akheron Gothikar says we need magicians," Leto said, "I'd take his word."

Akheron smirked, and sat back into his Avernan seat.

A few hours later, he allowed Leto to teleport him home. They checked the guest list in the Tower, as was custom, to see if anyone else needed such a spell. Another lord went with Akheron, some upper-class man from his city that he did not know. He did not wait for the man after arriving in Avernus. The city was cold, though it did not yet have snow trails in its streets. Akheron descended the stairs from the Known Location with a shiver.

"Thank you, my Prince," said the short, fat man who had travelled with him.

"Think nothing of it," Akheron said.

He made his way through the quiet streets as quickly as he could. It was too late for the markets to stay open—Avernus had a lot of vacant real estate since the Grey Night, and with the winter came a sharp decrease in business. Many of the buildings in the expensive residential district were made of stone, but the people and furnishings within were not.

It was not past dinnertime though, so Akheron joined his sister's family for their evening meal. Tam asked him about the Buccaneers and the Council Meeting he had attended. Her frown tugged at his conscience, but neither of them spoke openly in front of their uncle. Akheron asked Tam if she had seen a healer or magician yet. He did not say openly why, but they had talked about it before; Tam was having trouble conceiving. Both she and Barun wanted children. Sometimes, a concoction could help, other times a spell. Though, often, nothing could be done for a barren woman.

After dinner with Tam, Akheron retired to his castle on the hill. The infamous Three Towers of Avernus was larger than it used to be. Akheron had heard a conversation in a bakery recently that the Commoner Prince had conducted heavy renovations of the Palace only to spend his time elsewhere. After all, his blood family had chosen not to move into the spacious grandeur of the Prince's wealth.

Haekus reached the Palace gate at about the same time as Akheron. He had become skilled at giving the Prince some distance to walk on his own, but remaining close enough to uphold his vows of protection. The lanky warrior's red hair had a small line of sweat in front of it and Akheron wondered how much work he put into such a preposterous task.

The gate's guards waved them through without question. Akheron nodded his head to their bows.

Once they were through the building-tall outer wall, the rest of the Palace came into view. An angular courtyard of cobblestone surrounded the three colloquial Towers: the now enormous Keep dwarfed both the Barracks and the Library. As the sun set, the city to the west cast its shadows up at the Keep, so only Akheron's two added storeys gleamed in the twilight. The narrow steeple of the Library caught a ray of golden light, while the Barracks, bustling with soldiers and guards, fell into the dark.

Akheron led Haekus into the mess of the barracks and joined him for a short meal. He had already eaten, but he wanted to make sure Haekus was satisfied too. "I worry for Tam," he told his friend. "We have no family left... and she doesn't want to move here."

"Have you thought of moving there?" Haekus asked.

Akheron shrugged. "She's got her own family. They're trying to have kids. They don't want me bringing my life and issues into things."

"They have a spare bedroom," Haekus said.

"What about Mavas?"

"What about her?"

"Tam has never approved of her."

Haekus shrugged and spooned soup into his mouth. He picked up his loaf, paused, and said, "What's more important, family or Mavas?"

Akheron shook his head and failed to meet his friend's eyes. Since when had Haekus had a problem with Mavas? *Before long, he'll insist he's my only friend...* Akheron sometimes wondered if he should enforce an even more strict relationship with Haekus. The man had sworn fealty to Akheron. If Akheron insisted, he would obey. The distance of his protection, in the streets earlier, was proof enough of that. "What would you have me do? Move out of my own Palace? I can't be the Commoner Prince forever."

"Can you be the Prince forever?" Haekus asked.

"Until I die," Akheron said. "Then they'll choose a replacement, someone who makes a better Prince."

Haekus lifted the remainder of his soup to his lips and drank it right from the bowl. "Let him live in your Palace, then." He wiped his lips with the sleeve of his shirt, and then took a drink of his ale.

"Let him live in your Palace, then, *sir,*" Akheron said.

"Don't concern yourself with him. Concern yourself with yourself."

Akheron laughed. "Would you like to be Prince? Haekus, enough life advice. Your job is to protect me from threats to my person, not ensure the peacefulness in my head."

"I remember making no such distinction when I swore my oaths."

"But you did swear oaths," Akheron said. "Any man who tries to protect my state of mind is destined to fail, and I would not have accepted such a vow. Now, protect me from knives and leave the rest to me."

"Very well," Haekus said. He scratched his chin.

"Very well, *sir.*"

Haekus shook his head without looking at his Prince. "Very well, sir."

On the second storey of his Keep, he commanded Haekus to wait. The transition to the third floor was smooth. The masonry matched, by his order. Additional sculptures and artwork had been made to fit the old style, though not enough to fill all the spaces on the walls.

The third floor was abandoned. There were no guards and only one in every four torches was lit. Past empty walls and across cold stones, Akheron strode. He breathed in, and clenched his fists. He felt alive here. He felt invincible.

He stuck his head inside his quarters, and saw Mavas curled up on his bed. Her eyes were closed. He withdrew quietly, and returned to the hallway.

For some reason, he wasn't ready for her yet. He paced down the corridor again. This place would fill with time. The empty rooms would eventually have families within. From the new royal quarters, he turned right and paced down the hallway. The door on his left opened to a small empty room. *This would make a good nursery, one day,* he thought. He imagined a father cradling his son on that bed one day. A good father.

There was another room across the hallway, beside his quarters. He had already started using it as a small storeroom. He expected a servant would move into it soon enough, whoever attended the royals.

"Akheron?" a voice asked sleepily. Mavas meandered down the hallway, wearing only a sheet from the bed. She stretched her arms across the empty hallway, as much as she could without falling out of the cloth.

"I tried not to wake you," Akheron said. He gave her a little kiss when they met. "You went to sleep early."

"I was tired of waiting for you," she said.

"Did you eat?" he asked.

She shook her head. "Why are you out here?"

"I just wanted to walk around. These hallways... I like them."

"I do too," she said. She leaned in for another kiss, and he gave it to her.

"Do you want to find some food?" Akheron asked.

"No. I want you."

"Oh," Akheron said. He stepped closer, so their legs and waists were touching. Her bed-sheet started to waiver.

Another voice echoed down the hallway. A woman servant. "Apologies, highness, and milady. I will return after—"

"No, it's fine," Akheron said, stepping back from his woman. Haekus was standing down the corridor too.

Mavas pulled the sheet closer around herself. "I'm not a lady."

"Apologies, mistress," the servant corrected herself.

"What is it?" Akheron asked.

The girl bowed and said, "There is a member of the Maker's Kin below. He desires to speak with you, highness."

"Haekus," Akheron called. His guard approached briskly. "See that Mavas gets something to eat. I will go and see what this is all about. Damn late for an audience..." He followed the servant down the hallway.

"What if I don't want to eat?" Mavas asked, in her playful voice.

"You heard the Prince. Put on some clothes."

Akheron glanced back down the corridor, to see Mavas drop her bed-sheet as she entered the royal chambers again. Haekus immediately averted his eyes, while Mavas gave Akheron a comical wink. It was not the first time that Haekus had seen Mavas's skin, but he had not looked away in the past. Akheron kept walking.

"Oh my," the servant muttered, under her breath, immediately, turning back down the hall with the Prince.

"Oh my, indeed," Akheron said.

As they descended the stairwell, he thought about Haekus's reaction. The guard had seemed angry. Was he angry with Mavas? He had never been one to be bothered by such. Then Akheron understood, though it frustrated him like his earlier conversation with the guard had. Haekus felt responsible for Akheron's wellbeing and he was smart enough to see the relationship for what it was.

Mavas appealed to all of Akheron's sinful wants and none of his pure ones. If there were any pure ones left.

"Where is this Kin?" Akheron asked, as they reached the Great Hall on the Keep's first floor.

The servant pointed across the enormous room.

"Ah, yes," Akheron said. He strode between the ornate wooden tables. There were two massive pillars at each third of the Hall's length. The priest was sitting with his back to the pillar furthest from Akheron. It was Kin Geanar.

The priest bowed and said, "Prince Akheron. I hope you are well today."

"I'm tired," Akheron said. "And you've disturbed my evening. What's this about?"

"The Maker," the priest said.

For some reason, Akheron felt suddenly nervous. His stomach clenched. He had to consciously think: *It is not that. He means something else.* Then he thought about how troubling it was that he *hoped* the Kin would one day confront him for his crimes. "What about the Maker?"

"You have no dedication to him under you roof here, none that fits the scope of your Palace. You spent a fortune to add storeys to the Keep, but you have not yet added the Maker to it."

"Does he really need wealth to be a part of my house?" Akheron asked.

"Of course not. He sees within all rooms. He sees behind all closed doors," Geanar said. The man's white beard was braided today. "But it would speak well to your people, to the piety of our divine Nobles, and it would speak true praise to the Maker's ears."

"My people appreciate that I was a commoner, not a

priest," Akheron objected. Geanar's words rung in his ears though. *He sees behind all closed doors.* "My Nobles are hardly religious, let alone divine. And the Maker does not want to hear my praise... certainly not from a shrine."

"You *must* give the Maker his due. You did not come by your wealth, nor your position, without his favour."

"What do you want?" Akheron asked. "My coin? Have it. Put up a shrine then. Glyphs, put up a golden one."

Geanar frowned. "There is already a shrine in the Keep. I feel called to set one up on your added storeys. A chapel, on the top storey. It is the only action that is right."

"The Maker would not want a chapel up there, on my storeys. He would not like to see what goes on up there," Akheron said. He wasn't sure why he enjoyed Geanar's anxiety so, but he did. "You have my leave and my treasury to do whatever else you desire."

"It is not about my desires," the priest stuttered.

"Have a good evening." Akheron turned his back and briskly returned to the corner stairwell. The second floor was busier than the third. There were guards at all the doors and a servant cleaning the stonework on the floor.

Haekus nodded to him when he passed, on his way to the third floor. "I had a servant bring her some food."

"Were you tempted by her?" Akheron asked.

"What? Glyphs, no."

"Glyphs, no, *sir*." Akheron corrected. He had not tried that *sir* correction until today, but he was appreciating its wit.

"Glyphs, no, sir." Haekus shook his head.

"Go find a woman," he told Haekus, and gave him a coin pouch.

Haekus tried to refuse it, holding the coins back out and shaking his head.

"The other guards can protect me tonight. I won't have you standing here thinking about Mavas's body while I'm up there... Glyphs, no." Akheron chuckled and started to climb the stairs again. As he went, the steps became colder.

In the empty hallway he loved, he ran into the priest's words again. *The Maker sees behind all closed doors.*

On the doorstep to his quarters, he stopped. *The Maker sees.* Mavas was sitting on the elaborate four-poster bed, naked and ready for him. The silk looked soft, but not half as soft as she. All around him was the splendorous filth he adorned upon himself. *The Maker sees.* His hands felt so tainted. He stretched his palms and looked at them.

"What?" Mavas asked, smiling. "Get over here."

"Not tonight," he said. He felt ill. *Some priest did this to me,* he thought. It was a curse of some kind. A glyph-cast curse. He should kill Geanar.

"What?" Mavas asked. She stood up, with a bounce. He pulled off his shirt. She touched his back. "Really?"

"Really. I...." He closed his eyes. "I'm sorry. Maybe in the morning."

"I'm all worked up already," she said.

"I know," he jested. "I'm sorry."

She shook her head. "It's fine."

He took off his boots and pants, and pulled his nightgown on. It got cold at night in the nearly abandoned third Tower of Avernus. Akheron did not sleep, even after Mavas had calmed herself down and dozed off. He lay awake, staring at the canvas canopy of his bed.

The Maker sees me. And he always has. These were practised thoughts for him. He was, and always had been, a firm believer. *The pain of belief,* he recalled.

That was not what kept him awake. *The Maker knows. I thought Aristorn was the only witness. I thought I had finished. I thought I was done, once Aristorn was done...*

He had put one of the witnesses in the ground, but had not realized who the second witness was. He wiped his dry eyes, and rolled away from Mavas. He wanted to get to sleep, but could not.

The Maker knows.

24

Akheron lounged in his study. The cramped room occupied a corner of the Avernan Keep's second floor, full of bookshelves and treasures of the Princedom. He rested his booted feet up on the table, intentionally ignoring the dirt he knocked across the treasures there. On some days, he felt protective of his wealth, or at least, objects that held wealth. He was particularly fond of books. Though he had never been much of a reader, he treasured a carefully protected tome more than almost any trinket. How a fragile collection of sheets could stand the test of time astounded him, and he did not mind paying the fortune that most books sold for.

"I'm bored," Mavas said. She sat in a cushioned armchair nearby, looking around the dusty little room.

Haekus coughed. He was standing in the door.

"What do you want to do?" Akheron asked. He was currently looking through an extendible eyeglass. He had used a monocular like it before, at the wheel of a ship. He had never used one made of gold, though. He noted the initials near the eyepiece: "V.A." He tossed it aside. Another treasure he would not keep in the *Gothikar* fortress. It rolled across the floor with a hollow echo.

"I don't know," Mavas whined. "Fight?" She picked a small glass sphere off the wall and proceeded to look through it.

"Fight or flirt," Akheron said. "Sometimes, there's more to life than just those..." He knew she did not like it when he spoke like that. She had once told him that she was a simpleton and he could take her or leave her as she was. He had taken her repeatedly.

She rolled the glass ball across the floor. Haekus sighed, and picked it up before it exited the trophy room. Next, she found a knife on the shelf. It was a wicked weapon, with a black handle and a snaking silver blade. She ran a finger along its length and then winced. "Glyphs, the thing cut me!" The knife whirred through the air at a bookshelf nearby. It interrupted the pages of *After Vyndrel* with a sickening thud.

Akheron sighed, watching her lick the blood from her index finger. He pulled the knife—book and all—from the bookshelf. After separating it from the pages of the Triumvirate's early history, he lifted the blade for his own examination.

He knew which knife this was. There were glyphs along the blade, and a ring of them around the black metal grip. It was not a comfortable weapon to hold, but the winding blade looked deadly. It was likely kept sharp by magic. But these glyphs did much more than keep the edge. He had read about this dagger in one of the few books he had sunken time into. "This is Wither's blade," he remembered, *"Ethaanos."*

"Ethay what?" Mavas asked. Haekus listened with unveiled interest. Had he heard these stories already?

Akheron turned the blade over in his hands. "It means 'persuasion'."

Mavas shrugged, standing up impatiently. "What does it matter? It's a knife."

"Not just any knife," Akheron said. "This weapon played a role in the founding of the Triumvirate. An assassin wielded it against Tiberon Odyn himself."

"Really?"

Akheron ran his own finger along the blade. He felt a small tug, and then he was bleeding too. He had done it on purpose. *Do I feel different?* he wondered. He wasn't sure which stories of *Ethaanos* were true and which were myth. He watched the blood ooze on his thumb.

When he looked up, Haekus met his eyes. He *must* have known the tales.

Akheron slammed the knife down into the tabletop. "I wonder how this came to be here. Oh well, it's mine now. All of this is mine. But it's all got Telvyn Aristorn's fingerprints.

Mavas, you want something to do?"

"Yes."

"Take anything from this room that has his initials or sigil upon it. Take them all outside and burn them." Akheron stood up and winked at Haekus. "If anyone asks what you're doing, Haekus can tell them."

"Sir?"

"I have to meet with my Nobles, and they can do me no harm that would require your services," he said. "If they need to be strong-armed, I can do it myself."

Haekus regarded Akheron with a frown.

"I'll just take this along with me," Akheron said. He picked up the curved knife.

"If anyone asks us to stop burning treasures," Haekus said, "I'd be better off with it." His guard's eyes were like beads of ice, all of a sudden; his face was expressionless.

Why do I feel like this is an argument I'd lose? He reluctantly handed over *Ethaanos,* and said, "Don't use it. But don't let anyone else get their hands upon it. Ever."

"Of course," Haekus said. "You won't see it again."

Akheron looked at the black hilt that jutted past Haekus's belt. He had only just discovered the relic, but was immensely fascinated with it. "Fine."

"Glyphs," Mavas said, lifting a handful of books. "This is going to be a *good* fire."

There was a small meeting room on the other side of the second floor. Akheron got there before anyone else. The guard bowed to him as he arrived. Within sat a small table with a platter of grapes and cheese, a glass wine bottle of Elysia's finest and four cups. Akheron poured himself some wine while he waited.

He did not have to wait long. Lord Ahryn appeared first. He had likely spent the night in Avernus, having journeyed from the Marsh during the last few weeks. They only had meetings with all Three Nobles once per year, due to the logistical difficulty.

"Prince Akheron!" Lord Ahryn shook his hand firmly. He was a young man, perhaps even younger than Akheron, with long brown hair and catching brown eyes.

"Lord Ahryn."

"How are you settling into your new house?" Ahryn spread his arms.

Akheron chuckled. "It's incredible," he confessed. "There's so much to do, and so much to see. I'm looking for ways to leave my own unique footprint in this place. So much of it bears the signs of an age now passed."

Ahryn pursed his lips. He picked up the wine bottle to inspect it. The vintage was older than both of them. "Do not be quick to put the old age to rest," Ahryn said. "I may still be a young man, but the opportunities that define me might have been lost without my father's assistance and my Kin's guidance."

Akheron pushed the platter of food toward the lord. "Please, enjoy."

Lord Ino was the second to arrive. His family hailed from the most western lands of the Avernan Fief. He was so distant, he often spent a majority of the year in Avernus. Across the Triumvirate, it was not unusual for the Imperial Nobles to live away from their homelands to stay up-to-date on politics and matters of court. The Princes themselves were expected to live in their capitals, without question. Ino had family in Aninos and Lydion, but most of his year was in an Avernan estate.

"Akheron. Ahryn," Ino said. He gripped their hands and then seated himself across the table from Akheron. He had short black hair and the scars of a badly broken nose.

Edemar was late. While the other Nobles discussed the upcoming winter, Akheron worried what could cause his friend's tardiness. Edemar held many of his secrets, and though Akheron could not imagine him ever speaking of them, the very concept turned the Prince's stomach.

"Akheron, should we expect a wedding announcement soon?" Ahryn asked.

"What?"

"The rumours are deafening," Ino said. Akheron gave him a blank look.

"Come now," Ahryn said. "You live in a Palace with a young woman of common birth.... You have to know everyone is talking about your mistress."

"My mistress?" Akheron asked. "Mavas is a... friend of mine. I have known her for years. My sister has expressed a disinterest in castle-life, so why not fill her rooms here?"

Ino chuckled. "Perhaps if you put signs up around the city explaining that, some of your citizens might believe it."

"Glyphs," Akheron muttered. He leaned back in his chair. He should have brought Wither's *Persuasion* with him, instead of giving it to Haekus. "What are you saying then? That I have some *who*—"

"Easy, Akheron," Ahryn said. "We all have a special woman in our lives."

"I am not one of *you*," Akheron said. "I am a commoner. Why then wouldn't I have friends who aren't lords?"

"We didn't mean insult," Ino said. "I meant my question genuinely: should we expect anything serious to come of this?"

By the Maker, I hope so... Akheron thought. Mavas was *his*. Not Demetas's, not Haekus's, no one's but his. As much as any man could lay claim to her—Mavas was a fighter with passion that rivalled Akheron's. She lived by her own wants, not his.

"Akheron," a deep voice said. "Ino, Ahryn."

Edemar had arrived. Akheron's old friend had finally started to bald, though his short brown hair still looked sharp and well kept. He shook Akheron's hand first; rather than release it promptly, he held Akheron's attention for a moment, though his expression was blank. Then he greeted his peers.

I told him I would marry his daughter, Akheron thought. It was pertinent information to add to his prior conversation—information he deemed best left untold. *I'll have to deal with it at some point...*

"Shall we get to business?" Edemar asked.

Akheron poured himself more wine.

For the first topic, they discussed the treasury. Akheron had added a fortune to it, when he became Prince. He could remember Ahryn's reaction. The Noble was not the wealthiest of the group, and he had not expected the Commoner Prince to bring a treasure trove with him. *Blood coins and corsair's iron,* Akheron thought.

Ino brought up an issue of deteriorating infrastructure in the south, a dilemma that Ahryn added his relieved voice to. The roads out of Agwar were some of the worst in the Dominion, according to the Nobles. Akheron had little trouble deciding to commit some of his income to keeping them in proper shape.

Edemar suggested raising taxes to help; he explained that the people's morale was high, a result of Akheron's elevation to Princehood and the good weather. He thought that they could raise taxes without causing enough unrest to drop below the break-even point.

"No," Akheron said. "The commoner Prince's first act of state will not be to exploit his brethren."

"Well," Ino said, cautiously, "What will his first act be?"

Akheron leaned back from the table. He took a drink of his wine. "To usurp the upper class from within."

They looked at him, trying to understand his words. No matter what he meant, he *was* one of them by all the standards that defined them. But for a moment, his Nobles must have wondered if it was a declaration of antagonism.

"I'm going to do what *you* do, but to its extreme," Akheron said. "I will spend wealth on things that serve no purpose but to declare my greatness. Because declaring my greatness will be further declaring that *any* man can be that great. That any commoner can be me."

"A lie," Edemar said, flatly. Akheron quieted the errant question of why Mar was acting so... oddly.

"Of course, a lie," Akheron said. "That's what men do. We lie." They would say he seized and lived by the things that he hated. If they were even that smart, they would say he was a hypocrite. It was not about living by his failures, but about burning the world for them—that's what it had *always* been about, since the day he had decided to stop hiding.

For a moment, the meeting room was silent. Only a moment. Then Ahryn took a drink of his wine and Ino asked, again, "How?"

"First, I'll make myself a bigger castle," Akheron said. He had been planning this for most of the year. "I'm going to add a storey or two to the Keep. I'll have the craftsmen mimic the old architecture. The point is to be the old age, but *better*. I'll strike off all of Aristorn's words and sigils and replace them with my own new House words. Conquest and all that. The commoners will tell tales of how complete my victory was."

"Glyphs," Ahryn muttered.

Ino was less depressed by Akheron's ideas. He had been the first to be won over by Edemar's persuasions. He had been

Akheron's second vote. "And then what?"

"We'll raise some more lords," Akheron said. "Commoners who support us, of course, but we'll make it look like I'm genuinely building a government out of the poor."

"So, lords in the outlying towns, then?" This was something Ahryn could get behind. The more titles given to the fief the more evenly wealth could be distributed. Ahryn's Marsh was a profitable enough region—there was nowhere in the realm like it. The resources that only Ahryn exported had made him a Noble, not his father or Kin. But he lacked the society and civilization that his peers enjoyed.

"Of course," Akheron said. "I imagine that Nallar ten Eldian would be at the top of that list..."

"He's been breathing down my neck," Ino said.

Edemar was just lounging in his chair. Though he sat to Akheron's right, he was just staring at the Prince, expression guarded. Their last one-on-one conversation had been fierce. Akheron tried not to think of it.

He instead thought of Mavas, and his treasury, and his castle. By the time winter's winds bade the workers rest, they had finished the exterior of the new storeys of his Palace. Large portions of the construction were cast with magic over the span of a few days, while the masons spent weeks perfecting the designs upon the rock. The exterior was simple brickwork, while every dozen feet or so it had a column of granite with lavish sculptures at its head and toe.

Above the door were laid the words, *"Korbios decadus abyron,"* Conquest stands alone, and alone stood Akheron's victory. All sign of Aristorn was stripped away. All sign of the Maker, too. By the time that the season's snows fell on Avernus, Akheron wandered his enormous Keep with Mavas and Haekus and all his ghosts, alone.

25

Akheron knew the Crown Magician by her clothing. As Edemar led him, Mavas, and Haekus onto the roof of an aged stone building, he quickly sized up the one woman standing on its dusty surface. She was wearing an elaborate orange and red robe; though its colours were similar to the coat Mavas wore, its style was not. Mavas's coat was wide in the shoulders like a soldier's jacket, but narrow in the torso and hips. It was designed to attract the eyes. Orange was the traditional colour of the Magician's Order, while red spoke to Imperial tones and the colours of the Odyn dynasty—the robes of the Crown Magician were lined with both, trimmed with a burnt orange, and ornately patterned with red beads on the bosom, ruby buttons, and a high, raised collar. It was garb designed to lower one's eyes.

"Akheron Gothikar, I presume." The woman's voice was practiced with authority. A few wrinkles bespoke her middle age, tucked below her temples and across her forehead. Her eyes were little cubes of ice, giving Akheron's breath a freeze with their stoic analysis. She was by no means a beautiful woman; she had none of the proportions for attractiveness, nor any softness about her. But she was certainly not an ugly woman. She defined her stately position with her certainty, power, and acuity. "I am Leto of Delfie. I currently serve as the Crown Magician of the Triumvirate, and will be happy to associate you with your peers to ensure the four of us lead the Triumvirate properly."

"Well met," Akheron said, and extended his hand.

She looked at his hand for half a breath before she took it.

"I assume these are your... comrades?"

Akheron turned to see. Mavas stood next to him, and Haekus a few steps back. Edemar was climbing the steps to join them on the old rooftop. The former, Akheron's lover, gave Akheron a small smile and a nod. She was a woman corsair, meeting one of the most powerful ladies in the realm. *Meeting. I suppose I should introduce her, then.* "Yes, milady—"

"Sir," Leto said. "I haven't gone by Lady Leto in a long time. Of course, you will soon be a Prince, so you may call me whatever you wish."

Akheron blinked. "I suppose you're right. This is Mavas, my..." he searched for the word, before awkwardly going with the one Leto had suggested, "comrade. And Haekus, my guard."

Haekus smirked, then corrected himself and bowed with Mavas to the Crown Mage.

"Greetings," said the magician. "We will have more time to talk in Galinor. Please stand still, and I will write the Known Location."

Edemar bowed to the Mage and came to stand beside the Prince to be.

Akheron had read enough books to understand the basic principles of travelling with magic. Spells could only be written for areas that had been interpreted into glyphs, a process long since lost to the Order. However, the spell to travel to one of the Known Locations could be cast anywhere. The only reason to venture up to this building—the Location for Avernus—was to shorten the Crown Magician's trip. This rooftop was where she would arrive when coming to the east to fetch the planned Prince Gothikar.

And then it happened. There was a flicker to the air. The colours of Avernus—dark stone and dark wood, with a hint of green—seemed to blur and when they settled back into place, they were all different. The masonry was white now, the wood rich and the plants gold.

Akheron found himself standing on a circular stone platform, beneath artistic white arches. Everywhere he looked was a design or decal of some kind, whether it were the heavy brass rings wrapped around the base of the columns or carvings of knights and magicians on the surfaces of the walls. Akheron was standing in an open balcony, and every detail called his eyes. His head started hurting again, like it had earlier that morning, and he found himself overwhelmed. He couldn't focus, so he forced himself to look *outward*... and then he saw the city.

Galinor, the Imperial City, was not quite as large as Avernus, but it was stunning. The main street that Akheron could see was lined with enormous trees, trees with golden leaves and white blossoms. Everwoods. He had heard tales, but had never seen them. With the Buccaneers, he hadn't sailed far enough across the Mydarius to reach the capital, and such incredible trees only grew here, so far as he knew. The buildings were all between two and three storeys, crafted from light grey or smooth white rock, like the tower balcony that Akheron looked out from.

"Welcome to the Tower of the Throne of Midgard," Leto announced, raising her arms. Haekus and Mavas were staring off the balcony, too, though Leto faced Akheron and his friends, as they had been standing before the spell.

Akheron smiled to Leto, then walked right up to the ornate railing, complete with its eagle-head decorations. He leaned out and craned his neck to look up. "How tall is this building?" he gasped, pulling back in.

"We are on the third storey. There are twelve storeys in all," Leto said. "It is thought that an ancient spell must support the Tower, for, even with the most modern methods of construction, we cannot raise a new tower past six or seven storeys."

"What is that tower?" Akheron asked. He pointed into the cityscape. It was the second tallest building in Galinor, crafted out of an older rock, darker than most of the materials around it.

"That is the Keep of the Order, our old headquarters. As Crown Magician, and a resident mage of the Delfie School, I have transitioned the order out of that cold tower to my home."

Akheron glanced at Leto and raised an eyebrow. "But the job of the magicians is to keep the government on its toes. Shouldn't your Order reside here?"

"The job of my Order is to guard and govern the use of magic, not the policies of mankind," Leto said. "The Crown Magician accepts the extra responsibility of approving or disproving certain decisions of the Princes, but that is not associated with the Order."

"I see," Akheron said. "Where to now?"

"Up," said Edemar, skulking behind them. "But I'll speak to you after. It is a meeting for only Princes. Your friends can go for the sights, but I've already seen them."

Leto led the way, while Mavas slunk beside Akheron and Haekus stoically took up the rear. It was a lavish adventure through the Tower of the Throne, one with far too many steps, but Akheron spent the time in silence. He was still coming to terms with the favour of the commoners, his kind, as far as he saw them. *I may be Prince,* he thought, *but I have always been one of them.* Now his brothers and sisters of the underclass only stared at him, when they recognized him.

Leto seemed to be such a firm and calculated leader, but Akheron had begun feeling her impression of him. She respected him, and he wasn't yet certain why. *Maybe I'm just imagining it,* he thought, and took Mavas's hand.

She raised an eyebrow. Neither of them were really into hand-holding or anything so... innocent.

Close to the top of the Tower, they reached their destination. Akheron had lost track of what storey they were on. They were higher in the sky than he had ever been. What if some magician's spell or errant ocean storm struck, knocking the Tower across the city. Akheron smirked, as they climbed the stairs into a lavish antechamber, ringed with unlit torches and servants. *What a way to perish that would be, strewn through the golden streets with white rubble...*

"You will have to wait here," Leto said to Akheron's comrades. Sunlight was streaming in the windows, but from here, they could see the coast of their island beyond the streets of the capital and the arms of the Cerden Mountains, across Galinor's Crossing.

Across the room from the stairwell was an elaborate archway. The ancient phrases written there were indistinguishable to Akheron—they could have been Ancestral proverbs and blessings or spells written with glyphs to guard the divine throne within.

"Bow at each of the statues and do not approach the guard until he invites you," Leto said, nodding down the corridor. There were three, carved of everwood perhaps, with a cushion in front of each. The cushions were ornately woven, with various

House colours and emblems upon each of them. At the end of the hall, a single guard stood before hefty wooden doors. He had gold armour that Akheron had never seen, carved with lines and the phrase "Sacred is the unified throne," in Ancestral. Leto touched Akheron's shoulder. "And answer, 'Akheron Gothikar, named Prince by the Nobles of Avernus,' when he asks you. I will follow you."

Akheron met her eyes. She bowed her head to him. Akheron swallowed, and then started his progression. First was the likeness of a man a little taller than Akheron. He had short hair and a small beard around his chin. The wooden eyes were what caught Akheron off guard. For some reason, even without pupils, he felt the statue watching him. Accusing him. This was Tiberon Odyn, and the government that sat in the chamber beyond was his greatest achievement. Akheron was a usurper and a liar and a fraud. He bowed to Tiberon, driving his knees into a cushion that bore the colours of House Odyn.

The second pillow was that of Syril Ivos. Akheron took to his knees again before the second founding father. The man was shorter than Akheron expected, assuming these statues had been carved to scale.

Thirdly, Valik Aristorn. Lord Aristorn had receding hair and a thick, long beard. He looked stronger than the other two, and nothing at all like old man Aristorn had, when Akheron had come for him. The Aristorn line had ended with the recently deceased Telvyn Aristorn. His ancestor did not look as fatherly as Akheron's predecessor had, covered in hair and fierce edges. Akheron stumbled as he took the knee, but corrected his movement and descended upon the blue and white cushion.

When he rose, with his head hung, he didn't step away.

"Who approaches the Throne of Midgard?" asked the sentry.

Akheron raised his head and shuffled his feet away from Aristorn's statue. He tried to remember the words Leto had given him. "I am Akheron ten Gothikar, whom the Nobles of Avernus have named Prince."

There was a pause, and then the guard intoned, "Welcome Prince of Avernus. The Throne bids you approach. May you receive your new duty."

As he walked forward, his shoulders and his chin rose. The

guard swung open the everwood doors and admitted the fury of Avernus into the Chamber of the Throne.

He took in his surroundings quickly, before moving on to the room's inhabitants. The fabled wooden throne sat to his left—every father, mother and child in the Dominion knew that their throne was an unadorned frame of wood with simple gold lines poured into the arms. It was not supposed to be a trophy, but a task. The only time anyone sat in the throne was when all three Imperial Princes elected one of themselves to shoulder sole responsibility for the entire Triumvirate. Akheron was mildly surprised to see that the actual throne was as mundane as the tales suggested.

The everwood table in the centre of the room was an equilateral triangle, allowing each of the Princes to sit in equal proportions to one another. Two of the seats were occupied, though the men seated there rose at Akheron's arrival. Across the table from the Throne, to Akheron's right, was a window angled toward the Mydarius. And that was it. A simple council room, in a tower that could bankrupt the Known World, inhabited by the men who held all that wealth.

"Welcome," said one of the men. He was a giant, close to Akheron's age, with a rectangular beard and short, military hair. "I am Prince Odyn."

Akheron nodded, his mouth dry. "Akheron Gothikar," he said. He could scarcely believe he was meeting the Princes. These men were legends, when Akheron was a young boy. The anger he had permitted within himself to survive House Aristorn rose for the first time in months. *You are the men who permitted such atrocities. Each of us suspects the truth of me—a usurper and a murderer. Yet here I stand, in the centre of your holy house.* He clenched his hands.

"I am Verin Theseus," said the second man. He was more proportionately human, without the torso-thick neck and towering visage. He had combed hair and was clean shaven, though his cheeks and chin bore a whiskery shadow. He reached out a hand, and Akheron had to release his fists to embrace it.

"Well met," Akheron said. *Glyphs, one day, the Maker will end us. This golden age of sin.*

"Leto!" boomed Odyn, embracing her bodily. She seemed distressed by this, when the mass of muscle released her.

Akheron wished he could fight Odyn. The man was physically superior, beyond any doubt.

"Crown Mage," Theseus said, with a bow.

This got a sly smile out of the influential woman. Her only task on the Council was to stop infighting among the Princes, and offer her advice, but they treated her as an equal.

The first order of business was to formally raise Akheron to the rank of Prince. It was a ceremony like the raising of a lord. The two Princes placed their blades upon Akheron's shoulders, to symbolize the weight of his new responsibilities. Words were said, in both languages, and then Akheron was no longer 'ten Gothikar', but 'Akheron Gothikar.'

The second change was the words of Akheron's House. As a lord, he had the authority to change the words of his family. The Gothikars' words were, *"Tu grunay nassi tu grunay ayen welkos,"* or, "The greatest passion wakes the greatest pain." Leto explained that his new words could be of his choosing or composed by a translator. Akheron had thought about this. He had researched extensively, but could never find the original Gothikar motto. It had been lost in the annals of time, though it had to do with *conquest* like most of the original Imperial Houses did. "Conquest stands alone," Akheron said. "I don't know the translation yet, but those words seem fitting." Their government was about unity and community, but that was not how Akheron had become Prince. Leto seemed to accept the phrase.

The first issue they discussed as the three Princes was the bandits inhabiting the ruins of Vyndrel. Akheron remembered its broken walls, debris strewn from the city's heights into the Mydarius itself, where the Trident River poured into the Sea. He had visited those men, seen the squalor of their lives and wondered how humans could exist in such a place, sharing their dirt with earth spawn.

"We should show up with a couple good Imperial troops," Odyn said. "I'll go myself, if no one else desires to. An Imperial with true military men will scare the rabble out of there before it becomes a den for rebellion."

Akheron raised an eyebrow. "They are miscreants who have no better place to live. If we scare them out of Vyndrel, they'll hide in some other hole. Better to burn them. That's what you do with pests."

Odyn seemed to consider his point, while Theseus gaped at him. The Prince of Athyns shook his head. "Those men are not all criminals. No doubt there are some, but they should be given trials and—"

"All men are criminals," Akheron said. "Kill them." *Perhaps that is where Demetas is hiding.* The great captain of the Buccaneers had disappeared.

"Listen to yourself," Theseus said. "Did we invite this opinion?"

"What?"

"You're a guest here, until you learn your place," Theseus said. "What do you know of how to treat rabble? You've called yourself a criminal within your first ten minutes as Prince! We've given you a place here, commoner, yet you would have us repay your kin with—"

"Verin!" Leto snapped, rising from her chair. It was near the window, not at the table. "You may not speak to a fellow Prince like that. Akheron is your equal."

"Bah," Theseus said. "He is a usurper and a schemer."

"What are you going to do about it?" Akheron asked, putting his hands on the table. *Are these the real men I've been looking for?* He had searched the Dominion for what he had always tried to be, but never found it. A good man would throw Akheron from this very window.

Leto overlooked Akheron's comment. "He was elected Prince by his Nobles, as your grandfather was. His words have as much right to be spoken here as yours."

Odyn chuckled, and said in jest, "Mine are the only words that have more right. An Odyn has sat here since the beginning of the Triumvirate."

The joke was lost on Theseus who was still shaking his head and staring at Akheron. "He doesn't even deny it," Theseus said.

Leto exaggerated a shrug. "The people of our realm *need* to know that this is possible. They need the hope and they need to see one of *theirs* with us."

"Even if he's a common criminal? Even if it's a delusion, not a hope?" Theseus asked.

"Yes," Leto said.

Akheron trembled as he sat back down. He had told them to burn the men living in Vyndrel's skeleton; he should have told them to burn themselves while they were there. He barely listened to the remainder of their discussion. He just kept his fists clenched as the Council ran its course.

Afterward, he bowed to the statues of this Maker-cursed government and said not a word to Mavas as he took her hand and led her downstairs. Edemar was waiting for them, presumably having wrapped up his own business.

Together they were sent back to Avernus. Leto left them with the words, "Akheron, I'm sorry for the difficulty with Theseus. He'll come around." She did not ask him if the other Prince's accusations held merit, like Ahryn had when the Nobles decided to elect him their leader.

On the rooftop in Avernus, Akheron breathed a sigh of relief. His city was still here, waiting for him. Embracing him. He felt the hairs on his arms stand up as he inhaled the smell of salt water and baked bread. The sun felt better here, and the colours were less... fake. This was his place. Now he was the Prince, and it was truly *his*.

"Wait with me, Akheron," Mar said, bringing Akheron's wandering mind back to the rooftop. Mavas and Haekus were already at the staircase on the side of the old stone building.

Akheron gave his friends a wave. "I'll meet you at the inn," he told Mavas. She knew the place.

Once they were gone, and Edemar and he were alone, the latter finally met his eyes. It seemed they had been avoiding each other recently. They had been friends for a long time, but things had somehow changed. Edemar had dark eyes, to go with his short dark hair. He was several years older than Akheron, but that had never been mentioned during their friendship.

"You will marry Reya."

"Glyphs, what?" Akheron asked, stepping back.

"Reya. She is one of my daughters. You've met her, when you last visited my estate. I have three. She's the oldest."

Akheron did not remember, though it seemed Edemar had started having children as soon as he had stopped being a corsair. "I do not want to marry your daughter," he said. "I don't want to marry anyone."

Edemar smirked. "You can't keep bedding Mavas forever.

You're a Prince now. You'll need a wife, and an heir. The Nobles will insist. The Princes will insist. The world will insist."

"No," Akheron said. "Why are you asking this of me?"

"You owe me," Mar said. Except, it wasn't Mar anymore. It was a lord, not a seafarer.

"This is all wrong," Akheron said. He shivered. The sun seemed more distant now, and the smell of saltwater had become bitter. "You're my friend, not my political competition."

"Exactly," Edemar said. "That's why you'll bind my family to yours, and not some other lord in this city."

Akheron closed his eyes. "I won't bind anyone's family to mine. The Gothikar family line ends with me."

"Glyphs, are you that far gone?" Edemar asked. "You're really one of those Buccaneers. A broken man, living a broken life. Get over it, whatever it is. You're a Prince. You're on top of this whole Dominion. If you're really so unsatisfied with your bloodline, bring an heir into this world and teach him how to be better."

Akheron shook his head again.

"Listen, Akheron. There are countless reasons for this favour. Whether we are friends or peers, whether it's political or a personal debt, swear to me that you will marry my daughter."

"Don't," Akheron said.

"Swear it, Prince. You think there is no threat here? I can't hurt you, is that it? Because you just don't care about your life or your status or anything. You care about family. I can have Tamese arrested. I could have Mavas hung for being the damn whore she is," Edemar saw his reaction, saw the fist clenching. "You know what she is. She's been with all of us. She's the Navy's personal—"

Akheron swung his fist at Edemar, but the man simply stepped aside. He knew Mar's words were true. It was the betrayal that threw that punch.

"Akheron, don't make this blackmail. Just accept my offer and your debt to me will be paid."

"We are friends. Friends do not deal in terms of debts and payments," Akheron said. "Mar, what happened? I thought you were making me Prince because you believed I could help. I never bought it, but otherwise it was simply because of our friendship."

Edemar laughed. "Friends then! We deal in terms of gifts. Gift me this favour. You'll marry my daughter, Akheron. Swear it."

"Glyphs." Akheron said. He turned his back on Edemar and stared out into the Valharyn ocean. It was his favourite water. The Mydarius was more accessible, it was warmer, and it was more colourful. The Valharyn was an endless grey prairie, and, every morning, Akheron wished to ride across that prairie into the rising sun. He shook his head again. He would not live long enough to marry Mar's daughter—she was not of age yet, and by the time she was, Akheron would be in the ground. *I must be,* he thought, *else the world will burn.* He remembered the conversation at the bar in the Royal Rogue that first day with the Buccaneers.

"I swear it," he said at last. "I'll marry your daughter, when the time comes."

Edemar clapped him on the back and said something jovial. Then Akheron was alone on the balcony. When he returned to Mavas, at the inn, he said nothing. He simply took her, like the "whore" she had been called, and then took her again. He was a Prince of the Triumvirate and a delusion for the commoners, like Leto had said. He might as well play the part.

26

At noon, a messenger came to fetch Akheron from his home in Avernus. The young boy, scarcely more than ten, had sandy hair and small eyes. He waved at the narrow porch where Akheron sat with Tamese. "Akheron ten Gothikar?" he called.

"That's me," Akheron said, standing up, "I suppose."

"They're ready for you at the Palace," the runner said. He was short on breath, but his words were easily understood. He must have been doing this for a year already.

Akheron closed his eyes. *At last. Mar, you'd better have done what you said.*

"Thanks," Tam, his sister, said. She stood up; she was not quite as tall as Akheron, but had kept the proportions desired of attractive women in their land since first coming of age. "We'll head up shortly."

The boy bowed and started to leave.

"Wait," Akheron said. He tossed the messenger a silver coin. "You're a good lad. Keep it."

The youngster bowed and jogged off.

Tamese patted Akheron's arm. "Are you ready?" she asked. She put her dark hair in a knot behind her head and smoothed the wrinkles in her dark green dress.

"I don't know what you got me into," Akheron said. "I know... it was as much circumstance as anything. But, glyphs... can you really see me as Prince?"

"No." It was Barun, standing in the doorframe of the Gothikar estate, who spoke. He was smiling, but his words held real criticism.

Tam rolled her eyes. "We're going now, sour face."

Barun chuckled. "Maker's blessings, Akheron."

Akheron pursed his lips and started down the stairs from the deck to the wide cobblestone street in front of their house. The Gothikar estate was built in the Residential District of Avernus, close enough to the Palace to take advantage of the comfortable avenues and pristine keeping. Akheron had been living in his father's old chambers since his public return to Avernus. When he wasn't in the way of his sister or her husband, he was finding an ale with Haekus or Mavas. More often than not, he slept in an inn with the latter, rather than intrude on his older sibling.

"A thanks or 'likewise blessings' might have been appreciated," Barun called, returning indoors.

The Maker's blessings, Akheron thought. "Must you have invited him to move in?" he asked.

Tam descended the steps and joined Akheron in the street. She wore a stylish dress, narrow from shoulders to toes. It was a dark green, with white folds that started at her flaunted hips. Sometimes, the brotherly urge within Akheron would rise up and he would wish she would hide her womanly curves. Her dark hair matched his, but she was easily the most attractive Gothikar. "Humorous," she said. "He asks me the same thing about you."

The comment, though intended in jest, hit too close to home. For a few steps they glided toward the Palace gate in silence. They passed one of the wealthiest estates in the district. It belonged to one Lord Ivos. It was only a few more blocks to the Keep. "Tam, you know my bitterness is false..."

"No, it's not," she said.

He never could lie to her. *Except that once,* he thought. "Be that as it may—my point is, I could not be more undeserving of, nor more thankful for, your hospitality."

She smirked. "That's kind. Did it take you long to figure out the right words?"

He winced.

"Sorry," she said, noticing. "I can't joke with you, not like I used to."

"What do you mean?" he asked. They passed the pride of the Residential District, the Bard of the Valharyn. The inn sat on the edge of the Merchant District, near one of the baileys that admitted passage to the Palace grounds. Someone had set up a games table in front of the inn, where a group of men were playing a game that looked similar to King's Gambit, an age old game with different names and sets of rules across the Dominion.

"Ever since you left... you've been different. I'm glad I convinced you to come home, but you're not the little brother you were," Tam said.

Akheron had nothing to say. He simply nodded, and they continued. Ahead, he saw something in the road, shining bright as the sun. It must have been a puddle of water, catching enough radiance to blind him. The closer he got, the less bright it was, until he reached it. When he looked down at the puddle, it was full of gravelly mud. There was no light at all, just dirt. *Is this true of great men?* he wondered. *The further away you are, the brighter they look. But if you look close enough, we're all just scum.* They were already calling him the great commoner and nodding to him in the streets or the Stead. Would he shine across the timeline as a hero?

He and Tam soon reached the guards of the Palace grounds. He had been within the Three Towers of Avernus a few times, over the years, but only once since the Grey Night. He shivered.

"'Morning," a guard said, approaching them with his helmet in the nook of his arm. He had more hair on his chin than his head, making his age difficult to place. "What brings you to the Palace today?"

"I've been summoned by the Nobles," Akheron said. "I'm Akheron ten Gothikar."

"Oh, you're him," the guard said. He glanced at one of his friends and nodded. The other sentry came closer, giving Akheron a look over. "I had heard you were a commoner, but I had yet to believe it."

"And now you do?" Akheron asked.

"Well..." the guard trailed off, flushing slightly. He had not intended insult. It could have been Akheron's manner, speech, or garb that gave away his position. Beyond the 'ten' in his name, of course. "I'm sorry, Master ten Gothikar. The Nobles have summoned you, as you say. We'd best not delay your arrival. Sir."

Akheron smirked. "Thank you, and, at ease."

Tam elbowed him once they were through, and whispered in his ear, "Listen to you! *Now* I can imagine you as a Prince!"

Akheron shook his head and led the way toward the Keep. There was still fire damage along the west side, where workers were hammering and sawing new wood for framing. There was an enormous stack of bricks against the front of the building, presumably to replace those that had blackened in the fire. Akheron shook his head and looked away from the damage. "Will you just wait in the Hall, then?" Akheron asked.

"Whatever you want," Tam said.

Akheron nodded. "I'll owe Mar," he said. "I already do."

Tam blinked. "I've never heard you say anything so, uh, responsible."

Akheron shook his head. "Wait here," he said, as soon as they entered the Hall.

A servant approached Akheron as soon as he entered. The short man smiled to him and asked, "Master Gothikar?"

Akheron swallowed. "That's me."

"The Nobles are waiting for you. This way, please."

Akheron followed the short man to the back of the Great Hall. There was a short stairwell here. As Akheron climbed it, he examined the stone tiles. The last time he had seen them, they had been stained with blood. The memory startled him, so he grabbed the hand rail to steady himself as they climbed. *How many men and women have climbed these steps without seeing such a thing?* he wondered.

They reached the second floor and the servant led him to a meeting chamber of some kind, on the far side of the Keep. The room had a small table in the center, surrounded by four chairs. Three of them were occupied by the most powerful men in Avernus, while the fourth was empty. The servant bowed and left, and the men stood up, one by one, to greet Akheron.

Edemar clasped his hand first. "I hope you slept," he said, with a wink. They had shared a beer the night before, with Yory and Haekus, down at the Gatehouse.

"Akheron," Ino said. They had met a few times over the past few months. They gripped palms.

"We meet again," said Ahryn, when Akheron turned to him. They had only met twice, and Edemar had told him last night that convincing Ahryn would be the trickiest part of his job. Ino had already been swayed. Weeks ago.

"Please, sit," Edemar said. They all claimed their chairs again. As Akheron sat at the table, he decided he would be one of the most powerful men in Avernus. After all, he sat at their table.

They offered him wine, which he declined. "Business first," he said.

Ahryn smiled. "You were right," he said to Ino.

Edemar appreciated this, so Akheron let the corners of his mouth rise too. "Very well," Mar said. "As you know, the election of a Prince must be unanimous among the Three Nobles."

"We may elect a Governor by a majority vote, but a true Prince may only be declared with the votes of all three of us," Ino said.

"And we've decided, together," Ahryn said. "That you may be the man for the job."

For a moment, no one said anything. They were waiting to see his reaction. Most of the time, the heirs of Princes were elected to replace their predecessor's without question. A hundred years ago, House Theseus—lords already—had replaced House Ivos as the Princes of Athyns, by the unanimous vote of the Nobles. But a commoner being elected was unheard of. It was legal, as Edemar had explained to Akheron, but had not transpired since the founding of the Triumvirate.

The Nobles thought they were giving a child an unexpected award and were hoping for laughter, smiles, and thanks.

"Glyphs," Akheron said, "I 'might' be? This is a lot more important than 'might.' Voice your doubts, then. There cannot be any doubts if you make me Prince."

Edemar raised his eyebrow. "We are already convince—"

"No," Ahryn said. "I would like to hear a few words first. There have been... allegations made, concerning your whereabouts during the Grey Night."

Akheron blinked. Edemar lowered his head into his hands. He looked like a man who had wasted away a fair bit already. Ino did not look defeated. He looked interested. Their thoughts and the truth had drifted too close together. "I watched my home burn," Akheron said. "My estate survived, though my uncle was slain and robbed. My sister had to hide in our cellar, while the raiders ruined her world. My friends were beaten and bloodied. But my home is none of these... the raiders burned *Avernus*, while I watched. I will not watch again. I will act."

Ahryn nodded. He bought it. Enough of Akheron's words expressed how he really felt that they rung as truth for Ahryn.

Akheron was not certain if the same could be said for Ino, but Ino did not seem to care. Edemar had won him over already, and he was not in it for truth.

"Any other *allegations* I need to lay rest to?" Akheron asked.

Ahryn folded his arms. "I'm more convinced than ever," he said. "Akheron ten Gothikar, you are our Prince."

Akheron sat back, satisfied at last.

"We will conduct the ceremony in Galinor, on the morrow," Edemar said. He took a sip of wine, and then began to pour Akheron some.

"Tomorrow?"

"Is that a problem?" Ino asked, amused.

Akheron shrugged. "How will we get there?"

"Leto, the Crown Magician, will teleport here with magic, and then bring us to Galinor with her. You will meet the other Princes and swear the oaths of the Triumvirate," Edemar said. He slid the wine glass across the table to Akheron with a smile. "But for now, take a breath. We trust you more than the other three contending houses. And you've got the people on your side, which is what really counts." Mar didn't add, though his eyes seemed to say, *"Unless they knew the truth..."*

If the people ever found out the truth it would be the end of Akheron.

Akheron took a breath, though. And he even took a drink of the red wine. He had done it. It had never been part of the plan. But he had done it.

"I did it," he said, in the Great Hall. Tam threw her arms around him. She had dreamed it first, and he had made it happen. For some reason, he wanted her to be proud of him. And she was.

That evening, before he joined Edemar and Mavas for a drink, he wandered out onto the piers in the Harbour. The sun had dipped below the horizon but the sky over the Mydarius was swollen and red. He looked east, into the Valharyn Sea. A small sliver of moon had set itself above the waves and was beginning its long climb. It would be a long time before it reached its heights.

A man was standing at the end of the dock, looking north. He held his hands behind his back, with his feet set firmly apart. At his waist hung a short sword and a dagger, uncovered by the red half-cape he wore. He didn't even stir when Akheron stepped up to the edge beside him.

"*Prince* Akheron, I presume," Sathius Miroso said, with a smile.

Akheron nodded. Sathius and a few of the other ships had been boarding and burning most of the ships that set out from the Avernan Port, so that Akheron could make good on the promise to end the Buccaneers' grip on Avernus. "You should get out of here, corsair."

Sath gave him a raised eyebrow and the two suppressed a chuckle. The raider extended his hand. "It's been an honour," he said.

"There's no honour among men like us," Akheron said. "If we catch Yory or you, it'll be during the last daylight you'll ever see. Nothing I can do about it. I've certainly enjoyed sailing with you, my friend."

Sath lowered his hand. "Daylight? I'll just make sure to sail at night."

"Have you heard from Demetas? He set sail at night."

Sath's face became dark. "No one's seen him, nor his crew, not since the raid. Mavas with you?"

"She is," Akheron allowed. "But you'd best keep that quiet amongst the others."

Sath nodded. "Good. Be seeing you, Akheron."

"And you, Sath." Akheron turned and walked back off the pier. As shadows descended on the port, the path along the Avernan cliffs became illuminated by its torches. Beneath it was Akheron's destination, one of his favourite water-front common rooms. It was a square structure built right against the rock, while the steps up to the other city districts wound above its shoulders.

In front of the Gatehouse, Haekus was waiting. The bulky stone alehouse was wrapped in the growing shadows and the evening smoke of the Harbour town, like an ember in a dying fire. The front door was set between two unshaped stone pillars, enormous grey slabs with braziers drilled into them. Haekus was leaning against the left one, underneath the flickering firelight. When he saw Akheron, he stood up. "Akheron," he said, "Well done!"

Edemar appeared in the doorway, smiling.

Akheron and Haekus gripped hands. "That's no way to talk to a Prince," Akheron said.

Haekus laughed, and Akheron forced a smile. "How's this then?" his friend said. He drew his sword and went down on one knee.

"What's this?"

"Akheron, my friend, you are now my Prince also. I have never had a cause to support, but went wherever I might challenge my blade," Haekus said.

"This isn't necessary," Akheron said.

"But now I have grown tired of my travels. I am ready to give my sword a purpose. I hereby swear fealty to Prince Akheron Gothikar. I will protect your life with mine and will obey all your commands. As my leader, I will serve you, and, as my friend, I will follow you."

"Glyphs," Akheron said. He grabbed Haekus's arm, past the sword, and pulled the fool to his feet. "Why would you swear something like—"

"Akheron!" Mavas shrieked, as she came flying through the open wooden door of the Gatehouse. She ran at Akheron and threw her arms around him. "You're a *Prince!*"

He hugged her back, stepping away from Haekus. The small dark-haired girl clung to him, and only pulled back to adjust her angle and press her lips against his. He kissed her as long as she wanted, ignorant of whatever his friends might be saying.

The next morning, he awoke in an inn room and untangled himself from her limbs. It was barely dawn, though he could hear the sounds of the harbour outside—voices shouting and wood being hammered. He leaned close to her, and pressed his nose into her hair to whisper, "I have to go," into her ear.

She didn't respond. He pulled on his tunic and then sat down on the bed to lace his boots. "Why?" she mumbled sleepily.

"I'm going to Galinor today. To become Prince." He stood up.

"Great Glyph, how are you going to Galinor *today?*" she pulled herself up against the pillows, the bed sheets draped against her.

Akheron turned at his waist and kissed her. "Magic," he said. "Want to come with?"

Mavas nodded sleepily. "Wait for me."

"Fine. I'll be downstairs." He realized belatedly that this couldn't be the Gatehouse. The Gatehouse had no rooms. *Where am I?* He remembered very few details of the prior night.

He closed the door quickly when he stepped into the hallway for Mavas had stepped out from under the bedcovers. The corridor was empty, however, and he slowly made his way towards the door at the end. It turned out to be a one-storey inn. He did not descend any stairs, simply stepped out of the hallway into a small, cluttered common room. A few bodies were asleep at their tables. The innkeeper was awake, quietly trying to clean up the mess. Akheron stared once he noticed that the man's back was more than bent over to clean.

"Your friend is waiting out front," the hunchbacked man said.

Akheron left the tiny sleeping house feeling rather dirty. It must have been the lowest, dullest place to stay in the city. "I'm a Prince now..." Akheron said. "What am I doing here?"

Haekus was the friend in question. He was sitting on the three steps that led to the front door of the inn. Many of the buildings in the Harbour district were raised buildings to help them in the stormy winter season. The Gate—the span of water between the Mydarius and Valharyn seas—was dangerous that time of year. "You said you just needed a bed," Haekus said, standing up. "And that you didn't care where."

"Mar?"

"He went back to his estate," Haekus recounted. "Wherever that is."

"Huh." Akheron held his head. The sun had blinded him, and only now his surroundings revealed themselves. The inn, which was named "Orinar's Back" by a wicker sign nearby, sat as close to the shore as a building possibly could. A span of rough black rocks were the only semblance of a bank to divide the property of Orinar's Back from the ocean itself. The nearest wharf, no more than a hundred feet away, was bustling with fishermen and sailors, who were loading the nearest galley or manning the small fishing rafts docked at it.

"Are we heading up to the city? You said we were teleporting to Galinor today..."

"We?" Akheron asked. He had never been a heavy enough drinker to warrant the morning consequences, but he imagined this was as close to that feeling as he wanted to get. His head was killing him. "Did you really swear your life to mine last night?"

Haekus nodded. The man had let his beard grow a bit more, recently, so his head was covered in tightly curled red hair. He could have any wife he wanted or any military position he requested, but he had made a fool's oath to Akheron. "I did."

"Glyphs," Akheron said. He sat down where Haekus had been sitting, and found the sea-salt smoothed wood to be most comfortable, despite its dampness. "All the others are quick to leave me, like Demetas and Sath, while others seek to use me, like Mar is. You're the only one who's here just to stick with me... Why?"

"Mavas is sticking with you, too," Haekus pointed out, avoiding the question. Akheron felt like they weren't seeing eye to eye, the way they had for the past few months. Haekus's vow had changed things, no matter what he had intended it to mean.

"Yes, because we sleep together!" Akheron exclaimed. One of the sleeping men from inside had chosen that moment to leave, and he laughed at Akheron's words. Akheron shook his head and then pressed his palm to his forehead. "I hope you are not interested in..."

"Certainly not," Haekus said. They looked away from each other, uncomfortably. "It is exactly how I said it last night. I became a master of all the things I wanted to, and that's left me looking for something. I've never changed anything big before. Now we've changed the government itself. Glyphs, I want to keep being a part of something. And I want you to continue being a part of it as well. Swearing to defend you is the most sincere solution."

"Sincere? Glyphs." Akheron had no idea where his life was

going anymore.

"'Morning Haekus," Mavas said, coming out of the inn. Her short dark hair was brushed back and she was now wearing her long, dark red coat, almost like a cloak, with thin black pants beneath. "What are you doing here?"

"Going to Galinor, apparently," Haekus said. Akheron groaned. Before the sun set, he would become an Imperial Prince in the Tower of the Throne.

27

He had to see Tam again. He had been in Avernus for a week, watching them rebuild. At noon, the day after the corsairs left, the army arrived. Within two days, the rubble had been cleaned from the streets. The Nobles—Edemar included—had offered a gold coin to any man, woman, or child, for *each* day they helped. On the third day, timber was brought in and repairs began.

One of the few buildings that had remained untouched by the raid was the Stead of Avernus. There was actually a handful of holy meeting places in the city, but only one of them bore the title of Stead. The others were considered mere Chapels, to help the Kin meet the demand of a much larger population. At the top of the common class, the Gothikars had long attended the titular Stead.

On the Eve of Reflection, the building was packed. Everyone was terrified. The Buccaneer Navy had sacked the city and killed hundreds, including their Prince. The Stead had turned away more refugees on that night, but had defended its sanctum from the corsairs with elite soldiers—they had stood strong where even the Prince's guards had failed. Likely, most of the corsairs had decided it was not worth the trouble.

But now, the people wanted answers. Their homes had been invaded, their safety proven an illusion. They demanded that the Kin and the Maker himself explain.

Akheron did not seek such answers here. He sought his sister.

"The Maker was with us, a week ago," the Kin preacher

said, translating the words that another man spoke in the Ancestral Tongue. "Each of us who survived was blessed by the Maker to do so."

"My son wasn't blessed?" a man's voice demanded, as Akheron pressed, shoulder-to-shoulder, toward the seating within the building. The antechamber was packed, the hallway packed, the aisles packed. The seating area ran in a circle around the central dais, where beams of sunlight reached down from the sky to enclose the priests in a golden glow. "Why not?" the townsman demanded.

Akheron noticed Mar and his fellow Nobles sitting across the circle, in the front row. If Akheron's friend saw him squeezing through the crowd, he did not show it.

"The Maker does not approve of the Buccaneers, yet they have drawn the admiration of many commoners."

"Not my son!" the man retorted. Akheron finally got his eyes on the red-faced speaker. It was Ban ten Kear, the tailor. Sometimes, he had bought leather from Akheron or his father. Years ago.

"Of course not," the Kin said gently. "The Maker wished no harm upon your son. He made your son a hero. It is only by allowing such a grievous offence to transpire that something will be done about such bandits."

"The Maker made your son a martyr, Master Kear," said the Ancestral speaker, in the common tongue. He had interrupted tradition to give a more sensitive word of comfort to the mourning father.

But so many of the crowd were mourning, that the kind words were lost in a flurry of other examples. The people wanted to know *why* their loved ones had been chosen. Did their loved ones find peace at the Maker's side?

There can be no peace. Not in this life, nor the next, Akheron thought. *For it is our nature to sin.* The thought faded sourly, as he began to notice more familiar faces in the crowd. He had grown up with these people. The elderly had been working citizens when Akheron was growing up. They had attended the Kinship's services together. This was the community who raised him—their cobbler, Tonan ten Uris; Janfar, the best blacksmith in Avernus; the baker who had lived two doors from Veldar ten Gothikar's tannery, Balmah ten

Rysarius. Balmah's husband had been one of the chief merchants for the repairs, procuring tools, nails and furnishings for many citizens who could not afford it. These were the same people they had been all along. Where had Akheron gone? Whom had he become?

He finally noticed Tam. She was not angry, though she was wiping her eyes. She had been involved in some of the clean-up efforts, but Akheron had avoided her until now. He touched another woman on the shoulder, so she would shift away from Tam's side. Then, he sat down beside his sister.

She was listening intently, and didn't look around for a moment. When she finally started to notice that her peripherals had changed, she glanced sharply at him and then her hand went to her mouth. "You're back," she breathed, and then embraced him. "Thank the Maker, you're back!"

Her explanation drew the attention of those nearby. She didn't care though. He started to blink back tears as she sobbed into his shoulder. "Uncle was killed," she told him. "But Barun is fine. When did you get here?"

He tried to answer, but one of the men standing nearby gave them a loud, "Shh!"

"This is Akheron Gothikar," Tamese told him. She stood up and glanced around her. "Returned at last."

The man blinked. His wife raised a hand to her mouth, staring at Akheron. Another man clapped Akheron on the shoulder. He recognized the man, but had never spoken to him before. "Welcome home," said the woman who had moved to allow Akheron near his sister.

"Is there a problem?" asked Ban Kear, standing at the front row. He noticed Akheron and his jaw dropped. Akheron weakly raised his hand and gave his best attempt at a smile.

Even the Kin recognized Akheron. "Welcome back, wayward traveller," said the translator, though his fellow speaker had not made a noise.

"Everyone!" Tam raised her hands. "This is Akheron Gothikar. He was the favourite of our beloved late Prince, and he has returned home from across the Dominion in our time of need. If you look for work or stories, ask him. If you look for advice, I'm sure he'll have something sensible to say. The Kin claim that the Maker provides—they have provided yet another natural leader to our community. Akheron?"

Akheron stared around. Everyone in the crowded hall was staring at him. *Why? Do they know?* The thought flitted across his mind and nearly drove him mad. He sent it through that dark doorway in the corner of his head, where it could disturb no one.

As he stood up, he leaned close to Tam's ear and asked, "Why?"

"You told me you couldn't come back without a purpose, and that you thought you had found a purpose *out there*. So, now you've got a purpose here," she said, with a smile. Then she winked, and added, "Sorry."

Akheron turned back to the waiting crowd. He glanced at Mar, seated twenty feet away. His friend's expression was unreadable. He was watching with an analytical eye. Akheron looked away, and took a deep breath. "I don't know how I can help," he said. The Maker knew that Akheron had a lot of dishonesty in his life, but there were no reasons to lie in this circumstance. "But I'm here now, so that's a good first step. I left for a few years. To get my head on straight, I guess. I can certain help with building. I've always been good with my han.... I've always been skilled at that sort of thing." He consciously rubbed his palms against his tunic.

The community continued to wait. He tugged at his collar. He had been wearing the same clothes for a few days; combined with his poorly chosen words, he positively *itched.* "It's not right, what you've all been through. Not right at all. I'll try to do something about that. Might be some way to convince the corsairs to leave our city be. I guess my sister is right though. I hope I can help enough. We've got to put things back together."

Someone clapped. Then another joined in. Tam was the third, but before long, the whole crowd was clapping their hands. Akheron awkwardly bowed. When he rose, he saw Mar clapping his hands lazily. Now his friend had a sly smile on his face. But he did not give any familiar reaction to Akheron.

Tam tugged on his arm. She was crying, again. He decided to forget about Mar for a bit. He was home. He forgot about the crowd, grabbed Tam's shoulders and pulled her close.

28

At no point was the Grey Night like any other night to have passed or yet to pass. It was during the end of the winter, when the Valharyn storms relented and risky captains might set sail. Ten such set sail from the Elysian Point at dawn. They sailed south, across The Gate. It was a hundred-and-fifty miles to Avernus, and the ships—flying only black flags—made the journey in a little over fourteen hours. The Grey Night began then, like many nights did, with a red sun sinking across the Mydarius Sea and the moon peaking its crooked head above the grey Valharyn.

Akheron Gothikar stood at the helm of one of the ships that evening. Twilight slowly crept upon him, tendrils of grey and blue that claimed the sky from the sun's golden glow. He was wearing the dark rain-proof coat Sath had once bought him, and the tall leather boots he kept clean with saliva and a cloth. At his waist hung the sword Mavas had given to him, a short weapon with a wide blade—too wide for a sheath—and an old knife he had kept from his days growing up in Avernus. Avernus. As the night began, he watched for it on the horizon.

Beside him stood Demetas, his hands on the wheel. He was a truly ugly man, with a bulbous nose, a wide chin, and deep eyes. Since the foundation of the Navy, he kept his head completely shaven, though it had sideburns and a band of scruff across the bottom half of his face. The wheel was gripped in one of his hands, while the other fidgeted with the ring it habitually tortured. His legs were spread apart, and he rode the waves with an admirable ease.

Edemar stood behind them, leaning against the rail of the deck. He was sharpening his sword on a small whetstone.

"No turning back now," Demetas said. His ship, the *Astral Arrow*, led the voyage, with Sath's *Salty Shadow* close behind. The *Sky Hound* was a few ships back, with Yory at its helm and Haekus at her side. The legendary blade-master rarely got along with Sath. A handful of other ships had been chosen to accompany them on this particular raid. Almost half the Buccaneer Navy, though two ships would remain on the fringe of Avernus' harbour in case things went wrong.

Akheron wished he could tell Demetas to stop, to turn the ship around. But he couldn't. "No turning now," he said, quietly.

Before long, the islands came into view. Half an hour after that, and the Avernan harbour did. The sound of waves was louder than the hushed voices of the corsairs. They were waiting for the city. Then they would make noise.

Above the harbour, looming out of the night with crackling torches and glowing lanterns, was the Imperial City of Avernus. From the ocean, it looked like it clung to the cliff with dangerous risk of falling in. There was a single-storey wall against the rocky edge, with a well-lit gate where the line of torches descended the cliff to the harbour. Above the short wall loomed two-and-three storey buildings—wealthy inns and estates of the upper class who wanted to watch the sea. From the water below, the small castles looked precariously balanced on the edge. But from the other side of the city, miles away, the view revealed the hills and flats that the city spanned. It did not cling to the edge of the Gate, but seemed to determine the very passage of the ocean and the sun. It was said that a hundred-thousand citizens lived in the Residential District, and that could not have been much more than a third of the city's populace.

The harbour that the ships approached was tiny in comparison, though it was an ambitious trading centre. It held a dozen enormous wharfs, countless warehouses and the business headquarters of many merchants. Not to mention the inns. Akheron had bragged to Mavas that they could spend the night in a different inn every night for the first year they stayed in Avernus. If she stayed that long. The matter was still under undecided.

The *Astral Arrow* was the first ship to throw its lines onto a wharf. The harbour boys didn't know any better; they pulled the ship in slowly, and tied the galleon against the berths. Akheron was the first over the side. He leapt down onto the quay—this was not the first port he had raided—and proceeded to stride toward solid ground. The ropers stared at him, when he slammed onto the dock. There were three guards on duty, clustered around a fire pit in the middle of the harbour's yard.

Akheron and Demetas killed them without noise. Akheron grabbed one from behind, covering his mouth with a palm while he slit the guard's nearest companion's throat. There was only a gurgle and a horrified grunt from the man he held. Then that man joined his comrade in the water. Demetas's target was already in the salt.

The city would be a quiet infiltration, but they had to unload seven ships, and there was no way to do that without owning the marina entirely. With the guards out of the way, the crew of the *Arrow* kicked in the doors of the buildings at the bottom of the cliffs. Even the warehouses admitted a corsair or two. Every building here had to be watched, and any man or woman who attempted to flee the harbour would be called back or killed. Demetas positioned a few of their rare archers on the stairs themselves.

Up, they marched, to the wide gate into Avernus. Akheron walked with his hand around Mavas's hips. Ahead walked Demetas and Sath. Behind marched Haekus and Mar. Together, one last time, the Buccaneer Navy entered the city.

When Akheron had at first reached the Palace of Avernus, the looters, raiders corsairs, and Mavas had nearly finished pillaging all the streets. Houses lay in ruins, their organs and intestines pulled out into the street—overturned upholstered chairs, varnished tables, burning paintings and bloodied books. Their inhabitants, like little hearts, dotted the carnage with blossoms of dark red. Some citizens had joined the attackers, embracing the anarchy to find some way to survive it. Many had simply fled.

There was already someone wailing inside of the Avernan Palace. Akheron, Haekus and half a dozen raiders approached through the main street. It led toward the gate, where someone's shrieks were echoing through the haze. Above them, the murky sky reflected the fires in the city's innards; through the smoke and the glow of this abyss, the world had turned grey. Before the night was done, Akheron decided, all light would fade from Midgard.

"Akheron!" a voice called. A woman's voice. Mavas came out from an adjoining street with three bloodied corsairs under her wing. She pressed through Akheron's makeshift entourage and kissed him. They had brought the shadows upon the city, the sort of shadows left in the Maker's absence. Akheron had felt it before. He shivered, and pulled away from Mavas's mouth. "I love you," she said. "You wanted to hear it, but I wasn't ready. But *this* is right. We are taking what we deserve from these... tyrants." Her eyes were alive, like the crackling fires in the nearby inn—the Golden Stallion, which catered to the upper class of the city—and her breath was panting.

"No," Akheron said. He wished that cursed screamer would quiet. The sound was truly horrid. "We cannot be redeemed for this."

"Redeemed?" Mavas asked. Even Haekus had snorted at his words. "Glyphs, if you're not an odd one."

"I told you," Akheron said. His escort was getting anxious. "When I told you I loved you, I told you I can't tonight. Go find Demetas or Sath... there's plenty to be done in Avernus, for corsairs. Only one thing left for the true sinners like me."

"Glad to be added into that summation," Haekus said dryly.

Akheron gave him a glare. The lanky warrior could certainly be infuriating when he wanted to be.

Mavas shrugged. "Fine. I just wanted to tell you... Oh, forget it."

Akheron grabbed her to stop her from turning away. *This could be the end. The last night. If the Maker permits it.* Akheron would kill or be killed, a dilemma he would be forced into eventually, no matter what. *No matter what happens, there will be peace for me, after this.* "I hope to see you again," he told Mavas. It felt honest. "I'll love you unhindered on the morrow. But tonight... tonight I have only one name in my head."

"Telvyn Aristorn."

Akheron pursed his lips and looked past her, into the grey void of his destruction. "Something like that." He started to walk away.

"Come back to me, Akheron," Mavas said. "I'll be here, even if there's only ruin left!"

He spun on his heel, grabbed her in his arms and enveloped her into his torso. The tears came unbidden. In another life, another world—a far less cruel phantasm—she was the first woman he had loved. And he had not failed her. He had not lost her. Together, they had faced the world and become everything they could be. Now instead, Akheron was a shade of the Maker's dream, and Mavas was just his fix. He wouldn't release her, when she gently tried to pull away from his embrace. "Glyphs, I wish it wasn't this way," he whispered. He never let anyone see him like this, let alone Haekus and the other raiders. "I wish..."

"Don't wish. Go kill that earth-spawn on the hill," Mavas said. "And then come back to me."

He kissed her briefly, and then turned away. He did not trust himself to look back. He led his men up the hill. The Palace guards must have seen them already, for the wailer had been silenced, and steel gleamed in the firelight ahead. Mavas didn't say anything more as he left her in the grey night.

Like a mug of overturned ale, the corsairs fell upon the Palace guardians. Akheron killed two himself—the first with a sudden thrust against an unaware opponent, the second with a shield, bashed against his head with enough force to break the cobblestones. Haekus must have defeated five, on his own. He was still the *Red Dancer*, even after all of these years out of the public sphere; he shifted eloquently between men, educating them on the afterlife as he made a work of art out of their innards. The other raiders gave him a wide berth.

Once the guards had been dealt with, the raiding party split up. Most of them were sent to ravage the barracks of any off-duty guards. Haekus and Akheron strode through the Keep's double doors.

There, they were besought by two other soldiers. These wore enormous plate armour, and strode with the determination of loyalty. These were Aristorn's most trusted. *I was once Aristorn's most trusted...* Akheron thought. The thought of what was to come filled him with a black dread, weighing him down.

Haekus charged the first of these knights. The man wielded a mace, allowing the dextrous blade-master to duck past. The knight was forced to turn and continue facing his enemy, leaving

Akheron with only one soldier.

The bulky man made the first attack, lunging forward as though to keep Akheron off guard. His sword, wielded with ease despite it being a two-handed weapon, was easy to see coming. Akheron effortlessly stepped out of range, coincidentally back into the courtyard. Their duel became a game of spacing; the knight would swing his blade in a wide circle, and Akheron would step back or duck under. His own attacks, when he could risk them, glanced harmlessly off of the shiny plate armour. This was likely the finest armour that money could buy—Akheron had seen many sets of plate, but never one so effective or manoeuvrable as this.

He could hear Haekus cursing, and the echo of blades within the Great Hall. There was an overturned table already, visible from outside.

The knight came at Akheron again. This time, his swing was a feint and he used his mass to ram into Akheron. The plate armour sent Akheron rolling across the cobblestones. Dazed, he tried to reclaim his feet. He got one foot under him, and then pushed upward. A fist was there, clad in shiny steel.

The gauntlet dropped Akheron against the stones and everything went black. *I need to get to Aristorn before I die,* he thought. The Prince. The greatest Prince. *I need to tell him, before I go. Please, Maker...*

For once, the Maker answered his prayer. The knight stood over Akheron, with his feet on either side. He raised his sword for a killing thrust, and then a mace knocked his head against his shoulder. The ringing of steel echoed off of the two-storey Keep.

The soldier stumbled to a side, his head ringing. Haekus dropped the mace beside Akheron and lifted his own weapon's hilt up to his ear. The narrow sword slid into the visor of the knight's helm as the warrior tried to reclaim his balance. Haekus yanked the blade free and Aristorn's guard tumbled over with a painful crash.

Akheron shook his head, and put a hand to his ears. He stood up. His eyes felt dry, though he had been weeping already. He rubbed them gingerly with his dirtied hands. Then he inspected his palms. There was a lot of dirt, from the cobblestones, the ships, the fights... it had been a long, long day. He tried to rub them clean on his treated coat—the hide one tempered to be waterproof—but it was as dirty as they were.

"Are you alright?" Haekus asked, wiping his sword on the corner of his tunic. He was drenched in sweat and blood.

Without a word, Akheron reclaimed his feet. "Where is Telvyn?" he asked.

His friend shrugged.

Together, they approached the Keep again. The second knight lay against a blood-streaked wall. Haekus had found a weak spot in the armour, where he could jam his sword between two plates.

The Great Hall was completely abandoned. There were cold meals on some of the tables, though some were scattered from the commotion of the night. Other tables had been knocked over completely. The high roof of the Palace's first floor felt like Akheron's innards, stretched out and gaping like the maw of some starved monster.

As they climbed the steps to the second floor, Akheron shouted, "Aristorn! I've come for you! Where are you? Aristorn!" His words echoed through the halls. A servant scurried away from the top of the stairwell, just a meek little face that peeked down and then vanished. Akheron could hear footsteps and the latching of doors.

"Aristorn!" he bellowed again. They reached the second storey. Akheron used the hand rail to steady himself. His feet missed the steps occasionally. He ignored Haekus's concern.

"Face me!" he shouted, marching past the servant quarters. "Face me like a Prince!"

The servant quarters opened and a woman tried to run out. Akheron ran her through the side, and turned back down the hall. "Aristorn!" he shrieked.

A door opened, down the corridor. He did not know what room it hid.

The man that stepped into the hallway was close to Haekus's height. He had eyes so blue, they looked blue even from this distance. His hair was a mess, half of it tied behind his head. He looked like the Aristorn that Akheron remembered, the man Akheron had admired, but older and more angry. This was a man defined by fury and loss. His skin was wrinkled with age, but the smile lines had been crossed by the lines of a perpetual frown. And the blue eyes were no longer welcoming. They were glacial pits, offering to freeze Akheron.

"Aristorn," Akheron said.

"Don't move," Telvyn Aristorn said. The Prince was armed, but had not yet drawn his weapon. His blue eyes flicked to both sides of Akheron, where two guards stood. They had flanked both Akheron and Haekus.

"I'm going to move," Akheron said. He was forced to inhale. His eyes no longer felt dry. Now they stung. "Telvyn, I'm going to move."

"They'll kill you," Telvyn said. "Glyphs, you deserve worse for what you have done."

"I do," Akheron said, calmly. He took a step forward, followed by another.

Telvyn stepped back, but his eyes flicked toward the soldier that was nearest Akheron. The man must've raised his blade by now.

Without hindering his shuffle, Akheron swung his blade back, twisting at the waist and shoulders. The guard went down without a noise, slashed open from shoulder to hip.

Telvyn stepped back again. Haekus and the other guard clashed, behind Akheron, but the sound seemed distant. He glanced behind him; the hall seemed to stretch on for a mile, and at the end of the mile, his friend fought a common guard.

He switched his gaze back to his target. Telvyn was almost upon him though, slamming his sword downward.

Akheron leapt to the side, and the blade missed. He swung his own bloodied sword, and Prince Aristorn knocked it aside with a block. Akheron did not stop walking forward. Telvyn Aristorn did not stop walking backward.

They entered the room with the open door. Again their swords met. They were just testing each other.

A woman ran at Akheron from the side. She was holding a short blade of some kind. Akheron knocked her aside, easily. She tripped on a chair, and rolled on the wooden flooring. The Prince leapt to save her, but Akheron fended him off. It was Lady Aristorn. She was a wrinkled old snake now, nothing like the motherly hen he had once known. She stared up at him, cradling her hand and whispered, "You should never have come back here..." Her volume raised. "You were our very best! You took her! Oh, Eth—"

He slid his sword into her, sobbing as he did so. Telvyn came at him in a frenzy, shouting and cursing and knocking Akheron off his wife. Blood splattered across the floor and the murderer found himself pinned against the wall. Where had Aristorn's sword gone? Where had Akheron's?

"Glyphs! You killed her! Magician! Someone! Great Glyph..." A fist found Akheron's face. Then another. He felt blood bubbling from his nose. The next blow stuck his stomach and he doubled over. Telvyn pulled Akheron away from the wall. "Why? Oh, Akheron, why?"

Akheron had no words to say. He faced his fate with a raised chin.

Telvyn wrapped his hands around Akheron's throat. "Maker burn you," he prayed. He was a highly religious man, and never cursed with the Maker's name. Save now.

The air became short. Akheron had expelled almost all of his before the Prince's hands had found him.

"Is nothing in this world worth it?" Telvyn asked.

Mavas. And the one before.

Akheron lashed out with a hand, and caught Telvyn's chin. The man's head dazed sideways, and Akheron slammed his forearm against his assailant's, breaking his stranglehold. *I came here to finish this. To close this chapter. I came here to face my accuser. Not to die.*

He slithered free of the stunned Prince and kicked him backward before trying to reclaim his feet. He found Telvyn's sword against the leg of a table and scooped it up.

In the wreckage of the room, in the shadows of the grey night, Akheron faced his enemy. "It's over, Telvyn."

"Why did you come back here?" the old man mumbled. He had Akheron's sword in his hands and the hilt was now red with Akheron's own blood, smearing the Prince's hands.

"You left, which is far more than you deserved. You left, after it all, and I *let you.* Glyphs, I should have hunted you across both seas, through the Gate and into the shadows where the Maker doesn't see."

"Why didn't you?" Akheron asked. The Keep seemed eerily quiet, after the battle in the streets. Where was Haekus?

"You were like a son to me!" Telvyn said. "We would have been family... we could have been! You... look at this!" Spittle flung with his words, and his hand swung around him. "You have taken everything from me! My city, my wife, my family. Is this how you repaid your debt to me?"

"Glyphs," Akheron said, "It was never supposed to be this way."

"No! It was not. Why, Akheron?"

"Because it's what I am," Akheron said. "And the Maker did not see fit to save me when he had the chance."

"My son, my son," Telvyn whispered. "There is no rest where the Maker will send you. You cannot persevere through this life in hopes of a better one beyond. For beyond this world are only the fires of our God's wrath."

"I know," Akheron said. He lifted his chin. "This world is no fit place for me. If the Maker ever sees fit to give me what I should get, I will burn for a thousand years. You, you will get to see your family again."

Telvyn nodded. "You've taken it all from me, all save my life. Go on then, get it over with."

Akheron nodded. He closed his eyes for a moment. *It has all gone so wrong... I was never supposed to meet Mavas, let alone be saved from the edge of death by thoughts of her.* He took a deep breath and slowly exhaled it. *Stop me, Maker.* But Lady Aristorn already lay dead. And her blood was on Akheron's hands along with that of a hundred men and women of Avernus. The Maker had not stopped Akheron. He had let Akheron desecrate the human form, he had let Akheron ruin the human society, he had let Akheron stomp out his own soul. *Curse you, Maker. Curse you to your own shadows.*

Telvyn Aristorn was the last person to know what Akheron had done, and he would die for it.

He opened his eyes and advanced on Telvyn, slashing at him with the sword. Telvyn put up a good fight. He parried the first blow and ducked under the second. Perhaps he wanted to bring Akheron into the next world with him, send him down to the pits of the Maker's fury personally. But the Prince of Avernus could not hold his ground against Akheron.

They passed through a curtained door, which was slashed to pieces. Beyond was Telvyn's bedchamber; a four-poster bed held the center of the room, surrounded by shelves and drawers.

Akheron thrust and nicked the Prince in the upper thigh.

The man limped back a step, dropped to one knee, and then stabbed outward with his sword. The misleading move caught Akheron off-guard and his intestines were nearly impaled upon his adversary's steel.

He slid to the right, earning himself a gash along his left side, under the ribcage. His dodge sent him off balance, and he steadied himself on a short wardrobe. Telvyn, spry for his age, slammed bodily into Akheron, his blade swinging too wide, thanks to Akheron's off balance lean. Together, they tumbled to the floor tiles along with the entire wardrobe. Akheron recovered first. He shoved himself to his feet with a rough heave of muscle. Telvyn was slower to stand, trying to lift Akheron's sword to ward himself.

Akheron drove Telvyn's downward, over top of the angled parry, and into the Prince's torso. Aristorn hung upon his blade, took a bloody last breath, and then oozed sickly off the steel weapon.

Akheron stood alone in the bloodied room for a long moment. Outside he could hear the sound of combat. There was still no sign of Haekus. Perhaps he had left Akheron to his fate, like a wise man would. There was smoke on the air, stronger than it had been outside. Someone had set fire to this Keep.

Akheron found the deep breath he took to be most refreshing. He had to try not to cough on the fumes, but he felt great. He dropped Aristorn's sword on the old man's corpse, and inhaled again. No one knew now. The creature of evil that Akheron had created was alone in his head now, and could finally give the world some peace. No one knew. He was safe. He exhaled and went to find his friends.

With Aristorn out of the way, there was one loose end to tie up. He had to make sure the world could have some peace now. He descended through the grey night. It was not simply grey from the smoke, but from the glow that kept the night's darkness at bay. He journeyed through the wreckage, from the heights of Avernus to the port where the raiders were celebrating their victory. There were women, some by choice, some by coin, some by force. There was gold, coins and trinkets that filled the hands of the corsairs and adorned their clothes. The smoke of the city made a low roof over their heads. The quiet breeze of the

Avernan plateau pushed the sickly fog out of the city and over the cliffs, leaving the harbour under its belly. The writhing party of men and monsters was slowly waning as the galleons filled their holds with the spoils of the raid. Akheron saw Yory, shouting from her deck at some stubborn raiders.

"So we're done?" Demetas asked when Akheron found him. The chief Buccaneer had his arm around a woman with bright blonde hair and bright white skin. Akheron had never seen her before. In his other hand, Demetas held his sword, *Snake,* with its blade only covered by a robe of blood. He released the harlot when he saw Akheron, and firmly clasped his hand. "You finished off the Prince himself?"

"I did," Akheron said. He folded his arms and smiled.

"And you return to me with no sword!" Demetas finally decided to clean his Snake. He grabbed hold of the woman's shirt, a garment torn to be revealing, and wiped the dry blood off on it. He ignored her protests, and simply gave her one of his distasteful smiles. Demetas was the furthest from an appealing man, but he had the charisma to dwarf most politicians and the coin to back it.

Akheron shrugged. "I don't think I've a need for a sword anymore."

"Glyphs," the corsair said. He led the way onto one of the docks. The woman did not protest at this; perhaps she was joining the crew of the *Astral Arrow.* "Glyphs, you really are done now, aren't you? I didn't think you were serious when you said you had one task left to do. I thought it was all talk."

Akheron sighed. "I'm sorry, Demetas. I've got my own way to go."

"You and Haekus both," he said.

"Haekus?" Akheron asked, surprised. He hadn't seen the fighter since they reached the Palace. Even now, it seemed like a day ago.

"He says he's staying in Avernus," Demetas said. "I don't know why. We've made a campfire out of it! Those obsessed with their feet on solid ground do love fire, so we gave them some more."

"Wait, where's the *Arrow?"*

Demetas glanced at him. "I said we set the place on fire— the embers and ashes that rained on this port, well, I wouldn't risk my livelihood on it. Most of the ships pulled back to the Northern Rock, though we've called a few to the port for the sake of transporting our goods..."

Akheron nodded. "I need to talk to you before—"

"Come to the *Arrow* with me," Demetas said. He raised a hand to block Akheron's interruptions. "I'm taking this rowboat, but I've no place for it with my fleet. Row there with me, we'll talk, and then row back to the cinders of your city."

Akheron nodded. "Very well," he said. It had been a while since he had been alone with Demetas; Mavas or one of the others was always around. Mar had become particularly nosy of late. He glanced at the prostitute; she had lost the look of seduction and now looked confused. The rowboat was not large enough for three. At least, not in a comfortable way.

"Yes, you're staying here. I'm sure you can find some other man to pay for your night," Demetas said. He stepped into the rowboat, steadying it against the side of the wharf. "Toss me the statue, love."

"But, you said—"

"I never said the statue was yours to keep," the corsair said. He held his hands out for it, though the woman made no statue appear.

"No, I mean, you were going to take me to see—"

"There's no romantic sights where we're going. Trust me, the women I can tolerate for a whole voyage are the ones as greedy and deadly as myself," Demetas said. "You wouldn't last the journey. Not like Mavas." He gave Akheron a sly wink. *'The woman we share',* he had often said.

The whore pouted, mockingly shrugging her arms down to her sides. For some reason, Akheron felt it might be funny to kiss her, so he grabbed her shoulder, pulled her against him, and put his mouth on hers. He pulled apart, shrugged, and said, "I tried to cheer you up, but it might not be possible. Now, you'd better give the pirate his gold before he kills you or tells me to."

Demetas split his sides with laughter, while the woman pulled at her skirts in frustration. From a cord around her waist hung a golden statue of Tahelion, the Maker's man who had preached of how to follow their God in the best way. As a corsair this was not a fact that Akheron was supposed to recognize, so he said nothing. He merely snatched the statue from the woman and tossed it down to Demetas's waiting hands before releasing the mooring and climbing down into the boat with his friend.

"Remember the girl we found in Vero Port?" Demetas asked.

Akheron smiled. "The redhead?"

"Glyphs, we'd have made space for her in this boat," the corsair said, his eyes distant. He shoved off from the dock, after setting his gold trophy on the bench next to him and grabbing two oars.

Akheron seated himself facing Demetas on the second bench. He grabbed hold of the rudder and steered them around Sathius's *Salty Shadow*. Their friend waved to them from the stern of his two-deck galley. "See you someday!" he shouted to Akheron; the distance was too far to be certain, but Akheron swore he saw the corsair's signature wink.

"What if Mavas was with us?"

Demetas smirked. "What if she was? She'd have made space for that redhead too. I know she would have."

Akheron sighed. "I'm certain she would have..."

"Where is Mavas anyway? With Haekus?"

"She's staying in Avernus tonight," was all Akheron replied with.

"I assumed as much. She'll help you get on your feet here," Demetas said. "Maker, I'm going to miss having you around."

The question *Where will Mavas stay?* did not disturb the sound of the waves. They drifted away from the busy harbour. Akheron thought he knew the answer: *Mavas does not stay...* but part of him thought that things between them were different. She had told him she would stay when she had said, "I'll be here, even if there's only ruin left." But would Demetas leave it alone?

Soon, they couldn't hear any of the port's din. It was just the two of them, in the Avernan channel. Above, the smoke of the city blurred the bright stars.

"Listen, Demetas," Akheron began. He needed to convince the Buccaneer Navy to back off now. "I've been by your side since the start, but people will be watching me when I get back to Avernus."

"What people?" Demetas asked.

"People," Akheron shrugged. "The Imperials. Whomever they make Prince."

For a few moments there was silence. Demetas swished the oars again, and their rowboat surged forward another dozen feet. He didn't care what Akheron was saying. He was the wind in the sails of the most dangerous armada in history, and Akheron was just his friend and occasional rival.

"The Navy should lie low for a while," Akheron said.

"The Navy should do what we set out to do. We're teaching the world a lesson about themselves. More and more recruits join us."

"Not after this," Akheron said. "We burned them. The commoners joined us before because they could escape their lords that way. The 'Free City of Tarroth' and all that. Now, though, they will hate us. They will turn to the Prince or the soldiers or anyone who tells them they are safe. Anyone who can protect them."

"Fine. And sooner or later, they'll realize their protectors have abused them, yet again. Then they'll look for the Buccaneers again," Demetas said. "I've said it every time, we are the—"

"I know what you say," Akheron said. "But you said that before the Navy. There will be corsairs after the Navy. But there need not be a structure, like the one you set in place."

"*After* the Navy?" Demetas asked. He paddled again, with slightly more strength. "I'm not disbanding my crowning achievement, Akheron. We did your task, and you should be thankful. Enough of this argument."

Akheron looked out across the waves. He hated that gold ornament beside his friend. It reminded him of... He interrupted the thought. "My task? I gave you the chance to raid an Imperial City!"

"Ha, you *gave* us the chance? We sailed to Avernus and killed your enemies, Akheron. That's what this was. Just once, could you speak at face value? Stop acting like there's some disguise hiding what you do."

Demetas wasn't looking at him anymore. "What did you do to make such an enemy out of Prince Aristorn?"

Akheron closed his eyes and took a deep breath. He hated it when people asked questions like that, because he could not give them an answer. He could not think of the answer.

"Is that the big secret? The one you always stop questions about? 'Don't ask me that question' you always say." Demetas made a gruff voice for the mocking phrase, and then chuckled to himself. He glanced up at Akheron. Their eyes only met for a moment, and then Akheron looked away. That statue of Tahelion was staring at him. So was his friend. He ignored them both.

They were probably two thirds of the way. Akheron could see lights in the distance, reflecting off the gentle waves of the ocean beneath the black backdrop of the Avernan isle. After a lapse of silence, Demetas lifted his oars out of the water, sliding them in, across his lap.

"I'm sorry, Akheron," he said. "That wasn't called for. The Navy is going to stay together, though. It's important to me, important like going home was important for you."

Yes, this whole return home has been so fulfilling... he thought to himself, sarcastically. "Will you visit?" Akheron asked. "Sath said he might."

"Well, I'll be back in a fortnight or so to pick up Mavas."

There was a moment of silence. Akheron felt a hundred thoughts scrape through him in that moment. He gripped the sides of the boat, staring Demetas in the eye. *Everything leaves me eventually,* was one thought that reached the surface clearly. It broke the quiet waves of the sea with a crash. *Mavas is mine. Demetas knows my secret. Demetas holds the Navy together. Everything has to leave.*

Demetas glanced away, as he started to extend the oars again.

Akheron grabbed the knife from his belt. The leather whispered, but Demetas only turned back to him at the lurch of the rowboat under Akheron's feet. He stepped forward as Demetas leaned backward. He stabbed his knife into Demetas's throat. The blood immediately welled around the narrow steel blade.

His friend sagged back against the edge of the boat, gurgling as he tried to speak. He released one of the oars and it drooped into the sea. It dragged against the current, gradually pulling them into a broad circle. A drop of thick blood plopped into the ocean behind Demetas, while two red snakes made their way down his neck.

Demetas made a sound that roughly mimicked the word "Why?" Blood was leaking through the holes in his clenched teeth.

Akheron, still clinging to his knife, could scarcely speak, let alone release his friend. He exhaled, when he had to, breathing into the dying corsair's face. "Why?" he asked. He quoted the man's motto, which had not been said earlier. "Like you always say, 'We are men who act how men are.' We don't hide what we do. We take what we want, when we want it. You, of all people, should understand. I killed Aristorn because I had to. In that way, I hide, I hide everything that I am. I had a brief respite with you and your scum, Demetas, but even then, I was hiding from something. But I still take what I want. I want Mavas."

Demetas's eyes were wide. Was it the horror that he saw in Akheron's face, sheer shock, or the sight of the Maker leaving him? Certainly, the man's soul would not find respite at the Maker's side. He managed one short nod, as though to say, *You've taken her*, and then he was gone.

Akheron finally pulled his knife free. He liked this knife. Or rather, he had liked it. He threw it overboard with a splash. Next went the statue of Tahelion. It reminded him too much of the day his life had changed. The day he had learned Demetas's lesson: men will always be men. *We're all the same.*

Lastly, he threw Demetas over the side. He was sobbing by the time he let go of his friend. The body drifted on the waves. Slowly, it drifted away from the boat. The Buccaneer was dead.

And so was House Aristorn.

Akheron closed his eyes for a long moment. When he opened them again, he began paddling back to his home in that blood-stained rowboat. But after the Grey Night, no one would question such a boat. Would anyone ever know what had happened to the leader of the Navy? Would anyone ever learn the fate of the great captain? *No*, Akheron decided. *No one will know what happened to Demetas.* He blinked. "I don't know what happened to Demetas."

He had been invited to return home and now, at last, he could. But he couldn't imagine what he might say to his sister, after the night's killings.

Every thief had to canvas their target first. It was also this way for corsairs who sailed the two seas and took what they would from weak, pitiful men. For Avernus, an Imperial City, they decided a cautious approach might be run smoother than their usual raid tactics. So, according to a plan laid out in Vyndrel, they sailed to Avernus on Demetas's *Arrow*, or on other ships that departed Tarroth that month, before the harsh ocean winter struck. Akheron and Mavas went last on one such vessel. The *Jorggeh*, a small schooner captained by the bold Coden Bastyl, made the voyage across the Gate on Akheron's blood coins. The smuggler had a firm handshake, and swore to be ready to leave whenever Akheron's business was done. They had to get back across the Mydarius a few times before winter storms closed the passage.

They arrived in Avernus when the sun was rising on the horizon. Through a tiny porthole window, they watched the golden glow rise above the Valharyn; Akheron held Mavas in his arms, wrapped inside his warmth. Neither wanted to stir, when the boy in the crow's nest shouted, "Land!" As the blinding orb of light let slip an inch of blue between its brilliance and the horizon, Akheron kissed Mavas's shoulder. She had freckles on it. It reminded him of the near nudity she preferred while working on deck. She had never captained a vessel, though her word was as strong as Demetas's on the *Arrow*. Often, however, she did the tasks of the crewmen, from rigging, climbing, to scrubbing the deck itself. And she often dressed as the crew did. It turned Akheron's stomach into a knot, even laying there in their cabin simply thinking about it.

"I don't know how you can be so..." Akheron trailed off.

Mavas swung her legs away from his, and sat up on the narrow bed. He could see the curve of her, where her back met the mattress. "What?" she asked, glancing over her freckled shoulder at him.

"Sorry," he said. He winced, on purpose.

"This again?" she asked. "Listen, I'm going to be seeing Demetas while we're in Avernus."

"I know you are. And I know there'll be more than seeing involved."

Mavas shook her head. "Why do I get the impression you're about to try persuading me not to?"

"Demetas is a corsair, to the bone," Akheron said. "One day, he'll leave you on land and never return for you."

"There'll always be other men that can keep up with me. Like you. But will you leave me on land, one day?" She stood up. She was already wearing breeches, though she pulled on a small white undershirt before donning her tunic, and a heavier pair of trousers. The air outside was cold, and without Mavas in his arms, Akheron could feel cool tendrils fingering their way in from beneath the door.

"Never," Akheron said. "You know that already. I just can't understand how you can be so casual with..."

"With *my* body?" Mavas asked. She tossed him his pants. "I'm a corsair, to the bone, Akheron. Like Demetas says, 'We're humans who don't hide what humans are.' I do what I want. Kill whom I want. Take what I want. That won't change."

Akheron closed his eyes. He fumbled blindly into each pant leg. When he opened his eyes, Mavas was putting on her cloak. "I've been with more men than you and Demetas," she said. "And a few women besides that. Why do you think I have no place to go home to? You do. And I respect that. I honestly do, Akheron. But, you were not my first, as I was yours."

"I'm sorry," he said again. *What else can I say?*

"You don't have to be. I understand how you feel. And if it makes you feel better, you are important to me. You *are* special to me," she said. "More than almost all of those in my past."

"Thanks," he said. Her words did start to calm his stomach. *They may be a comfort, but that is only half the problem.* It was all wrong. There was no holiness. No separateness. No distinction between her, him, and the rest of the sinning world. *But she would think me mad, if I said it.*

The deck was windy, and, despite the sun, most of the working crew wore shirts. Mavas and Akheron wore cloaks; he wore the water-resilient one Sath had bought him.

Captain Bastyl was almost a wiry man, though it was easy to see that he had worked as hard as his crew did for most of his life. He nodded to his passengers as they came above deck. "We'll be moored within the hour," he said.

As they walked down the plank and onto solid ground, Mavas glanced back at Akheron and asked, "This is your home?"

"Yes," he said. "Glyphs, it has been too long." He inhaled the sea salt and the smell of fish, felt the tang in the back of his throat. The sun was above the cliffs, casting angular and broken shadows across the Avernan port.

"I could live here," Mavas said. "It's like Tarroth, but not as cold and not as rocky." It might seem like an odd thing to say, standing on a rocky beach underneath rocky cliffs. But she was right—Tarroth was an enormous city carved into the rock. Avernus was full of elaborate wooden houses, mixed with stonework, but it was so much *warmer* here.

And as Mavas, smiling, led the way into the busy courtyard, Akheron thought, *I have to find a way to keep her.*

They met the others in the Gatehouse, a drug and drinking den built against the cliffs. Akheron had never been inside of the square building, though he had spent the first twenty years of his life in the streets of Avernus. His father had been a successful tanner—the best in Avernus. He had been at the top of his class by the end, enough that Prince Aristorn himself had attended Veldar ten Gothikar's funeral, and had met Akheron there. His status had only improved from then, and he had never had an interest, nor an opportunity, to enter such a disgusting place as the Gatehouse.

Everyone was there, in a secluded side-room. Sathius cheered when Akheron arrived, and gave him a quick hug. Demetas shook his hand, and Yory held hers out as though she wanted Akheron to kiss it. He chose to simply squeeze it. The stubbly corsair shook her jowls and sat down at a table with seven chairs. Mar patted Akheron's shoulder as they embraced hands. "I haven't seen you since Vyndrel," Mar said. "I trust you've enjoyed the fall?"

"It's been a long wait," he said. "I can't believe I'm back here, in Avernus. I've been gone for what, three or four years now?"

"I know how you feel," Mar said. They had been friends since Aristorn had invited Akheron into his circle. Comparable in age, Lord Edemar had enjoyed the young commoner's comradeship. "When you left, we all felt a hole. Well, two. I've never blamed you for needing to leave. Everything here reminds me of—"

"Now you're back too." Akheron interrupted him without thought. He had parts of the truth, but had assumed such a false motivation for the circumstances they had now made. "Must be different without your father."

"To be honest," Edemar said, "I'm glad he's gone. Don't tell the court that though. My court. I've already told Demetas I'm staying in Avernus after this is done."

"I am too," Akheron said, without thinking. Everyone had come to a natural lull in conversation before the words left his mouth, so they had all heard. Mavas knew already, but not the rest.

"What?" Demetas asked.

"Glyphs!" Haekus blurted. It seemed very un-Haekus-like.

"I'm sorry," Akheron said. He calmly sat down at the table, across from Yory. Her mock irritation with his greeting had been replaced by true surprise.

The rest of his friends fell into their chairs like dazed or wounded people. Mavas sat beside Akheron and grabbed his hand under the table to lend him courage. He began to explain, "I know I have helped you with these raids—"

"You've practically built the Navy!" Sath seemed angry at his announcement. At a dry glance from Demetas, he added, "You and the great captain too, of course."

"I know I have helped with the Navy," Akheron said, "and that you all consider me one of you. But I have waited for a long time to return home, and this assault we are planning will cause enough chaos for me to return without drawing too much attention. Unwanted attention."

"Is this because of your sister's visit?" Haekus asked. He was not angry, but looked ponderous. Akheron wished that his friend would stop trying to understand him.

"No. I would have reached this point, even if she did not visit me. I told you before we left Vyndrel that I had unfinished business here. And we agreed to finish it. If I put an end to it—" He realized that they would not appreciate such thinking, the anticipation of failure, so he corrected himself. "When I put an end to it, I will finally have a measure of peace here."

"Peace?" Demetas asked. "You know what we are going to do to this city, right? Are you changing that plan too?"

"Of course not," Akheron said. "Like I said, that is *my* plan."

"There's not going to be any peace after this. There is going to be war."

"War?" Sath said. He lowered his voice. "We're corsairs, Demetas. We sail where we want and do what we want; we can't be bound by a struggle when we don't care about the cause."

"The cause is freedom against shackles and lies," Demetas said.

Sath fell silent. He lived by the words that left the great captain's mouth.

"Who will choose our targets?" Yory asked. "Demetas hasn't seen a scrap of real news in a decade."

"What about speeches?" Sathius asked. "Demetas, you've got great ones. But Akheron started it. I still remember finding him in Tarroth and inviting him to the Royal Rogue. You wanted to throw him out, but he basically repeated your own code to you, word for word, without knowing a scrap of it. Who will give the speeches, if you jump ship?"

Demetas groaned. He dragged his hands across his face. Mavas said nothing, though everyone knew how torn she was now. At least, Akheron hoped he knew how torn she truly was. *What if it's a game, and she'll just leave me when I step off the* Arrow *for good.*

"How's this for a speech?" Haekus said. He stood up and then it was Akheron's turn to moan. He took a drink of ale, as Haekus began. "I've never really known what to do with myself. Since I picked up a sword, I've been able to beat any animate or inanimate object into submission, except Akheron. He is the deadliest of us, the smartest of us, and the truest 'free man' I know. If he wants to come home to Avernus, then that's what he'll do. The Navy never signed a charter. We're corsairs, and he may not be the great captain, but he's the best of us."

Lies, Akheron thought. *No good speech can be so full of lies.*

Haekus raised his mug. "A toast to Akheron, the greatest Buccaneer in the Navy!"

Even Demetas clapped his palm against the table. They slammed their cups together and drank merrily, and when it was done, they got down to business.

"We'll set sail with only enough ships to complete the task. Secure this port first, and then move into the city," Mar said.

"Six ships maybe?" Mavas asked.

"Closer to eight," Akheron said. "There will be plenty of loot, trust me."

Demetas's eyes gleamed. "Let's choose ten, then."

"Ten?" Sath asked. "Half the fleet?"

The Buccaneer Navy had twenty-one ships, but their crews were all exceeding efficient capacity.

"So it'll be myself, Sath, Yory," Demetas said, as they nodded to their names. He continued his list with those that were not present. "Captain Bozlay, Caw One-Eye, Captain Peke, Shamillard, Rye Baley, Quinen... and who else?"

"We could offer Coden Bastyl a share?" Akheron suggested.

"He had a lot of cargo space, and has proven reliable thus far," Mavas said.

"Done," Demetas said.

Later, after they made some other logistical plans and agreed upon a date for the complex raid, they spit in their hands and shook on it. A humorous custom, but customs were important. Akheron knew that.

Outside, a cold breeze caught Akheron's breath. He stood there on his own. Mavas had said she was going with Demetas tonight, so he did not expect her to slip an arm around his and lean her head against him. Startled, he waited a moment before snuggling his cheek against her dark hair. Together, they stared out at the waves. The port was almost entirely abandoned, though a man with no home slept in the middle of the courtyard.

Akheron inhaled. "This is *my* city," he whispered.

"I wish I knew that feeling," she said.

"What about the *Arrow?*"

"I've served on many ships. I love Demetas's, but I've never had a place to just call my own."

Akheron nodded. "I wish I could impart the feeling, but it's just mine. I've walked in these streets. I've ridden horses over these lands. I've worked in these shops. I've wept in these nights. I've run on these rooftops."

"You ran on the rooftops?" Mavas asked, raising her head to stare at him. She was a little shorter than he, so she tilted her face up.

"It's a long story."

"You'll have to tell it to me, someday," Mavas said.

A frown settled on Akheron's mouth. "No," he said. "I don't."

"Oh. It's that story. Have you told anyone? Will you ever?" Mavas pulled her arm away.

"Two men know it. One, well... he won't survive our attack on Avernus, unless he kills me." Akheron stared down at the dirty cobblestones beneath his boots.

"And the other man?" Mavas asked.

"I don't truly know what he knows. I don't know how he found it out either. But he spoke to me as my own soul might. He *understood* me, the way I want to be understood. Even with you, there's things in the way." He remembered his conversation with Arad in the Royal Rogue that day.

"Perhaps," Mavas said, "if you told me, I could try to connect with you more."

"Maybe someday," Akheron said. "But this man, he is a traveller. I will likely never see him again. So I need not kill him."

"Why do you have to kill everyone who knows where you came from?" Mavas asked. "I kill when I want to. I don't let anything or anyone convince me that I sometimes *have* to."

"And that's one of the things between us," Akheron said.

She drifted further away from him. He had almost lost her to Demetas, he knew. But she would end this night with him, regardless. He glanced at her, and touched her arm before he lost her attention. "I have to kill them, so I can be at peace. I would

love for you to someday know me—when I am at peace."
　　Mavas smiled. "Me, too."

30

As the sun rose over the Mydarius, Akheron sat in the crow's nest of the *Salty Shadow* with his legs hanging over the edge and his chin resting on the bottom slat of the railing. His chin itched—he had not shaved in a week—so he rubbed it against the wood. *That's much better,* he thought, as he watched the coast come closer. He had first spotted land by paying attention to the dull clouds overhead, but now the rocky points were visible, clawing into the ocean like a wolf ravaging a carcass. The northern coast of the Mydarius Sea, where the Sinai Mountains gradually declined into the ocean, was all rock. It was still quite distant, but they knew they were close to their destination. He could feel the crew's excitement, even from way up on top of the ship.

He removed his chin from the rail, and glanced behind him. The *Astral Arrow* sailed there, as well as Captain Baley's *Goldrunner*, a deck-and-a-half caravel. Another group of three ships, led by Yory, would be a day's voyage behind. The rest of the fleet was completing other raids on Orlin Isle. The Navy would not reunite until they returned to Tarroth in a few months, to plan their next big score.

"Can you see the inlet?" Sath shouted up. He held his hand on his hat when he raised it, so the wind wouldn't steal it away.

"We're heading straight for it!" His call was almost carried away but Sath waved and returned to the wheel.

Over the next hour, they sailed into a wide bay. They were looking for the mouth of the Trident. They were looking for the ruins of Vyndrel. After the Vero job, they had set sail from the jungle shores of the Olympian Point through the west channel. From there, they followed the coast the whole way to the hill-covered point of Galin. Rather than sailing onward to Galinor, the capital, they had followed the line of the point of Galin on a north-east trajectory, straight across the Mydarius Sea. The entire voyage had taken eight days, with their holds so laden— the *Stellaris* had surrendered enough treasure to fill half the cargo space for *six* ships.

Soon though, it became clear that this was not the Trident inlet. There was no river, just a wide cove.

"I know where we are," declared a sailor. Sath went to talk to him. After a few moments, Akheron saw his hat nod, and then the pirate barked more orders.

"We sailed too far east. The Trident lies to the west. Raise the sails and lower the oars!" This was met with a groan, but the crew jumped to it and the sails were raised. Akheron rode the rest of the journey lazing in the crow's nest. Now that the coast was in sight, he felt useless. He was no sailor. For the Navy, he was a soldier. He had been on the previous oar shift, so he was not expected to join them this time.

The inlet they sought was clouded with a thin fog. As the *Salty Shadow* slid through it, the walls of Vyndrel came into sight. Akheron had heard stories of it, but nothing had prepared him for this. He pulled his knees up and rose to his feet.

The Outer Wall of Vyndrel was more than four storeys tall, but it was burned at the top and Akheron could not tell how tall it had stood before whatever battle had broken it. The mist drifted through holes in the walls, enormous craters caused by something much more deadly than catapults or ballistae. Within, the Inner Wall rose, still standing. It was taller than the Outer Wall, but also more ruined. Entire sections seemed to be missing.

"Quite a sight, isn't it?" Sath asked. He had climbed into the crow's nest without a word. "The fearsome might of a Skin Caster, sending out spells with the speed and ferocity of a dozen warrior wizards. The last Skin Caster helped Tiberon win his war, until the Emperor declared it a crime to write glyphs upon one's skin."

"Emperor? Skin Caster?" Akheron asked.

"The stories that have been erased from the books," Sath

said. "They live on *here*, in the ashes of civilization."

The walls extended across the Trident River, with a three-storey opening for ships to pass through. Within was a surprisingly busy port. A dozen ships were docked, and, though the buildings were full of holes or surrounded by rubble, every place seemed occupied. The rock was grey, but Akheron could not tell how much of it had been coloured by age or the embers of its catastrophe.

"What was it like before?"

Sath smiled. "They say the city was full of gardens and vineyards. Out in that bay, the walls looked green—that's how overgrown they were. The Vyndi were proud of their paradise. It was said that they had the best wine, women, and wonders in all the lands of Midgard."

Akheron shook his head. The *Salty Shadow* was almost at an empty wharf, and the men on the dock shouted welcoming words to the crew. Akheron had always marvelled at the size and wealth of Tarroth, but he felt like he stood inside the earth itself right now. The harbour was dark, lit by torches, for the walls were so tall they hid the sun and the holes in them were masked by fog. "Who were the Vyndi?" he asked.

"There were twelve Kingdoms," Sath explained. "Not counting the Mountain Men. They didn't want to be counted, you see. Not back then. Three hundred years ago. The Kingdom of Vynd was the greatest in the north, but it was the first in the north to fall."

"To the emperor?" Akheron repeated, flatly.

"Listen," Sath said. "This city is not like any other you've been to. Even in Tarroth, we have laws. Not in Vyndrel. Watch your back. Watch your purse. And don't be afraid to kill, if things get heated."

Akheron blinked and opened his mouth, but Sath Miroso was in one of his enigmatic moods and was already descending the rigging. Reluctantly, Akheron followed. He grabbed his sheath that sat against the railing of the crow's nest and belted it to his back. He preferred to keep his blade at his waist, but it was not usually conducive to climbing nor many other tasks on a ship.

The deck of the *Shadow* was a commotion of crew and corsairs getting ready to enter the ruins. "Find somewhere to sleep!" Sath bellowed. "You five, stay onboard and make sure no one touches our beauty! Akheron, Orbo, and Jallyn, with me!"

"Captain," Orbo said, as he smoothly leapt onto the wharf from the wall of their ship. Sathius waited for Akheron to follow suit, and then the four of them strode into the port.

It reminded Akheron of the lower end inns he had seen. Out in the open, men were smoking and inhaling various substances that were illegal. There was alcohol everywhere, cards and dice being played on the ground. Some legitimate business seemed to be going on in front of some of the buildings, but on the other hand, he could see at least three couples showing much more affection than he would consider... normal, for a port.

He tried to ignore the shock of it all as he followed Sath, but that was not Captain Miroso's plan. "Attention!" Sath called. "The Buccaneer Navy is hiring! Any man or woman here who wants to get off their sorry backsides and fight for glory should speak to one of our ship's captains before we set sail. We have the coin to pay, and the skills to protect it and you. Should you cast your lot in with us, of course. Else-wise, stay out of our way!"

Behind him, the *Astral Arrow* made a spectacular entrance. It came paddling through that incredible stone arch and the grey fog with its crew cheering the chorus of a shanty, and the great captain of the Navy standing proudly at its bow.

Their corsair counsel met with the fence in a derelict feast hall. The black market merchant brought close to twenty guards to surround the building, though he wore an air of comfort and ease when he sat with them inside.

"Two hundred gold coins," he said. He held a glass of Trident wine in his hand and sipped it gingerly. The finest alcohol in the Dominion, Akheron had always heard. He had no taste for alcohol, but he understood the irony of the merchant's choice of beverage. The villages on the Trident rivers brewed it, from all over Sinai. Once, Vyndrel must have been their greatest achievement. Now it was their greatest obstacle.

"Four," Demetas replied. He had steel eyes, and looked ready to skin the merchant alive. "I've already explained the scope of our prize. We would be ill pressed to fit it on a single ship; five cargo holds would be required to move it quickly. And this sampling," he waved at the selection of gold and gem-adorned trinkets on the table, "was selected at random. These are not even the finest treasures we have collected."

"But it is the method of collection I worry about," the fence said. He set the wine glass on the table and folded his hands on top of his sizeable gut. "How is it that five jewelers stowed all of their wares on one cargo vessel for you to steal?"

"Organization," Akheron said. "We are not scallywags and bandits. We're a Navy. We knew there would be decoy ships, and we knew there would only be one true one. As for why the craftsmen of Vero saw fit to secret away their goods... that took a year of subtle thievery and political suggestions. We collected it with intelligence, not luck."

"I don't like it," the merchant said. "Three hundred coins."

"Intelligence and planning are timely and expensive," Demetas said. "Three hundred twenty five. I will not go lower."

The criminal shook his head, his chins waving. He stood up and shrugged exaggeratedly. "You'll have to take your business elsewhere, I'm afraid."

As he began his timely shuffle toward the door, Haekus and Edemar, seated near Yory, seemed to glare at Demetas. They had been the ones arguing to take their treasures home to Tarroth, to fences they trusted. But they did not break the silence, for they trusted their great captain. They let things play out.

"Akheron and Sath, see if you can find Master Yyn," Demetas said, quietly.

Akheron stood up.

"Sit down, you," said the merchant. He turned around with a look of pained exhaustion on his face. "Three hundred twenty five. Theeren, go and find my treasurer. Bring us the coin."

One of the man's guards bowed and left.

Later that evening, the Buccaneers carried a keg of ale up into one of the towers. It was a long hike up the stairwell, but was well worth it.

As they drank to their fortune, they watched the sun set on the ruins. The city of Vyndrel, though surrounded by such enormous walls, was the size of Galinor. It was not larger than Olympus, but it was too large for comprehension. How long would it have taken to build those walls? Did they use slaves? Or did they pay craftsmen?

As shadows grew, so did the noise of the city. Akheron heard the sounds of fighting and the screams of rape. How many women were kept here against their will? Were they a resource like the treasures, the gold, or the supplies that Akheron's comrades had bought? How many men grew up in this debris and died in it, too?

"So what do we take next?" Mavas asked. She sounded restless already. She had sailed on the *Arrow* for the last few days. But tonight, she had told Akheron she would be with him.

Demetas smiled. Everyone was watching him for the answer. He was their great captain.

"Avernus," Akheron said.

Sath glanced at him. "What?"

Demetas's smile faded, though Akheron could feel the rise of excitement in the others. "Did you say Avernus?" Haekus asked.

"I did," he said.

"We're going to score some merchant's goods again?" Yory blinked.

"No. We're going to raid an Imperial City."

The musty, smoky air was quiet for a few breaths. They could hear the waves far below, but the noise of rotten men was louder. Vyndrel might've been the corsairs' paradise, as it had once been the elitists', but it was not somewhere that Akheron wanted to be.

Demetas chuckled quietly. "We're going to raid Avernus," he said, nodding.

"Can we?" Sath asked.

Mar put down his ale. It was his home, too, but instead of objecting, he said, "Do we have the manpower?"

"We will," Demetas stated bluntly. As he answered their questions, he smiled at Akheron. They were the sort of brothers that only kindred spirits could be. They thought the same, and desired the same. Underneath it all, Akheron was a different man. But the corsair he was acting as now, well... that was Demetas.

"What about ships?"

"We can buy five, with this payout."

"What about military?"

"Akheron?"

Akheron smirked. "The armies of the Avernan fief are divided between five castles, none less than a day from Avernus itself. There's a garrison there, sure. Plus the Defenders of the Kinship, and the Prince's personal soldiers."

"So we can get in and out before the army arrives," Demetas said.

"A day's raid?" Sath asked.

"A night's," the great captain decided. "Just one night's."

Akheron closed his eyes. They had bought it. One night, to finish this. One night to kill the man who knew him. *Aristorn,* he thought, *I'm coming for you.*

He opened his eyes and stepped to the edge of the lofty rampart. Almost a dozen storeys dropped below him to the rough coast, ruined by jagged bricks and debris. As he watched the waves, he thought of his long lost love, the one who had left him before he met Mavas. Later that night, when he gave Mavas something similar to love, something that usurped it, he preferred not to think about the woman he had loved. He thought about Prince Aristorn and decided that one of them would die when Akheron brought his Navy down upon his home. Then he would not have to be like Demetas anymore. Then he would be free.

31

The *Stellaris* set out from Vero Port amongst a fleet of twenty ships. Each set out on a separate trajectory, while a group of nine moved in three eastward-bound groups. Each group was half a day behind the previous one, so Akheron watched two of the groups sail toward Olympus before he sailed on the *Stellaris* out of the port. As they lowered their sails and caught the wind out of the harbour's waters, Akheron clutched the amethyst in his palm. Anyone standing close enough might see it glow briefly, signalling their position to his corsair-friends.

The captain of the Buccaneer's target was an inhumanly tall man. When the six ships of the Navy appeared on the horizon, he gave the order to divide his group of three. The *Stellaris* sailed due east—the least likely path—to throw off their pursuers. The ship travelling north east, around the Olympian peninsula was the prime target, although sailing south the quickest path to land and potential safety.

When all six ships with full sails continued in pursuit of their particular transport, the *Stellaris* captain frantically ordered men to start rowing. Perhaps if they made it to the shore of Olympus they could hide their treasure in the jungle and escape harm.

Akheron tossed the gemstone over the side of the boat, and grabbed an oar. He hated the idea of magic, and hated using it. It was too literal of a connection to the Maker—when had any good come of that? The homing spell was useful and expensive, but their score would dwarf that cost.

The *Stellaris* sported two masts and two decks. The deck

below was only storage and quarters, while oars were stored against the rails on the top deck. Akheron carried an oar to an empty bench and slid it into the pin in the rail. He was one of the first to lower it into the water, so he waited for the others before he began oaring. He had spent a lot of time on ships for the past five years... his arms were covered in bulbous veins and angular muscle. He wore no shirt; the black hair on his chest and arms protected him from the sun. He kept his chin clean-shaven, however, for the stink of sweat when he oared and for Mavas's nether. The thought called a smile to his lips.

The crewman ahead of him, who was still running the oar through its slot, gave him a raised eyebrow—what sort of man smiled when they were given a task like this?

Akheron Gothikar did, though these crewmates did not know that name. He put his back into the heaving motions, and welcomed the pain.

The chase across the water continued in vain. By the afternoon, the Buccaneer Navy was upon them. The tall captain ordered a full stop when there were black-flag ships ahead and behind them. Within minutes, they were boarded. The captain surrendered to Demetas personally, who then clasped Akheron's hand before executing the surprised captain with a swift thrust to the heart. To the rest of the crew Demetas shouted, "The rest of you can go free, or join us for some gold and glory—or join him, if you wish."

None of them took the last option, though several took the second.

After all hands had boarded Navy ships or survival rafts, the treasure trove in its lower deck was carried by more than fifty men to the various corsair cargo holds. Then, fire was set to the *Stellaris*. The sails went up quickly as the Navy sailed west. By the time the burning ship faded into the horizon behind them, the decks were ablaze and they lit the twilight that chased them.

Akheron watched it from the wheel of the *Astral Arrow*. Demetas captained the ship, though Akheron leaned nearby, and watched the light fade from the horizon. "We did it," he said.

Demetas grinned. He flicked the gold ring he had been toying with all evening—the trinket caught the nearby lantern light as it spiraled up and then fell back into his palm. "Yes, we did, brother."

N A VREUGDENHIL

"Are you sure you want to stay at the helm all night?" Akheron asked. "I could send her to you later—"

"No, no," Demetas said. "That's the difference between you and I. This ship, these waves, this night... I love it as much as I do any other pleasure. I'm glad you've come to terms with... uh... sharing, though." He flicked the ring again, and caught it.

Akheron bit his lip. The light of their passage shimmering on the waves behind looked like a flock birds, playing in the sky. At last, he admitted, "I haven't, really."

"What's that?"

"It just doesn't feel right..."

Demetas frowned. He slid the ring onto a finger, and then grabbed a stool from the edge of the deck. Plopping down in front of the helm, he again flicked his gold ring up. "Why?"

"There's nothing quite like what we do. This freedom, this attitude—the world is ours, and we take what we want!" Akheron's voice echoed overboard. Some of the crew gave a "Hear! Hear!" but the call quickly died down. It was getting late and everyone was half drunk. They would follow the coast past Olympus with caution tonight, but then pursue the dawn most of the way to the Galin river on the morrow, if the winds were in their favour.

"But?" Demetas's ring shot upward.

"But," Akheron said.

The corsair caught his gold with a smile. "But, the Maker."

"It's not just how I was raised," Akheron said. "It became part of me. It became who I am. And then I lost it all."

Demetas shrugged. "And you never want to talk about that."

"Never," Akheron said. "But with Mavas..."

"With Mavas, you remember. You have doubts," Demetas was paying no attention to their passage—just their conversation and his golden toy.

"But I've never felt so... welcome. So comfortable. So complete," Akheron explained. "And Mavas knows it. That's why she does it, that's why she's in all our lives in the way that she is."

"And that must feel especially wrong to you," Demetas said. "I get it. I did from the very start, Akheron."

"I know."

"You've got the curse of the believer," Demetas said, and caught his ring.

"Nothing could be worse," Akheron said, watching the waves.

Below deck, he found Mavas keeping his bed warm. She wore a handful of gold necklaces and a solid clasp around her thigh. With a smile, she pushed him into the blankets. She was on top for a while, then he was behind. He clawed at her short dark hair, holding it in a knot behind her head. He pulled at her, gripped her, kissed her, taunted her, pushed her, finished her. It was different than the first time—it was rougher than the first. They were both on par with one another now. Akheron was thick with muscle and Mavas strong enough to take him for all that he was. There were times that night when he wasn't sure which was tilted: the ship could be heaving on the ocean or it was all in his mind. He grabbed her chin and moved her mouth against his.

By the end, she wore no gold and he had no energy left. They lay side-by-side on the damp bed; their eyes were locked, save when he glanced at her body. In those moments, she would just smile and kiss him again. "I could stare at you forever," he whispered, "without wanting another thing."

"Sounds like love," Mavas whispered, with a wink.

"Does it?" Akheron groped her again, and she laughed. It didn't sound like love to him, but something much more base.

"Sometimes I forget how *new* this is for you," she said, indicating his active hands. "It's just me. All of it."

Akheron shook his head. "I know. It's... impossibly real."

"Careful," Mavas said. "Combine phrases like that and you'll start sounding like Sathius. He's a talkative one, especially when he's alone with—what?"

Akheron's hands had released her. "I don't want to hear about Sathius. Or Demetas. Or any of the others."

"So it is love!" Mavas laughed.

"No. Yes. I don't know," Akheron said. He closed his eyes and tilted his head back. "Glyphs, I don't know. I still love another. I will always love her."

"Who?" Mavas asked.

Akheron felt cold. His skin had become ice, he was certain. She was still tangled with him though, and seemed un-phased. "Don't ask me that. Please, don't."

"So if this isn't love, then what is it? You just want me all to yourself."

"I suppose it's in my nature," Akheron said.

"Well, alright then. Feel how you want to," Mavas said.

"But..."

"But it won't change me any," she said. "I'll do what I want."

"I'm so tired of hearing that," Akheron said. "Why are you really here, Mavas? There's got to be more to it than simple desire. You're so much more than Demetas. I'm sure of it."

Mavas frowned. She sat up, but her move warranted a reply from Akheron's body. She let a brief smile slip through, but then gave him a serious stare. "Do you really want to know?"

He propped himself up on his elbows, with the pillow between him and the headboard. "Yes."

"Fine. Though, please notice that I'm telling you my story, even though you get all gruff and tough about your history."

Akheron forced a nod. It was all he could manage. He briefly remembered her red hair in his hands. *Her* red *hair. Glyphs.* "Talk."

Mavas shook her head. Then, she took her sweaty hair in her hands and held it off her neck. They were both still steaming and sweating. "I grew up in Athyns, on the streets. I had to watch out for my sister until I was nine—I never knew my parents. When we were nine, we were taken in by a wealthy widow, but when she passed after only three years, her son sold us to..."

She fell silent for a moment, and Akheron managed a, *"Sold?"*

"We were sold to a brothel."

Akheron could barely breathe. He couldn't imagine that being someone's life. "You didn't stand a chance..."

"No, we didn't. My sister was only ten!"

"Shouldn't the Maker have given you a chance to escape? A potential good deed to rescue you? Glyphs, that's not right... I..."

"The Maker?" Mavas asked. She laughed. "He's never given me a second thought, until I met Demetas."

"How did you meet?"

Mavas shook her head. "Not yet. There's more. My sister

was killed by a client when I was fifteen. The guards were notified, but they never caught the man who did it. That was the darkest year..."

Akheron couldn't stand it anymore. He sat up, and gently embraced Mavas around the shoulders. Though he could feel parts of her that would usually arouse him, he felt only sick right now. "How can you say this without crying?" he asked. He had tears in his eyes.

"It was more than ten years ago, Akheron. I've cried all I can about it."

"I would never—" *become so callous...* Akheron cut his phrase short. It was not what Mavas needed right now. "... I *could* never imagine such a life..."

She pulled away enough to see his face. "Later that year, I was sent to another house. This one was down in the port. I didn't know anyone there, though a couple men from the first place would come to see me there. One of the girls there... Ierie, her name was... she looked just like my sister." Her eyes were distant and she gave a small chuckle as she remembered something. "The first time I saw her, I screamed, and someone dropped their wineglass. Made quite the mess. Of course, then I cried and everyone tried to comfort me."

Akheron managed a smile for her.

"That's how Ierie and I started. Comfort. But it became a lot more. Within the year, we were... together more than either of us was with clients. A Kin heard tell of it, somehow; maybe the owner of the brothel tipped him off. The guards came to arrest me—not Ierie, because I was newer."

"And that's how you met Demetas?"

She smiled, at last. "Yes! How'd you know?"

"He said he rescued you from the guards. That was how you met. Didn't say anything more."

"He doesn't know much more. No one does," Mavas said. "Keep it that way. Or I'll cut your tongue out."

Akheron knew better than to doubt her. Nor did he intend to share something she had told him in confidence. That was far too precious to him. "What about Ierie? Did you ever go back?"

"I did once. I cut my hair and wore fancy clothes so no one recognized me. But Ierie was not there. Everyone said she had a new job. A better one. I never did find her though. She's still out there somewhere... But the last time I saw her, before I was arrested, was eight or nine years ago."

"You sail across the Mydarius every year!" Akheron said. "If you try, you will one day find her. I'm certain."

"Thanks," Mavas said. "But I'm different now, and I don't doubt she is, too. I'm more confident. More grounded. I'm happier."

"Well, I can't take all the credit," Akheron said. He gave her a wink.

She leaned in close and gave him another kiss. It was a long, still one. When she pulled away, she said, "I've changed the mood, haven't I..."

"Doesn't matter to m—" Then he kissed her, and the ship started to tilt around him once more.

They didn't separate for an hour, but when they did, Akheron could not fall asleep as easily as she did. He was exhausted. He had been awake since the small hours of the previous night and had even spent a few hours oaring. He was certainly tired enough to sleep, but he had too many thoughts in his head. He knew what was right. It was etched into him. Mavas loving Ierie, that was not right. Not according to the Maker that Akheron knew. Mavas making love to Akheron, that was not right either—not now, not like this. His gut was full of fire, and when the sun touched the horizon, Akheron was as resolute as he could be on one statement, but that was not very resolute at all.

"The Maker's never given me a second thought," he whispered to the rising sun "So I'll let go. Enough of your rules, Deyvas." Mavas wrapped her arm around his abdomen, though she was still half-asleep. Akheron's words did not change a thing—what he knew to be right was a part of him, not some lofty ideal he could say 'no' to. *The curse of believing, Demetas called it.* Akheron closed his eyes. *It's a damn painful curse.*

He put his hand on Mavas's arm and waited for the next day to begin.

They devised the plan for the Vero robbery during the summer season of Tarroth, when the rains relented and the parties began. The nightlife of the free city was unlike any other, but in secrecy, the leaders of the Navy plotted. Their favourite den for such endeavours was called the Undertown, a sprawling establishment of inns, storage houses, and brothels. There were two basements beneath the main building, the Hall of Undertown. In one, the gang lord Ursiar Mandagg held his meetings and ran the 'town. The other was for rent, for the meetings of any whose nefarious dealings might brave the watching eyes of Undertown's self-proclaimed Mayor Mandagg.

Akheron waited in the doorway of the den one night, while Demetas and his inner circle discussed which town to enact their scheme upon. All the other details had been ironed out. The next year would involve more time and research than any of them were comfortable with, but Demetas had clung fast to Akheron's suggestion that the corsair Navy be run with the same regulation that a real army required.

With his arm resting on the soft driftwood doorframe, Akheron had a full view of their table. The room was only barely wide enough for the stone slab that they surrounded. It was all the same colour, the shade of Tarroth, grey like old, worn iron. A faded pattern adorned the red banner that separate the platter of drinks and breads from the rock table; the decoration resembled the linked hands of Tarroth's old kingdom. Before the Triumvirate, the men of the Valharyn Spine had called their lands the Joining. On their banner were two hands clasped. It was the design that repeated across the tablecloth, though the hands had been painted as skeleton hands, a change added by the criminals that now called the free city home.

"Cuross, it should be," said Sath Miroso. He sat in a backwards chair, his arms folded upon the back of it and his chin resting on his wrist. Shifting, he grabbed his drink from the table. "It's closest, and its wealth is well known."

"The closer it is, the stronger the response we might expect from the Royal Fleet. Across the Athynian Bay, the ships of Prince Theseus lie in wait," Haekus said.

Sathius swallowed a mouthful of ale.

"Better to choose a distant target," Haekus repeated.

"And lug our loot across the ocean itself!" Mar's sarcasm fell on deaf ears. He saw it right away, and adjusted his argument. "If we mean to sail across the Mydarius with our prize, let's hit Orlin Port or Eldius."

"Both of them are booming." That was Mavas's contribution.

Akheron shifted his weight, and rubbed his arm against the edge of the wood to itch it. He cleared his throat quietly, and wiped his palms on his shirt to clean them. "Where are we selling?"

"What?" Mar asked.

"We're talking about literal *boatloads* of gold and jewels," Akheron said. "A true pirate's trove."

"Where will we fence it?" Demetas asked, with a thin smile. He leaned back in his chair, with his sandaled heels resting on the red cloth, rippling its surface like the surface of the sea. He looked like he was proud of Akheron's insights.

"Here," Sath said.

"We could risk the black market in Athyns," Mar suggested.

Mavas had it this time. "Vyndrel."

Demetas nodded. "Even if we split the treasure to multiple buyers," he said, "We'll need to land in Vyndrel."

"Vyndrel?" Akheron asked.

"Call Tarroth the free city, if you like," Demetas said. "Vyndrel is so free, it's in rebellion against *being* a city."

"It's on the mouth of the Trident Rivers," Haekus explained. Akheron crossed his arms.

Eventually, their discussion shifted again to their target. With Vyndrel in mind, a more distant target made sense. Both Vero and Gev were suggested, but Gev was dismissed for the excessive river voyage it required.

After their meeting was adjourned, the Navy's captains sought out the ongoing feasts on Tarroth's waterfront district. The lowest tier of the city was usually referred to as its waterfront, though the three Points of Tarroth that supported it overlooked the docks and waters of the true harbour. At first glance from the ocean, Tarroth looked like the front half of a pyramid, built against a mountainous hill. But as one reached the city, the angle would reveal that the city was two arms of a pyramid that met at a sharp corner against the hill but reached out, arms open, to the water's edge.

The towering shape of the city had almost become a usual sight for Akheron over the last couple years, so he turned his eyes away from it as he exited the Hall of Undertown with Mavas clutching his arm and Haekus hugging his heels. Instead, he let his eyes wander upward. Some said that the heaven referenced in Tahelion's Teachings alluded to a literal heaven above the world. Was the Maker up there, somewhere? All that Akheron saw were the stars and the repeatedly amazing sight of darkness creating a trail across the night sky; that was Mount Aesiar's smoke, smouldering from the old volcano seaward. The moon was half obscured by those dark tendrils.

"Amazing, isn't it?" Akheron asked. "I'll never get used to it."

"Yes, you will," Mavas said.

Haekus said nothing, and Akheron took that to be his gentle way of disagreeing with Mavas's words. He was always too noble to openly contradict a woman. They taught blade-masters to be efficient and ruthless killers, but they also imbued them with a chivalrous disposition and a sense of honour. It made no sense to Akheron, but he still felt that he understood Haekus more than Mavas.

The buildings of Tarroth were built into the rock face of the city, like an enormous Keep. The open areas were not obstructed by buildings, but rather served as a courtyard and balcony. Each layer of the city could see the one below it, and from each overlook reached a dozen downward ladders and staircases into the shops and houses that occupied the block of the Keep beneath them. Here and there were ovens or campfires. A few bonfires dotted the stone plateau, too, where men and women danced and drank. The sound of cheers and shouts filled the air and a plethora of smells—some pleasant, some too intimate, all of them intrusive—filled Akheron's nostrils. He let himself kiss Mavas, when the whim took him. They were following Demetas and Sath to the Royal Rogue, their favourite drinking place. Akheron never touched alcohol, but the Buccaneer Navy practically owned the Rogue now and it was as close to a home as he had now.

Akheron had known both Mavas and Haekus in ways that he would never know the other corsairs—with Mavas, he had known her physically. They had become one flesh, or so Tahelion's Teachings instructed. Akheron still felt sick, thinking about it. But he also felt aroused.

He had come to know Haekus's heart intensely as well. It had also been through physical means, but much different ones. Together, they had found the gates of death. They had fought each other to the brink of the world, to see who was the stronger; both had returned unscathed and unified. They might not have learned who was the better man, but they had become brothers and it was something Mavas and Akheron would never share.

"Might I interrupt?"

Akheron turned away from Mavas to see a woman in a green cape. She had short dark hair and was perhaps a head shorter than he. Even in the dark he could tell she was sunburnt from the ocean, with dark bands of red on her neck and beneath her eyes. Finally, he managed to stir his voice. "Tam?"

Mavas let go of his arm in surprise.

Tamese Gothikar took the arm in her place, and hugged her brother. He was not ready to have a head nestled against his neck, and did not return the gesture in time. "Your sister comes to see you," Tam said, starting to pull away, "and you can't even manage two words?"

Akheron grabbed her this time, and pulled her against his torso. "What are you doing here! By the Maker!"

"I came to see you," Tam said.

"Again?" Akheron belatedly tried to bury the word with a chuckle, but it didn't really work.

Tam withdrew more forcibly this time. "I'm allowed to visit you," she said. "I'm still allowed to visit you!"

"Glyphs," Akheron said. "I didn't mean—of course you are. You're always allowed to. It's just not safe here."

"Akheron?" Sath asked. The others were standing in a bundle ahead, waiting for him. "Everything good?"

"Go on ahead." Akheron said. "I'll catch up with you at the Rogue."

Sathius shrugged and kept walking, while Demetas eyed Akheron. Did he think their acquaintance some big secret? What would it matter if Akheron did spill his secrets to his own sister? *Not that I've got any intent of doing that... her brother, the Buccaneer!*

"Mistress Gothikar," Haekus said, with a slight bow.

"Please, Haekus," Akheron's sister said, with a wink. "Tam will do."

"Tamese, then," Haekus said. "I'll give you three a moment." With that, he gave Akheron a sly glance and then quickened his pace to catch up with the other corsairs. Even with a sword at his waist, Haekus soared like an eagle across the uneven stone surface.

Mavas forced a smile. "He's said lots about you, um..."

"Tam is fine."

"I'm Mavas." She offered a hand, and Tam took it cautiously. "One of Akheron's closest friends here."

Tam raised an eyebrow, and glanced at Akheron. "How... lucky for him," she said. "If you don't mind, Mavas, could I have some privacy with my brother?"

"Of course," Mavas said. Hand on her sword pommel, she strutted away, not trying to be coy or indiscriminate at all. Dismayed, Akheron turned back to his sister and blinked.

Tam gripped the bridge of her nose as though she had a headache. "I was going to say something like 'You're still in the same group', but Mavas—she really improves the quality of *your friends.*"

Akheron shook his head. "So this is going to be just like the first time?" he asked. He turned to follow his friends. Over his shoulder, he called, "Go back to Avernus, Tam. There's nothing in Tarroth for you."

A nearby group of drunks let out some slurred chorus, and

Tam's words were lost. Akheron felt like turning back to hear what she had said, but he didn't. He continued on his way toward the Royal Rogue. It was built into the first row of chambers of the next tier of the city, rising like a wall. In front was a huge array of fire pits, tables, and feasters. Akheron saw a man standing on a table tossing up knives and catching them in some sort of juggling act. With a fluid move, he deposited the blades into the tabletop and took a drink from a vial on his belt. Grabbing the nearest torch, he let a curtain of fire ignite the spray he expended into the air. The crowd cheered.

"Akheron." Tam was still following him.

He put his hand on the door of the inn.

"Akheron!"

"What?" He rounded on his sister, and shoved her away from the Royal Rogue. He didn't want her to enter his sanctuary, his shrine, his *Stead.* "Do you want an apology?" he asked. "I got caught up with all this, and I'm sorry I'm not your little brother anymore? I'm sorry I walked away from you, just a few moments ago? I'm sorry I'm sleeping with a woman who could carve you up for breakfast? I'm sorry for failing your expectations, Tam? Nothing was worth it. Nothing that lasted anyway."

"What happened to you?"

"Don't ask me that!" Akheron thundered.

Her eyes flicked to his waist. He had not realized that his hand now gripped his sword. He had drawn the weapon on the last person to ask him that question. Tam shook her head. "I'm going to come see you every couple years. Because when you are ready to come home, we'll all be waiting for you."

"We all?" Akheron asked. "The way I see it... you're the only one in Avernus who would care if I even came home. The Aristorns would rather I be dead, and you and I don't have much blood family left anyway. I hear Aunt Iarn passed during the last winter."

"Enough," Tam said. "I don't believe what you're saying. Avernus is your home, and it is a part of you. Don't try to lie about it. Just answer this for me: do you love this Mavas girl? Is that what keeps you here?"

Akheron bit his lip. "Love? You know whom I love, but no captain can take me that far. It is love that keeps me here, Tam, but not love for Mavas."

She glanced where he pointed at the windows of the Royal Rogue, behind Akheron. There were two enormous windows at the front of the common room; perhaps Akheron's friends were watching their argument. Akheron didn't care.

"She's what, then?" Tam prodded. "A drug? A crutch? A rebellion?"

"A friend," Akheron said. "I've got a few more of those here. Mostly just enemies at home."

"I don't know what's between you and Aristorn, in truth," Tam said. "But you still call Avernus home. Please, come home. We can make a place for you there. A place that is not as 'unsafe' as this place."

"Tam," Akheron said. "I don't want safety."

Tam shook her head. "What happened to my brother?" she asked. "He used to make sense. He used to make me smile."

"I don't have patience for smiles anymore," Akheron said. "And only Prince Aristorn knows what *happened* to your brother. Why don't you go home and ask him?"

Tam's eyes, ready with tears, burned into him, but she could not argue with a man who refused all arguments. He was troubled by the thought of her actually asking Aristorn when she reached Avernus again, but he knew deep down she would not. She did not want to know what had happened. No one did, not even Aristorn. Perhaps, one day, Akheron could bring peace to that situation. But he did not want peace. He did not want safety.

That night was the first night he drank the drink of the corsairs, as he whispered a quiet prayer into the smoke-blocked sky. *Give Tam peace, so she will not come back here. Please, Maker mine, if you will not give peace to any other thing I touch, give it, at least, to her.*

33

Akheron's arms danced at his sides while the *Astral Arrow* shot across the bay as though fired from some heavenly bow. He was as taught as a bowstring. The sword at his waist seemed to throb against him, asking to be drawn. Behind him, he heard Sathius shout, "Ready!"

Above, the sails billowed in a full wind. The sky was cloudless. The sun had begun its course overhead. Akheron glanced back at their destination, a single wharf in front of a hill. Higher landward, a lumber village was nestled among the pine woodland. Had any of the town's inhabitants spotted the careening vessel?

For every two corsairs on board this day, there was a new recruit. The Navy's first order of business was to strengthen its ranks into a formidable force, like any true army might.

Akheron and Mar were both under the charge of Sathius, though Haekus also oversaw them. It was a tense squad, for Haekus had little appreciation for Sath's antics, and Akheron was still surprised by Edemar's arrival. He had been there, when they first found the Navy, but that was only three months past.

The *Arrow* shifted, suddenly, to starboard, and Demetas— legs spread beside the wheel of his galleon—bellowed, "Now! All hands overboard! Get up that hill!" He released his wheel and helped an enormous man named Turbus drop the anchor.

Akheron's feet landed on the wharf at the same time as Haekus's. They grinned at each other. Akheron drew his blade, and Haekus followed suit. Up the slope, a guard shouted, "To arms! Pirates!"

The Buccaneers were already halfway up the slope by the time any townsfolk that wanted to stay and fight had reached the streets. Akheron had to correct the thought—there were no streets here. Just a single dirt rut that cut between rows of houses. A slightly larger hut displaying the circular banner of the Maker was the village's Stead, and the warehouse on the far side of town was the corsairs' target.

The Navy was growing. New ships required new timber. And infamy was good for recruiting. This village sat on the Valharyn Coast of the Elysian Point. Elysia was a highland situated south of the Valharyn Spine, covered in farmland, forests, and wealthy orchards. It was close to Tarroth, in a zone that Demetas had decided was not fit for settlement. Not anymore.

"Halt!" shouted a mail-clad guardsman. Behind him, villagers formed a ramshackle line in front of the dry, white thatching on the rooftops. The sun was almost directly overhead.

"Flee!" retorted Sath. With his small metal shield, he smashed the guard to the ground and finished him off with a sword slash to the torso.

It appeared many villagers already were. As children shrieked, men and women, clutching their valuables, ran eastward. It was a long journey to the northland's military. Some were running seaward, though, with sticks and stones raised.

Akheron's first blood was a man in a stained butcher's apron. The man attacked him with a huge knife. Akheron stepped smoothly to the side, and broke the man's forearm with his sword hilt. As the knife tumbled, Akheron walked past the man. After a thrust through the back, the stunned man's blood mingled with the animals he had killed.

Akheron still felt a little ill after the kill. He closed his eyes for as long as he dared—corsairs were being swarmed by poorly armed townsfolk all around—and tried to think about what he was doing. *I'm not hiding anymore,* he thought, and forced his eyes open. This was not his first raid.

Another man rushed at him with a hatchet, and Akheron raised his sword to block it.

At one point in the fight, Akheron found himself back-to-back with Demetas. The man somehow wielding two swords. He blocked with one, and killed with the other. It was quite the spectacle, but not as much as Haekus was. Villagers were seen fleeing wherever he went.

It was not a long fight. Towards the end, another armoured guard emerged from one of the shacks in town. Two of Demetas's recruits were nearest. One found a short spear in his leg—he screamed until the guard slammed him against the wooden wall of the building. His friend turned to retreat as the guard yanked his spear free.

Akheron was the closest experienced fighter, so he raised his sword and stepped toward his opponent. The guard had no helmet, but had hurriedly tossed on a chainmail tunic. The sides were open to his undershirt. He had knee and shoulder plates, and chainmail covered his leather sleeves and trunks. At his waist was a knife.

Neither of them had a shield; the guard wielded his spear with both hands, as though it were a quarterstaff. A staff with a blade on one end. It whizzed past Akheron's face, jarring him into the fight at hand. He jabbed forward with his sword, and found his sword knocked skyward by the upward move of the guard's spear.

"I'm going to finish you, snake," the sentry sneered, swinging his spear with one hand in a wide slash. Akheron leapt backward, then rushed forward again. He didn't bother speaking. He had no use for words in a fight. Here, action was dialogue.

Every time he thrust forward, the guard's staff would knock his sword up, so the next time it happened, he let go of his sword altogether. With one hand, he forced the spear to continue upward, while he deftly grabbed the knife at the man's hip. The guard released his spear as quickly as he could, and caught Akheron's forearm as he drove the dagger's tip home into the man's side.

"Maker," the guard gasped. His breath smelled like garlic. Akheron forced the knife upward and then swiftly released the body. It spilled to the dirt below. His hands, now covered in blood, clenched and then released of their own accord. He wiped them on his grey cloak, leaving red streaks.

He looked over his shoulder. The entire crew was standing there, in the muddy streets, with smiles on their faces. A few cheers rang out, and, as the corsairs stormed past, they patted his shoulder. Demetas waited a few, with Sathius at his side.

Akheron then noticed Mavas, standing just behind Demetas. She had a small smile on her face, but it was fading. Her eyes were intent on Akheron, and he could feel so much more than a smile in them. Her nostrils flared as Demetas stepped through their locked vision. Akheron heard his friend say, "Good kill," as he walked by.

Then Mavas stepped up to him, kissed him on the cheek, and said, "I hope you don't have plans tonight."

She was gone, and Haekus was chuckling at the look on Akheron's face. Akheron blinked. "What?" he asked.

Haekus shrugged. "Poor guard, I guess."

"It was his choice. Could've fled like the others," Akheron said. Together, they strode after the corsair crew. The village's inhabitants had abandoned it to them, and now the real work began. The harvest. *I hope you don't have plans tonight?* he repeated in his head. The phrase wouldn't stop; like a chant, it defined his afternoon. Mavas had kissed him once, in the common room of the Royal Rogue, and he had been kissed by another woman. That felt like years ago. His cheeks were warm though, just from her little tease. What did she mean for that night? As he lugged a beam of tinder toward the wharf, he glanced at the Maker's Stead. *I'm not that kind of person. Everything I do, I would rather stand against... but I can't do this, can I?*

They sailed back to Tarroth as the sun set. It all passed in a blur. Akheron sat on the deck with his feet hanging overboard and sipped from a canteen of honey mead. The ship was heavily over-crewed, so many of them sang or gambled to pass the time. One man was drumming away on two drums, his hands a blur.

Mavas sat beside him, and slid her legs between the wooden slats of ship's rail. She didn't say anything at first, merely hugged the edge. "How long were you in Tarroth before you met us?" she asked at last. It felt like the smallest of small talk.

"No more than a day," Akheron laughed. "Do you know anyone named Arad?"

"Arad?" Mavas asked. She blinked. "Not familiar to me."

"He was quite an interesting man," Akheron said absently. He couldn't look at her without feeling anxious. "I met him the same day I met you, at the bar in the Rogue. Never saw him again, though."

"Is that why you're here?" she asked. "To meet interesting men?"

Akheron glanced at her sharply and his stomach seized up into a ball. With wide eyes and a humoured smile, she invited his attention. "No," he said.

"Then why are you here?" she prodded.

He glanced away from her and into the ocean. The Valharyn stretched to the horizon, grey and endless. It shimmered with the setting sun, but looked so cold and forlorn all the same. "Because I can't be where I was. Not anymore."

"Do you like it here?" she asked.

"On the *Arrow?*" he asked. "Or with all of you?"

"With me," she said. Her smile was gone, but she met his surprised eyes.

"I—uh."

"Do you like... me?" Mavas asked.

Akheron should've said no. He found her fun to be around. And he certainly desired her. But in his churning gut, he knew that what he said was a lie. "Oh. Yes, I do. Do you like me?"

She nodded, then glanced out into the ocean as he had. "You're a bit more noble than what I'm used to," she said.

"Noble?" he asked.

"And you're certainly better looking," she said.

"Better looking?"

Mavas glanced back at him. "I mean, look at him. Demetas. He's up there at the wheel. Bold and striking as any corsair ever was. You've got the same scruff as he does, you're the same sort of ruffian, I think."

"What?"

"But you don't have all those bad looks," Mavas said. "The thrice broken nose, the missing teeth..."

"I thought you and Demetas were..." Akheron struggled to find the words. "I thought you two were together."

Mavas shrugged.

Akheron did his best to not invite her further. He couldn't find the words to tell her that he was a Maker's man, and that he didn't believe he should want her the way he did. He didn't have the confidence to say how things were.

He was quiet as they walked back to the Rogue that night.

Demetas led their entourage, with Sath between him and Akheron. Sath was still singing a tune, and a smiling Edemar occasionally joined in. Other members of the Navy, indicated by the blue badge they wore, covered the port. They waved and clapped at the return of the successful raid—not that there had been much doubt about their chances. Ursha, one of Sath's favourite night girls, came over to him.

Mavas walked behind Akheron. She must've sensed his nervousness. She must've known what thoughts wormed within his brain.

In the Rogue, the upper circle of the Navy had private quarters. Akheron's were on the second floor, and he had a small window that looked out from the block of Tarroth's structure into the Valharyn. He had arm-wrestled Edemar for the quarters. The Noble's son had felt entitled to them, but that was not how the Navy decided matters.

Akheron stepped inside and closed his door. Finally alone, he took a deep breath and stepped out of the anteroom. The large chamber had two halves—a big bed, a chest, and a wardrobe spread across the room's left walls, while a makeshift kitchen and armchairs lay to the right.

He sank into a chair. The room was dark; the distant sunset was glowing against the closed translucent curtains. He put his head in his hands. *Maker, she's not the one. Why put her here? Why advertise her to me?*

A quiet knock echoed on the door. Akheron thought of Mavas's eyes, and the smooth skin of her belly that she often left bare on hot days. She thought he was good looking. Since when had Akheron let his beliefs restrict his actions? *I thought that was me... but this world taught me the truth.*

He stood up from the armchair. *Self-control is a paradox.* He walked toward the door. The door's latch was cold.

Men are all the same. Who was I to think I was above that? He opened the door.

Mavas smiled at him. "Good, you're here."

"Where else would I be?" he asked.

Mavas shrugged nonchalantly. "Haekus and Edemar run a dice ring out front. Demetas has paid for a couple whores. Sath and his friend are halfway through a pitcher of beer."

"I don't do any of that."

"What do you do?" she asked. She had a raised eyebrow, and a crooked smirk. She didn't even blush, though her advance was clear.

Akheron shrugged, but didn't bite. "Read, sometimes."

Mavas laughed. "May I come in?"

"Yes." Akheron wasn't sure what he was thinking, but he stepped back from the door.

"It's sparse," she said, when she saw his living quarters. "Cleaner than most though. Do you ever open the curtains?"

"Not often," he replied.

"Open them."

He turned his back on her, thankful for a breath on his own, and pulled the veil open. He could see the edge of this level of Tarroth, dotted with rings of loud socialites and cooking fires. Beyond, the ocean had turned red, as the sun set.

He turned back to Mavas, and she was no longer near the other side of the room.

She had been wearing a cloak when she came in, but, as she stepped up close to him, she was wearing only a small white undershirt and tan breeches. She pressed her mouth against his. He allowed it, and after a moment, he started to kiss back. She pressed herself against him until he stumbled against the edge of the window. She felt nervous, too, but she was also full of passion. She bit his lip and pulled his mouth towards her.

After a moment, he forced her away from him. "I thought you and Demetas were together."

"More often than not," she said, "we are. What about it?"

"Then, why are you doing *this?*"

Mavas met his gaze and calmly said, "Because I want to. Don't you?"

Her wide eyes were hazy with desire, and her smile so welcoming. He wanted to say something else, but he could not organize any words quickly enough. He didn't say anything before he started kissing her again.

When she started pulling off her shirt, Akheron thought, *Please, Maker, no. Don't let this—* Then she showed herself to him and all of his resistance evaporated.

"I haven't done this before," he said, when she pulled him to the bed.

"It's alright," she said. "I'll show you." And she did.

Later that night, after they had finished, doused the lantern and slipped beneath the blankets, he writhed beside her calm body. He could not sleep, though she was sound in her dreams. His thoughts were so confused that he was barely thinking anything. An occasional argument bubbled through his mind, only to be dismissed for its late timing. Any of his issues were in vain now. In his heart, stomach, and below that, he felt an uneasiness that he had not felt in a long time. He liked her. He really did.

In his head, he felt something else. He whispered under his breath as he fell asleep, "I love *you*, Etheas. I think I always will."

34

Captain Rye Baley did not stoop for Demetas. The bold, wide-shouldered corsair looked down his nose at Akheron's friend and, without stuttering, said, "I demand to know why I am here, Demetas. Tarroth is too... public, for a shark like me. You've summoned us all here—some of us with bloody water between us—and you have yet to offer an explanation."

Demetas gave Akheron a blunt look, and, with a wink, took a sip of his wine. "Go outside, Captain. I'll address you with the rest."

There was a rasp of steel and a wide scimitar came to rest on the table between Akheron and Demetas. The Royal Rogue tavern fell silent. Blades were drawn frequently in the rowdy establishment, but it was still against the innkeeper's rules. If it came to a fight, the patrons would do their best to steer it outside. Someone at the six-person dice table coughed as Rye Baley glared at his rival captain.

"You've wasted my time and patience, and the time and patience of my crew," Captain Baley drawled. "I ought to—"

Demetas quietly put down his wine cup. "I've wasted no time, and your patience will be repaid tenfold. I have a... business proposal for you all, and I don't intend to repeat myself. Any captain who wants none of it will be paid ten silver pieces and a piece for every member of his crew, and sent on his way with no ill wishes. But if any of you draw another blade on me," Demetas licked his lips, "You'll be getting only more steel from me and mine."

Baley set his jaw and quietly withdrew his sword. "A

business proposal?" he asked. He wore a tattered black cape that gathered stylishly about the black leather holster for his silver spyglass. "What sort of business involves fifteen of the most notorious..." His syllables dropped below his breath as he sheathed his sword again and paced away from them. To the dice players, he boomed, "Better get that cough taken care of!" It was not until the shuttered wooden of the Rogue creaked closed that the hubbub of conversation returned to normal.

"Are you sure about this?" Demetas asked Akheron. "I ordered wine, not swords, for our table."

Akheron shrugged. He had not touched his glass and did not intend to. "You know the nature of our kind as well as I do."

"Our kind? Corsairs?"

"No, humans. The only thing to surpass our... anarchy is our selfishness." Akheron glanced into the nearby fire. The words sounded so heretical to his own ear. *This is not the discourse of the Maker's teaching.* Had the great matriarch of the Kinship, Malya, ever spoken of the selfish nature of humans? Akheron sincerely doubted it.

"Selfishness is a solitary mindset," Demetas said. "I'm asking selfish men to work together, aren't I?"

"Like I've pointed out since we first started discussing an organized fleet, the benefits cannot be understated. If we do this right, our navy will last two hundred years. Our children and theirs will know of your piracy," Akheron said. "Tell the captains that, if you want."

Demetas nodded. He poured a little more wine. "Will you have children, one day?"

Akheron shrugged. "I haven't thought much of it." He slouched lower in his chair. What sort of spawn would he bring into the world? *All of us are wrong-doers; and I'm the worst.* "Maybe not," he muttered.

"If you meet the right girl," Demetas said.

"I—" *won't,* he meant to say. He didn't think even Demetas would appreciate such bluntly discouraging words. "I hope I do, someday," he said. *I already love her.* He remembered her fair red hair and those deep blue eyes. Blue as the Mydarius, he had once told her. He reconsidered the glass of wine, but he couldn't move. He was frozen. He *longed* for her, as the moon longed for the sun.

"You will," Demetas said, and finished his glass.

Mar waved from the door, where their friends sat at a table. Haekus and Mavas were there too, waiting. Sath nodded his head toward the door. The last of their guests had arrived.

"It's time I guess," Demetas said. "Will you stand with me?"

Akheron stood up. "I'm afraid that's a bad idea. I'm still a newcomer, to that lot."

Demetas groaned as he rose to Akheron's level.

"Have Sathius stand with you."

Demetas nodded and led the way to their friends' table. Haekus hurriedly finished a mug, while Mar clapped hands with Demetas. "Are you ready?"

"'Course," Demetas said. "Sath, will you stand with me?"

"Aye," the corsair said. He put on his wide black hat. "I hope we aren't strung up on account of poor humours or some such."

"I'm sure we'll be fine," Demetas said.

Outside, Caw One-Eye and Captain Peke were ferociously engaged in a game of five finger fillet, a knife dancing between their fingers. A heavyset but well-armed woman and Matthias Bozlay were busy shouting at each other, while a few others laughed at their antics. The assortment of captains, along with their bristling selection of crewmates, had dominated the entire deck of the Rogue. There were many empty tables, but none of the inn's patrons desired to occupy them. *Selfishness,* Akheron thought, with a dry smile. He hung back with his friends. Haekus gave him a reassuring nod. He had discussed Akheron's philosophies with him a bit, before the latter brought the suggestion to Demetas.

Demetas grabbed a nearby chair, dragged it away from its table and slammed it down on the deck with a loud slam. Then, he put one boot on it and heaved himself up into the air, clearing his throat as he did. "Friends and rivals!"

A few glanced at him, but mostly just to snort in derision.

"Attention!" Demetas shouted. The din began to die down. "Be seated."

Gradually, they all took their seats. Mostly, it was just curiosity that had driven them to this meeting. Everyone knew Demetas was one of the most successful raiders and his exploits were synonymous with the word corsair. What did he want, then, with the rest of them?

Akheron found himself sitting next to the heavy-set woman. She had short brown hair and a perpetually raised eyebrow. "Yory," she said as she sat down. "Captain of the *Sky Hound*."

"Akheron," he replied. "And I don't captain a ship, yet."

"Hah," she said. She glanced back to Demetas.

From the lofty height of that wooden chair, Demetas opened his mouth and preached to his Stead. "Who are you?" he asked. Someone gave their name and chuckled sarcastically, only to be elbowed to silence. "Are you all true corsairs? The wolves among the sheep pen of the two seas?"

"Aye," Captain Shamillard said. "I speak for myself, though."

Captain Peke guffawed. "Silent, you. We're all corsairs here, Dem. Why else would you send for us?"

"Well, what is it that you seek the most? Gold? Jewels? Infamy? Women? Men?" The last one he aimed at Yory, who smirked but said nothing. "I've come to understand the bottom line of the corsair's life. Or so I think. I'll humble myself, but please, consider: we are the men who do not hide what men are."

There was a moment of silence, then Rye Baley slammed a mug against his table and cried, "Here, here!" A few more cups slammed in reply, and a few drinks were had.

"We take what we want, with salt and steel. Let no man tell us where to live, for the open sea is our home. And, look around! We do not live there alone."

"I've got to share it with this lot," One-Eye drawled.

"Hey!" Captain Peke said. "You'd be dead if I hadn't saved you last year."

"I would not—" A brief scuffle ensued, until Sath stepped down from his place beside Demetas's chair and separated the two.

"Here is my proposal," Demetas said. "Any soldier on land knows that there is more plunder to be had by a troop than a single warrior. Even the most dangerous battler needs comrades, if not to help conquer his target, then to help carry the loot afterwards."

"You want us to work for you?" Yory asked.

"Not work *for* me," Demetas said. "Work with me. Together, we can make scores a hundred times what we can apart. They'll tell tales of our quests in the most secluded northland tavern!"

"What could we do together, that we can't do apart?" Baley asked.

Demetas shrugged. "I want to scheme the wealthiest merchants out of their trinkets by surrounding them, on all sides! I already share the bond of brotherhood with my crew; I want to share it with all of you! I want to spit in the face of the Imperial Navy. I don't want to raid little villages any more. I want to raid a proper city! I want to raid the Triumvirate itself! And, like we've agreed—we are the men who do what men want!"

Men were nodding before he was done. The corsairs were clapping as he listed those wants. His audience cheered when he resounded that last declaration.

"I'll have union on the terms of fair shares," Captain Bozlay announced.

"Agreed." Baley folded his arms. "You're not the captain of us all, Demetas."

"We're brothers at arms," Demetas said. "And we share the spoils of our victories. But we will treat this fleet like the army treats theirs. This must not be a raft of drunken scum. We will be a Navy, stronger than the Imperial. We will be the Buccaneer's Navy."

"Here, here!" shouted Captain Peke. All the captains drank, and some began standing up, clasping hands.

"What is our first target?" Caw One-Eye asked.

"Unity," Demetas said, with a laugh. He stepped down from his chair. "I think we work our way from joint raids to a careful scheme. We'll see what comes of that."

"Fair," Shamillard declared. "I'll nominate you the Great Buccaneer."

"We're all equals here," Demetas said, before the other captains interjected. Surprisingly, Shamillard's comment did not conjure much discomfort among the others.

Akheron stood up with a lightness that surprised him. They had done this, Demetas and he. He had set his mind to making himself safer, and had done it. If Aristorn came for him, new the Navy would defend him. *If, if, if,* Akheron thought. *Maybe, one of these if's might eventually let me return home.* He wanted to sail to Avernus right now, like Tam had suggested. But he knew what awaited him there. Aristorn's fires and blood-ready blades. *I loved her, I truly did,* he thought. Again he asked himself that question: *Maker, why?*

Demetas sought him out first, and embraced him like a true brother. "I did it," he said. "We did it. We've built something, today, Akheron. I'll hold you to that word—the Triumvirate will still be fighting us two hundred years from now, when we're all dead and in the drink."

Akheron gripped his friend's hand and smiled.

35

"I'm not done yet," Tam said.

Akheron couldn't even remember their argument. They'd been exchanging angry words all day it felt like. Angry, wanting, depraved words. Tam seemed so healthy, so whole. It attracted Akheron like a moth to the light. The closer he got, the more he felt the fire. "I am," he said, quietly.

His sister had sailed across the sea to find him, in Tarroth. Even a den of murderers, crime lords, and scum could not hide him, it seemed. A termite on a rotten log full of swarming bugs, and she had found this particular bottom-feeder. They sat across from each other on two stone benches on the ramparts of the second tier of Tarroth. From here, the slopes of Mount Aesiar seemed fuzzy, as though a short, ash-choked grass grew upon it. There were nearby hills, but the mining town was built beneath the shadow of the smouldering volcano. It had not been active since the age of myth, when a mighty wizard had supposedly quieted it in order for the builders to raise up their stone-tiered city.

Tam held out her hands as though to grasp what he had said with mock warmth. "Someone has to keep fighting for you."

"I don't need anyone to fight for me, Tam. I can do all the fighting I need to."

"You've let your friends and preachers be replaced by bandits and murderers!" Tam stood up. "Look at this place, Akheron. These are not the warm streets of Avernus. This place is a cave of rock, under a mountain of fire. You've gone as far from the Maker as you can, and I don't know why! What has gotten into you? What has taken you or tempted you?"

"Nothing is tempting me. Tam, this is who I am."

"No," Tam said. "I refuse to believe it."

Akheron looked out at the lazy waves. From here, only the white-capped ones sparkled with light, while the rest were only shifting around. He took a deep breath and let it out through his mouth. Someone was baking bread in the building block below them, and it smelled delicious. "Tam, in Avernus, I have only memories. I miss it, of course. There're so many *good* memories there. But they're all gone. Etheas is." He nearly choked on the name. Quietly, he pulled at the scruff of his beard for a moment and then rubbed the sweat and grease on his shirt. "Prince Aristorn has no fondness for me, anymore. And you've got your own life. I can't bear to look at the Maker's Circle again, not now. Maybe not ever. So I won't come home for the Stead. There're just all those memories."

"Then what's so great about this place? You surround yourself with these people," she said, standing before him. "Haekus seems honourable, but you yourself said that he almost killed you!"

"It was... fun," Akheron said.

Tam craned her neck and rested her palms against her forehead. "Then there's the crowd at the Royal Rogue! I can't believe you would just stay there, even when I sailed across the Gate to find you!"

"Mar was there too."

"Glyphs," Tam said. She leaned back onto the opposing bench. Each of the stone rests was sanded to a cold, smooth surface, and had a large block at the end for an armrest. "Edemar is such a staple of comradeship, is he? You haven't told him to return to Avernus, like you're telling me to! Why should he get to stay with you, here?"

"Let me speak," he said, swiftly, when he could. He met her red-rimmed eye. "I *did* tell Mar to go home, but Demetas decided otherwise. He's one of us. If you can convince Demetas to keep you, then there's not much I can do about it. But Tam... I don't care about Mar. If he lives or dies, or suffers in between, it makes no difference to me. I wouldn't want anyone I love to be here, to be amongst Demetas's circle, and you are—"

"Akheron," she said, leaning forward. Her chestnut bangs

fell to either side of her narrow forehead and she regarded him with a wide frown. He shook his head and tried to look away, but she had her elbows on her knees and one hand grabbed his. "Akheron," she repeated, "I am not done fighting for your soul."

His avoiding eyes became a glare. *Why not?* he wanted to demand. *Why haven't you finished fighting? The Maker's given up on me. Aristorn has given up on me. Give up on me, Tam!* But he didn't speak those words. If he shared even a handful of the cargo-hold he carried on his shoulders, she would be crushed by it. If he told her the truth about Etheas, or the truth about the Maker, the truth about himself... she would spit in his face and damn him to the lowest of earthly places, if only to ensure her own survival.

He did not look away from his sister. He made his voice as cold as the depths of the grey Valharyn below. "It's a fight you've lost, Tam," he said, with raised eyebrows. "Now, leave me."

She quietly released his hand, and regarded him with tears in her eyes. Then she shrugged brokenly, her shoulders sagging and head shaking, and got up from the bench. As the summer sun beat down, Akheron decided to cheer himself up with a game of dice. Sath would have some coins to lose before the end of the eve.

36

The winter wrapped Tarroth in the folds of its cloak as the maritime temperatures plummeted and the snow line crept down the mountain slopes towards the city folk. The season walked through the tunnels of rock unhindered; it was wary of the fire braziers and furnaces, but feared nothing else. Tendrils of smoke continued to rise above Mount Aesiar, but the mountain did not share any warmth with the free city.

Somehow, the city's populace remained free of even the cold's clutches. Markets remained open except during the storms. There was a winter fair, serving food delicacies and unusual entertainments—a man walked with tamed wolves around a large enclosure, a trickster performed illusions with glyphs that changed the light and fooled the mind, and a fighting ring was set up for any who wished to duel or wrestle. At night, the children were locked within the tiers of the city, and the adults continued to feast and party into the darkness. The cages were no longer occupied with wolves, the foods were spicier, the drinks heavier, and the wrestling was not limited to the men.

Akheron took little part in such venues. He gambled, mainly for the fun of the game, and occasionally watched the daytime entertainers. He spent most of his days with his newfound friends, Demetas, Sathius and Mavas. They shared freely of their wealth, and, in return, Akheron helped when he could. Once, he went on a raid with them, and watched as their corsair crew fought a town's guards to seize loot. It had been more violent and criminal than Akheron was prepared for, but he wanted to earn his keep and there was something about them that drew him. Perhaps it was their freedom.

One day, as the sun made its short, crooked journey across the sky, Akheron went for a walk to the second tier of the city. He had never been to the third tier, but he didn't particularly care to. *My days of royal courts and lordly friends are done,* he told himself. Once, he had called a Prince friend. Aristorn, the Wise. The memory brought only sadness, and he brushed past it like the dead, dried leaves near one of the city's potted-tree gardens.

It had been almost two years. This was his new life.

"Akheron!" It was Mavas, running to catch up to him.

He turned. She was wearing a blue shawl around her shoulders and a lopsided cloth hat hung toward her ear. Where was she off to, in the middle of the day?

"Demetas and the others are already at the ring."

"The ring?" Akheron asked. "At the fair?"

Mavas smiled and started to walk past. Akheron hurried to keep up. "The Red Dancer is fighting today," she said. "It'll be quiet the show, lordling!"

Sath and she had started calling him "lordling" as a joke, though Akheron ten Gothikar had always been a commoner. Once, the Gothikars had been kings, but that was before Tiberon had put them down. Personally, Akheron did not find the joke humorous.

"Who's the Red Dancer?" Akheron said, walking alongside her. A few feet from the battlement of the second-tier of Tarroth, a torch-lit stairwell descended to the first tier, where most of the fair was set up. It was the widest of the tiers.

Mavas stared at him. "Who's the Red Dancer!"

Akheron shrugged and followed her between two covered market stalls. Beneath a blue banner, a man selling candies and baked goodies tried offering Akheron some, but he ignored the haggle and kept walking.

"That's the Red Dancer!"

The fighting ring ahead was surrounded by the largest crowd Akheron had seen so far. It had four wooden corner posts, slats of wood forming a squared fenced area. Rising about four feet from the ground, the duelling platform was occupied by two men locked in a fast-paced bout. One stocky man, armed with a broadsword and shield, seemed to be taking the offensive. Calmly retreating away from his opponent's onslaught, a lanky redheaded man, wielding only a single sword, defended himself.

Akheron watched in fascination as the fight continued. It was clear which one was famous; the lesser armed man had no trouble turning the shield-banger in circles. He even moved like a dancer.

Mavas and he reached the back of the crowd. "There's Sath," she said, and started cutting the way through the crowd to where he stood.

The Red Dancer decided to stop playing with his opponent. In a fluid motion, his blade seemed to wrap around his opponent's. The first slice cut deep enough into the man's blade arm that the weapon slipped from his hands. The second slice, at the man's leg, sent him spilling across the fight ring. He crashed onto his hands, and rolled over, raising his shield as quickly as he could. The victor of the fight gently stepped on the shield arm, forcing it out of the way.

"Yield!" cried the defeated warrior. The victor spread his arms and stepped off him. "I yield. Now, heal me!"

There was a small wooden gate built against the side of the ring. It slammed open, and a handful of people stormed into the ring.

The Red Dancer restlessly strode away. He yanked a tattered cloth from his belt and wiped the blood from his weapon as he paced. "Come on, Tarroth!" he boomed. "You can do better than that!"

One of the ring's attendants knelt by the wounded dueller and put a hand on his shoulder. A moment later, both reclaimed their feet. The warrior was unharmed, though his clothes sported a few holes. Undoing a strap on his left arm, the warrior shoved his shield into the hands of one of men on the dais.

"Mavas," Akheron said, as they reached the other corsairs. "Was that magic?"

Sath chuckled. "You bet. They heal the wounded... but the Red Dancer has already killed two today. Can't heal deceasement."

"Deceasement?" Demetas asked. They were pretty close to the ring. From here, the Dancer looked larger than life, swinging his sword at the air impatiently. Sathius shrugged at Demetas's incredulity.

The ring's master, a man in a burgundy coat with big blue

earrings and a black tattoo under his eye, raised his hand at the Dancer. "Haekus is once again our champion!"

"No way." With dry sarcasm, the fighter dragged his finger across his throat. "I expected more out of you lot!"

The game keeper laughed awkwardly. Even he seemed out of his depth. Rubbing his hands together, he asked the crowd. "Do we have any more contenders?"

To Demetas, Sath said, "Let me, Dem—"

"No way," Demetas said. "He'll carve you up in short order."

"But they can just heal me."

Mavas laughed. "It *would* be entertaining."

Akheron was barely paying attention. He was still just a *lordling* to these bandits. He'd been waiting for a chance to shine. Maybe this was it. But he didn't really know how to fight. His experience was only from a raid with his friends, and a few sessions with the Avernan Master of Arms, when Aristorn had suggested it.

"He's a blade-master," Demetas said. "That means he was trained by the Academy of Swordplay in Olympus. And he's not just any blade-master. He's the *Red Dancer!* He hasn't been beat."

"You're too fat," decided the ring keeper. A line of shabby half-drunk old men had formed in front of the wooden gate. "You don't even smell human anymore," he said to another.

The Dancer was standing with his long legs spread and his sword held behind his head like a yolk. He circled impatiently. "Come on..."

Akheron shook his head. It was a dare. *I want some real action. I have since the start of all this. I realized I'm nothing more than all this rabble. All this scum.* He remembered it as clearly as his name. *I'm nothing anymore. I was once so much more. Aristorn's friend. Etheas's love. I was a champion of sorts. I was a good man.*

The Red Dancer scanned the audience quietly. His short red hair seemed to have no sweat in it, like defeating these fighters was nothing more than walking or eating breakfast was. His eyes met Akheron's briefly, and then continued through the crowd of bleakly-dressed miners and merchants. He was looking for something. For someone *more* than all this. "Come on,

Tarroth," he said again. "Where are the legendary corsairs? Where are the dangerous criminals that cannot fit in the delicate Triumvirate? Where's a decent match for me?"

"Please," Sath said to Demetas, as Akheron started to walk forward. *There's no such thing as* more *than all this scum. This is us. Humankind, the dirt of this forsaken rock.* Someone needed to tell the Red Dancer this.

Mavas was the first to notice that Akheron was walking. "Wait," she said, trying to grab him. He pulled himself out of her grip. *There is no* more *than this,* Akheron wanted to say. If there was, Akheron would use it to show Etheas that he *was* a good man. He was staring at this fighter, though. He wanted to say, *You're no better than all of us. You're cut from the same cloth.*

"What are you doing?" Demetas asked, grabbing his arm. When Akheron didn't stop, he walked alongside him. "Where are you going?" The miners ahead of Akheron gently made way for him.

"Is there no one here with a desire for glory?" the fight keeper demanded.

"I'll fight him," Akheron called.

Everyone seemed to react to this. The keeper pointed, with a wide, greedy smile. Demetas cursed and tried to pull Akheron to a stop. Mavas laughed.

And the Red Dancer? He locked eyes with Akheron.

"Are you sure, lad?" the ring keeper asked. He stepped off the platform and down to Akheron's level. "You willing to pay? There's no good gambling in a one-sided fight. Two crowns, and I'll let you in the ring, or one corsair."

Akheron absently handed him a single iron coin. Tarroth was the only city to accept the illegal currency.

The Dancer was swinging his sword again, and getting himself pumped up.

"Alright," the ring keeper said. "You fight much?"

Akheron shrugged. "I've used a sword a few times."

"A few times?" the man had a lot of flesh below his chin which swayed with his words and nods. He calmly put a hand on Akheron's arm. "You're thin as the fog, and just as pale, too. Are you sure about this?"

"I said I'll fight. And I paid you," Akheron said. He showed the man his scabbard and the cheap blade he had bought before leaving Avernus last year. "Do I use my own sword?"

"Do you have a death wish?" the ring master asked. The tattoo under his eye was just a mix of swirling lines, but it looked faintly like the contour of a woman's body.

"What?"

The crowd was making a fuss, listening and talking about the new contender. Demetas was still trying to speak to him, while Sath was complaining that it wasn't him fighting.

The man grabbed Akheron's shoulders with both of his hands and met his eyes. "Listen, that blade-master, he's killed a few men already today. We have a healer, but if he nicks you too close to something vital... you'll be dead before you hit the ground. This isn't some game, young man. This is life or death. So, do you want to die today?" There was no humour or softness in the voice.

Jarred, Akheron found himself facing the question that had defined the last two years of his life. He blinked. When Demetas had asked him that same question, he had joked his way out of answering it. There was no avoiding it here and now, so he dug inside and found an answer. "No," he said firmly. The strength of the reply surprised him. *I'm not done with this world.* "I'm not going to die today. Count on it."

The fight keeper grinned and said, "There we go. That's the spirit. You can use one of our swords if you would prefer."

Hands removed his scabbard from his waist. It was Demetas, who gave him a smile and said, "If this is what you want... make me smile." Then he spun Akheron toward a rack of weapons. Akheron shrugged out of his grey cloak, assuming Demetas would also take that.

There were three swords. The broadsword wielded by the first warrior had already been replaced, though Akheron favoured a longer, lighter blade. "And a shield?" prodded one of the attendants.

Akheron glanced at the Dancer again. The blade-master wielded only a single weapon. "No," he told the squire. The ring keeper snorted. Akheron repeated himself. "It's not a fair fight if I'm more armed than he."

The ring keeper's bulbous earrings swayed like his jowls. "It isn't a fair fight! He's been training his whole life."

"No shield," Akheron said. He had never been trained with

one, anyway.

The Red Dancer smiled and nodded when he saw Akheron, climbing the steps with just a single sword. "Well met," the dueller said, extending his hand. "Think you've got the skill? I'm not sure if you've got steel nerves or are just a fool."

"Neither," Akheron said. "I'm just one of them." He nodded toward the crowd, then took the man's hand. The air was icy, but that would not be a problem for long. The floor of the fighting ring was stained red, and not a lot of it looked old.

"I'm Haekus of Olympus," the redhead said, as he stepped away. He flexed his sword hand, while his blade still rested in the crook of his free hand. He wore a sleeveless tan tunic, and didn't appear cold at all. He seemed completely comfortable.

"Akheron ten Gothikar." Akheron gently gave his sword a shake. He wanted to be used to its weight as much as he could before the duel began.

"Attention onlookers!" boomed the ring master. "We have another bout for your bets. Akheron thinks his short fighting experiences from the past will give him what it takes to survive the Red Dancer..."

A few boos resounded, but there was more laughter than anything. Demetas and his friends remained silent. Akheron tried not to look their way. He could make out enough words from the crowd that they were not betting on a winner. They were betting on whether Akheron would die or not.

Typical, heartless men, Akheron thought, and then smirked at the thought. Thankfully, Haekus didn't see it.

"Best of luck to you both," said the ring keeper. It was still a stage for him, and he wasn't really talking to the fighters. He was talking to his audience. "Or, if you have the faith, Maker's blessings. Now... fight!" He scurried for the gate, as though the duel would begin with swords a-flurry.

Haekus circled Akheron, as the latter kept his guard up. He angled the sword at what felt like a good position. To the blade-master's trained eye, he probably looked ridiculous.

After a moment of analysis, the Red Dancer delivered a direct slash at Akheron, clearly a testing attack. Akheron blocked it easily, but the clash of steel-on-steel almost made him bite out his tongue. After that, he kept his teeth clenched. *I felt that in my spine!* Again, the truth sunk in: this was not a game.

This was life or death.

Haekus attacked again, and, this time, Akheron retaliated with a thrust of his long blade. Haekus didn't bother blocking. He just stepped aside. He could've delivered a dangerous blow in the opportunity, but didn't.

They circled again, then exchanged steel once more. This bout lasted a few clangs of sword longer, but again, they separated. Though it felt like their game of cat-and-mouse continued for a long time, Akheron was certain only a few moments had passed. He started to sweat.

And so, Haekus taught him how to fight.

Akheron was surprised he had it in him. *I thought I had given up,* he said. But the way he defended himself... the resounding blow or the slow grind of crossed blades felt so... *alive* to him. He had some fight in him, and, suddenly, he really wanted to let it all out.

The next time that Haekus relented his assault, Akheron did not. He pursued his opponent with an angry hack.

Haekus moved quicker than Akheron had ever seen a man move, and he felt something cold against his left arm. Somehow, the blade-master had stepped under his attack, and nicked him as he danced past. Without thinking, Akheron swept his sword downward and caught the blade-master's weapon before it could cleave the back of his leg muscles.

Haekus grunted in surprise and tried to step away. Akheron swung his sword in an upward arc, leaning off balance to account for Haekus's backward motion.

He wasn't sure how much he hit, but he felt the tug of meat on the end of his blade. The Red Dancer glided away, hiding one side from Akheron so he could not see the damage he had done. Meanwhile, Akheron gingerly glanced at his left arm. He had received more than a nick—there was a line of blood dribbling down his arm.

"Didn't expect that," Haekus said, showing a blood-stained hand. Akheron's blade must have made a good mark on his right side, under his ribs. The beige tunic was stained. "Let's play, then."

He thrust forward as fast as lightning. Akheron stepped to the side as he had seen Haekus do. And he took advantage of the opening, swinging his sword down at Haekus's arm. The Red

Dancer parried and tried an uppercut. Again, Akheron just stepped away and followed with his own attack. Haekus blocked the slice again, and again, went on the offensive. His blade cut the air as Akheron ducked below the slash.

"Glyphs," Haekus said, stepping back on the balls of his feet. "You are fast, I'll give you that."

Akheron smirked. The crowd was cheering. When had they started cheering? He didn't dare look around, but kept his eyes locked on his deadly opponent. Sweat dripped off him and his breath fogged the cold air. Now he was glad it was winter.

Haekus touched his side wound to check it, but as abruptly as he had stopped fighting, he was rushing at Akheron once again. His blade moved in a spiral, slashing again and again at his opponent's left side. Akheron had blocked the first, but the speed of the assault prevented him from then trying to dodge. He kept his sword angled on that side of his body, parrying blow after blow. He was stepping backward as he blocked, and there wasn't much space left.

Then, out of nowhere, Haekus's spinning blade did not land on the left side. Akheron found himself lying face first against the wooden fence. Alarmed, he rolled to the right—ignoring the pain—as Haekus's blade slashed down on the fresh wood. Bark splintered through the air, as Akheron's thrust blindly with his sword. He hooked the point into the Red Dancer's arm and pushed, as hard as he could, away from him.

Haekus grunted and stumbled away.

Akheron's shoulder was killing him. When Haekus's blade had not spiraled toward the left side, it had landed on the right side. Blood was coursing down his blade arm, and it hurt to move the muscle. Biting back the pain, Akheron advanced on his opponent.

Haekus shook his head; his left arm now resembled Akheron's right. He saw Akheron coming for him, and pulled himself through the pain. As Akheron jabbed his blade straight again, Haekus arched his back forward and thrust as well. Both blades hit flesh, and both duellers did not separate this time. Akheron felt the sword slash along his left hip, as he drove his own blade at his opponent's shoulder. Then, as they came close enough to touch, Akheron slammed his shoulder into Haekus's side.

They both ended up on the ground, rolling away from one another. The sky was white, the shouting of the crowd a distant buzz.

Akheron rolled to his feet, favouring his right leg, to find Haekus already bearing down on him. They crossed blades, shoving against one another. Then, the swords separated and became a flurry of attacks and parries once more. For countless painfully-inhaled breaths, their melee continued. Akheron received cuts on his other leg, another gash on his left arm. At one point, Haekus separated from a clash by elbowing Akheron in face, and after that he tasted blood in his mouth. Haekus didn't fare any better; he had a proper hole in his shoulder—his left arm didn't even move, and was bleeding from a dozen other injuries too.

Akheron *was* this fight. In this moment, as he slammed his sword ruthlessly against his opponent's, he was more alive than he had been in a year. He no longer wanted to hide in Tarroth. He wanted to go home. He no longer wanted anything to do with Demetas and the corsairs; he wanted to be as noble and wise as Aristorn. As he twisted a slash against Haekus's back, he became something *more* than this crowd. Something that was stronger than any betrayal. *I'd make you proud, Etheas,* he thought.

And with that thought, he made a mistake. He stepped too far forward. Haekus dragged his blade in an uppercut, up Akheron's left leg, before the commoner's sword could protect down that far. Akheron's leg gave out from beneath him, though he could barely feel the pain, and he found himself lying on his back. Before he even saw Haekus stepping over him, he thrust upward.

The blade pierced the advancing torso, spraying blood onto Akheron. Haekus cursed, loudly, and back stepped quickly.

Akheron tried to climb to his feet, but his left leg wouldn't work at all. He dragged himself after the wounded blade-master. The Red Dancer was leaking from a hole between his ribs. It didn't look deep, but there was a lot of red.

Haekus spit blood to one side, amidst a cloud of frost. He saw Akheron and shook his head. With scuffing feet, he stumbled forward.

Akheron used his sword to push himself to up. He couldn't

move his left leg, but he used it stiffly like a crutch. When his opponent raised his own blade, Akheron was ready. He knew he could not move around—he would just fall over—so he took the offensive whenever Haekus came into range. A slash here and a jab there kept Haekus wary. The blade-master again spit up blood.

The next time that Haekus stepped in for the attack, Akheron used his right foot to force himself forward. They crossed blades, and Akheron shoved Haekus off his feet.

Together, they plummeted to the floor, and hit it hard. Akheron found the crossed swords in his face, grazing his cheek and shaving him. He pressed his own blade down with both hands, as blood welled up from one palm. Haekus angled his weapon to save himself, and the blades pressed into his right shoulder. He cried out, but Akheron did not relent. Had he been in Haekus's shoes, he would not want his oppressor to give an inch. *Bring it all on!*

Then, up came Haekus's elbow again, releasing his sword enough to slam Akheron away. The unhindered swords slashed past his shoulder until they met the wood beneath and Akheron rolled out of striking range. He spit up his own blood this time. He didn't think he could move anymore. But he would not yield.

"A match," Haekus whispered. "You've given me... a refreshing fight."

Akheron laughed, but started to choke and quit. They were both just staring up at the sky without the strength to face each other. "I'm not dying today. Not unless you are, too."

"I say, we both live another day."

"Sounds fair," Akheron decided. "Got you good, there. When I fell on my leg."

"You did," Haekus laughed. "I think, if they don't heal us soon, I might bleed out."

Akheron raised himself up on one arm, though it hurt to do that. He wasn't in great shape either. He felt weak and nauseous. "Healer!" he called.

The ring-master was already on the stage, staring down at their bleeding bodies. "I don't believe it," he said, quietly.

"Healer," Akheron gagged. He fell back to the ground. Had he broken something, inside?

"I declare this fight a draw!" the man shouted.

At last, the healer arrived, and with a silent rush of syllables healed Haekus. Then it was Akheron's turn. The words felt alien, as did the wash of ice that sunk into Akheron's extremities. At least the physical pain went with it. And the scars, too.

Haekus was crouched, examining their chipped and scratched swords. "Who are you?" he asked.

"Just one of them," Akheron said, staring out at the crowd. "As are you."

"No," Haekus whispered, turning to stare at him. During the fight, they had been connected like a single confused identity. The *fight* itself. Haekus smiled through bloody teeth. "No, you're something more than this rabble."

Akheron closed his eyes against the bright white sky. *That means I'm something worse.*

37

Akheron turned the iron coin over in his hands and then tried returning it to the corsair. *Glyphs, she doesn't even mind being grabbed by a stranger,* he thought of the woman whose waist he clasped; Ursha's bare midriff was smooth and warm.

Sathius Miroso would not accept the corsair coin back. He raised his hand and smiled. "No, you keep that for a drink. If only to buy Ursha a drink, should you be too *honourable* for alcohol."

"Too inexperienced, in truth."

"I am rich with experience, with women, with coin, with life!" Sath declared, drawing looks from the passersby. "Just a sip is all you will need."

Akheron glanced out at the ocean. He had just arrived in Tarroth, and that sea called to him. Avernus. *My city... and I left it in shame.* The iron coin was cold and so much more real than Akheron's memories. He glanced back at Sathius. "To the Royal Rogue, then."

"Excellent!" the corsair took Ursha's hand and led the way.

It was not far. Built against the side of the pyramid-like wall was a wooden deck. It served as the face for a stone building with sharp, crisscrossing lines carved into its walls. An elaborate etching read, "The Royal Rogue—All welcome!" The cursive script was weathered by years of winter storms and was barely legible. The tavern looked anything like 'royal', as Sath led him across the freshly sanded deck between two enormous sailors that smelled like beer and sweat. He got a glance through the front window at a packed table of card players. There were more beverages on their table than coins.

Akheron kept turning over the coin in his hand, as Sath held the door open for Ursha, and then led Akheron within. "Welcome!" boomed the corsair. "To our den of inequities!"

There were as many women as there were men, though the latter were more thoroughly garbed. Akheron tried not to meet eyes, but many of the prostitutes smiled at him and tried to meet his. Sathius seemed to have some destination in mind, leading Akheron through the low-hanging haze of smoke. He coughed, and tried not to show the tears that welled up to protect his eyes from the sting of it all. He had set foot in a few places like this before, over his last week in Avernus, but most of these men were hardened criminals, not dispossessed commoners. Men waved to Sathius, or grabbed his hand. At last, Sathius stopped at a table.

"Twelve. Twelve to do the job," said the man at the head of the table. His muscular arms crossed on the table, though his skin was pale and malnourished. He smiled to the people he was speaking to, and Akheron had to stare at all the holes in his teeth. The man pulled his wiry brown hair out of his eyes as he looked up at Sathius. He had a scar on his forehead. "Where've you been?"

"With her," Sathius said, pinching Ursha's bottom.

"You should try it sometime," the whore said, smiling at the ugly man.

Sath shook his head, though the man at the head of the table merely winked, and extended his hand to the woman sitting next to him. There were others at the table, but Akheron could no longer look at anyone else than her. She had short brown hair, knotted behind her head and sharp facial features. She glanced at the man who had touched her; she was breathtaking in the opposite way than he was. "I don't think anything could compare, Ursha. Not to this one," the man said. "Sath, who's this, anyway?"

All eyes turned to Akheron. The ugly man wasn't smiling anymore. Akheron glanced to the man's right; that stunning woman was staring at him too, and she stole all his words away.

"This is... Akheron," Sath said. "He's fresh off a boat from Avernus, and he seems to have fallen on hard times. He's one of your twelve, I suspect."

"What do you say?" the man said. "Do you want a job?"

"A job?" Akheron asked. He had an epiphany that he was standing in a drunken tavern, surrounded by pirates, and that he was being offered a job. Suddenly, the good looks of the woman at the table meant very little.

"Give him a chance," Sath said. "He's not sure what he's looking for yet."

The ugly man made his crooked smile again. "Of course, of course. Akheron, I'm Demetas, captain of the *Astral Arrow*. This is Mavas. That's my first mate, Thord, and Captain Peke, of *Peke's Oasis.*"

"How do you do," said Thord.

Mavas smiled and said, "Akheron."

Sath gave him a grin. "Why don't you go buy Ursha that drink?" he asked.

Akheron shrugged. "I don't know what..."

"Just a beer," Ursha said.

"Get me one, too," Mavas said, with a wink. She reminded him of Etheas, but her hair was not red and not as long.

Akheron had no other option than to comply. He looked around for the bar, which was crowded with miners and fishermen. *It's only the middle of the day!* he thought, as he made his way toward it. There was a table of men laughing obnoxiously loud nearby, so he walked the long way around the room to avoid them.

He found a spot near the end of the bar and waited for the barkeeper to come by. She was a short buxom woman with curly black hair. Her complexion implied she was a native of Tarroth—hair that black was not found in many other places. She came his way and asked, "What can I get you?"

"Two beers," he said.

She grabbed a pair of mugs and stepped up to the keg behind the bar. As she filled them, he lifted his iron coin to the ready.

"Hello," said the man next to him. He was as tall as Akheron, with short sandy hair and a scar under his left eye.

Akheron nodded to him, then looked back at the barkeeper.

"I'm... Arad," said the man. His tone had almost an inquisitive quality.

"Akheron." The barkeeper brought over the two beers, and

Akheron held up the iron coin. "Will this pay for it?" he asked.

She raised an eyebrow. "You, a corsair!...Yes, it's enough. Do you want change?"

"I suppose so," Akheron replied. She handed him a silver coin. *Glyphs, is corsair currency really worth so much here?*

"I think I spoke to you once before," said Arad. He had his own mug, but didn't seem very interested in it. He seemed more concerned about Akheron.

"I don't think so." Akheron started to get up from the bar.

"You've just come from Avernus?" asked the odd man.

Akheron turned back, and sat down on the bar stool again.

Arad was smiling. "The first time, *I* seemed confused and you did not. This time, it's *you* who doesn't know me..."

"Glyphs, what?" Akheron asked. "How did you know I'm from Avernus?"

"I know lots about you," Arad said. "The first time we met, you asked me why I *studied* you. If it was to be like you."

"No man should want to be like me," Akheron said.

"That's what we agreed upon then."

"I've never met you before."

Ruthlessly, Arad continued. "But I was wrong, in that conversation. There is something to learn from you. How to keep evil at a distance, how to think about what is wrong, like it's a curse."

"I don't keep evil at a distance. It's in my soul, simply because I walk upon the face of this world," Akheron said. "And how do you know what I think?"

Arad's eyes seemed to know so much more than that, and though he had a short smile on his face, he did not seem happy. He seemed empathetic. "You will find redemption one day," Arad said.

"Don't." Akheron's voice dripped with venom.

"And if you didn't fight inside, if you didn't wrestle with what you've done with every last fiber of you... you would not be able to see forgiveness, and you would not be able to ask for it," Arad said. "When the time comes."

Akheron put his hand on his sword, and drew the blade out an inch. "Do you know what I've done?"

The words hung in the air for a moment. If Arad knew as much as he seemed to, he knew that this was a life or death question. Right here and now, in the middle of this noisy sinful pit, Akheron would have no trouble drawing his sword and damning his soul with another crime.

There were tears in Arad's eyes now. *"You* know what you've done," he said. Then he stood up. "And that's enough, for now."

Was he just going to walk away? After this? Akheron released the hilt, put a hand on Arad's shoulder and quietly asked, "But what about all the people I'll hurt? If I stay on this world *and* keep knowing what I've done—I will burn this world before I find peace. I swear it. Aristorn must forget, the Maker must forget... I will make them forget. I have to. What about all the death?"

Arad shook his head. "I don't know. It's a tragedy," he said. "I wish... It doesn't matter what I wish, does it?"

"I'm afraid not," Akheron whispered.

"Akheron!" Sath shouted. "Come on, already!"

Arad stepped away, and when Akheron tried to follow he realized he had lost track of the mysterious man. He scanned through the crowd of lost people and did not find Arad there, for the man was nowhere close to being lost.

He looked down at the two beers he was holding and he remembered that woman, Mavas's, dangerous smile. "It's a tragedy," he repeated, and went to find his new friends. That iron coin was worth almost as much as gold; how much would this new job pay?

38

The main street divided into three others that toured the Residential District. To prolong arriving at his old house, Akheron took the southern prong, and walked throughout the estates that overlooked the Gate of the seas. It was autumn, and errant leaves decorated the roadway with brilliant orange and rusty yellow. The sun was low enough to occasionally blind Akheron when he looked straight ahead. There was a breeze blowing through the street, scattering the dead foliage droppings and chilling him to the bone.

Occasionally, through the divide between buildings, he spotted the gleaming water. He could see a little of the channel between the Valara Isles and the Point, and beyond those large rocks in the channel, he could see the ocean proper, sparkling under the sun's afternoon rays.

The ship was departing soon; they were probably already waiting for Akheron. He had paid the captain enough that the ship would not set sail until he arrived, however late that may be.

He just wasn't ready to say goodbye to his home.

The buildings were tall in this part of town; most were two big storeys, and one or two had an attic above that. The fronts usually had white marble columns and vine-covered lattices, while some even had an iron gate in front of that. On the corner of another avenue, an enormous mansion rose three storeys high. Two columns rose on either side of its front doors, reaching the whole way to the top of the second floor before meeting the eaves they supported. How much was this estate worth? It seemed unbelievable, even after Akheron's regular appearances at court. Telvyn Aristorn's Keep and private estate were even fancier, of course, but he had a royal treasury to fund his properties. As far as Akheron knew, this mansion just belonged to some citizen who had a lot of money.

At last, his feet brought him back to the main street. He stopped avoiding the route he knew so well, and followed the roads toward his house. He had not been home in a week, and he did not intend to stay.

The Gothikar household was barely two storeys; though it had been renovated recently, it was one of the poorer houses on the block. Of course, the Gothikars were commoners. Many of those living here were lords and ladies. When Akheron had been a child, his father had purchased this home, and separated his house from his workplace. Most of the commoners in the city could not afford such extravagance; they lived where they worked.

Absently, Akheron thought to thank his late father for the opportunity. He never would have met Telvyn's family if he had been just another commoner.

Before last week, he was on a track toward the upper class, but now he was stuck with a 'ten' article in his name for good.

"Akheron?" Tamese was in the kitchen, staring at him out of the window. She ran to the front door, and the warmth released pressed against Akheron's face. "Oh, Akheron!"

He allowed her to embrace him, but it was clear to them both that he did not share the emotion she did.

"Where have you been?" she asked. "We'd started searching for you!"

"I know," Akheron said. "But you have to stop."

"What? Akheron, you've been gone for a week! We were worried..." Tam lowered her voice, "We were worried you had done something rash."

"I've lost her," Akheron mumbled.

"I know," Tam said. "Everyone does."

"I can't stay here."

Tam raised an eyebrow. "What do you mean?"

Akheron took a deep breath. He tried to look away from her, but the sun was blinding, and he met her eyes again. "Tam, I'm leaving for a while. I'm leaving Avernus."

"Glyphs!" Tam shook her head in disbelief. "Please, just come inside. We'll talk it over first."

"No," Akheron commanded. "This isn't like getting in an argument with Mar, or placing a bad bet. This isn't like our parents' deaths. We can't just 'talk this over'. I'm leaving."

"Are you going to be alright?"

"I hope so," Akheron said. "I just need to stretch my legs, and get some fresh air. You know?" It was a blatant lie. He wanted to get away from here. He wanted to forget about Telvyn. He wanted to forget about Etheas. He wanted to forget that truth he had learned—*You're only a man*—that repeated again and again in his head.

Besides, Aristorn would have his head if he found Akheron in the city. He was the true witness, not Rel, another of his fictive sons. Rel though, Rel had seen Akheron's sin with his eyes, instead of hearing word of it from spies.

"I have to do this, Tam," Akheron repeated.

She hugged him again. "Thanks for telling me, I guess."

"I'm many things, but I won't be heartless," Akheron said, with a sad smile.

"I'll see you soon, right?" Tam said.

Akheron shrugged and started to back away.

"You'll come back here, right?"

Akheron took another deep breath. "I don't know. Glyphs, I just don't know. Goodbye, Tam."

"'Bye," she said. She didn't go inside though. Akheron turned and forced himself to walk away. He tried not to look back, but he couldn't stop himself. He glanced over his shoulder when he was twenty paces away; Tam was still there. She waved.

He looked straight ahead and didn't turn back again. It was the year 507, and he was going to Tarroth, a rock on the edge of the world where no one cared about the world's refuse. He hoped it would be a new home, because he felt like he was leaving *himself* in Avernus.

39

The door creaked open, a hole into Akheron's abyss. How long had he been in that room, before the door admitted eyes to see that dark, dark place? He had lost track.

The man who stepped inside witnessed it all. He saw Akheron's sin, he saw the blood, he saw it all. It was Rel, blessed Rel. He had been like Telvyn's son long before Akheron had entered the picture. Rel ten Asirus was an apprentice blacksmith in the Prince's Palace; after forging a marvelous helm for Prince Aristorn, he had begun a friendship with Prince Telvyn Aristorn. Akheron may have been a comrade of the Prince, but Rel was like a son.

And he was the first witness.

"What have you done?" Rel whispered. "Glyphs, Akheron, why?"

Akheron stared up at him—he was lying on the ground—and trembled. He had no answer. "Don't tell him."

"Him? Who? Aristorn?" Rel's eyes were wide with horror. "I'm going to him right now."

The door closed.

Akheron pulled himself to his feet. There was blood everywhere. He wiped his hands on his pants, but they would not clean. There were red lines in the cracks of his palms that would never clean. He stumbled to the doorway, without looking down at his stained clothes.

This was in Telvyn's house, his mansion in the Residential District. The Prince was still at the Keep though; he had stayed there for a political dinner.

In the corridor, Rel was dashing for the stairwell. Akheron blinked. It was brighter in the hall than in that cursed room. He ran after the blacksmith with all the strength he could muster.

At the bottom of the stairwell was a wide, circular anteroom. Rel grabbed the door, yanked it open, and Akheron collided with him.

"Let me go," Rel whispered, trying to squeeze through.

Akheron clung to Rel's sleeve and tried to force the door closed on the man. "Please, I'm sorry, please don't, please..." he mumbled. He was weeping still.

"Maker, let me go!" Rel cried, and shoved Akheron off him. He stepped outside and took off at a run. Where were the servants? If they saw Akheron, drenched in red, he would have to stop them from telling the Prince too.

Thankfully, as he pulled himself to his feet, the room was still empty. The heavy wooden door was ajar. Through it, he could see Rel pulling open the gate of the estate's grounds. He had made it to the street.

Akheron sprinted through the door without shutting it. He blurred through the garden, disregarding the winding stone walkway and reached the street as Rel took off in the direction of the Palace grounds. A woman and her son were shoved out of Akheron's way as he gave pursuit. "Stop!" he shouted in vain. *Please Maker...* The prayer was met with silence of course. The Maker would have nothing to do with a sinner like Akheron.

There were three streets through the residential district, and Rel took the most direct one toward the Palace. Akheron was lighter on his feet, he was barely anything but skin and bones. His best muscles were his legs though, and he started to gain on the stocky young blacksmith.

It was night. The sun had set. Had he been inside that long, in that dark chamber? The guards were lighting the street lanterns. A couple shouted, "Stop!" as they saw Rel and Akheron dash past, but even though they gave chase, they fell far behind. Ahead was the evening market, shining with light. The noise of the merchants, entertainers, and the crowd was so loud it drowned out Akheron's rushing footsteps and pounding heartbeat.

Rather than trying to fight his way through the clutches of the busy market, Rel twisted to the right, and sprinted up a staircase. Akheron was moving forward too fast, and he skidded too far to make the stairs. After colliding with the brickwork on the front of an apothecary's shop, he stumbled back a few steps, and chased up the stone ramp.

Rel was already across the wooden rooftop above, so Akheron sucked in his breath and sprinted after him. He couldn't tell if his hand was bleeding from the rough bricks, or if it was blood from earlier.

He leapt across the alleyway ahead and landed on the next rooftop. They were more than halfway to the Palace grounds now, and Akheron was still several arm's-lengths behind. He bit back the pain in his lungs and pushed himself after Telvyn's friend. "Please," he gasped again, but talking made it harder to run.

Rel leapt another alley, this time onto a stone rooftop. His sandaled feet thundered across the surface. Before he reached the other side, Akheron's feet slapped the rock too.

The next rooftop was shingles, and Rel landed on it off balance. He fell to one knee, sliding down the tilt toward the edge.

Akheron landed on the top of a gable and slid down it to the roof proper, where Rel had fallen. He desperately grabbed at the shingles to stop his fall, as Rel was doing. At the window of the gable was a small, mock balcony. Akheron's bloody hands grabbed the metal rail of it and did not slip.

Rel reached the edge of the roof, his skinned knee squealing along the plaster shingles. With a cry, he slipped over the edge and was gone.

Moments later, someone screamed.

Akheron inhaled painfully. *I'm dying,* he thought. It felt like all the air he sucked in turned to fire as it passed his throat. He could barely process what was going on. *Rel went over...*

He let his muscles slack a bit, and stood up on the shingles gently. He wouldn't slip if he was careful. He leaned over the edge, just enough to see below. Rel lay in the street, his legs buckled beneath him. The building was only a storey and a half tall, but the blacksmith did not appear to be moving. A group of men and women had surrounded him. "Someone help!" cried a woman. A man said, "Go get a healer—this man might survive!"

Akheron gingerly stepped away from the edge. Rel

wouldn't be telling anyone now, would he? *You can't heal death,* he whispered. If Rel was dead. *Of course he is. I'm a killer.* He already knew this. He stared down at the body one last time and then climbed back to the top of the shingled roof. Above, the night sky's silence seemed to drown out the pounding beat in Akheron's chest. He had killed the witness.

40

The dawn began with clouds, but by midday, the sun broke through the cover and shone down upon Akheron's city in glorious, golden rays. *The city seems quiet, somehow*, Akheron thought, as he strode through the streets. A baker was setting loaves of bread on his sill, and Akheron said, "Good morning to you," as he passed. The air smelled alive, like the city did. It was a calm, quiet morning. It was the Day of Preparation, when the good folk of the Triumvirate prayed for the coming days.

At the end of the tranquil street, the tower of Avernus's Stead rose. With a warm smile, Akheron strode within. He clasped palms with the Kin who stood at the door, and said, "Blessings upon you."

The Stead was not as full as it would have been earlier. Akheron had had such a full night's sleep that he had lazed for the first part of the day. It was not a good custom to have for the Eve of Preparation, but it was rare. Akheron knelt at the side of one of the aisles and simply basked in the beam of sunlight that descended through the circular opening above the Maker's shrine.

At last he bent his head in prayer. He whispered the words beneath his breath; they were for him and the Maker alone. "Thank you for your blessings, my Maker," he began. "I have so much to be thankful for. The ongoing faithfulness of my sister. The favour of my Prince and friend, Telvyn. The love of his daughter, Etheas, my betrothed. It is not the Eve of Reflection, but I cannot stop myself from praising you for your unending blessings."

He took a breath. Some days, it felt like the Maker was right there, in front of him. It seemed as though, if he opened his eyes a little, he would see a man clothed in light smiling and embracing him. "Alas," he said, "It is the Day of Preparation now. Bless my heart in the coming week. Guard my mind from sinfulness. And, above all, give me the wisdom to praise you even when you take away what you have given me. You have blessed me ten times more than my brothers and sisters, and I pray that, even if you bless me as you bless them, I will see your love in my life. Praise to you, Maker."

The final phrase was customary for closing prayer.

Akheron waited a moment, and then opened his eyes. Ahead of him, the Four Elements sat as they always did, and the Circle of the Maker shone with the sunlight. He climbed to his feet quietly, and left the Stead, again taking the Kin's hand as he went.

A few columns of dark smoke were making their way into the sky now, but it was not a work day and not many jobs were being done.

Etheas had sent her servant, Olia, to tell Akheron to come see her today, though he would have anyway. She had something to discuss with him. With his prayers attended to, he sought out her family estate, a mansion in the Residential District. He considered returning home for something to eat first—his house was nearby—but decided against it. *I've wasted enough of a good day, already,* he thought, as he followed the middle street through the town.

The Aristorn's estate rose three storeys into the Avernan skyline. It was built out of old grey stone, though decorated with dark, rich wood and marble. The entryway was sided with a wall of columns. They were white as quartz, with a half-wound scroll sculptured at the top and bottom.

He strode between the pillars, and knocked gently on the front door. It was an old tradition—the servants had told him a hundred times he did not need to knock before entering. He was a regular guest on these premises and favourite of the Aristorn family.

The door creaked open, and then swung wide. "Why do you always knock?" Olia asked. She was a foot shorter than Akheron, with long brown hair and a white gown on. "Enter, guest, or I will tan your rear!"

Grinning, Akheron mocked fear, and jumped across the threshold. "Where is she?"

"Upstairs," Olia said. "Don't tell me I need to show you the way."

"Oh, you're no fun," Akheron said. "Fine. I'll show myself the way! Get back to your duties, then."

"Shall I?" Olia asked, with a wink.

"Go on!" Akheron commanded, as he stepped across the circular antechamber. The floor was alternating granite tiles, between a dark and light shade. A few cloaks and such hung from the hooks, and a lush fern from the Royal Chase grew in a nearby pot that was so polished it shone.

Up the stairs was a long corridor that cut straight through the Aristorn's mansion. The first door was Prince Aristorn and his wife's, while the second and third were his servants' quarters.

Across the hall from the servants' was a living room, with a table, half a bar, cushioned chairs, and a hearth for the winter. Akheron paused in front of the door, and ran a hand through his hair. He patted the sides, making sure he would be presentable. He tugged at his collar, lastly, then cracked the door inward enough to look within.

And there she was. Etheas Aristorn sitting in an armchair reading a book, and with rays of sunshine in her hair she was as glorious a sight as Etheas Aristorn was in any light. She defined Akheron's desires and completed his senses, even without being aware of him. Her red hair hung down past her shoulders. The soft green gown she wore seemed only to make it more vibrant. Her nose was long, but not bulbous or hooked. It was a soft, cute nose. Her lips were wide, and smiled now, as she read something pleasant in the thick, dusty book. He must have creaked the door, for she glanced up suddenly. Her smile faded until her blue eyes spotted him, with only his face peaking within, and then she smiled again.

But her smile slipped away too fast after that, and he stepped inside, concerned. "Good morning," he said.

"Indeed," she said, and set aside the book. "Did you sleep well? I think you ate too much at dinner last night."

"Eat too much?" Akheron asked. He patted his stomach.

"Me?"

She laughed and stood up. Akheron rested his hands on the chair between them. The bottom hem of her gown draped all the way to the floor, but it did not conceal all her curves completely. She was slim, but not skinny, and she had the full shape of a woman.

"I slept perfectly well," Akheron said. "Did you?"

"I was up late, talking with my father and a couple of the guests," she said, with a weak smile. She did seem tired.

Their dinner had welcomed a few lords from court, Akheron recalled, though they had been seated at a separate table. He glanced around the room. The walls were made of the same grey stone. To his left was a tapestry of some historic battle, though a painting of a beautiful, motherly woman hung on the wall behind Etheas. There were two small pillars on the wall to Akheron's right; between them, a windowed door accessed the balcony. The estate outside was quiet and abandoned today.

Akheron glanced back at Etheas, and stepped around the armchair. Taking her hand, he pulled her closer to him and whispered, "Maybe you should have a nap? I don't want you feeling too tired."

She smiled and looked into his eyes. "I love it when you get all concerned," she said. "I'm the Prince's daughter. If I need something, it's not going to require your attention to remedy."

"But you're everything to me," he said. "I'll go out of my way to remedy whatever ails you, and count myself lucky!"

"Oh, Akheron," Etheas murmured. "We're not married. You can't make me your *everything*, I'm sorry. Which brings me to.... There's something I need to talk to you about."

He stepped back a pace.

"It's the result of some ongoing discussions..."

"What?" he asked.

"We're not going to be married, Akheron."

His heart stopped. "What?"

"It's got nothing to do about our feelings," she said. "I love you, Akheron. You need to remember that."

"What do you mean we're not getting married?"

"I'm going to marry Lord Ryven's son. I'm my father's only child, Akheron! Politically, that is a dangerous situation.

The Nobles have more say in who I marry than my father does. But I understand it. I do."

Akheron couldn't breathe.

"The Aristorn name will no longer be royalty, but there are a few other relatives who will be kept in the royal circle if I marry into House Ryven. They will inherit the Princedom, through me. If I have a daughter, she will marry a male cousin of mine."

Akheron closed his eyes. He was losing Etheas. He could not lose Etheas.

"Akheron," Etheas said. Her voice was strained. She sounded hurt. "Listen, this won't change anything. We can love each other as much as we want. Kelan Ryven knows it's political. He'll allow me to be with whomever I want."

"Glyphs," Akheron gasped. The room was spinning around him. The woman on the wall was laughing, and the battle in the tapestry was a din that deafened him. Why couldn't he breathe? He felt like he was falling. A thousand questioned pierced his head—what was she thinking? Did she even care about him? Did she understand what she was asking of him? Did she understand how betrayed his whole household would be? Did she know the pain he felt? Was their love some sick thing, hidden from the Maker, that they could continue in private?

"Please, say something," Etheas whispered. "Be sad. Be hurt. Be angry. Please, you have to feel this, like I do."

"Like you do?" Akheron's voice was hoarse. He forced his eyes open again. She was staring at him with tears in those heavenly eyes. Her orange eyebrows were angled with concern, and her mouth quirked with an unheard prayer of some sort. "You want me to get angry?" he asked. He did not have the strength to shout, though. He grabbed her arms, just under the shoulders.

"I'm sorry, I'm so sorry," Etheas said.

"This can't be happening. Maker."

Etheas's voice broke. "It has to."

The final straw. A pounding began in the back of Akheron's head. A beat that burned his molars and shook his knees. He strode toward Etheas, though she was already in his arms, and shoved her past the armchair toward the wall. The chair and the book toppled across the floor. Their bodies hit the wall. "It has to? It has to? You *have* to sin? To break your promise? To break my heart? Glyphs, what *has* to happen?" he demanded, shaking her.

Her head hit the wall. And hit it again. When had his hand grabbed her by the throat? Her eyes were locked on his, tears running down her cheeks.

"You don't even understand me," Akheron sucked the air for a breath, "Do you? I would *never* sleep with you in some private shack, pretending the Maker can't see. I wanted to shout at the world how much I love you. This is wrong, Etheas. This is—all—wrong."

She was no longer looking into his eyes, but looking down. Her whole head hung down.

Akheron saw blood on the wall.

He released her and stepped backward. His foot landed on the book and the spine tore, spilling pages and his mass across the floor. He toppled on the smooth wooden boards, landing with a bang and rolling toward the wall.

Etheas sank down to Akheron's level, her head lulling. The tears he saw were no longer tears, but drips of red that dripped on the floor, running from her hair.

"No, no." Akheron clawed across the floor and grabbed her. "Etheas, no." She rolled in his arms, her head hanging back and her shoulders still. There was a line of blood down the grey bricks, where she had slumped. He looked back down at her, praying for a breath.

"Etheas," he pleaded. He gently lifted her head, with one hand slipped amongst the hair behind her scalp and the other holding her shoulders against him.

Her eyes were wide and still, two green irises that had forever stopped.

"No!" He lifted her, pressing his forehead against hers. "No. No. How? Oh, Etheas..." He kissed her, but there was no life in her lips.

His muscles went limp, and she slid from his grasp. He slumped against the fallen armchair, right behind him, staring at her body through blurry eyes. Within moments, there was a pool of blood forming on the floorboards, staining the oak.

He had no words. No breath. No prayers.

"Why?" he asked. There were so many 'why's to ask. And

no answers. None from the Maker, none from his conscience, none from the Etheas.

Another sight: his hands, shaking before him, were covered in blood. Her blood, running through her red hair. Red on red. He shook his head, but when he looked again, his hands were still stained. He couldn't look away and he couldn't clean them.

"I'm just a man," he realized. His voice was nothing more than a whisper in the dark, empty room. "I thought I was a... champion of some kind. I was the greatest of my family. I was marrying a princess! I was blessed by the Maker. I was something... special."

But it was a lie. He stared at the blood on his hands. He had seen murderers once. Hung by the court of law, they had died for justice. When he had looked at their bodies, he had seen something else than humans. An odd alien entity. Who murdered? They were some blighted creatures, cursed by the Maker to crawl in sin.

Akheron choked. "I'm just one of them. I'm a man." He glanced back at Etheas, past his blood-stained hands, and he wept.

ACKNOWLEDGMENTS

First thanks go to the first reader and my editor this time around: James Vreugdenhil. Gramps, your feedback was exciting and timely! Glad to have help with this project, and so glad that you're enjoying my series. Love you Grandma and Gramps!

Again, thanks to my regular listeners: Joseph, I don't know how you can listen to all my random stories without losing track of them all... of course, then you'll enjoy rereading more! You actually do a great job of it! All the best, as always. Dylan, thanks for going over that first third of the book and continuing to support my writing!

Mom, I owe so much of passion to you. I've been blessed with other intense and intellectual people in my life, but you are an invaluable one! Whether it is your patience and interest in my ceaseless creativity or your understanding when I need to reel in Akheron's sorrows... I love you and always will! Dad, the same goes for your humour. How many times will I make a joke and then think, "that was a Dad joke."? I hope you catch up on the books ;) I look forward to hearing your thoughts on the direction of the series. And thanks for being my best promoter!

Deb Smit took the excellent cover photos and I'm so glad to have found them with her help after meeting her at a local crafts sale. I had an icy photo of my own with poor resolution but she had one that worked far better!

I'd also like to send a special shout out to Cameron McKillop for keeping the covers on display at the bookstore, as opposed to just the spines!

So much of my inspiration and support comes from friendly comments and connections (in person and online): thanks to my friends in BC: the Tangents (is this still a thing?); Sean Lawrence (it's so awesome to have a prof who likes my books!) & co at UBCO; Ron & Monica, and the community of the Well; Nicholas, Courtney, Jared, Sherry, Justin, and all you guys at Value Village! In Ontario: John and Aaron, great times; my brother, as always. Rock on, bro; Gerreke, glad to see you around again; the crew at Bulk Barn—Paul, Marjorie, Michael, Bryan, Stephanie, Matt, Bethany, the list goes on... I'm so glad to have all of the people in this huge list in my life and look forward to talking to you whenever our paths cross!

Once again, thanks to my readers! At local signings I've noticed a community, and it is so exciting and gratifying. Hang on—we've got two books left in the Shadow Glyph series, and they're both going to keep you on the edge of your seat!

N. A. VREUGDENHIL grew up in Trenton, Ontario, and graduated the University of British Columbia with a degree in Creative Writing. He started writing novels at age 10, and, ten years later, published the first of a series of five, *Shadow Glyph* (2012). *Aristorn* (2014) is the third.

facebook.com/shadowglyph

www.ithyka.com

Made in the USA
Charleston, SC
05 April 2015